Henry H. Smith, William E. Horner

Anatomical Atlas

illustrative of the structure of the human body

Henry H. Smith, William E. Horner

Anatomical Atlas
illustrative of the structure of the human body

ISBN/EAN: 9783337370886

Printed in Europe, USA, Canada, Australia, Japan

Cover: Foto ©Andreas Hilbeck / pixelio.de

More available books at **www.hansebooks.com**

ANATOMICAL ATLAS,

ILLUSTRATIVE OF

THE STRUCTURE

OF

THE HUMAN BODY.

BY

HENRY H. SMITH, M.D.

Fellow of the College of Physicians, Member of the
Philadelphia Medical Society, &c.

UNDER THE SUPERVISION OF

WILLIAM E. HORNER, M.D.,

Professor of Anatomy in the University of Pennsylvania, &c.

PHILADELPHIA:

HENRY C. LEA.

1867.

PREFACE.

In the performance of the duty which has been confided to me, of forming a set of Plates as an accompaniment to the text of the work entitled, "Special Anatomy and Histology, by Wm. E. Horner, M. D.," but which should, at the same time, be so extended and general, as to be consulted by all desiring the use of a complete set of Anatomical Plates, the present volume is now offered.

The utility of drawings in illustration of a purely demonstrative branch, is now too well established to require any argument in its favour. Separated from the centre of instruction, and deprived of the advantages of the Dissecting Room, the ideas once so thoroughly acquired soon begin to fade, and the images once so distinct, become confused and mixed. A recourse to plates, in the absence of dead bodies, is then the only means of refreshing our knowledge.

Numerous works, framed with these intentions, have long enjoyed a large share of professional approbation; some from the finished style of their execution; others from some striking feature of simplicity, or adaptation to the wants of medical men.

The claim of the present one is to have been selected from the most accurate of these, as well as from the latest Microscopical Observations on the Anatomy of the Tissues; and, where plates were not deemed satisfactory, to have been enriched by original drawings, from specimens furnished by the beautiful Anatomical Museum of the University of Pennsylvania. In these instances the cut is marked Wistar Museum, or W. M.

In the arrangement of the work, it will be seen that reference has been had to the production of a volume suited to general circulation, of such a size as could be conveniently used in the Lecture, Dissecting, or Operating Room; with a Terminology sanctioned by general usage in the United States, and with concomitant references on the same page, thereby saving to the young student much embarrassment and confusion. Lastly, it has been placed at such a price as will render it easy of acquiremer by all.

To the attention bestowed on the plates by the artists employed in their execution, is due much of their fidelity. The original drawings, as well as those which are copies in a reduced form, are from the pencils of Messrs. Pinkerton, French, and Weaver, gentlemen now most favourably known in this department of Anatomy. To say that the engravings are in Mr. Gilbert's best style, is a sufficient guarantee for their beauty, his name being now identified with some of the finest wood engravings made in this country.

HENRY H. SMITH,
1029 Walnut Street.

January, 1845.

INDEX

TO

THE ILLUSTRATIONS,

EMBRACING

SIX HUNDRED AND THIRTY-SIX FIGURES.

A Highly Finished View of the Bones of the Head ...... facing the title-page.
View of Cuvier's Anatomical Theatre .... vignette.

PART I.

BONES AND LIGAMENTS.

PART II.

DERMOID AND MUSCULAR SYSTEMS.

PART III.

ORGANS OF DIGESTION AND GENERATION.

PART IV.

ORGANS OF RESPIRATION AND CIRCULATION.

PART V.

THE NERVOUS SYSTEM AND SENSES.

PART FIRST.

BONES:
NINETY-TWO FIGURES.

LIGAMENTS:
THIRTY-SIX FIGURES.

FIG. I.

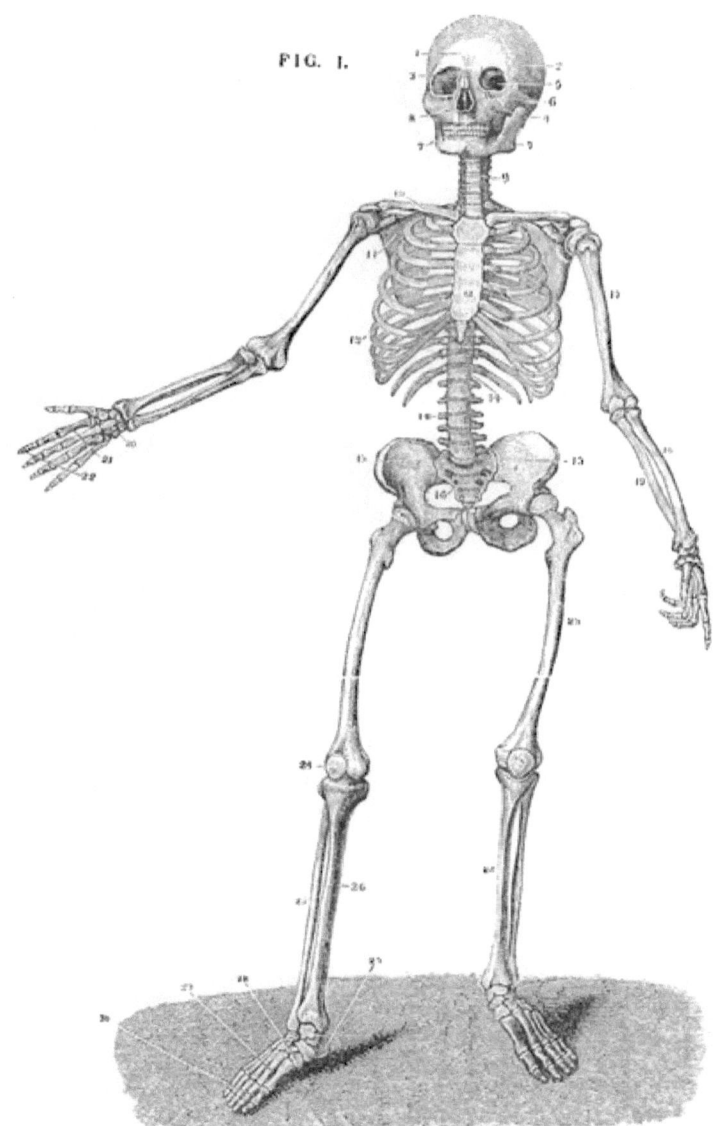

FIG. I.

A FRONT VIEW OF THE ADULT SKELETON.

1. Frontal Bone.	8. Nasal Cavity.	15. Innominata.	23. Femur.
2. Parietal Bone.	9. Cervical Vertebræ.	16. Sacrum.	24. Patella.
3. Nasal Bones.	10. Clavicle.	17. Humerus.	25. Fibula.
4. Occipital Bone.	11. Scapula.	18. Radius.	26. Tibia.
5. Orbits of Eyes.	12. Sternum.	19. Ulna.	27. Calcis & Astragalus.
6. Malar Bone.	13. Ribs.	20. Carpus.	28. Cuneiform & Cuboid.
7. Upper and Lower Maxilla.	14. 14. Dorsal and Lumbar Vertebræ.	21. Metacarpus.	29. Metatarsus.
		22. Phalanges of Hand.	30. Phalanges of Toes.

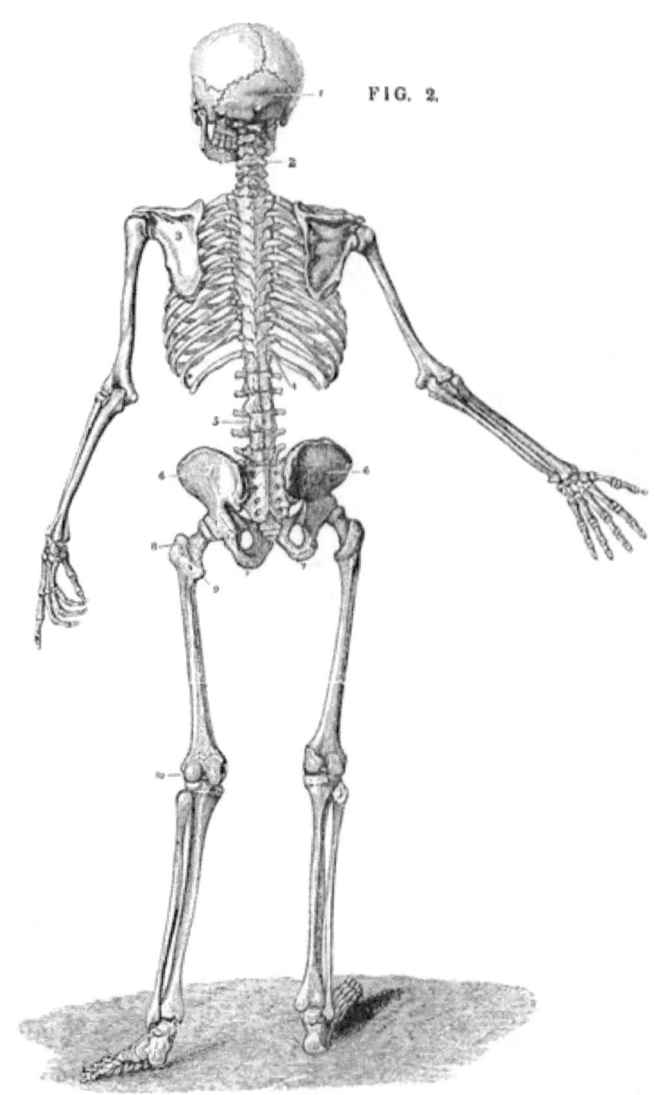

FIG. 2.

FIG. 2.
A BACK VIEW OF THE ADULT SKELETON.

1. Occipital Bone.	5. Lumbar Vertebræ.	8. Trochanter Major.
2. Cervical Vertebræ.	6.6. Ilia.	9. Trochanter Minor.
3. Scapula.	7.7. Ischia.	10. Condyles of Femur.
4. Dorsal Vertebræ.		

FIG. 3.

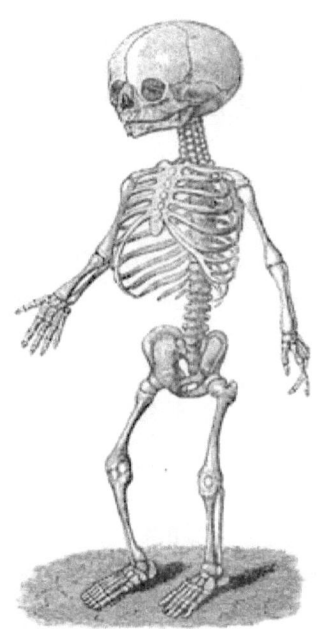

FIG. 3

A SIDE VIEW OF THE FŒTAL SKELETON. SHOWING THE
GREAT EXPANSION OF THE CHEST AND THE
IMPERFECT DEVELOPEMENT OF
THE BONES.

Page 19

FIG. 4.

FIG. 5.

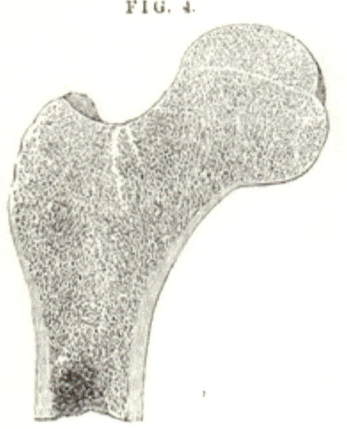

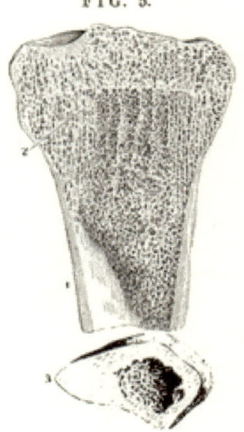

FIG. 6.

FIG. 7.

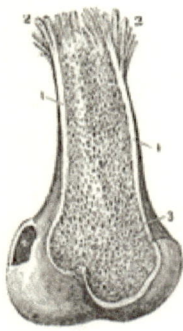

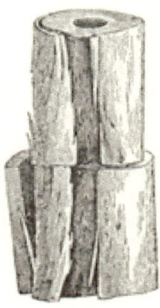

TEXTURE OF BONES.

FIG. 4.

A LONGITUDINAL SECTION OF A FEMUR, SHOW-ING THE CELLULAR STRUCTURE AT ITS EX-TREMITY.

FIG. 5.

A VIEW OF A SECTION OF THE TIBIA, SHOW-ING

1. The Compact Structure.
2. The Cellular Structure.
3. A Transverse section of the Femur, show-ing its Compact Substance, its Internal Cellular Structure, and the Medullary Canal.

FIG. 6.

THE TEXTURE OF A BONE AS SHOWN IN A HU-MERUS, AFTER MACERATION IN DILUTE ACID.

1. 1. The Compact Matter as usually seen.
2. 2. The same split, so as to show the Lon-gitudinal Fibres composing it.
3. The Internal Cellular Matter.
4. The Bone seen under its Articular Car-tilage. (*From the Wistar Museum.*)

FIG. 7.

A VIEW OF THE CONCENTRIC LAMELLÆ OF THE COMPACT MATTER OF A BONE. (*W. Mus.*)

FIG. 8.

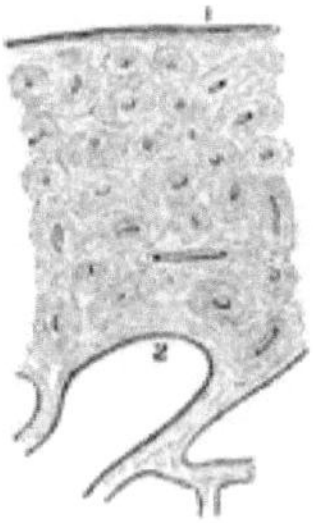

FIG. 9.

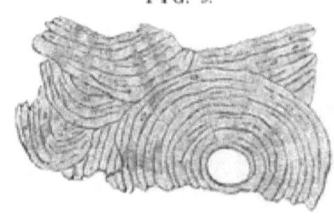

FIG. 10.

FIG. 11.

TEXTURE OF BONES.

FIG. 8.

A TRANSVERSE SECTION OF THE COMPACT MAT-
TER AS SEEN UNDER THE MICROSCOPE; MAGNI-
FIED FIFTEEN DIAMETERS.

1. Periosteal or Outer Layer.
2. Medullary or Internal Layer.

The intermediate Haversian systems of Lamellæ, each perforated by a Haversian
Canal, are also shown.

FIG. 9.

A TRANSVERSE SECTION OF AN OLD TIBIA,
SHOWING THE APPEARANCE OF THE LAMELLÆ
SURROUNDING THE HAVERSIAN CANALS, AND
ALSO THE APPEARANCE OF THE LACUNÆ,
WHEN THEIR PORES ARE FILLED WITH LI-
QUID; MAGNIFIED.

FIG. 10.

A LONGITUDINAL SECTION OF THE COMPACT TIS-
SUE OF THE SHAFT OF A LONG BONE SHOWING
THE VESSELS; MAGNIFIED.

1. Arterial Canal.
2. Venous Canal.
3. Dilatation of another Venous Canal.

FIG. 11.

THE MINUTE STRUCTURE OF A BONE MAGNIFIED
300 DIAMETERS.

1. A Haversian Canal surrounded by its
concentric Lamellæ.
2. The same with its Purkinjean Corpuscules and converging tubuli.
3. The area of one of the canals.
4. Direction of the Lamellæ of the great
Medullary Canal.

The outlines of three other canals, showing
their form and arrangement in the entire
bone, are also seen.

FIG. 12.

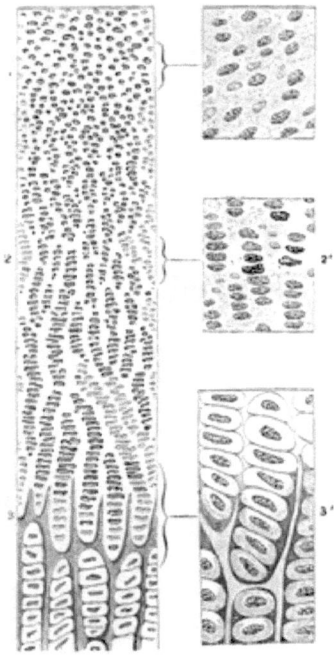

FIG. 13.

FIG. 14.

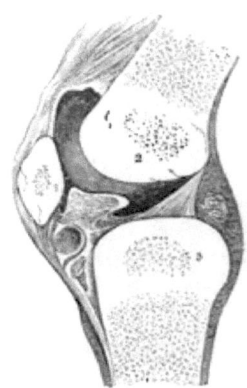

TEXTURE OF BONES

FIG. 12.

A MAGNIFIED VIEW OF A VERTICAL SECTION OF CARTILAGE FROM A NEW-BORN RABBIT, SHOWING THE PROGRESS TOWARDS OSSIFICATION.

1. The Ordinary appearance of Temporary Cartilage.
1. The same, more highly magnified.
2. The Primary Cells beginning to assume the linear direction.
2. The same, more highly magnified.
3. The Ossification is extending in the intercellular spaces, and the rows of cells are seen resting in the cavities so formed, the Nuclei being more separated than above.
3. The same, magnified more highly.

FIG. 13.

THE SCAPULA OF A FŒTUS AT THE SEVENTH MONTH, SHOWING THE LINEAR DIRECTION OF THE OSSIFICATION.

1. 2. 3. Are Epiphyses as yet in the state of Cartilage.

———

FIG. 14.

A VERTICAL SECTION OF THE KNEE-JOINT OF AN INFANT, SHOWING THE PUNCTA OSSIFICATIONIS IN THE SHAFT AND EPIPHYSES OF THE FEMUR AND TIBIA, AS WELL AS IN THE PATELLA.

FIG. 15.

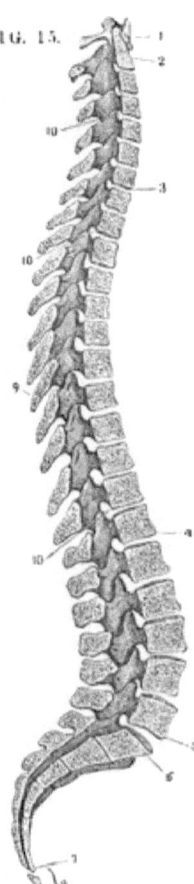

FIG. 16.

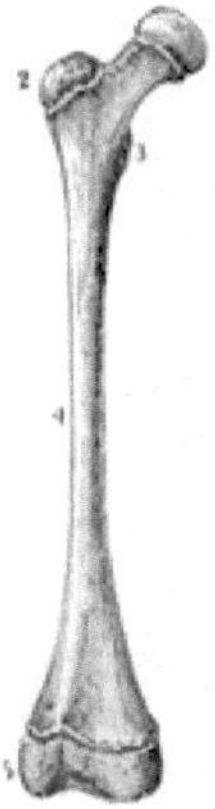

FIG. 17.

DEVELOPEMENT OF BONES.

FIG. 15.

A LATERAL VIEW OF THE SPINAL COLUMN, SHOWING ITS CURVATURES AND INTERNAL STRUCTURE.

1. Atlas.
2. Dentata.
3. Seventh Cervical Vertebra.
4. Twelfth Dorsal Vertebra.
5. Fifth Lumbar Vertebra.
6. First piece of Sacrum.
7. Last piece of Sacrum.
8. Coccyx.
9. A Spinous Process.
10. 10. Intervertebral Foramina.

FIG. 16.

A YOUNG FEMUR, SHOWING, AT

1. 2. 3. 5. the Epiphyses.
4. The Diaphysis.
2.3. afterwards become Apophyses.
(*Wistar Museum.*)

FIG. 17.

THE EXTERNAL PERIOSTEUM LAID OPEN AND TURNED OFF FROM A YOUNG HUMERUS. (*W. M.*)

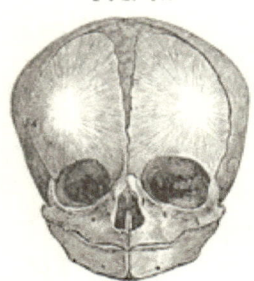

FIG. 18.

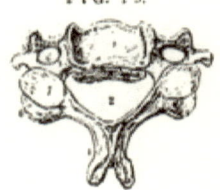

FIG. 19.

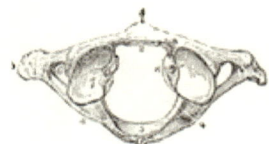

FIG. 20.

FIG. 21.

BONES OF THE TRUNK.

FIG. 18.

A VIEW OF THE PUNCTUM OSSIFICATIONIS IN THE FLAT BONES OF THE HEAD OF A FŒTUS— THE RADIATING LINES FROM THE CENTRAL POINT ARE ALSO SHOWN.

FIG. 19.

THE GENERAL CHARACTERS OF A CERVICAL VERTEBRA.

1. Upper Face of the Body.
2. Spinal Canal.
3. Half of an Intervertebral Foramen.
4. Bifid Spinous Process.
5. Bifid Transverse Process.
6. Vertebral Foramen.
7. Superior Oblique Process.
8. Inferior Oblique Process.

FIG. 20.

THE ATLAS.

1. Anterior Tubercle.
2. Articular Face for the Dentata.
3. Posterior Surface of Spinal Canal.
4.4. Intervertebral Notch.
5. Transverse Process.
6. Foramen for Vertebral Artery.
7. Superior Oblique Process.
8. Tubercle for the Transverse Ligament.

FIG. 21.

THE DENTATA ~ The Axis.

1. The Body.
2. Processus Dentatus.
3. Facet for Articulating with the Atlas.
4. Foramen for the Vertebral Artery.
5. Spinous Process.
6. Inferior Oblique Process.
7. Superior Oblique Process.

FIG. 23.

FIG. 22.

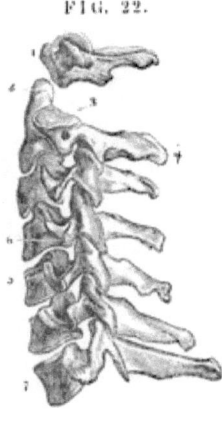

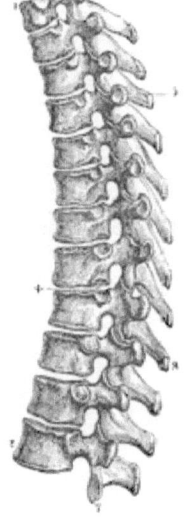

FIG. 24.

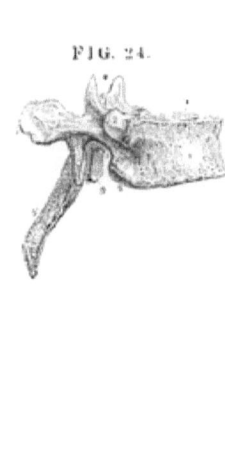

BONES OF THE SPINE.

FIG. 22.

A LATERAL VIEW OF THE CERVICAL VERTE-
BRÆ.

1. Atlas.
2. Processus Dentatus of the second Vertebra.
3. Its Superior Oblique Process.
4. Its Spinous Process.
5. 6. Upper and Lower Oblique Processes, showing their inclination.
7. Last Cervical Vertebra.

- - -

FIG. 23.

A LATERAL VIEW OF THE TWELVE DORSAL
VERTEBRÆ.

1. First Dorsal Vertebra.
2. Twelfth Dorsal Vertebra.
3. A Spinous Process.

4. Articulating Face for the Head of a Rib.
5. Articulating Face for the Tubercle of a Rib.
6. Superior Oblique Process.
7. Inferior Oblique Process.

———

FIG. 24.

GENERAL CHARACTERS OF A DORSAL VERTEBRA.

1. The Body.
2. Portion of the Face for the Head of a Rib.
3. Superior Face of the Body.
4. Superior half of the Intervertebral Notch.
5. Inferior half of the Intervertebral Notch.
6. Spinous Process.
7. Articular Face for the Tubercle of a Rib.
8. Two Superior Oblique Processes.
9. Two Inferior Oblique Processes.

FIG. 25.

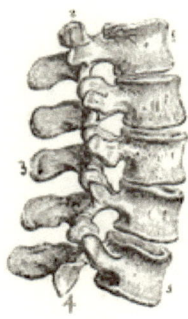

FIG. 26.

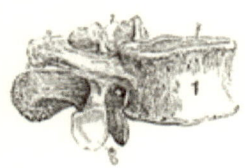

FIG. 27.

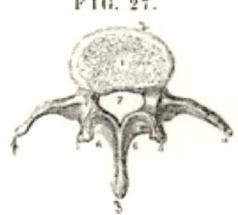

BONES OF THE SPINE.

FIG. 25.

A LATERAL VIEW OF THE FIVE LUMBAR VER-
TEBRÆ.

1. First Lumbar Vertebra.
2. Superior Oblique Process.
3. Spinous Process.
4. Inferior Oblique Process.
5. Last Lumbar Vertebra.

FIG. 26.

A LATERAL VIEW OF A LUMBAR VERTEBRA.

1. The Body.
2. Superior Articular Face of the Body.
3. Superior half of the Intervertebral Notch.
4. Inferior half of the Intervertebral Notch.

5. Spinous Process.
6. Transverse Process.
7. Two Superior Oblique Processes.
8. Two Inferior Oblique Processes.

FIG. 27.

A PERPENDICULAR VIEW OF A LUMBAR VER-
TEBRA.

1. Face for the Intervertebral Substance.
2. Anterior Surface of the Body.
3. Spinous Process.
4. Transverse Process.
5. Oblique Process.
6. A portion of the Bony Bridges.
7. The Spinal Foramen.

Page 26.

FIG. 28.

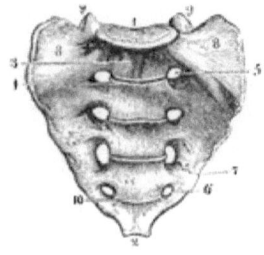

FIG. 29.

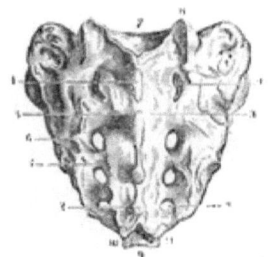

FIG. 30.

BONES OF THE SPINE

FIG. 28.

AN ANTERIOR VIEW OF THE SACRUM.

1. Articular Face for the Last Lumbar Vertebra.
2. Articular Face for the Coccyx.
3. Promontory of the Sacrum.
4. Line marking the former pieces of the Sacrum.
5. The First Sacral Foramen.
6. The Fourth Sacral Foramen.
7. A portion of the Sacro-Sciatic Notch.
8. Alæ of the Sacrum.
9. Oblique Processes for articulating with the Last Lumbar Vertebra.
10. Line of Separation of the last pieces of the Bone.

FIG. 29.

A POSTERIOR VIEW OF THE SACRUM.

1. First Spinous Process.
2. Fourth Spinous Process.
3. Roughness for the Muscles and Fascia of the Back.

4.4. Foramina for the Posterior Sacral Nerves.
5. Remnant of an Oblique Process.
6. Roughness for the Sacro-Sciatic Ligaments.
7. Articular Face for the Fifth Lumbar Vertebra.
8. Superior Oblique Processes of the First Piece of the Sacrum.
9. Articular Face for the Second Bone of the Coccyx.
10. Bifid Spinous Process of the Last Piece of the Sacrum.
11. The First Bone of the Coccyx.

FIG. 30.

THE FOUR BONES OF THE COCCYX.

1. First Bone.
2, 3. Processes to join the Sacrum.
4, 5. The Notches to form the Foramen for the Sixth Sacral Nerve.
6. The Last Bone of the Coccyx

Page 27

FIG. 31.   FIG. 32.

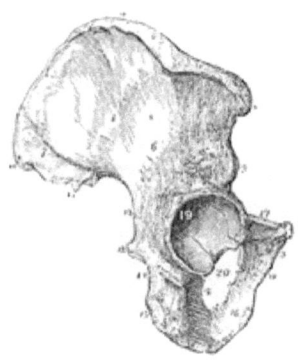 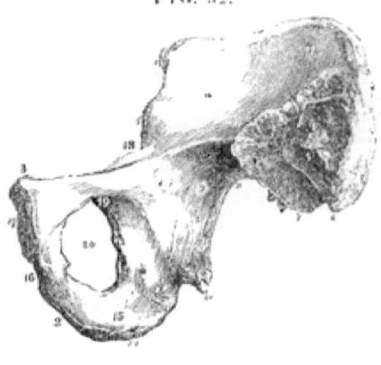

OSSA INNOMINATA.

FIG. 31.	FIG. 32.

OUTSIDE OF THE INNOMINATUM OF THE RIGHT SIDE.

1. Dorsum of the Ilium.
2. Ischium.
3. Pubis.
4. Crest of the Ilium.
5. Surface for the Gluteus Medius.
6. Surface for the Gluteus Minimus.
7. Surface for the Gluteus Maximus.
8. Anterior Superior Spinous Process.
9. Anterior Inferior Spinous Process.
10. Posterior Superior Spinous Process.
11. Posterior Inferior Spinous Process.
12. Spine of the Ischium.
13. Greater Sacro-Sciatic Notch.
14. Lesser Sacro-Sciatic Notch.
15. Tuber Ischii.
16. Ascending Ramus of the Ischium.
17. Body of the Pubis.
18. Ramus of the Pubis.
19. Acetabulum.
20. Thyroid Foramen.

INSIDE OF THE INNOMINATUM OF THE RIGHT SIDE.

1. Surface for the Sacro-Iliac Ligaments.
2. Ischium.
3. Body of Pubis.
4. Anterior Superior Spinous Process.
5. Anterior Inferior Spinous Process.
6. Posterior Superior Spinous Process.
7. Posterior Inferior Spinous Process.
8. Greater Sacro-Sciatic Notch.
9. Plane of the Ilium.
10. Venter of the Ilium.
11. The portion of the Venter which is continuous with the Alæ of the Sacrum.
12. Linea Ilio Pectinea.
13. Spine of Ischium.
14. Tuber Ischii.
15. Line of attachment of the Greater Sacro-Sciatic Ligament.
16. Point of attachment of the Erector Penis, or Clitoridis Muscle.
17. Symphysis Pubis.
18. Ilio-Pectineal Protuberance or Boss.
19. Groove for the Obturator Vessels and Nerve.
20. Foramen Thyroideum.

FIG. 33.

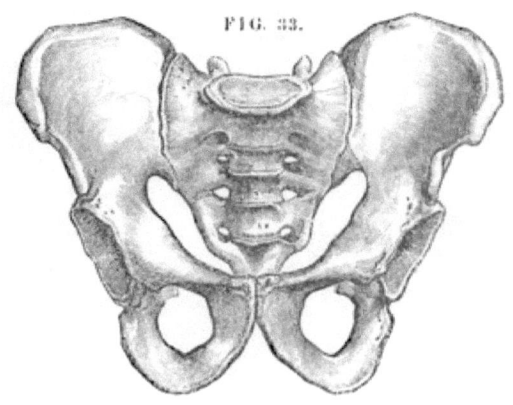

FIG. 34.

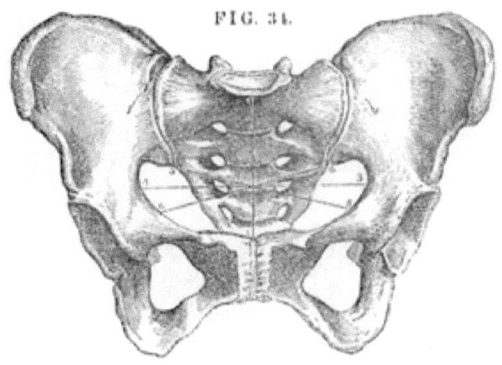

THE PELVIS.

FIG. 33.

AN ANTERIOR VIEW OF THE MALE PELVIS, SHOWING THE PECULIAR SHAPE OF THE SUPERIOR STRAIT; OF THE FORAMEN OVALE, AND OF THE ARCH OF THE PUBIS—WHEREIN IT DIFFERS FROM THAT OF THE FEMALE.

FIG. 34.

AN ANTERIOR VIEW OF THE FEMALE PELVIS, SHOWING THE SHAPE AND DIAMETERS OF THE SUPERIOR STRAIT.

1. 2. The Antero-Posterior Diameter, measuring 4 inches.

3. 4. The Transverse Diameter, measuring 5 inches.

5. 5. ⎫ The Two Oblique Diameters, measur-
6. 6. ⎭ ing 4½ inches each.

———

The difference in the Shape of the Arch of the Pubis, in the Foramen Thyroideum and in the Superior and Inferior Straits, are the principal objects of interest between the Male and Female Pelves.

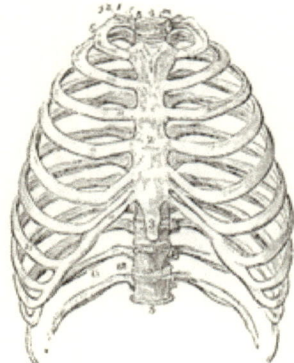

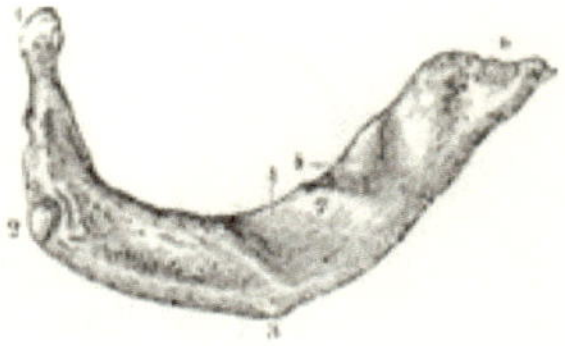

FIG. 38.

FIG. 37.

THE THORAX

FIG. 35.

A Front View of the Thorax.

1 First Bone of the Sternum.
2 Second Bone of the Sternum.
3 Third Bone or Ensiform Cartilage.
4. First Dorsal Vertebra.
5. Last or Twelfth Dorsal Vertebra.
6. First Rib.
7. Its Head.
8. Its Neck.
9. Its Tubercle.
10. Seventh or Last True Rib.
11. 11. Costal Cartilages.
12. False or Floating Ribs.
13. Groove for the Intercostal Artery.

FIG. 36.

A View of the Upper Side of the First Rib of the Right Side, Half the Size of Nature.

1. The Head.
2. The Tubercle.
3. Anterior Surface.
4. Groove for the Subclavian Artery.
5. Groove for the Subclavian Vein.
6. Anterior Extremity for the Cartilage.
7. Tubercle for the Scalenus Anticus Muscle.

FIG. 37.

General Characters of the other Ribs— seen on their Upper and Under Surface.

The Left Hand Figure is the Upper Face of the Rib.
1. Head of the Rib.
2. Its Tubercle.
3. Anterior Extremity for the attachment of the Costal Cartilage.
4. Groove for the Artery and Nerve.
5. Angle of the Rib.

The Right Hand Figure is the Under Surface of the Rib.
1. The Head.
2. Its Tubercle.
3. Anterior Extremity.
4. Groove for Intercostal Artery and Nerve
5. Angle of the Rib. (*Wistar Museum.*)

FIG. 38.

A Front View of the Sternum.

1. First Piece.
2. Second Piece.
3. Ensiform Cartilage, or Third Piece.
4. Articular Face for the Clavicle.
5. Articular Face for the First Rib.
6. Articular Face for the Second Rib.
7, 8, 9, 10. Articular Faces for the Last Five True Ribs. (*Wistar Museum.*)

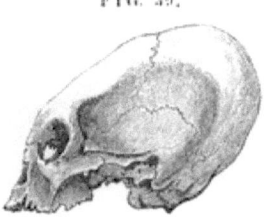

FIG. 39.

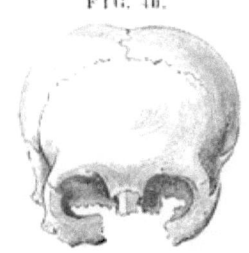

FIG. 40.

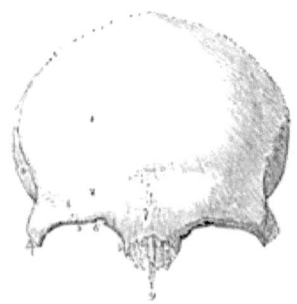

FIG. 41.

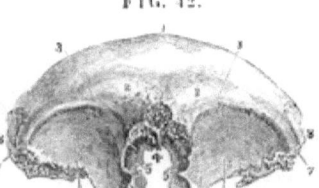

FIG. 42.

THE CRANIUM.

FIG. 39.

A LATERAL VIEW OF THE HEAD OF A PERUVIAN INDIAN, SHOWING THE FLATNESS OF THE OS FRONTIS AND OCCIPITIS, PRODUCED BY PRESSURE. (*Wistar Museum.*)

FIG. 40.

A FRONT VIEW OF THE HEAD OF A CHOCTAW INDIAN, SHOWING THE SAME; PRODUCED IN ACCORDANCE WITH THE FASHION OF THEIR TRIBE (*Wistar Museum.*)

FIG. 41.

A FRONT VIEW OF THE EXTERNAL SURFACE OF THE OS FRONTIS.

1. Frontal Protuberance of the Right Side.
2. Superciliary Ridge.
3. Supra-Orbitar Ridge.
4. External Angular Process.
5. Internal Angular Process.

6. Notch for the Supra-Orbitar Nerve.
7. Nasal Protuberance.
8. Semicircular Ridge for the Temporal Muscle.
9. Nasal Spine.

FIG. 42.

A VIEW OF THE LOWER PART OF THE OS FRONTIS. (*Wistar Museum.*)

1. Line of Junction of the two Halves of the Bone.
2. Frontal Protuberances.
3. Supra-Orbitar Notch.
4. Nasal Spine and Space, filled by the Ethmoid Bone.
5. Frontal Sinuses.
6. Orbitar Plates.
7. External Angular Process.
   The depression for the Lachrymal Gland, is seen in the dark surface just within the line of reference.
8. Surface for the Temporal Muscle.

FIG. 43.

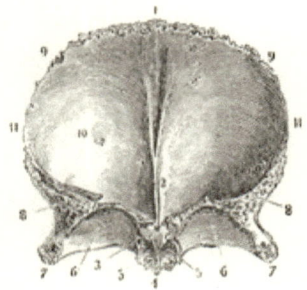

FIG. 44.

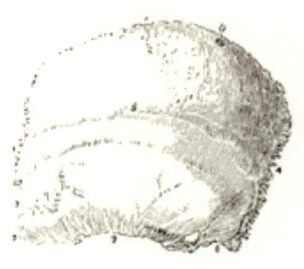

FIG. 45.

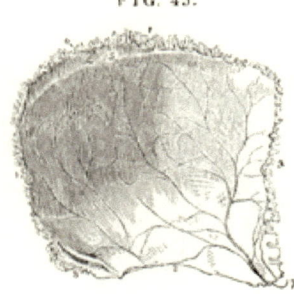

THE CRANIUM.

FIG. 43.

A VIEW OF THE INTERNAL SURFACE OF THE OS FRONTIS. (*Wistar Museum.*)

1. Serrated Edge for Junction with the Parietal Bones, and Groove for the Superior Longitudinal Sinus.
2. Ridge for the attachment of the Falx Major.
3. Foramen Cœcum.
4. Nasal Spine and Surface for the Ethmoid Bone.
5. The Openings of the Frontal Sinuses.
6. The Orbitar Plates.
7. The External Angular Process.
8. Serrated Surface for the Sphenoid Bone.
9. The Line of Junction of the Parietal Bones.
10. A Depression made by the Glands of Pacchioni.
11. The Surface for the Squamous portion of the Temporal Bone.

FIG. 44.

THE EXTERNAL SURFACE OF THE LEFT PARIETAL BONE.

1. The Superior or Sagittal Surface.
2. The Inferior or Squamous Surface.
3. The Anterior or Coronal Surface.
4. The Posterior or Lambdoidal Surface.
5. The Ridge for the attachment of the Temporal Fascia; the Parietal Protuberance is at the point of the Figure.
6. The Parietal Foramen.
7. The Anterior Inferior, or Elongated Angle.
8. The Posterior Inferior, or Truncated Angle.

FIG. 45.

THE INTERNAL SURFACE OF THE LEFT PARIETAL BONE.

1. The Surface for the Bone of the opposite Side.
2. The Surface for the Temporal Bone.
3. The Surface for the Frontal Bone.
4. The Surface for the Occipital Bone.
5. Part of the Groove for the Superior Longitudinal Sinus.
6. The Internal Orifice of the Parietal Foramen.
7. Anterior Inferior Angle and Groove for the Middle Artery of the Dura Mater.
8. The Posterior Inferior Angle and Groove for a portion of the Lateral Sinus.

FIG. 46.

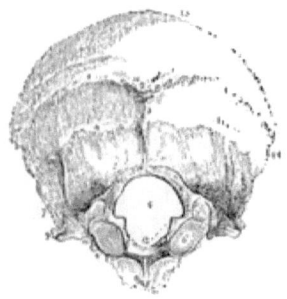

FIG. 47.

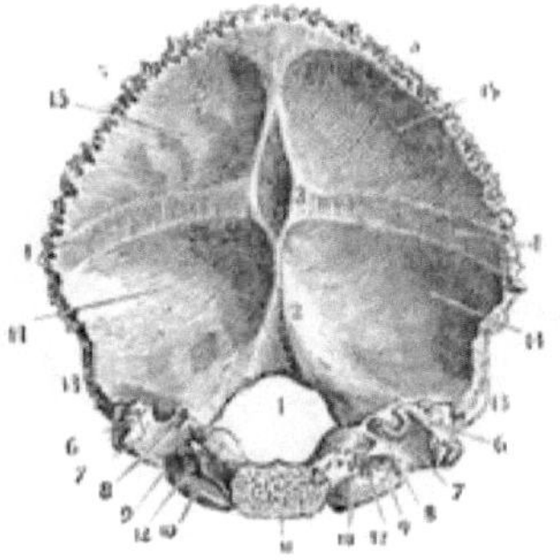

FIG. 48.

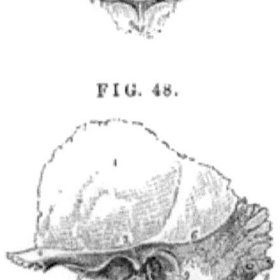

FIG. 49.

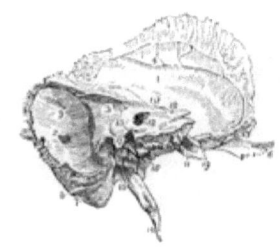

THE CRANIUM.

FIG. 46.

THE EXTERNAL SURFACE OF THE OCCIPITAL BONE.

1. Superior Semicircular Ridge.
2. External Occipital Protuberance.
3. Portion for the attachment of the Ligamentum Nuchæ.
4. Inferior Semicircular Ridge.
5. Foramen Magnum.
6. Condyle of the Right Side.
7. Point of the Posterior Condyloid Foramen.
8. Point of the Anterior Condyloid Foramen.
9. External Part of the Jugular Eminence.
10. Part of the Jugular Foramen.
11. Basilar Process.
12. Points of attachment of the Odontoid Ligaments.
13. Surface for the Parietal Bones.
14. Surface for the Mastoid portion of the Temporal Bone.

FIG. 47.

THE INTERNAL SURFACE OF THE OCCIPITAL BONE. (W. M.)

1. Foramen Magnum.
2. Ridge for the Falx Minor, and depression for a small Sinus.
3. Internal Occipital Protuberance, and the depression strongly marked in this Bone for the Torcular Herophili.
4,4. Lateral Limbs of the Occipital Cross, and depression for the Lateral Sinus.
5. Surface for the Parietal Bones.
6. Jugular Eminence.

7. Jugular Fossa, for the transmission of the Jugular Vein, and the Eighth Pair of Nerves.
8. Internal Orifice of the Posterior Condyloid Foramen.
9. Surface for the Petrous portion of the Temporal Bone.
10. The Condyles.
11. The Surface for the Sphenoid Bone; or, the Anterior Extremity of the Basilar Process.
12. Exterior Edge of the Basilar Gutter.
13. Surface for the Mastoid portion of the Temporal Bone.
14. Depression for the Cerebellum.
15. Depression for the Posterior Lobes of the Cerebrum. The marks made by its convolutions are also seen.

FIG. 48.

THE EXTERNAL SURFACE OF THE LEFT TEMPORAL BONE.

1. The Squamous Portion.
2. The Mastoid Portion.
3. Extremity of the Petrous Portion.
4. Zygomatic Portion.
5. Tubercle on which the Condyle of the Lower Jaw touches, when the mouth is widely opened.
6. Posterior part of the Temporal Ridge.
7. The Glenoid Fissure.
8. The Mastoid Foramen.
9. Meatus Auditorius Externus, surrounded by the Auditory Process.
10. Fossa for the Digastric Muscle.

11. Styloid Process.
12. Vaginal Process.
13. Glenoid Foramen.
14. Part of the Groove for the Eustachian Tube.

FIG. 49.

THE INTERNAL SURFACE OF THE LEFT TEMPORAL BONE.

1. Squamous Portion.
2. Mastoid Portion and Foramen.
3. Petrous Portion.
4. Groove for the Posterior Branch of the Middle Artery of the Dura Mater.
5. Bevelled Edge of the Squamous Portion.
6. Zygomatic Process.
7. Digastric Fossa.
8. Occipital Groove.
9. Groove for the Lateral Sinus.
10. Position of the Superior Petrous Sinus.
11. Opening of the Carotid Canal.
12. Meatus Auditorius Internus.
13. Supposed Aqueduct of the Vestibule.
14. Styloid Process.
15. Stylo-Mastoid Foramen.
16. Carotid Foramen.
17. Spine separating the Eighth Pair of Nerves from the Jugular Vein. The dark depression immediately in advance of the number, is the Opening of the Aqueduct of the Cochlea.
18. Points to the Vidian Foramen, on the Anterior Surface of the Petrous Portion.
19. Origin of the Levator Palati and Tensor Tympani Muscles.

Page 33.

FIG. 50.

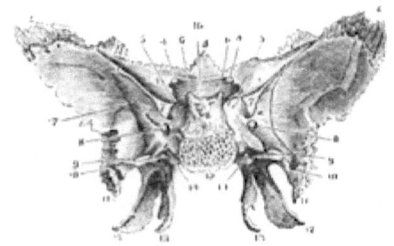

FIG. 51.

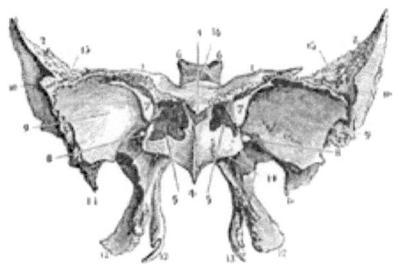

FIG. 52.

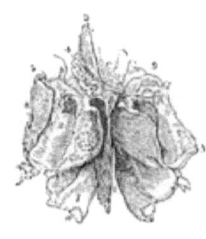

THE CRANIUM

FIG. 50.

THE INTERNAL OR CEREBRAL SURFACE OF THE SPHENOID BONE.

1.1. The Lesser Wings or Apophyses of Ingrassias.
2.2. The Upper extremity of the Greater Wings.
3. Ethmoidal Spine.
4. Optic Foramina.
5. Anterior Clinoid Processes.
6. Posterior Clinoid Processes.
7. Sphenoidal Fissure for the transmission of the 3d, 4th, First Branch of the 5th and the 6th Pairs of Nerves.
8. Foramen Rotundum, transmitting the Second Branch of the 5th Pair.
9. Foramen Ovale, for the Third Branch of the 5th Pair.
10. Foramen Spinale, for the Middle Artery of the Dura Mater; its course is shown by the dark line.

11. Styloid Process.
12. External Pterygoid Process.
13. Internal Pterygoid Process and Hook for the Circumflexus Palati Muscle.
14. Pterygoid Foramen for the Pterygoid Nerve.
15. Articular Face for the Os Occipitis.
16. Points to the Sella Turcica.

FIG. 51.

THE ANTERIOR AND INFERIOR SURFACE OF THE SPHENOID BONE.

1.1. Apophyses of Ingrassias.
2.2. The Great Wings.
3. Ethmoidal Spine.
4. Azygos Process.
5. Sphenoidal Cells, after the removal of the Pyramids of Wistar.
6. Posterior Clinoid Processes.
7. Sphenoidal Fissure.

8. Foramen Rotundum.
9. Depression for the Middle Lobes of the Cerebrum.
10. Surface for the Temporal Muscle.
11. Styloid Process.
12. External Pterygoid Process.
13. Internal Pterygoid Process.
14. Pterygoid Foramen.
15. Articular Face for the Os Frontis.
16. Points to the Sella Turcica.

FIG. 52.

AN UPPER AND POSTERIOR VIEW OF THE ETHMOID BONE.

1. Nasal Lamella.
2. Body or Cellular Portion.
3. Crista Galli.
4. Cribriform Plate.
5. Superior Meatus.
6. Superior Turbinated Bone.
7. Middle Turbinated Bone.
8. Os Planum.
9. Surface for the Olfactory Nerve.

FIG. 53.

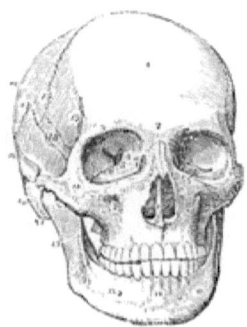

FIG. 54.

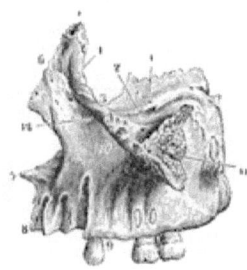

FIG. 55.

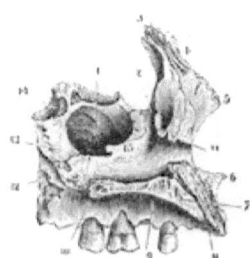

BONES OF THE FACE

FIG. 53.

A FRONT VIEW OF THE SKULL,
SHOWING THE BONES COM-
POSING THE FACE.

1. Os Frontis.
2. Nasal Tuberosity.
3. Supra-Orbital Ridge.
4. Optic Foramen.
5. Sphenoidal Fissure.
6. Spheno-Maxillary Fissure.
7. Lachrymal Fossa, and commencement of the Nasal
Duct.
8. Opening of the Anterior
Nares, and the Vomer.
9. Infra-Orbital Foramen.
10. Malar Bone.
11. Symphysis of the Lower
Jaw.
12. Anterior Mental Foramen.
13. Ramus of the Lower Jaw-
bone.
14. Parietal Bone.
15. Coronal Suture.
16. Temporal Bone.
17. Squamous Suture.
18. Great Wing of the Sphenoid.
19. Commencement of the
Temporal Ridge.
20. Zygomatic Process.
21. Mastoid Process

FIG. 54.

AN EXTERNAL VIEW OF THE
SUPERIOR MAXILLA OF
THE LEFT SIDE. (W. M.)

1. Orbitar Process.
2. Infra-Orbitar Canal.
3. Space for the Os Unguis.
4. Upper part of the Lachrymal Canal.
5. Nasal Process, and Surface for Articulating with
the Os Frontis.
6. Surface for the Nasal Bone.
7. Anterior portion of the
Floor of the Nostril.
8. Surface for Articulating
with its Fellow.
9. Alveolar Process.
10. Points to the Depression
just below the Infra-Orbitar Foramen.
11. Surface for the Malar Bone.

FIG. 55.

AN INTERNAL VIEW OF THE
SUPERIOR MAXILLA OF THE
LEFT SIDE. (W. Museum.)

1. Antrum Highmorianum.
2. Ductus ad Nasum.
3. Articular Surface for the Os
Frontis.
4. Articular Surface for the Nasal Bone.
5. Surface for the Nasal Car-
tilago.
6. Anterior Point of the Floor
of the Nostril.
7. Surface for the Bone of the
Right Side.
8. Foramen Incisivum.
9. Palate Plate.
10. Surface for the Palate Bone.
11. Anterior part of the Ridge for
the Inferior Spongy Bone.
12. Articular Surface for the
Palate Bone behind.
13. Surface for the Nasal Plate
of the Palate Bone.
14. Surface for the Orbitar Plate
of the Palate Bone.
15. Termination of the Nasal
Duct.

FIG. 56.   FIG. 57.

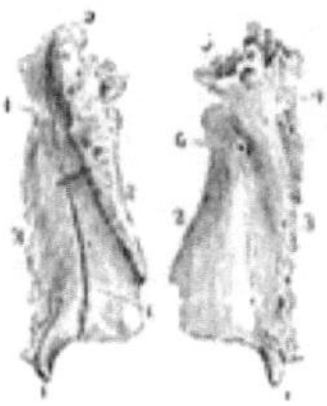

FIG. 58.   FIG. 59.

   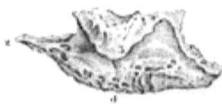

FIG. 60.

BONES OF THE FACE

FIG. 56.

A POSTERIOR AND HALF LATE-
RAL VIEW OF THE PALATE
BONE. (*Wistar Museum.*)

1. Palate Plate on its Nasal Surface.
2. Nasal Plate.
3. Pterygoid Process.
4. Surface for Articulating with its
Fellow.
5. Half of the Crescentic Edge and
Spine for the Azygos Uvulæ
Muscle.
6. Ridge for the Inferior Spongy
Bone.
7. Spheno-Palatine Foramen.
8. Orbital Plate.
9. Pterygoid Apophysis.
10. Depression for the External
Pterygoid Process of the Sphenoid Bone.
11. Same for the Internal Pterygoid
Process.

FIG. 57.

AN ANTERIOR AND POSTERIOR
VIEW OF THE NASAL BONES.
Right Hand Figure.

1. Anterior Inferior Extremity.
2. Articulating Surface for its Fellow.

3. Surface for the Nasal Process
of the Superior Maxillary Bone.
4. Points to the Groove on the Inner Side, for the Nasal Nerve.
5. Articular Face for the Os
Frontis.
6. Foramen for the Nutritious Artery.

Left Hand Figure.

1. Posterior Inferior Extremity.
2. Surface for its Fellow.
3. Surface for the Superior Maxilla.
4. Groove for the Internal Nasal
Nerve.
5. Surface for the Os Frontis.
6. Lower portion of the Groove
for the Nasal Nerve.

FIG. 58.

AN ANTERIOR VIEW OF THE
OS UNGUIS OF THE LEFT
SIDE. (*Wistar Museum.*)

1. Its Anterior Inferior Angle.
2. Orbitar Plate and Side for the
Os Planum.
3. Fossa for the Lachrymal Sac.
4. Superior Extremity.

FIG. 59.

AN EXTERNAL VIEW OF THE
INFERIOR SPONGY BONE OF
THE RIGHT SIDE. (*W. M.*)

1. Anterior Extremity for resting on
the Ridge of the Upper Maxilla.
2. Posterior, for resting on the
Ridge of the Palate Bone.
3. Hooked portion, for resting on
the Lower Margin of the Antrum Highmorianum.
4. Its Inferior Border.

FIG. 60.

AN ANTERIOR VIEW OF THE
MALAR BONE OF THE RIGHT
SIDE. (*Wistar Museum.*)

1. Anterior Orbital Angle.
2. Orbital Face.
3. Superior Angle for Articulating
with the Os Frontis.
4. External Angle for the Zygoma
of the Temporal Bone.
5. 6. Inferior Angle and Surface for
the Superior Maxilla.
7. Nutritious Foramen.

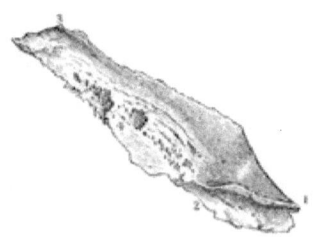

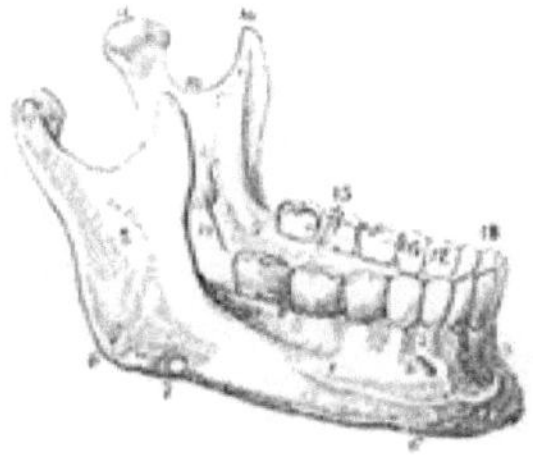

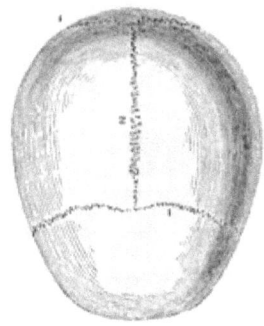

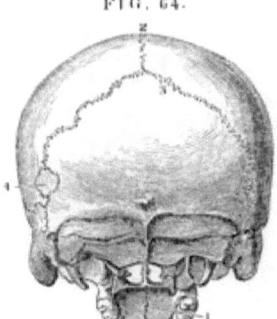

FIG. 63.

FIG. 64.

THE FACE AND THE SUTURES.

FIG. 61.

THE VOMER. (*W. M.*)

1. 2. Posterior and Superior Surface hollowed to receive the Azygos Process of the Sphenoid Bone.

3. Anterior Surface for the Cartilaginous Septum of the Nose.

FIG. 62.

THE INFERIOR MAXILLARY BONE.

1. The Body.
2. The Ramus.
3. The Symphysis.
4. Alveolar Process.
5. Anterior Mental Foramen.
6. The Base.
7. Groove for the Facial Artery.
8. The Angle.
9. Extremity of the Ridge for the Mylo-Hyoid Muscle.
10. Coronoid Process.
11. Condyle.

12. Neck of the Condyloid Process.
13. Posterior Mental Foramen.
14. Groove for the Inferior Maxillary Nerve.
15. Molar Teeth.
16. Bicuspate Teeth.
17, 18. Middle and Lateral Incisors.

FIG. 63.

A VIEW OF THE OUTSIDE OF THE VAULT OF THE CRANIUM, SHOWING THE SUTURES.

1. The Coronal Suture.
2. The Sagittal Suture.
3. The Lambdoidal Suture.

FIG. 64.

A POSTERIOR AND INFERIOR VIEW OF THE CRANIUM, SHOWING THE POSTERIOR SUTURES.

1. The Palate Suture.
2. Posterior end of the Sagittal.
3. The Lambdoidal.
4. An Additamentum Suture and Os Wormianum above the Temporal Bone.

FIG. 65.

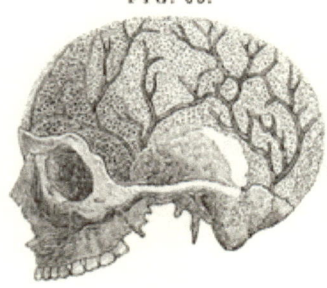

FIG. 66.

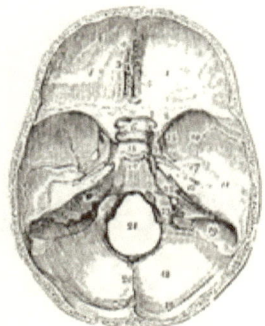

FIG. 67.

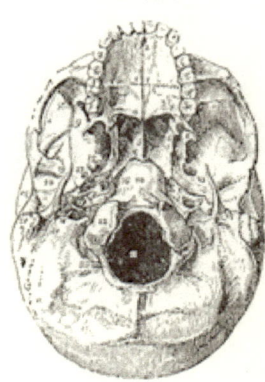

THE SURFACE OF THE HEAD.

FIG. 65.

A VIEW OF THE SKULL DE-
PRIVED OF ITS OUTER TABLE,
SO AS TO SHOW THE DIPLOIC
STRUCTURE. THE ARBORES-
CENT DARK LINES INDICATE
THE CHANNELS FOR THE
VEINS OF THIS STRUCTURE.

FIG. 66.

A VIEW OF THE INTERNAL
SURFACE OF THE BASE OF
THE CRANIUM, AFTER THE
VAULT HAS BEEN REMOVED.

1. Anterior Fossa for the Anterior Lobes of the Cerebrum.
2. Lesser Wing of the Sphenoid Bone.
3. Crista Galli.
4. Foramen Cæcum.
5. Cribriform Plate.
6. Processus Olivaris.
7. Foramen Opticum.
8. Anterior Clinoid Process.
9. Groove for the Carotid Artery.
10. Greater Wing of the Sphenoid Bone.

11. Middle Fossa for the Middle Lobes of the Cerebrum.
12. Petrous Portion of the Temporal Bone.
13. Sella Turcica.
14. Basilar Gutter for the Medulla Oblongata.
15. Foramen Rotundum.
16. Foramen Ovale.
17. Foramen Spinale.
The Hiatus Fallopii is just
below this number.
18. Posterior Fossa for the Cerebellum.
19. Groove for the Lateral Sinus.
20. Ridge for the Falx Cerebelli.
21. Foramen Magnum.
22. Meatus Auditorius Internus.
23. Posterior Foramen Lacerum
for the Jugular Vein.

FIG. 67.

AN EXTERNAL VIEW OF THE
BASE OF THE CRANIUM.

1. The Hard Palate.
2. Foramen Incisivum.
3. Palate Plate of the Palate
Bone.

4. Crescentic Edge for the Azygos Uvulæ Muscle.
5. The Vomer, separating the
Posterior Nares.
6. Internal Pterygoid Process
of the Sphenoid Bone.
7. Pterygoid Fossa.
8. External Pterygoid Process.
9. Temporal Fossa below the
Zygomatic Arch.
10. Basilar Process.
11. Foramen Magnum.
12. Foramen Ovale.
13. Foramen Spinale.
14. Glenoid Fossa.
15. Meatus Auditorius Externus.
16. Foramen Lacerum Anterius.
17. Carotid Foramen.
18. Foramen Lacerum Posterius.
19. Styloid Process.
20. Stylo-Mastoid Foramen.
21. Mastoid Process.
22. The Condyles of the Occipital Bone.
23. Posterior Condyloid Foramen.

FIG. 68.

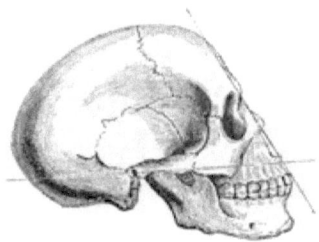

FIG. 69.

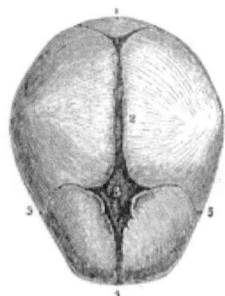

FIG. 70.

THE HEAD

FIG. 68.

A LATERAL VIEW OF THE SKULL, SHOWING THE LINES AND DIRECTION OF THE FACIAL ANGLE.

FIG. 69.

A VIEW OF THE FŒTAL HEAD, SHOWING THE FONTANELS.

1. Posterior Fontanel.
2. Line of Separation of the Parietal Bones.
3. Anterior Fontanel.

4. Line of Separation of the Os Frontis.
5.5. Coronal Suture in the Infant.

FIG. 70.

AN ANTERIOR VIEW OF THE OS HYOIDES.

1. The Anterior Convex Side of the Body.
2. The Cornu Majus of the Left Side.
3. The Cornu Minus of the same Side.

The Cornua were Ossified to the Body of the Bone, in this Specimen.

FIG. 71.   FIG. 72.

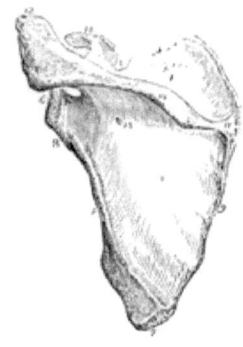

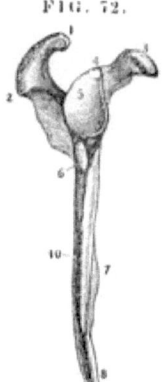

FIG. 73.

THE SHOULDER.

FIG. 71.

A POSTERIOR VIEW OF THE SCAPULA OF THE
LEFT SIDE.

1. Fossa Supra-Spinata.
2. Fossa Infra-Spinata.
3. Superior Margin.
4. Coracoid Notch.
5. Inferior Margin.
6. Glenoid Cavity.
7. Inferior Angle.
8. The Neck and Point of Origin of the Long
   Head of the Triceps Muscle.
9. Posterior, or Vertebral Margin.
10. The Spine.
11. Smooth Facet for the Trapezius Muscle.
12. Acromion Process.
13. Nutritious Foramen.
14. Coracoid Process.
15. Part of the Origin of the Deltoid Muscle.

FIG. 72.

THE EXTERNAL OR AXILLARY MARGIN OF THE
SCAPULA OF THE RIGHT SIDE. (W. M.)

1. Articular Face for the Clavicle.
2. Acromion Process.

3. Coracoid Process.
4. Origin of the Long Head of the Biceps Muscle.
5. Glenoid Cavity.
6. Origin of the Long Head of the Triceps
   Muscle.
7. Anterior Costa.
8. Surface for the Teres Major.
9. Surface for a slip of the Latissimus Dorsi.
10. Depression for the Teres Minor Muscle.

FIG. 73.

AN ANTERIOR VIEW OF THE CLAVICLE OF THE
RIGHT SIDE. (Wistar Museum.)

1. The Anterior Face of the Body of the Bone.
2. Origin of the Clavicular Portion of the Sterno-
   Cleido-Mastoid Muscle.
3. The Sternal extremity of the Bone.
4. The Acromial extremity of the Bone.
5. Articular Face for the Acromion Process of the
   Scapula.
6. Point of Attachment of the Conoid Ligament.
7. Point of Attachment of the Rhomboid Ligament.

FIG. 74.

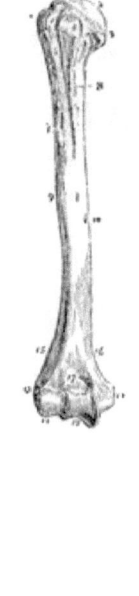

FIG. 75.

FIG. 76.

THE ARM AND FORE-ARM

FIG. 74.

AN ANTERIOR VIEW OF THE HU-
MERUS OF THE RIGHT SIDE.

1. The Shaft, or Diaphysis of
   the Bone.
2. The Head.
3. Anatomical Neck.
4. Greater Tuberosity.
5. Lesser Tuberosity.
6. The Bicipital Groove.
7. External Bicipital Ridge for
   the insertion of the Pectoralis Major.
8. Internal Bicipital Ridge.
9. Point of insertion of the
   Deltoid Muscle.
10. Nutritious Foramen.
11. Articular Face for the Head
    of the Radius.
12. Articular Face for the Ulna.

13. External Condyle.
14. Internal Condyle.
15. 16. The Condyloid Ridges.
17. Lesser Sigmoid Cavity.

FIG. 75.

AN ANTERIOR VIEW OF THE
ULNA OF THE LEFT SIDE.

1. Olecranon Process.
2. Greater Sigmoid Cavity.
3. Coronoid Process.
4. Lesser Sigmoid Cavity.
5. External Surface; just above
   the Number reposes the Anconeus Muscle.
6. Ridge for the Interosseous
   Ligament.
7. The Small Head for the Radius.
8. The Carpal Surface.

9. The Styloid Process.
10. Groove, for the Extensor
    Carpi Ulnaris Tendon.

FIG. 76.

AN ANTERIOR VIEW OF THE RA-
DIUS OF THE RIGHT SIDE.

1. Cylindrical Head.
2. Surface for the Lesser Sigmoid Cavity of the Ulna.
3. The Neck of the Radius.
4. Its Tubercle, for the insertion
   of the Biceps Muscle.
5. Interosseous Ridge.
6. Concavity for the Lower End
   of the Ulna.
7. Carpal Surface.
8. Styloid Process.
9. Surface for the Pronator Quadratus Muscle.

FIG. 77.

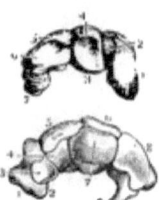

FIG. 78.

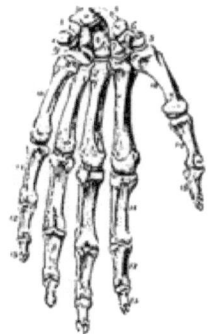

FIG. 79.

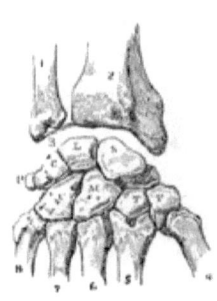

BONES OF THE HAND

FIG. 77.

THE TWO ROWS OF BONES OF THE CARPUS.

The Upper or First Row, viewed on its Inferior Articulating Surface.

1. The Scaphoides.
2. Its Articular Face.
3. The Lunare.
4. Its Articular Face.
5. The Cuneiforme.
6. Its Articular Face.
7. The Pisiforme.

The Lower or Second Row, viewed on its Superior Articulating Surface.

1. The Trapezium.
2. Its Tubercle.
3. Its Articular Face.
4. The Articular Face of the Trapezoides.
5. The Superior Surface of the Trapezoides.
6. The Magnum.
7. Its Head, or Articulating Surface.
8. The Unciforme.
9. Its Hook-like Process.

FIG. 78.

AN ANTERIOR VIEW OF THE LEFT HAND.

1. The Scaphoides.
2. The Lunare.
3. The Cuneiforme.
4. The Pisiforme.
5. The Trapezium.

6. Groove for the Flexor Carpi Radialis Tendon.
7. The Trapezoides.
8. The Magnum.
9. The Unciforme.
10.10. The Five Meta-Carpal Bones.
11.11. First Row of Phalanges.
12.12. Second Row of Phalanges.
13.13. Third Row of Phalanges.
14. First Phalanx of the Thumb.
15. Last Phalanx of the Thumb.

FIG. 79.

A POSTERIOR VIEW OF THE ARTICULATIONS OF THE BONES OF THE CARPUS IN THE RIGHT HAND.

1. The Ulna.
2. The Radius.
3. Inter-Articular Fibro-Cartilage.
4. Metacarpal Bone of the Thumb.
5. Metacarpal Bone of the First Finger.
6. Metacarpal Bone of the Second Finger.
7. Metacarpal Bone of the Third Finger.
8. Metacarpal Bone of the Fourth Finger.
S. The Scaphoides.
L. The Lunare.
C. The Cuneiforme.
P. The Pisiforme.
T. T. Trapezium and Trapezoides.
M. The Magnum.
U. The Unciforme.

FIG. 80.

FIG. 81.

FIG. 82.

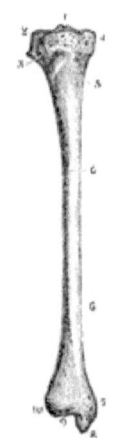

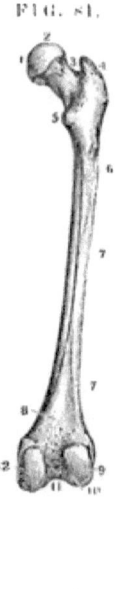

BONES OF THE INFERIOR EXTREMITY

FIG. 80.

AN ANTERIOR VIEW OF THE FEMUR OF THE RIGHT SIDE. (*Wistar Museum.*)

1. Depression for the Round Ligament.
2. The Head.
3. The Neck.
4. Trochanter Major.
5. Trochanter Minor.
6. Surface for the Capsular Ligament.
7. Shaft of the Bone.
8. The External Condyle.
9. The Internal Condyle.
10. Surface for the Patella.

———

FIG. 81.

A POSTERIOR VIEW OF THE FEMUR OF THE RIGHT SIDE. (*Wistar Museum.*)

1. Depression for the Round Ligament.
2. The Head.
3. Depression for some of the Rotatory Muscles.
4. Trochanter Major.
5. Trochanter Minor.
6. Roughness for the Gluteus Maximus Tendon.
7.7. The Linea Aspera.
8. Surface for the Gastrocnemius Muscle.
9. The External Condyle.
10. Depression for the Anterior Crucial Ligament.
11. Depression for the Posterior Crucial Ligament.
12. Point of Origin of the Internal Lateral Ligament.

FIG. 82.

AN ANTERIOR VIEW OF THE TIBIA OF THE RIGHT SIDE. (*Wistar Museum.*)

1. Spinous Process, and Pits for the Attachment of the Crucial Ligaments.
2. Surface for the Condyles of the Femur.
3. Articular Face for the Head of the Fibula.
4. The Head.
5. The Tubercle.
6.6. The Spine and Shaft of the Bone.
7. Internal Malleolus.
8. Process for the Internal Lateral Ligament of the Ankle.
9. Tarsal Surface.
10. Face for the Lower End of the Fibula.

FIG. 83.

FIG. 84.

FIG. 85.

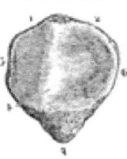

FIG. 86.

FIG. 87.

BONES OF THE INFERIOR EXTREMITY.

FIG. 83.

AN ANTERIOR VIEW OF THE FIBULA OF THE RIGHT SIDE.

1. Its Head.
2. Articular Face for the Tibia.
3. Point of Insertion of the External Lateral Ligament and Biceps Cruris Tendon.
4. Shaft of the Bone.
5.5. External Face, for the Peroneus Longus and Secundus Muscles.
6. Interosseous Ridge.
7. Face for the Lower End of the Tibia.
8. Malleolus Externus.
9. Tarsal Surface.

FIG. 84.

AN ANTERIOR VIEW OF THE PATELLA.

1.
2. } Surface for the Quadriceps Femoris Tendon.
3. Lower Extremity and Point of Origin of the Ligamentum Patellæ.

FIG. 85.

A POSTERIOR VIEW OF THE PATELLA.

1.2. Its Superior Extremity.
3. Its Inferior Extremity.
4. Elevation for fitting the Trochlea of the Femur.
5.6. Internal and External Sides.

FIG. 86.

A LATERAL VIEW OF THE OS CALCIS OF THE LEFT SIDE. (*Wistar Museum.*)

1. Surface for the Tendo-Achillis.
2. Point, or Inferior Posterior Extremity.
3. The Lesser Apophysis.
4. Articular Face for Part of the Astragalus.
5. The Anterior Extremity, or Greater Apophysis.
6. Groove for the Flexor Longus Pollicis Pedis Tendon.

FIG. 87.

A LATERAL VIEW OF THE ASTRAGALUS OF THE RIGHT SIDE. (*Wistar Museum.*)

1. The Semi-Cylindrical Face for Articulating with the Tibia.
2. The Articular Face for the External Malleolus.
3. Surface for the Os Calcis.
4. Posterior Extremity.

FIG. 88.

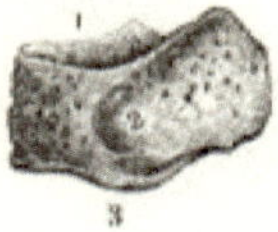

FIG. 89.

FIG. 90.
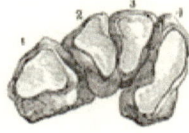

FIG. 91.

FIG. 92.

BONES OF THE FOOT

FIG. 88.

A LATERAL VIEW OF THE NA-
VICULARE. (*Wistar Museum*.)

1. Surface for the Astragalus.
2. Superior Face.
3. Surface for the Cuneiform Bones.

FIG. 89.

A HALF LATERAL VIEW OF THE
CUBOID BONE. (*W. M.*)

1. Its Superior, or Dorsal Face.
2. Surface for Metatarsal Bones.
3. Posterior Face for the Os Calcis.
4. Inferior Face and Groove for the Peroneus Longus Tendon.
5. Surface for the Cuneiforme Internum.

FIG. 90.

AN ANTERIOR VIEW OF THE
THREE CUNEIFORM BONES,
AND ALSO OF THE CUBOID OF
THE RIGHT SIDE. (*W. M.*)

1. The Cuboid.
2. The Cuneiforme Externum.

3. The Cuneiforme Medium.
4. The Cuneiforme Internum.

FIG. 91.

A VIEW OF THE UPPER SUR-
FACE OF THE LEFT FOOT.

1. The Astragalus on its Upper Face.
2. Its Anterior Face, Articulating with the Naviculare.
3. The Os Calcis.
4. Naviculare, or Scaphcides.
5. The Internal Cuneiform.
6. The Middle Cuneiform.
7. The External Cuneiform.
8. The Cuboid Bone.
9.9. Metatarsal Bones.
10. First Phalanx of the Big Toe.
11. Second Phalanx of the Big Toe.
12.12. } The First, Second and
13.13. } Third Phalanges of the
14.14. } other Toes.

FIG. 92.

THE UNDER SIDE, OR SOLE, OF
THE LEFT FOOT.

1. The Lesser Apophysis of the Os Calcis.
2. The Outer side of the Calcis.
3. Groove for the Flexor Longus Pollicis Pedis Tendon.
4. Anterior Face of the Astragalus.
5. The Naviculare.
6. Its Tuberosity on the Inner side.
7. Internal Cuneiform Bone.
8. Middle Cuneiform Bone.
9. External Cuneiform Bone.
10. The Cuboid Bone.
11. Groove for the Peroneus Longus Tendon.
12.12. The Metatarsal Bones.
13.13. The First Phalanges of the Toes.
14.14. The Second Phalanges of the Toes.
15.15. The Third Phalanges of the Toes.
16. The Last Phalanx of the Great Toe.

FIG. 93.

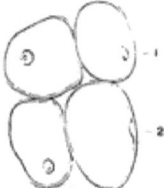

FIG. 94.

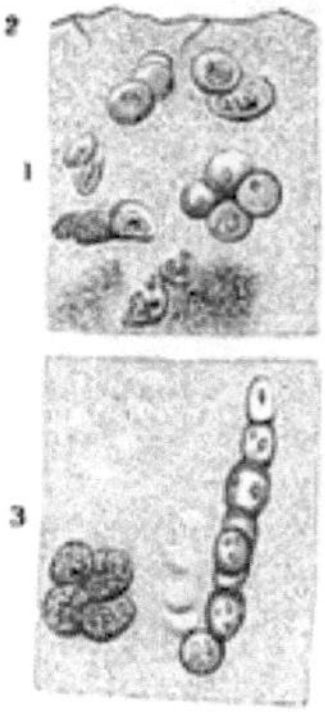

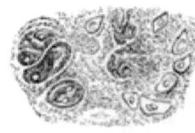

FIG. 95.

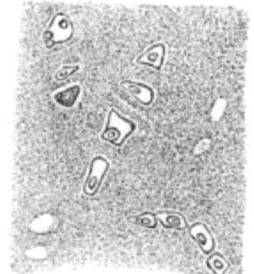

FIG. 96.

THE CARTILAGINOUS SYSTEM

FIG. 93.

THE NUCLEATED CELLS OF CARTILAGE, FROM THE LAMPREY; MAGNIFIED.

1. The Nucleus, with its Nucleolus.
2. Another, seen in Profile.

———

FIG. 94.

ARTICULAR CARTILAGE FROM THE HEAD OF THE HUMERUS, MAGNIFIED 320 DIAMETERS, VERTICAL SECTION.

1. Section close to the Surface.
2. The Surface of the Cartilage.
3. A Section far in the Interior.

FIG. 95.

A SECTION OF THE CARTILAGE OF THE RIBS, MAGNIFIED 320 DIAMETERS, AND SHOWING THE CELLS, THEIR NUCLEI AND NUCLEOLI. THE TRANSPARENT SPACES, RESULT FROM THE REMOVAL OF THE CELLS BY THE KNIFE, THEIR CAVITIES REMAINING.

———

FIG. 96.

A THIN SECTION OF THE THYROID CARTILAGE, MAGNIFIED 320 DIAMETERS.

FIG. 97.　　　　　　　　　　　　　　　FIG. 98.

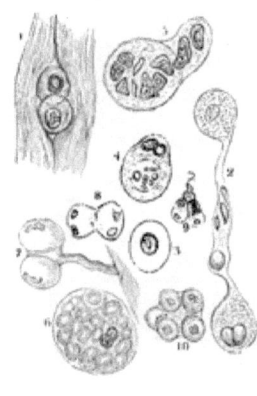

FIG. 99.

THE FIBRO, OR LIGAMENTO-CARTILAGINOUS SYSTEM.

FIG. 97.

A MICROSCOPICAL VIEW OF FIBRO-CARTILAGE.

1. Two Cartilage Cells, lying amongst the White Fibrous Tissue, in an Intervertebral Disc.
2. Fibro-Cartilage, as Laminæ, free on both Surfaces, and as placed in the Cavity of Diarthrodial Joints. They are the *Menisci* of Authors, and exist in the Temporo-Maxillary, Sterno-Clavicular, and Tibio-Femoral Articulations.
3. Fibro-Cartilage, as Triangular Edges to the Glenoid and Cotyloid Cavities, in the Shoulder and Hip-Joints.
4. 5. 6. 7. 8. 9. 10. Exhibit various Forms of the Cells in the Central Pulpy Substance of the Intervertebral Matter. In several there is an appearance of Multiplication by Subdivision of the Nucleus, and some seem attached by a Fibrous Tissue.

FIG. 98.

A MICROSCOPICAL VIEW OF THE WHITE FIBROUS TISSUE, MAGNIFIED 320 DIAMETERS

1. 2. The Straight appearance of the Tissue when stretched, as in Ligaments of the Funicular and Fascicular kinds.
3. 4. 5. Show the various Wavy appearances which the Tissue exhibits when not stretched.

FIG. 99.

THE YELLOW FIBROUS TISSUE, SHOWING THE CURLY AND BRANCHED DISPOSITION OF ITS FIBRILLÆ, THEIR DEFINITE OUTLINE AND ABRUPT MODE OF FRACTURE, MAGNIFIED 320 DIAMETERS.

1. The Structure undisturbed, and not moved from its natural position, as seen in the rest of the Specimen.

FIG. 100.   FIG. 101.

 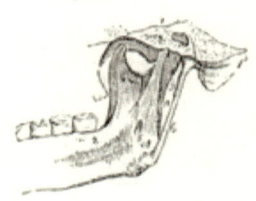

FIG. 102.

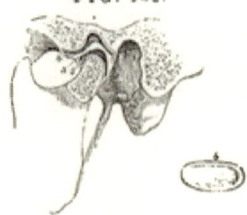

ARTICULATION OF THE LOWER JAW.

FIG. 100.

THE ARTICULATION OF THE LOWER JAW ON ITS
    EXTERNAL SURFACE.

1. Zygomatic Arch.
2. The Tubercle in Front of the Glenoid Cavity, on which the Condyloid Process rests when the Mouth is widely opened.
3. The Ramus of the Lower Maxilla.
4. The Mastoid Process of the Temporal Bone.
5. The External Lateral Ligament.
6. The Stylo-Maxillary Ligament.

FIG. 101.

AN INTERNAL VIEW OF THE ARTICULATION OF
    THE LOWER JAW.

1. A Section through a portion of the Temporal and Sphenoid Bones.
2. The Inside of the Ramus and part of the Body of the Lower Jaw.
3. The Internal Surface of the Capsular Ligament.
4. The Internal Lateral Ligament.
5. The Opening in it for the Mylo-Hyoid Nerve, a Branch of the Inferior Dental.
6. The Stylo-Maxillary Ligament.

FIG. 102.

A VIEW OF THE ARTICULATION OF THE LOWER
    JAW, GIVEN BY SAWING THROUGH THE JOINT.

1. The Glenoid Fossa.
2. The Tubercle for the Condyle in its Forward movements.
3. The Inter-Articular Cartilage.
4. The Superior Synovial Cavity.
5. The Inferior Synovial Cavity.
6. The Inter-Articular Cartilage removed from the Joint and seen from below.

FIG. 104.

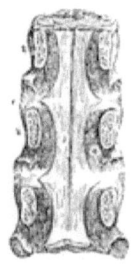

FIG. 103.

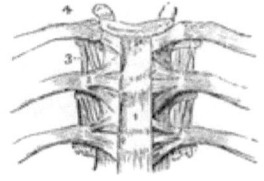

FIG. 105.

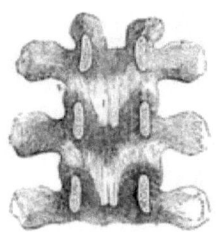

LIGAMENTS OF THE SPINE

FIG. 103.

AN ANTERIOR VIEW OF THE LIGAMENTS OF THE VERTEBRÆ AND RIBS.

1. The Anterior Vertebral Ligament.
2. The Anterior Costo-Vertebral Ligament.
3. The Internal Transverse Ligament.
4. The Inter-Articular Ligament, connecting the Head of the Rib to the Intervertebral Substance.

—

FIG. 104.

A POSTERIOR VIEW OF THE SPINAL CANAL, HALF OF WHICH HAS BEEN CUT AWAY IN ORDER TO SHOW ITS INTERIOR.

1.1. The Intervertebral Substance.

2.2. Surfaces of the Vertebræ from which the Bony Bridges have been removed.
3. The Posterior Vertebral Ligament.
4. An Opening for one of the Vertebral Veins.

—

FIG. 105.

AN INTERNAL VIEW OF THE BONY BRIDGES OF THE VERTEBRÆ, AFTER THEIR SEPARATION FROM THE BODIES OF THE BONES.

1.1. One Pair of the Ligamenta Flava, or Yellow Ligaments.
2. The Capsular Ligament of one side.

FIG. 106.

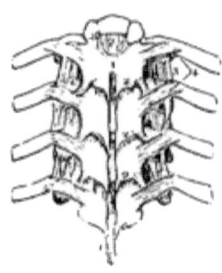

FIG. 107.

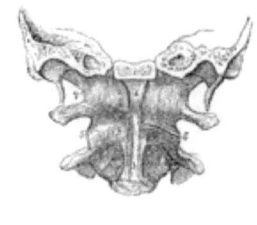

FIG. 108.

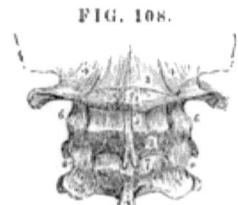

FIG. 109.

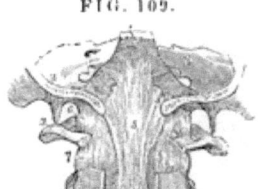

LIGAMENTS OF THE SPINE

FIG. 106.

A POSTERIOR VIEW OF THE THORACIC PORTION OF THE VERTEBRÆ.

1.1. The Ligaments of the Spinous Processes.
2.2.2. The Yellow Ligaments.
   3. The Anterior, or Internal Costo-Transverse Ligament.
   4. The Posterior, or External Costo-Transverse Ligament.

FIG. 107.

AN ANTERIOR VIEW OF THE LIGAMENTS CONNECTING THE ATLAS AND DENTATA WITH THE OS OCCIPITIS. THE BASILAR PROCESS OF THE OCCIPITAL BONE AND THE PETROUS PORTION OF THE TEMPORAL BEING DIVIDED BY THE SAW.

1. The Anterior Occipito-Atloidien Ligament.
2. The Membrana Annuli Anterioris of Caldani.
3. The commencement of the Anterior Vertebral Ligament.
4.5. The Capsular Ligament of the Oblique Processes of the Atlas and Dentata.
6. The Joint between the First and Second Cervical Vertebræ, after the removal of the Capsular Ligament.
7. The Outer Fibres of the Membrana Annuli Anterioris.

FIG. 108.

A POSTERIOR VIEW OF THE ARTICULATION OF THE OCCIPUT, ATLAS AND DENTATA.

1. The Atlas.
2. The Dentata.
3. The Posterior Occipito-Atloidien Ligament.
4. The Capsular Ligament of the Oblique Processes of the Atlas and the Condyles of the Occipital Bone.
5. The Ligament between the First and Second Vertebræ.
6. The Lateral Fasciculi of the same.
7. The First of the Yellow Ligaments.
8. The Capsular Ligament between the Oblique Processes of the Second and Third Vertebræ.

FIG. 109.

THE UPPER PART OF THE SPINAL CANAL OPENED FROM BEHIND, TO SHOW THE LIGAMENTS ON ITS FRONT.

1. The Basilar Portion of the Sphenoid Bone.
2. Section of the Occiput.
3. The Front Half of the Atlas.
4. The Front Half of the Dentata.
5. The beginning of the Posterior Vertebral Ligament.
6.7. The Capsular Ligaments of the Occipito-Atloidien, and the First and Second Vertebral Articulations, at their Oblique Processes.

FIG. 110.

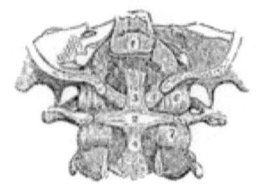

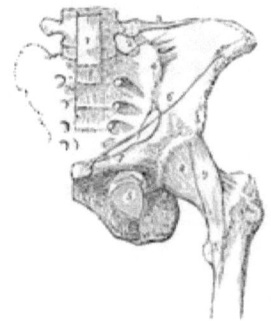

FIG. 112.

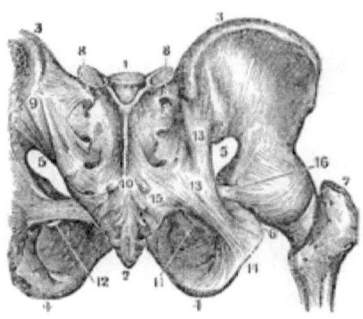

LIGAMENTS OF THE SPINE AND PELVIS.

FIG. 110.

A Posterior View of the Ligaments connecting the Atlas and the Dentata with the
Occipital Bone.

1. The Upper Part of the Posterior Vertebral
   Ligament.
2. The Transverse Ligament.
3.4. The Upper and Lower Appendices of the
   Transverse Ligament.
5. One of the Moderator Ligaments.
6.7. Capsular Ligaments belonging to the Oblique
   Processes of the First and Second Vertebræ.

FIG. 111.

An Anterior View of the Ligaments of the
Pelvis.

1. The Lower Part of the Anterior Vertebral Ligament.
2. The Sacro-Vertebral Ligament
3. The Ilio-Lumbar Ligament.
4. The Anterior portion of the Sacro-Iliac Ligament.
5. The Obturator Ligament.
6. Poupart's Ligament.

7. That portion of the same which is known as
   Gimbernat's Ligament.
8. The Capsular Ligament of the Hip-Joint.
9. The Accessory Ligament of the Hip-Joint.

FIG. 112.

A Posterior View of the Ligaments of the
Pelvis.

1. Base of the Sacrum.
2. The Coccyx.
3.3. The Crista Ilii.
4.4. The Tuber Ischii.
5.5. The Greater Sciatic Notch.
6. The Lesser Sciatic Notch.
7. The Femur.
8. The Posterior portion of the Sacro-Iliac Ligament.
9. The Sacro-Spinous Ligament.
10. The Posterior Sacro-Coccygeal Ligament in
   its whole length.
11. The Obturator Ligament.
12. The Obturator Foramen.
13.13. The Origin of the Greater Sciatic Ligament.
14. Its Insertion.
15. The Origin of the Lesser Sciatic Ligament
16. Its Insertion.

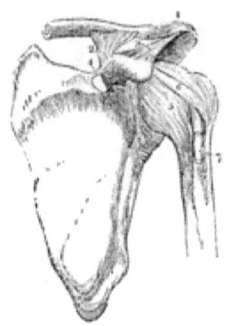

FIG. 114.

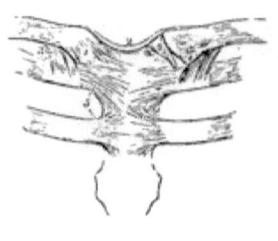

FIG. 113.

FIG. 115.

FIG. 116.

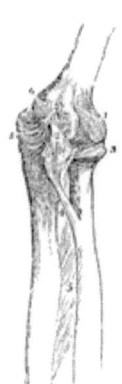

ARTICULATIONS OF THE UPPER EXTREMITIES.

FIG. 113.

THE LIGAMENTS OF THE STERNO-CLAVICULAR AND COSTO-STERNAL ARTICULATION.

1. The Capsular Ligament, of the Sterno-Clavicular Articulation.
2. The Inter-Clavicular Ligament.
3. The Costo-Clavicular, or Rhomboid Ligament.
4. The Inter-Articular Cartilage.
5. The Anterior Costo-Sternal Ligaments of the First and Second Ribs.

FIG. 114.

THE LIGAMENTS OF THE ACROMIO-CLAVICULAR AND SCAPULO-HUMERAL ARTICULATIONS.

1. The Superior Acromio-Clavicular Ligament.
2. The Coraco-Clavicular Ligament.
3. The Coraco-Acromial Ligament.
4. The Coracoid Ligament.
5. The Capsular Ligament of the Shoulder-Joint.
6. The Ligamentum Adscititium, or Coraco-Humeral Ligament.
7. The Tendon of the Long Head of the Biceps Muscle. issuing from the Capsular Ligament.

FIG. 115.

AN EXTERNAL VIEW OF THE ELBOW-JOINT.

1. The Humerus.
2. The Ulna.
3. The Radius.
4. The External Lateral Ligament.
5. The Coronary Ligament.
6. The Insertion of the Coronary Ligament at the Posterior Part of the Lesser Sigmoid Cavity of the Ulna.
7. 8. The Portions of the Capsular Ligament known as the Accessory Ligaments.
9. The Interosseous Ligament of the Fore-Arm.

FIG. 116.

AN INTERNAL VIEW OF THE ELBOW-JOINT.

1. The Capsular Ligament.
2.2. The Internal Lateral Ligament.
3. The Coronary Ligament.
4. The Ligamentum Teres.
5. The Interosseous Ligament.
6. The Internal Condyle, which conceals the Capsular Ligament behind

FIG. 117.

FIG. 118.

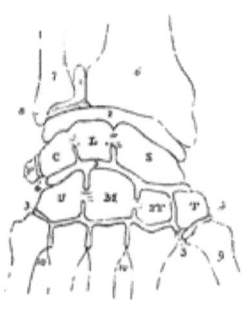

ARTICULATIONS OF THE UPPER EXTREMITIES.

FIG. 117.

AN ANTERIOR VIEW OF THE LIGAMENTS OF THE
WRIST, ON THE LEFT SIDE.

1. The Lower Part of the Interosseous Ligament.
2. The Radio-Ulnar Ligament.
3. The portion of the Capsular Ligament known as the Anterior Ligament.
4. The External Lateral Ligament.
5. The Internal Lateral Ligament.
6. The Capsular Ligament of the Carpal Bones.
7. The Pisiform Bone.
8. The Ligaments connecting the Second Row of the Carpus with the Metacarpus.
9. The Capsular Ligament of the Carpo-Metacarpal Joint of the Thumb.
10. The Capsular Ligament of the Metacarpo Phalangial Joint of the Thumb.
11. The External Lateral Ligament of the same Joint.
12. The Capsular Ligament of the Metacarpo Phalangial Articulation of the Index Finger.
13.13. Lateral Ligaments of similar Articulations.
14. The Inferior Palmar Ligaments.
15. The Phalangial Joint of the Thumb, with its Capsular and Lateral Ligaments.

16.16. The same of the Fore-Finger. The Capsular Ligaments have been removed in the other Fingers.

FIG. 118.

A DIAGRAM SHOWING THE ARRANGEMENT OF
THE FIVE SYNOVIAL MEMBRANES OF THE
WRIST JOINT.

1. The Sacciform Membrane.
2. The Joint between the First Row of Carpal Bones and those of the Fore-Arm.
3.3. The Synovial Membrane between the Two Rows of Bones.
4. The Joint between the Pisiform and Cuneiform Bones.
5. The Synovial Membrane at the Meta-Carpal Joint of the Thumb.
6. The Radius.
7. The Ulna.
8. The Interarticular Cartilage, or Triangular Ligament.
9. The Metacarpal Bone of the Thumb.
10.10. Those of the Fingers. The Capital Letters indicate the separate bones of the Carpus, thus, S. Scaphoides—L. Lunare, &c ,&c.

FIG. 119.

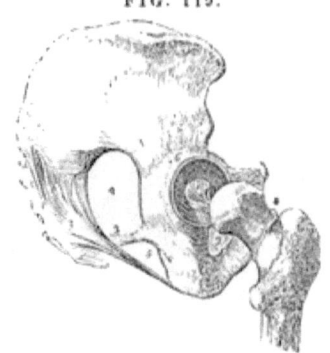

FIG. 120.

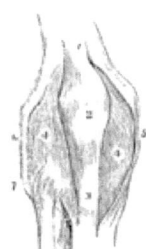

FIG. 121.

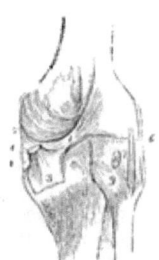

ARTICULATIONS OF THE LOWER EXTREMITIES

FIG. 119.

A LATERAL VIEW OF THE LIGAMENTS OF THE HIP-JOINT AND PELVIS.

1. The Posterior Sacro-Iliac Ligament of the Pelvis.
2. The Greater Sacro-Sciatic Ligament.
3. The Lesser Sacro-Sciatic Ligament.
4. The Greater Sacro-Sciatic Notch.
5. The Lesser Sacro-Sciatic Notch.
6. The Cotyloid Ligament around the Acetabulum.
7. The Ligamentum Teres.
8. The Line of Attachment of the Capsular Ligament of the Hip-Joint, posteriorly. The Ligament has been removed, in order to show the Joint.
9. The Obturator Ligament.

FIG. 120.

AN ANTERIOR VIEW OF THE KNEE-JOINT OF THE RIGHT SIDE.

1. The Tendon of the Quadriceps Femoris Muscle.
2. The Patella.
3. The Ligament of the Patella.

4.4. The Synovial Membrane, after the removal of the Involucrum.
5. The Internal Lateral Ligament.
6. The External Ligament.
7. The Anterior Ligament of the Superior Peroneo-Tibial Articulation.

FIG. 121.

A POSTERIOR VIEW OF THE KNEE-JOINT OF THE RIGHT SIDE.

1. The Ligament of Winslow.
2. The Tendon of the Semi-Membranosus Muscle.
3. Its Insertion, showing the Expansion of its Fibres.
4. The portion which passes beneath the Internal Lateral Ligament.
5. The Internal Lateral Ligament.
6. The External Lateral Ligament.
7. A Fasciculus of the same, sometimes called the Short External Lateral Ligament.
8. The Tendon of the Popliteus Muscle cut short.
9. The Posterior Superior Peroneo-Tibial Ligament.

FIG. 122.   FIG. 123.

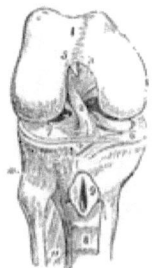

FIG. 124.   FIG. 125.

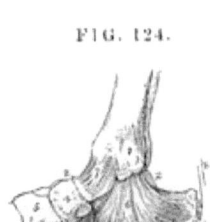

ARTICULATIONS OF THE LOWER EXTREMITIES.

FIG. 122.
THE RIGHT KNEE-JOINT LAID OPEN.

1. The Lower End of the Femur covered by its Articular Cartilage.
2. The Anterior Crucial Ligament.
3. The Posterior Crucial Ligament.
4. The Transverse Fasciculus adhering to the Semilunar Cartilages.
5. The Point of Attachment of the Ligamentum Mucosum, the rest of it has been removed.
6. The Internal Semilunar Cartilage.
7. The External Semilunar Cartilage.
8. A part of the Ligamentum Patellæ turned downwards.
9. Its Bursa laid open.
10. The Superior Peroneo-Tibial Articulation.
11. The Interosseous Ligament.

FIG. 123.
A LONGITUDINAL SECTION OF THE KNEE-JOINT OF THE LEFT SIDE.

1. The Cellular Structure of the Lower End of the Femur.
2. The Tendon of the Quadriceps Femoris.
3. The Patella.
4. Its Ligament.
5. The Cellular Structure of the Tibia.
6. The Bursa Mucosa between the Ligament of the Patella and the Head of the Tibia.
7. A mass of Fat projecting into the Joint below the Patella.
8. The Synovial Membrane; the Stars show its Reflections in the Joint.

9. One of the Ligamenta Alaria, the other being removed with the opposite Section,
10. The Ligamentum Mucosum.
11. The Anterior Crucial Ligament.
12. The Posterior Ligament.

FIG. 124.
AN INTERNAL VIEW OF THE ANKLE-JOINT OF THE RIGHT SIDE.

1. Internal Malleolus.
2.2. Part of the Astragalus, the rest being concealed by Ligaments.
3. Os Calcis.
4. Scaphoides.
5. Internal Cuneiform Bone.
6. Internal Lateral, or Deltoid Ligament.
7. The Synovial Capsule, covered by a few Fibres of a Capsular Ligament.
8. Tendo Achillis. A small Bursa is seen between this Tendon and the Tuberosity of the Os Calcis.

FIG. 125.
AN EXTERNAL VIEW OF THE RIGHT ANKLE-JOINT.

1. The Tibia.
2. The External Malleolus of the Fibula.
3.3. The Astragalus.
4. The Os Calcis.
5. The Cuboides.
6.7.8. The Anterior, Middle, and Posterior Fasciculi of the External Lateral Ligament.
9. The Imperfect Capsular Ligament.

FIG. 127.

FIG. 126.

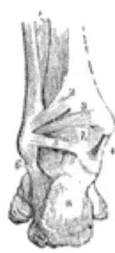

FIG. 128.

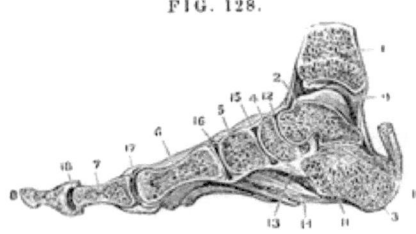

ARTICULATIONS OF THE LOWER EXTREMITIES.

FIG. 126.

A POSTERIOR VIEW OF THE ANKLE-JOINT OF THE LEFT SIDE.

1. The Interosseous Ligament of the Bones of the Leg.
2. The Posterior Inferior Ligament connecting the Tibia and Fibula.
3. The Transverse, or Long Fibres of the same Ligament.
4. The Internal Lateral Ligament.
5. The Posterior Fasciculus of the External Lateral Ligament.
6. The Middle Fasciculus of the same.
7. The Synovial Capsule.
8. The Os Calcis.

FIG. 127.

A VIEW OF THE LIGAMENTS OF THE SOLE OF THE FOOT.

1. The Under Surface of the Os Calcis.
2. The Astragalus.
3. The Scaphoides.
4.5. The two Planes of Fibres of the Calcaneo-Cuboid Ligament.
6. The Calcaneo-Scaphoid Ligament.
7. The Plantar Ligaments.
8.8. The Peroneus Longus Tendon.
9.9. The Tarso-Metatarsal Plantar Ligaments.
10. The Capsular Ligament of the First Joint of the Big Toe.
11. The Lateral Ligaments of the First Joints of the Toes.

12. The Transverse Ligament.
13. Lateral Ligaments of the Last Joints of the Toes.

———

FIG. 128.

A VERTICAL SECTION OF THE ANKLE-JOINT AND FOOT OF THE RIGHT SIDE.

1. The Tibia.
2. The Astragalus.
3. Os Calcis.
4. The Scaphoides.
5. The Cunciforme Internum.
6. The Metatarsal Bone of the Great Toe.
7. The First Phalanx of the Great Toe.
8. The Second Phalanx of the Great Toe.
9. The Articular Cavity between the Tibia and Astragalus, with its Articular Adipose Matter.
10. The Synovial Capsule between the Astragalus and Calcis.
11. The Calcaneo-Astragalian Interosseous Ligament.
12. The Synovial Capsule between the Astragalus and Scaphoides.
13. The Calcaneo-Scaphoid Ligament.
14. The Calcaneo-Cuboid Ligament.
15. The Synovial Capsule between the Scaphoides and Cunciforme Internum.
16. The Synovial Capsule between the Cunciforme-Internum and the First Metatarsal Bone.
17. The Metatarso-Phalangial Articulation of the Great Toe, with the Sesamoid Bones below.
18. The Phalangial Articulation of the Great Toe.

END OF PART FIRST

PART SECOND.

DERMOID AND MUSCULAR SYSTEM:

NINETY-ONE FIGURES

FIG. 129.

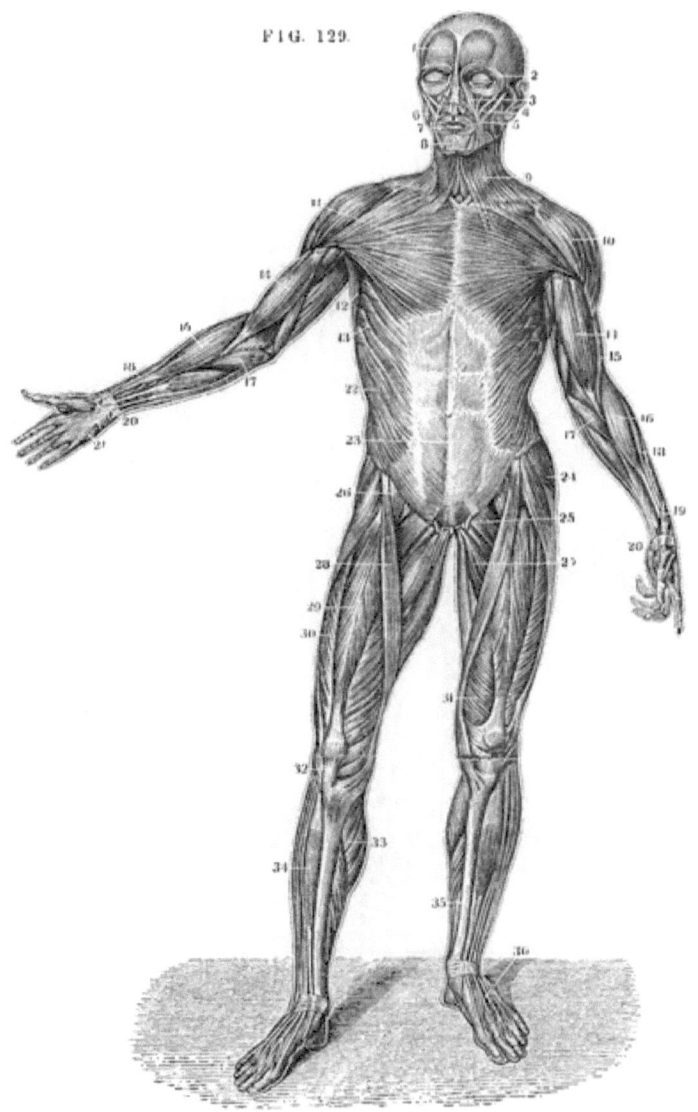

THE MUSCLES.

FIG. 130.

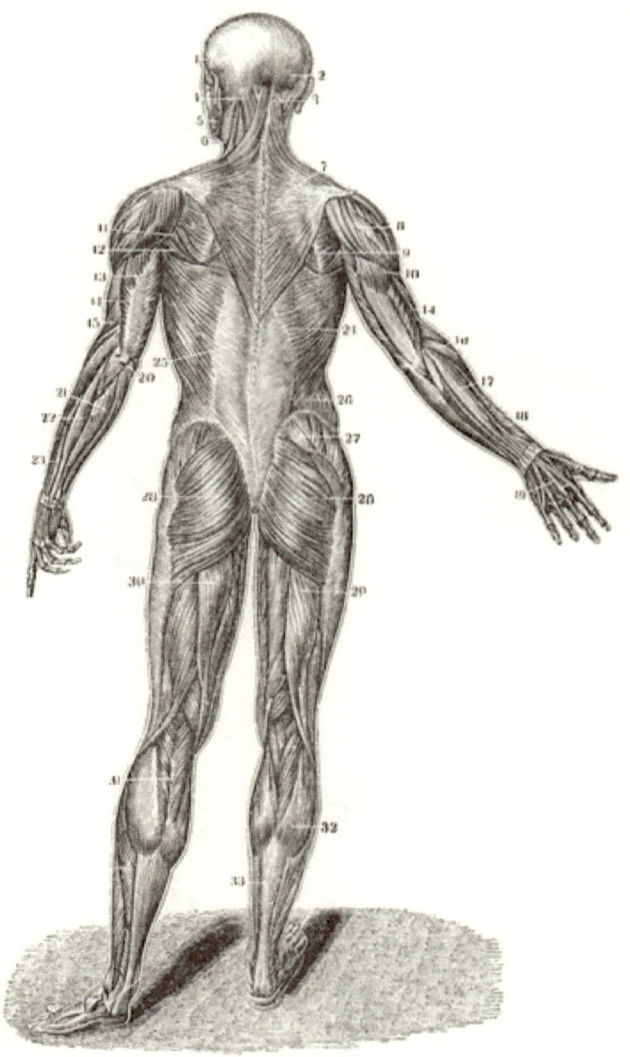

THE MUSCLES

FIG. 130.

POSTERIOR VIEW OF THE MUSCLES OF THE BODY.

1. Temporalis.
2. Occipital portion of the Occipito-Frontalis.
3. Complexus.
4. Splenius.
5. Masseter.
6. Sterno-Cleido-Mastoideus.
7. Trapezius.
8. Deltoid.
9. Infra-Spinatus.
10. Triceps Extensor.
11. Teres Minor.
12. Teres Major.
13. Tendinous portion of the Triceps.
14. Anterior Edge of the Triceps.
15. Supinator Radii Longus.
16. Pronator Radii Teres.
17. Extensor Communis Digitorum.
18. Extensor Ossis Metacarpi Pollicis.
19. Extensor Communis Digitorum Tendons.
20. Olecranon and Insertion of the Triceps.
21. Extensor Carpi Ulnaris.
22. Auricularis.
23. Extensor Communis.
24. Latissimus Dorsi.
25. Its Tendinous Origin.
26. Posterior part of the Obliquus Externus.
27. Gluteus Medius.
28. Gluteus Magnus.
29. Biceps Flexor Cruris.
30. Semi-Tendinosus.
31. } Gastrocnemius.
32.
33. Tendo Achillis.

FIG. 131.

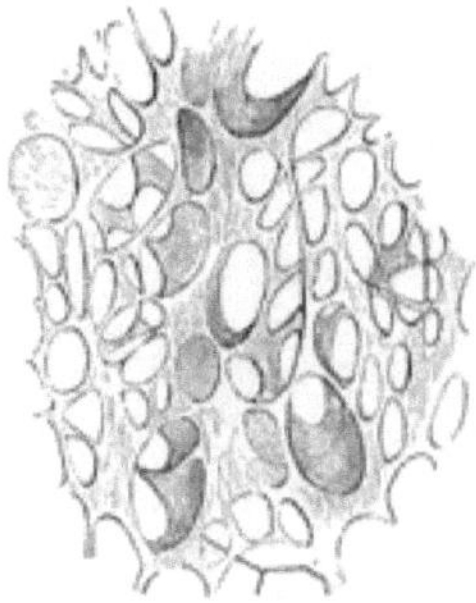

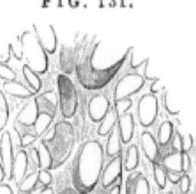

FIG. 133.

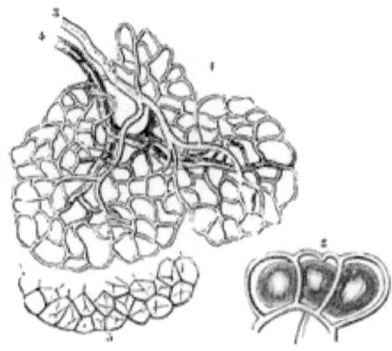

FIG. 132.

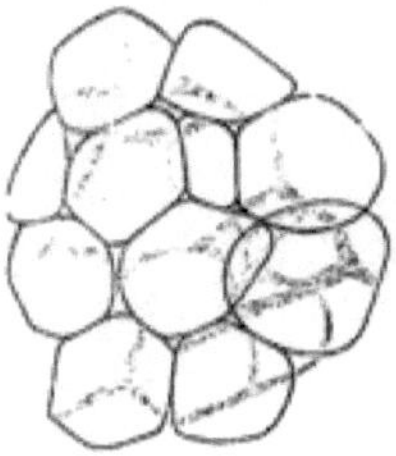

FIG. 134.

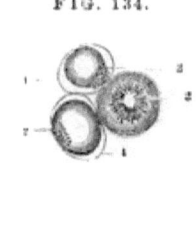

THE CELLULAR AND ADIPOSE TISSUES

FIG. 131.

A View of a Portion of Areolar or Cellular Tissue, Inflated and Dried, showing the general Character of its larger Meshes; magnified twenty Diameters.

——

FIG. 132.

Fat Vesicles from the Omentum, magnified about 300 diameters, and assuming the Polyphedral form, from pressure against one another. The Capillary vessels are not represented.

FIG. 133.

The Blood-vessels of Fat, magnified 100 Diameters.

1. Minute flattened Fat Lobules, in which the Vessels only are represented.
2. Plan of the arrangement of the Capillaries of the exterior of the Vesicles, more highly magnified.
3. The Terminal Artery.
4. The Primitive Vein.
5. The Fat Vesicles of one border of the Lobule separately represented.

FIG. 134.

Fat Vesicles from an emaciated Subject.

1.1. The Cell Membrane.
2.2.2. The solid portion collected as a star-like mass, with the Elaine in connexion with it, but not filling the Cell.

FIG. 135.   FIG. 137.

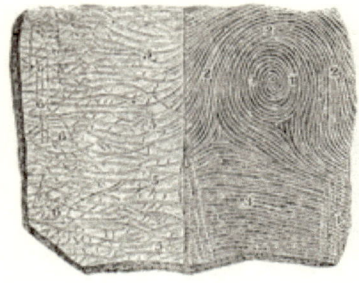 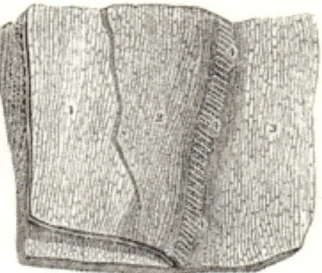

FIG. 136.   FIG. 138.

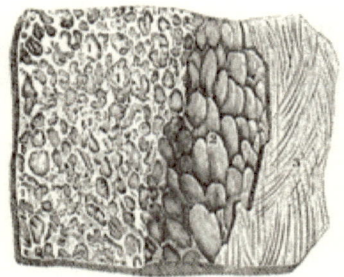 

THE INTEGUMENTS OF THE BODY.

FIG. 135.

THE EXTERNAL SURFACE OF THE EPIDERMIS, AS SEEN UPON THE FRONT EXTREMITY OF THE FORE-FINGER, AND UPON THE ULNAR SIDE OF THE BACK OF THE ARM, SLIGHTLY MAGNIFIED.

1.1. The circular Wrinkles on the front of the Fore-Finger.
2.2. The curvature of the Wrinkles and Lines on the outer surface of the circular ones.
3. The Transverse Wrinkles.
4.4. Wrinkles made by the Sudoriferous Canals.
5.5. The oblique Wrinkles on the Ulnar side of the Back of the Arm.
6.6. The peculiar Diamond-shaped Wrinkles on the Back of the Hand, with a few of the Hairs found at their angles.

FIG. 136.

THE CELLULAR TISSUE ON THE INTERNAL SURFACE OF THE SKIN, WITH ITS ADIPOSE LAYER AND THE FASCIA SUPERFICIALIS. FROM THE INTEGUMENTS OF THE ARM; MAGNIFIED.

1.1. The large and smaller Cells of the Skin deprived of the Fat which filled them.
2. The Sub-Cutaneous Adipose Matter.
3. The Fascia Superficialis.

FIG. 137.

THE EPIDERMIS, RETE MUCOSUM AND CUTIS VERA ON THE SOLE OF THE FOOT.

The Epidermis and Rete Mucosum have been detached and drawn back, so as to shew the Sudoriferous Canals passing from the Cutis Vera into the Rete Mucosum and Epidermis.

1. The Internal Surface of the Epidermis with its Lines and Transverse Furrows.
2. The Rete Mucosum in connexion with the Internal Face of the Epidermis.
3. The External Surface of the Cutis Vera separated from the Rete Mucosum and Epidermis.
4.4. Sudoriferous or Spiral Canals, so stretched by the withdrawal of the Epidermis that they appear like very thin and straight Filaments.

FIG. 138.

THE EPIDERMIS AND RETE MUCOSUM OF THE HEEL SEPARATED FROM EACH OTHER AND SEEN ON THEIR INTERNAL SURFACES, MAGNIFIED SIX TIMES.

1.1. The Internal Face of the Epidermis.
2.2. The Rete Mucosum.
3.3. On the sides of these Figures are the elevated Lines as adapted to the Furrows of the Derm.
4.4. The deep-seated Furrows corresponding to those on the External Face of the Epidermis.
5.5. The smaller Eminences which sink into the Furrows between the different series of Papillæ; seen in the Furrows.
6.6. The Cells of the Rete Mucosum in which the Papillæ of the Derm rest.
These Cells are of the same order as the Cells of the Papillæ of the Derm, seen in Fig. 139, to which they correspond.

FIG. 139. FIG. 140.

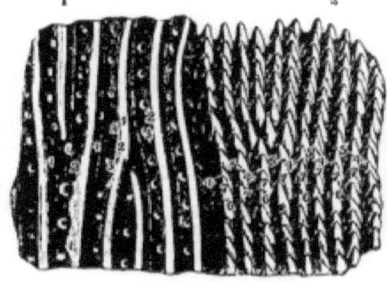
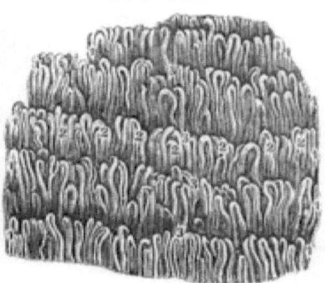

FIG. 141. FIG. 142.

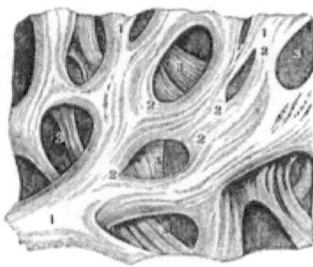
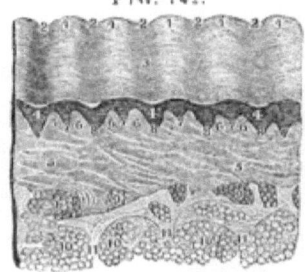

THE INTEGUMENTS OF THE BODY

FIG. 139.

THE EXTERNAL SURFACE OF THE EPIDERMIS AND CUTIS VERA, ON THE SOLE OF THE FOOT, MAGNIFIED SIX DIAMETERS.

(1.) Represents a portion of the Cutis Vera with the Epidermis.

1. The Wrinkles, or Furrows.
2. The prominent Lines.
3. The Funnel-shaped Orifices of the Sudoriferous Canals or the Pores of the Skin.

(2.) Represents a portion of the Cutis Vera deprived of the Epidermis and Rete Mucosum.

4.4. The deep Furrows which correspond to the elevated Lines on the Internal Surface of the Epidermis as seen in Fig. 138, at 3.
5.5. The smaller Furrows between the Papillæ, in which the small Prominences of the Rete Mucosum are inserted.
6.6. Orifices of the Sudoriferous Canals of the Cutis Vera seen between the Papillæ and corresponding to the Funnel-shaped Orifices of the surface of the Skin.
7.7. Ranges of the Papillæ which are inserted into the Rete Mucosum.

FIG. 140.

THE LOOPS OF VESSELS IN THE CUTANEOUS PAPILLÆ OF THE HAND. THE ARTERIAL INJECTION HAS SUCCEEDED ADMIRABLY, AND THE WHOLE IS REPRESENTED AS SEEN UNDER THE MICROSCOPE.

1.1. The Salient Lines of the Cutis Vera formed by the Papillæ (2.2.)
3. The Furrows.

FIG. 141.

THE INTERNAL RETICULATED AND CELLULAR FACE OF THE CUTIS VERA, MAGNIFIED CONSIDERABLY.

1. The greater and smaller Bands of Fibres.
2. The junction and intaercrossing of these Fibres.
3. The greater and smaller Cells from which the Cellular Substance which fills them has been removed.

FIG. 142.

A PERPENDICULAR SECTION OF THE INTEGUMENTS OF THE SOLE OF THE FOOT, AS SEEN UNDER THE MICROSCOPE.

1.1. The Salient Lines of the External Surface of the Skin cut perpendicularly.
2.2. The Furrows or Wrinkles of the same.
3. The Epidermis or Cuticle, as formed by its Superimposed Layers.
4.4. The Rete Mucosum.
5.5. The Cutis Vera, with its Cellular Fibres pressed into Fasciculi and each directed towards the Papillæ.
6.6. The Papillæ, each of which answers to the Prominences on the External Surface of the Skin.
7. The small Furrows between the Papillæ.
8. The deeper Furrows which are between each couple of the Papillæ.
9. Cells filled with Fat, and seen between the Bands of Fibres.
10. The Adipose Layer with numerous Fat Vesicles.
11. Cellular Fibres of the Adipose Tissue, continuous with the Sub-Cutaneous Cellular Tissue, and with that of the Cutis Vera.

FIG. 143.

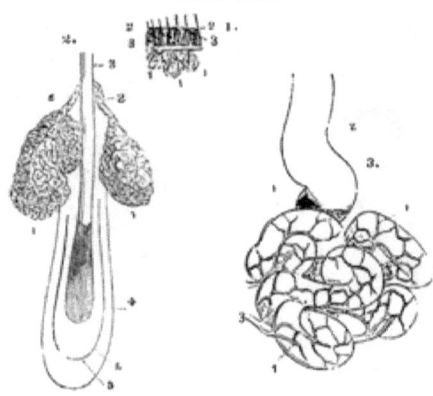

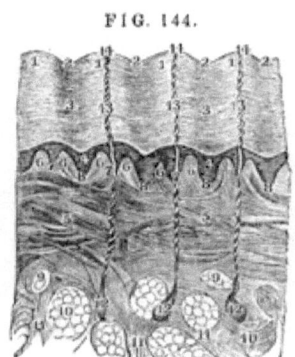

FIG. 144.

FIG. 145.

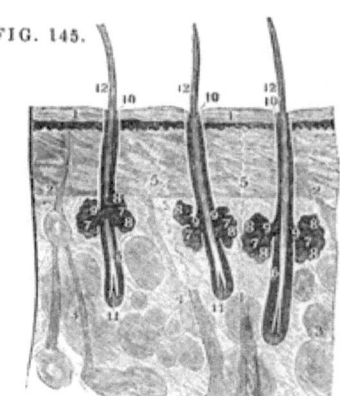

THE SEBACEOUS AND PERSPIRATORY ORGANS OF THE SKIN.

FIG. 143.

A HIGHLY MAGNIFIED DRAWING OF THE CUTANEOUS GLANDS OF THE EXTERNAL MEATUS AUDITORIUS.

(FIG. 1.) A Section of the Skin magnified three Diameters.

1.1. The deep-seated Glands which secrete the Cerumen or Ear-Wax.
2.2. The Hairs on the Surface.
3.3. The superficial Sebaceous Glands.

(FIG. 2.) A Hair perforating the Epidermis, highly magnified.

1.1. Sebaceous Glands.
2.2. Their Excretory Ducts.
3. The Epidermis.
4. The Base of the Hair.
5.5. Its Double Follicle.

(FIG. 3.) A view of the Cerumen Gland as formed by the Contorted Tubes.

1.1. The Tubes.
2. The Excretory Duct.
3. The Vessels supplying it.

FIG. 144.

A MAGNIFIED VIEW OF THE SUDORIFEROUS ORGANS OF THE SKIN ON THE SOLE OF THE FOOT.

This Figure from 1 to 11, inclusive, is the same as in Figure 142.

12. The Sudoriferous Follicles.
13. The Spiral or Sudoriferous Canals.
14. The Infudibular-shaped Pores or Orifices of these Canals.

FIG. 145.

THE PERSPIRATORY ORGANS—GRANULAR SEBACEOUS GLANDS AND FOLLICLES OF HAIRS IN THE SKIN OF THE AXILLA; HIGHLY MAGNIFIED.

1. Epidermis.
2. Cutis Vera.
3. Adipose Tissue.
4.4. Two Perspiratory Follicles.
5.5. Their Spiral Canals.
6.6. Follicles of Hairs.
7.7. Sebaceous Glands, two of which almost always belong to each Follicle.
8.8. The Acini of these Glands.
9.9. Their Excretory Ducts, continuous with the Cavity of the Follicle of the Hair.
10.10. The Orifices of the Follicles of the Hairs.
11.11. Their Roots.
12.12. The Hairs as seen under the Microscope.

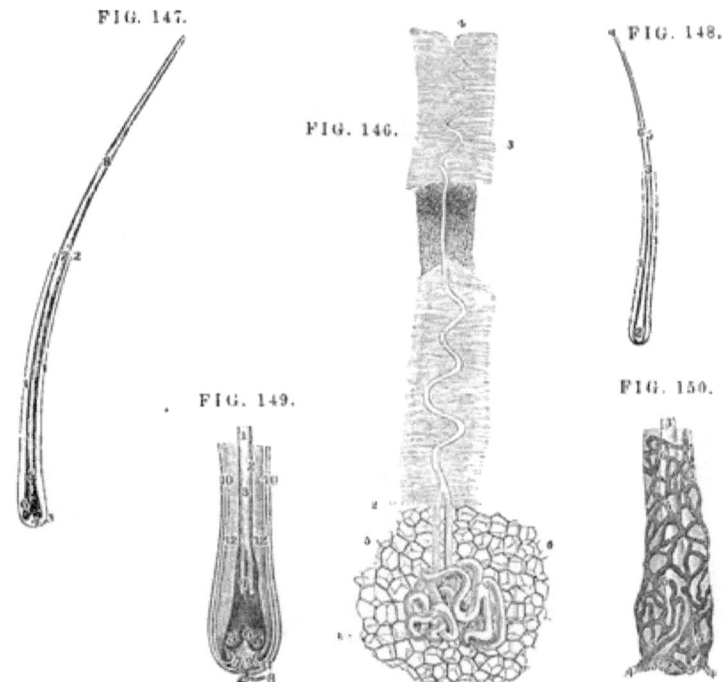

FIG. 147.

FIG. 148.

FIG. 146.

FIG. 149.

FIG. 150.

PERSPIRATORY GLANDS AND HAIRS OF THE SKIN.

FIG. 146.

A Sudoriferous Gland from the Palm of the Hand; magnified 40 Diameters.

1.1. The twisted Tubes composing the Gland.
2.2. The Excretory Ducts formed by the union of these Tubes.
3. The Spiral Canal formed by the Excretory Ducts perforating the Epidermis.
4. Its Opening on the surface.
5.5. The Fat Vesicles in which the Gland is imbedded.

FIG. 147.

A Hair from an Adult as seen under the Microscope.

1.1. The Follicle of the Hair.
2. Its Orifice.
3. The Base of the Follicle.
4. Pulp of the Hair.
5. Its Root.
6. The Bulb in which the Pulp is inserted.
7. Trunk of the Hair.
8. The portion which projects beyond the Skin.

FIG. 148.

A magnified View of a small Hair from the Face of a Man — removed with its Follicle and seen under the Microscope.

1.1. Its Follicle.
2. Root of the Hair.
3. Its Trunk.
4. Its Extremity.
5. Its Cortical or External Substance.
6. Its Internal or Medullary Substance.

FIG. 149.

The Root of one of the Hairs of the Beard with its Pulp and Follicle, considerably magnified.

1. A small portion of its Trunk.
2. The Cortical Substance.
3. The Medullary.
4. The Root of the Hair.
5. The Bifid portion of the Root called the Bulb.

6. Its excavated Base, in which the Pulp, 7, is inserted.
8. A small Artery.
9. Its distribution to the Pulp.
10. The Membrane of the Follicle of the Hair.
11. Its Base placed in the Pulp of the Hair.
12. The Cuticle or Epidermis of the Follicle, which joins with the Bulb of the Hair.

FIG. 150.

A small portion of the Follicle of a Hair of the Beard, with the Arteries supplying it—very highly magnified.

1. Its Follicle.
2. Its Pulp.
3. The Trunk of the Hair without the Follicle.
4.4. Two Arteries going to the Base of the Follicle.
5.5. Their Distribution.
6.6. The Reticulated Tissue of the Follicle.

FIG. 151.

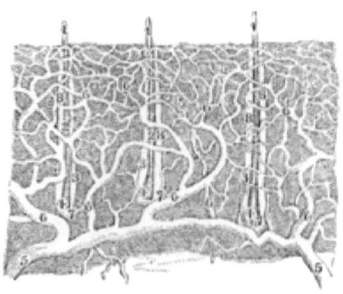

FIG. 152.   FIG. 154.   FIG. 153.

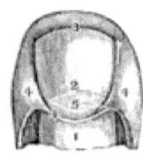  

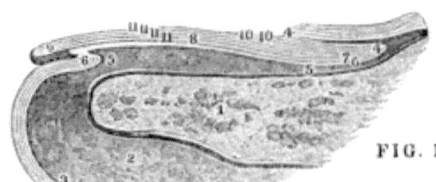

FIG. 155.

THE HAIRS AND NAILS

FIG. 151.

A SEGMENT OF THE SKIN OF THE BEARD ENCLOSING THREE HAIRS, AS SEEN UNDER THE COMPOUND MICROSCOPE, WITH THE ARTERIES INJECTED.

1.1. The Hairs without the Skin.
2.2. The same in their Follicles.
3.3. The Follicles.
4.4. The Follicles in the Pulp.
5.5. Two Arteries in the Internal Surface of the Skin.
6.6. Branches which are distributed around the Hairs in the Skin.
7.7. Branches to the Pulp.
8.8. The Arterial Net-work around each Follicle.

FIG. 152.

THE THUMB-NAIL DETACHED FROM THE THUMB AND SEEN ON ITS EXTERNAL SURFACE, WITH THE EPIDERMIS OF WHICH IT IS A CONTINUATION.

1. Root of the Nail deprived of the Epidermis.

2. Its Body.
3. Its Summit.
4.4. The Epidermis covering the sides of the Nail.
5. The Crescent or Lunula of the Nail.

FIG. 153.

THE SAME NAIL SEEN ON ITS INTERNAL SURFACE, WITH THE EPIDERMIS.

1. The Root.
2. The Body.
3.3. The Sides of the Nail.
4.4. A portion of the Epidermis near the Nail.
5. The Crescent.

The Internal Face of the Nail has been freed from the Rete Mucosum. The prominent Lines and Furrows corresponding to the Lines and Wrinkles of the Cutis Vera, and covered by the Nail, are seen arranged in parallel Lines.

FIG. 154.

A LONGITUDINAL SECTION OF THE NAIL OF THE RING FINGER.

1. The Third Phalanx.
2. The Adipose Tissue.
3. The Skin.
4. The Root of the Nail and Fold of the Skin in which the Root is inserted.
5. The Cutis Vera covered by the Nail.
6. The Epidermis.
7. Root of the Nail.
8. Its Body.
9. Its Summit or free End.

FIG. 155.

THE SAME FIGURE VERY HIGHLY MAGNIFIED.

The References from 1 to 9 inclusive as in Fig. 154.
10. The thin Laminæ of the Epidermis placed between the Nail and the origin of its Matrix. They are detached from the Epidermis by nature and then add to the proper thickness of the Nail itself.
11.11.11.11. The Laminæ of the Nail arranged in superimposed layers.

FIG. 156.

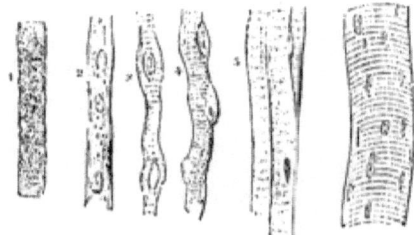

FIG. 158.

FIG. 157.

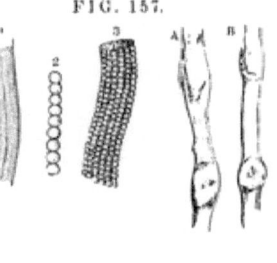

FIG. 160.

FIG. 159.

GENERAL ANATOMY OF THE MUSCLES.

FIG. 156.

THE STAGES OF DEVELOPEMENT OF MUSCULAR FIBRE.

1. Arrangement of the Primitive Cells in a Linear Series.

2. The Cells united. The Nuclei separated and some of them broken up—Longitudinal Lines becoming apparent.

3.4. The transverse Stripes or Bands beginning to show.

5. Transverse Bands fully formed and dark, with the Nuclei disappearing.

6. Elementary Fibres from the Adult, treated with acid, to show the Nuclei.

FIG. 157.

ANOTHER VIEW OF THE STAGES OF DEVELOPEMENT OF MUSCULAR FIBRE.

1. A Muscular Fibre of Animal life enclosed in its Sheath or Myolemma.

2. An Ultimate Fibril of the same.

3. A more highly magnified View of fig. 1., showing the true nature of the Longitudinal Striæ, as well as the mode of formation of the Transverse Striæ. The Myolemma is here so thin as to permit the Ultimate Fibrils to be seen through it.

4. A Muscular Fibre of Organic life with two of its Nuclei ; taken from the Urinary Bladder, and magnified 600 Diameters.

5. A Muscular Fibre of Organic life from the Stomach, magnified the same.

FIG. 158.

A VIEW OF THE ARRANGEMENT OF THE FASCICULI OR LACERTI OF VOLUNTARY MUSCLE, THE FIBRES SEPARATED AT ONE END INTO BRUSH-LIKE BUNDLES OF FIBRILLÆ.

FIG. 159.

A PORTION OF HUMAN MUSCULAR FIBRE, SEPARATING INTO DISKS BY CLEAVAGE IN THE DIRECTION OF ITS TRANSVERSE STRIÆ.

FIG. 160.

A VIEW OF THE FIBRES OF HUMAN MUSCLE BROKEN TRANSVERSELY. THE FRAGMENTS ARE CONNECTED BY THE UNTORN SARCOLEMMA OR MYOLEMMA.

FIG. 161.

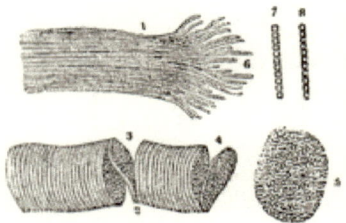

FIG. 162.　　　　FIG. 163.　　　　FIG. 164.

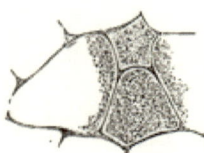

FIG. 165.

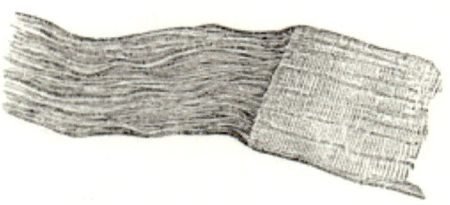

GENERAL ANATOMY OF THE MUSCLES.

FIG. 161.

A VIEW OF THE FRAGMENTS OF STRIPED ELEMENTARY FIBRES, SHOWING A CLEAVAGE IN OPPOSITE DIRECTIONS — MAGNIFIED 300 DIAMETERS.

1. The Longitudinal Cleavage.
2. The Transverse Cleavage, the Longitudinal Lines being scarcely visible.
3. Incomplete Fracture, following the opposite surfaces of a Disc which stretches across the Interval and retains the two Fragments in connexion. The Edge and Surface of this Disc are seen to be minutely granular, the Granules corresponding in size to the thickness of the Disc and to the distance between the faint Longitudinal Lines.
4. Another Disc nearly detached.
5 A detached Disc more highly magnified, showing the Sarcous Elements.
6. Fibrillæ separated by violence from each other at the broken end of the Fibre.
7.8. The two appearances commonly presented by the separated single Fibrillæ; more highly magnified, at 7 the spaces are rectangular, at 8 the borders are scalloped and the spaces bead-like.

FIG. 162.

A FRAGMENT OF MUSCULAR FIBRE FROM THE MACERATED HEART OF AN OX, SHOWING THE FORMATION OF THE STRIÆ BY THE AGGREGATION OF THE BEADED FIBRILLÆ.

FIG. 163.

A TRANSVERSE SECTION OF THE ULTIMATE FIBRILS OF THE BICEPS, SHOWING THEIR POLYGONAL FORM AND THE ULTIMATE FIBRILS COMPOSING THEM.

FIG. 164.

A MASS OF ULTIMATE FIBRES FROM THE PECTORALIS MAJOR OF THE HUMAN FŒTUS AT TERM. THESE FIBRES HAVE BEEN IMMERSED IN A SOLUTION OF TARTARIC ACID, AND THEIR NUMEROUS CORPUSCULES TURNED IN VARIOUS DIRECTIONS, AND SHOWING SOME NUCLEOLI.

FIG. 165.

A VIEW OF THE ATTACHMENT OF TENDON TO MUSCULAR FIBRE, AS SHOWN IN THE SKATE. THE COMPONENT FIBRES OF TENDINOUS STRUCTURE ARE ARRANGED WITH GREAT REGULARITY, PARALLEL TO EACH OTHER, AND ARE ATTACHED TO THE END OF THE SARCOLEMMA, WHICH TERMINATES ABRUPTLY AND WITHOUT THE TAPERING OF THE MUSCULAR FIBRE, AS SOME HAVE SUPPOSED.

FIG. 166.   FIG. 167.

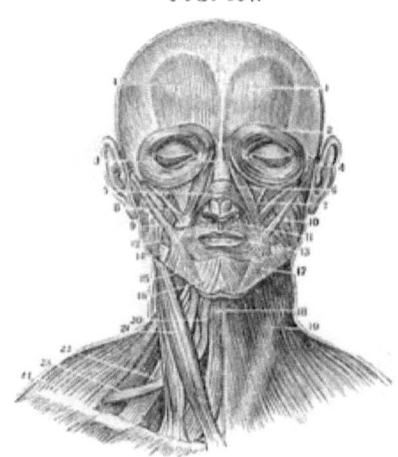

MUSCLES OF THE FACE AND NECK.

FIG. 166.

A VIEW OF THE MANNER IN WHICH THE NERVES
SUPPLYING THE MUSCLES TERMINATE.

FIG. 167.

A FRONT VIEW OF THE SUPERFICIAL LAYER OF
MUSCLES ON THE FACE AND NECK.

1.1. Anterior Bellies of the Occipito-Frontalis.
2. Orbicularis or Sphincter Palpebrarum.
3. Nasal Slip of Occipito-Frontalis.
4. Anterior Auriculæ.
5. Compressor Naris.
6. Levator Labii Superioris Alæque Nasi.
7. Levator Anguli Oris
8. Zygomaticus Minor.
9. Zygomaticus Major.
10. Masseter.

11. Depressor Labii Superioris Alæque Nasi.
12. Buccinator.
13. Orbicularis Oris.
14. The denuded Surface of the Inferior Maxillary Bone.
15. Depressor Anguli Oris.
16. Depressor Labii Inferioris.
17. The portion of the Platysma-Myodes that passes on to the Mouth, or the Musculus Risorius.
18. Sterno-Hyoideus.
19. Platysma-Myodes. It is wanting on the other side of the Figure.
20. Superior Belly of the Omo-Hyoideus near its insertion.
21. Sterno-Cleido-Mastoideus.
22. Scalenus Medius.
23. Inferior Belly of Omo-Hyoid.
24. Cervical Edge of the Trapezius.

FIG. 168.   FIG. 169.

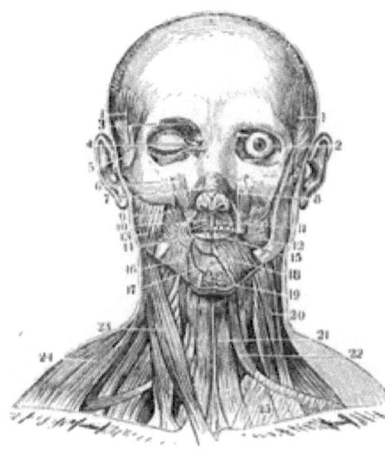
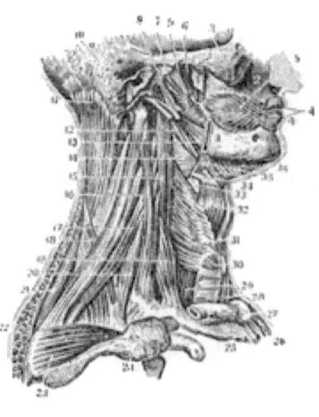

MUSCLES OF THE FACE AND NECK.

FIG. 168.

A Front View of the Deep-seated Layer of Muscles on the Face and Neck.

1.1. Temporalis.
2. The Eye-Ball in the Orbit with its Oblique Muscles in situ.
3. Corrugator Supercilii.
4. Points of insertion of the Orbicularis Palpebrarum.
5. Anterior Auriculæ.
6. Orbitar portion of the Levator Labii Superioris Alæque Nasi.
7. Compressor Naris.
8. Levator Labii Superioris in its Lower Third, showing its intermixture with the Orbicularis Oris.
9. Levator Anguli Oris.
10.11. Depressor Labii Superioris Alæque Nasi, seen on both sides of the Face.
12. Buccinator.
13. Masseter.
14. Orbicularis Oris at the angle of the Mouth.
15. Orbicularis Oris as shown in the edge of the Lower Lip.
16. Depressor Anguli Oris.
17. Levator Menti vel Labii Inferioris.
18. Depressor Labii Inferioris.
19. Adipose Tissue on the Chin.
20. Scalenus Medius.
21. Sterno-Hyoideus
22. Omo-Hyoideus.
23. Sterno-Cleido-Mastoideus.
24. Trapezius as seen on the Neck.
25 Attachment of the Fascia Profunda Colli to the Clavicle.

FIG. 169.

A Lateral View of the Deep-seated Muscles of the Face and Neck.

1. The Inferior Maxillary Bone.
2. Superior Maxillary Bone.
3. Malar Bone.
4.4. Orbicularis Oris Muscle.
5. Buccinator.
6. External Pterygoid.
7. Internal Pterygoid.
8. Glenoid Cavity.
9. Constrictor Pharyngis Superior.
10. Mastoid Process of the Temporal Bone.
11. Splenius.
12. Stylo-Pharyngeus.
13. Stylo-Glossus.
14. Constrictor Pharyngis Medius.
15. Longus Colli.
16. Scalenus Medius.
17. Levator Scapulæ.
18. Serratus Superior Posticus.
19. Scalenus Anticus.
20. Scalenus Posticus.
21. Rhomboideus Minor.
22. Section of the Trapezius.
23. Supra-Spinatus.
24. Acromion Scapulæ.
25. First Rib.
26. Sterno-Clavicular Articulation.
27. Clavicle.
28. Trachea.
29. Œsophagus.
30. Crico-Thyroideus.
31. Constrictor Pharyngis Inferior
32. Thyro-Hyoid.
33. Thyro-Hyoid Ligament.
34. Os Hyoides.
35. Hyo-Glossus.
36. Mylo-Hyoid.

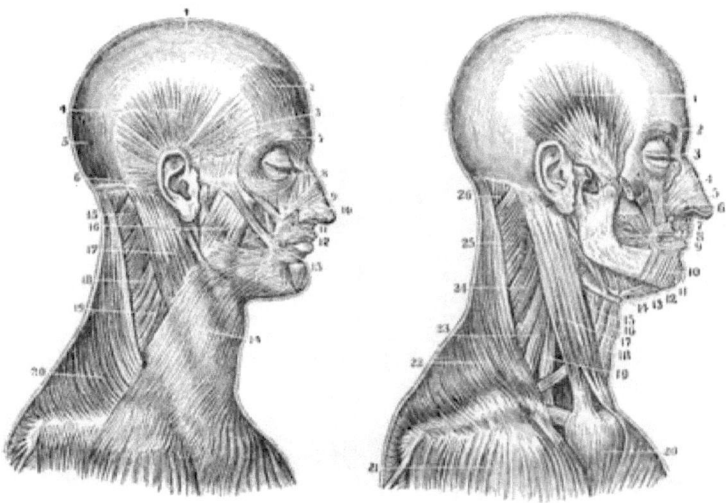

FIG. 170.

FIG. 171.

MUSCLES OF THE HEAD AND NECK.

FIG. 170.

A SIDE VIEW OF THE SUPERFICIAL LAYER OF MUSCLES ON THE FACE AND NECK.

1. Tendon of the Occipito-Frontalis.
2. Its Frontal Belly.
3. Anterior Auriculæ.
4. Attollens Auriculæ.
5. Occipital Belly of the Occipito-Frontalis.
6. Retrahens Auriculæ.
7. Orbicularis Palpebrarum.
8.8. Levator Labii Superioris Alæque Nasi.
9. Compressor Naris.
10. Levator Anguli Oris.
11. Buccinator.
12. Zygomaticus Minor.
13. Orbicularis Oris and Zygomaticus Major.
14. Platysma Myodes.
15. Splenius.
16. Masseter.
17. Sterno-Cleido Mastoid.
18. Levator Scapulæ.
19. Scalenus Medius.
20. Trapezius.

FIG. 171.

A LATERAL VIEW OF THE DEEP-SEATED LAYER OF MUSCLES ON THE FACE AND NECK.

1. Temporal Muscle deprived of its Fascia.
2. Corrugator Supercilii.
3. Nasal Slip of the Occipito Frontalis.
4. Superior or Nasal Extremity of the Levator Labii Superioris Alæque Nasi.
5. Compressor Naris.
6. Levator Anguli Oris.
7. Depressor Labii Superioris Alæque Nasi.
8. Buccinator.
9. Orbicularis Oris.
10. Depressor Labii Inferioris.
11. Levator Labii Inferioris.
12. Anterior Belly of the Digastricus.
13. Mylo-Hyoid.
14. Stylo-Hyoid.
15. Thyro-Hyoid.
16. Upper Belly of the Omo-Hyoid.
17. Sterno-Cleido Mastoid.
18. Sterno-Hyoid.
19. Scalenus Anticus.
20. Pectoralis Major.
21. Deltoid.
22. Trapezius.
23. Scalenus Medius.
24. Levator Scapulæ and Scalenus Posticus.
25. Splenius.
26. Complexus.

FIG. 172.

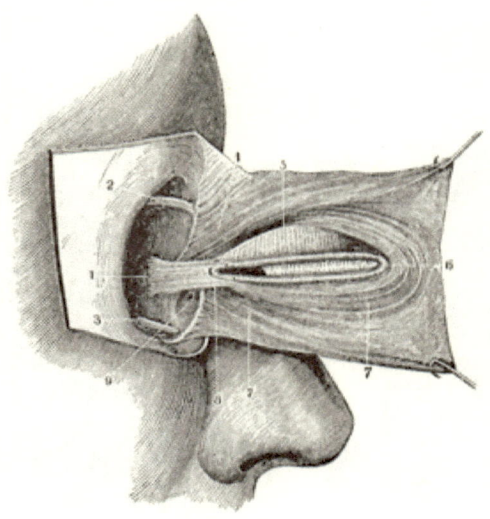

MUSCLES OF THE EYE-LID.

FIG. 172.

A VIEW OF THE TENSOR TARSI OR MUSCLE OF HORNER, AS SHOWN BY A DISSECTION OF THE INTERNAL SURFACE OF THE EYE-LIDS.

1. Origin of the Tensor Tarsi Muscle, from the superior part of the Os Unguis, just in advance of the Vertical Suture, between the Os Planum and the Os Unguis.
2. Superior Oblique Muscle of the Eye-Ball.
3. Inferior Oblique Muscle of the Eye-Ball.
4. Origin of the Orbicularis Palpebrarum, from the Nasal Process of the Os Maxillare Superius, Internal Angular Process of the Os Frontis and the contiguous part of the Os Unguis—also along the whole Superior Margin of the Internal Palpebral Ligament.

5. A portion of the Palpebral Conjunctiva.
6. External Palpebral Ligament and Canthus of the Eye-Lid.
7.7. Lower Portion and Terminating Fibres of the Orbicularis Palpebrarum.
8. Bifurcation of the Tensor Tarsi Muscle at the Base of the Caruncula Lachrymalis. The Insertions of the Muscle near the Puncta are also shown.
9. Lachrymal Sac.

FIG. 173.

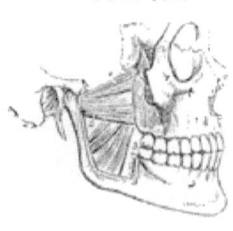

FIG. 174.

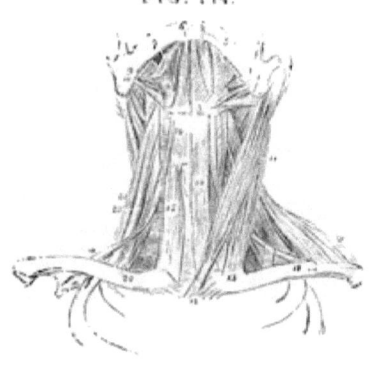

FIG. 175.

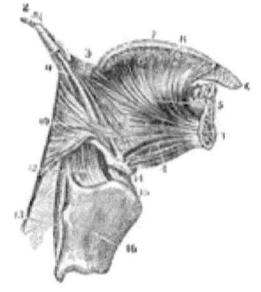

FIG. 176.

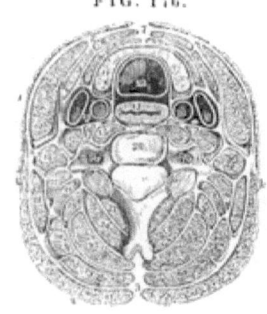

MUSCLES OF THE HEAD AND NECK.

FIG. 173.

A VIEW OF THE PTE-
RYGOID MUSCLES, AS
SHOWN BY THE REMO-
VAL OF THE ZYGOMA-
TIC ARCH AND THE
GREATER PART OF THE
RAMUS OF THE JAW.

1. Sphenoidal portion of the
External Pterygoid.
2. Pterygoid portion of the
External Pterygoid.
3. Internal Pterygoid.

FIG. 174.

A VIEW OF THE SUPERFI-
CIAL AND DEEP-SEAT-
ED MUSCLES ON THE
FRONT OF THE NECK

1. Posterior Belly of the
Digastricus.
2. Its Anterior Belly.
3. Ligamentous Loop on
the Os Hyoides through
which its Tendon plays.
4. Stylo-Hyoideus.
5. Mylo-Hyoideus.
6. Genio-Hyoideus.
7. The Tongue.
8. Hyo-Glossus.
9. Stylo-Glossus.

10. Stylo-Pharyngeus.
11. Sterno-Cleido Mastoid.
12. Its Sternal Origin.
13. Its Clavicular Origin.
14. Sterno-Hyoideus.
15. Sterno-Thyroid of the
Right Side.
16. Thyro-Hyoideus.
17. Hyoid Belly of the
Omo-Hyoid.
18. Scapular portion of the
Omo-Hyoid.
19. Anterior Edge of the
Trapezius.
20. Scalenus Anticus of
the Right Side.
21. Scalenus Posticus.
22. Scalenus Medius.

FIG. 175.

A VERTICAL SECTION
OF THE TONGUE AND
LOWER JAW, SHOW-
ING THE MUSCLES AT-
TACHED THERETO.

1. A Section of the Lower
Jaw.
2. Styloid Process of the
Temporal Bone.
3. Stylo-Glossus Muscle.
4. Lower portion of Ge-
nio Hyo-Glossus.

5. Upper portion of Genio-
Hyo-Glossus.
6. Tip or Point of the
Tongue, showing the
Vertical Lingual Mus-
cle.
7. Surface of the Tongue.
8. Transversales Linguæ.
9. Superficialis Linguæ.
10. Superior Extremity of
the Constrictor Pha-
ryngis Medius.
11. Stylo-Pharyngeus.
12. Its Insertion.
13. Constrictor Pharyngis
Inferior.
14. Os Hyoides.
15. Thyro-Hyoid Ligam't.
16. Thyroid Cartilage.

FIG. 176.

A TRANSVERSE SEC-
TION OF THE NECK,
SHOWING THE FASCIA
PROFUNDA, AND ITS
PROLONGATIONS AS
SHEATHS FOR THE
MUSCLES.

1. Platysma Myodes.
2. Trapezius.
3. Ligamentum Nuchæ.
4. Sheath of Sterno-Cleido-
Mastoid.

5. Muscle itself.
6. Point of Union of its
Fascia.
7. Point of Union of the
Fascia Profunda Colli
of each side of the Neck.
8. Section of the Sterno-
Hyoid Muscle.
9. Section of the Omo-
Hyoid Muscle.
10. Section of the Sterno-
Thyroid Muscle.
11. Lateral Lobe of the
Thyroid Gland.
12. Trachea.
13. Œsophagus.
14. Blood-vessels and Pneumogastric Nerve in their
Sheath.
15. Longus Colli.
16. Rectus Anticus Major.
17. Scalenus Anticus.
18. Scalenus Medius and
Posticus.
19. Splenius Capitis.
20. Splenius Colli.
21. Levator Scapulæ.
22. Complexus.
23. Trachelo-Mastoid.
24. Transversalis Cervicis.
25. Cervicalis Descendens.
26. Semi-spinalis Cervicis.
27. Multifidus Spinæ.
28. A Cervical Vertebra.

FIG. 177. FIG. 178.

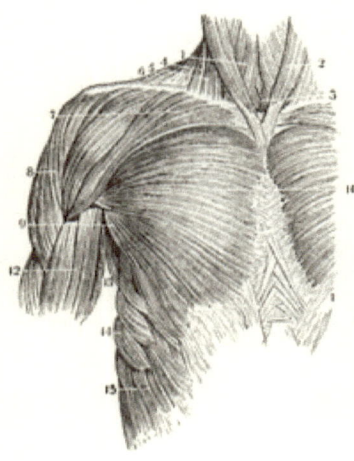 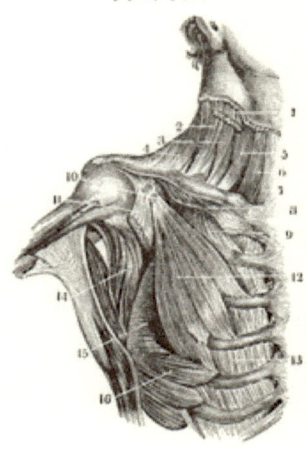

MUSCLES ON THE FRONT OF THE THORAX.

FIG. 177.

A VIEW OF THE SUPERFICIAL MUSCLES OF THE
UPPER FRONT OF THE TRUNK.

1. Sterno-Hyoid.
2. Sterno-Cleido Mastoid.
3. Sterno-Thyroid.
4. Clavicular portion of the Sterno-Cleido Mastoid.
5. Anterior Edge of the Trapezius.
6. Clavicle.
7. Clavicular Origin of the Pectoralis Major.
8. Deltoid.
9. Fold of Fibres of the Pectoralis Major on the Anterior Edge of the Axilla.
10. Middle of the Pectoralis Major.
11. The crossing and interlocking of the Fibres of the External Oblique of one side of the Abdomen with those of the other.
12. Biceps Flexor Cubiti.
13. Teres Major.
14. Serratus Major Anticus.
15. Superior Heads of the External Oblique interlocking with the Serratus Major.

FIG. 178.

A VIEW OF THE DEEPER-SEATED MUSCLES ON
THE UPPER FRONT OF THE TRUNK.

1. Cut portion of the Sterno-cleido-Mastoid.
2. Scalenus Medius.
3. Scalenus Anticus.
4. Trapezius.
5. Omo-Hyoid.
6. Sterno-Hyoid.
7. Sterno-Thyroid.
8. Subclavius Muscle.
9. First External Intercostal.
10. Insertion of the Pectoralis Minor.
11. Cut portion of the Coraco-Brachialis and short Head of the Biceps.
12. Body of the Pectoralis Minor.
13. An External Intercostal Muscle.
14. Sub-Scapularis.
15. Latissimus Dorsi.
16. Serratus Major Anticus.

FIG. 179   FIG. 180

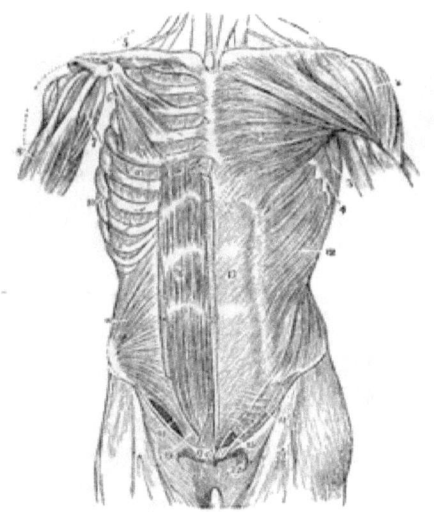
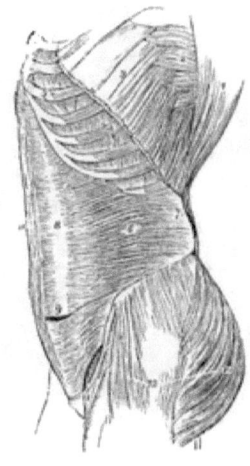

MUSCLES ON THE FRONT OF THE TRUNK.

FIG. 179.

A VIEW OF THE SUPERFICIAL MUSCLES OF THE LEFT SIDE AND OF THE DEEP MUSCLES OF THE RIGHT SIDE, ON THE FRONT OF THE TRUNK.

1. Pectoralis Major.
2. Deltoid.
3. Anterior Edge of Latissimus-Dorsi.
4. Serrated Edge of Serratus Major Anticus.
5. Subclavius Muscle.
6. Pectoralis Minor.
7. Coraco-Brachialis.
8. Biceps Flexor Cubiti.
9. Coracoid Process of the Scapula.
10. Serratus Major Anticus after the removal of the Obliquus Externus Abdominis.
11. External Intercostal Muscle of the Fifth Intercostal Space.
12. External Oblique of the Abdomen.
13. Its Tendon. The Median Line is the Linea Alba.—The Line to the Right of the Number is the Linea Semilunaris.
14. The portion of the Tendon of the External Oblique, known as Poupart's Ligament.
15. External Abdominal Ring.
16. Rectus Abdominis. The White Spaces are the Linea Transversæ.
17. Pyramidalia.
18. Internal Oblique of the Abdomen.
19. Common Tendon of the Internal Oblique and Transversalis.
20. Crural Arch.
21. Fascia Lata Femoris.
22. Saphenous Opening.

The Crescentic Edge of the Sartorial Fascia is seen just above fig. 22, and the Interior or Pubic Point of the Crescent is known as Hey's Ligament.

FIG. 180.

A LATERAL VIEW OF THE MUSCLES OF THE TRUNK, ESPECIALLY ON THE ABDOMEN.

1. Latissimus Dorsi.
2. Serratus Major Anticus.
3. Upper portion of the External Oblique.
4. Two of the External Intercostal Muscles.
5. Two of the Internal Intercostal Muscles.
6. Transversalis Abdominis.
7. Fascia Lumborum.
8. Posterior part of the Sheath of the Rectus or Anterior Aponeurosis of the Transversalis Muscle.
9. The Rectus Abdominis cut off and in its Sheath.
10. Rectus Abdominis of the Right Side.
11. Crural Arch.
12. Gluteus Magnus—Medius and Tensor Vaginæ Femoris covered by the Fascia Lata.

FIG. 181.　　　　　　　FIG. 182.

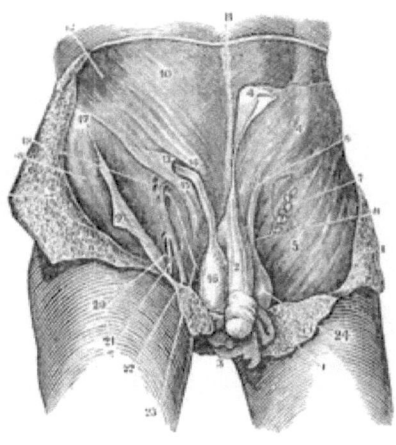 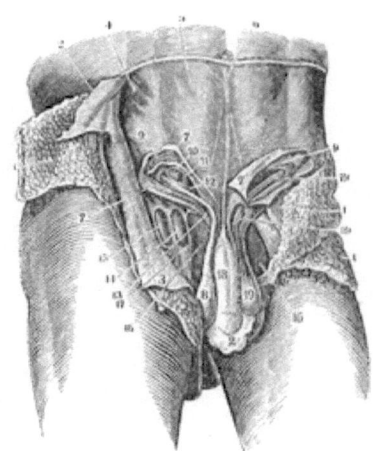

MUSCLES AND FASCIA OF THE ABDOMEN.

FIG. 181.

A VIEW OF THE EXTERNAL PARTS CONCERNED IN INGUINAL AND FEMORAL HERNIA.

1 1. The common Integuments and Adipose Tissue of the Abdomen turned back.
2. The Penis with its Suspensory Ligament deprived of the Integuments.
3. Integuments of the Scrotum drawn down.
4. Fascia Superficialis of the Abdomen.
5. The same on the Thigh.
6. The Left Spermatic Cord covered by the Fascia Superficialis.
7. The Inguinal Glands which are placed on the Fascia Superficialis.
8. Branch of the External Pudic Artery.
9. Fascia Superficialis turned off the Thigh.
10. Tendon of the External Oblique.
11. Linea Alba.
12. External Oblique Muscle.
13. External Abdominal Ring.
14. Its Superior Column.
15. Its Inferior Column.
16. Testicle covered by the Cremaster Muscle.
17. Anterior Superior Spinous Process.
18. Close Attachment of the Fascia Superficialis on the outside of the Thigh.
19. Cribriform Openings in the Fascia Lata Femoris.
20. Saphenous Opening.
21. Branch of the Saphena Vein.
22. Saphena Vein.
23. External Femoral Ring.
24. Testicle.

FIG. 182.

A VIEW OF THE DEEP-SEATED PARTS CONCERNED IN INGUINAL AND FEMORAL HERNIA.

1.1. Integuments and Adipose Tissue.
2. Integuments of the Scrotum.
3.3. Fascia Superficialis Abdominis and Fascia Lata Femoris turned off.
4. External Oblique Muscle.
5. Its Tendon.
6. Linea Alba.
7. Lower part of the External Oblique Tendon divided and turned back.
8. Right Testicle in the Tunica Vaginalis Testis.
9. Internal Oblique and Transversalis Muscles.
10. Epigastric Artery and Vein as placed between the Fascia Transversalis and the Peritoneum.
11. Points to the Surface of the Peritoneum through the Internal Abdominal Ring.
12. Cord covered by the Cremaster Muscle laying in the Abdominal Canal.
13. External Abdominal Ring laid open.
14. } Fascia Propria of the Vessels laid open so
15. } as to expose them.
16. Pectineus.
17. The Vessels in their Sheath.
18. Penis and Ligamentum Suspensorium.
19. Testicle and Cord in its entire length.

FIG. 183.

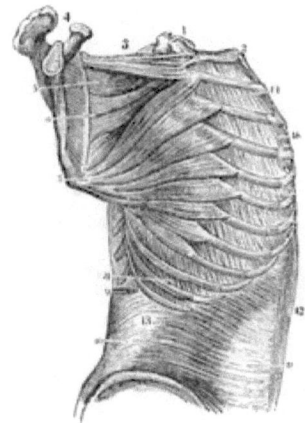

FIG. 184.

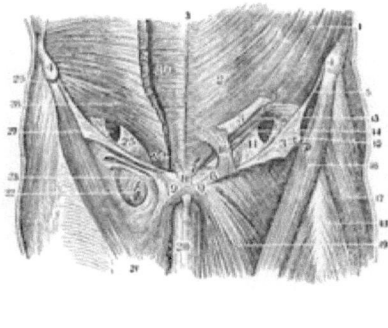

MUSCLES OF THE TRUNK

FIG. 183.

A LATERAL VIEW OF THE DEEP-SEATED MUSCLES
OF THE TRUNK.

1. Vertebra.
2. First Rib.
3. Superior Origin of the Serratus Major Anticus
4. Acromion Scapulæ.
5. Show the Convergence of the Fibres of the
6. Serratus Major and its Insertion into the
7. whole Base of the Scapula.
8. An External Intercostal Muscle.
9. Section of the Sacro-Lumbalis.
10. Transversalis Abdominis.
11. Abdominal Aponeurosis.
12. Rectus Abdominis.
13. Fascia Lumborum.
14.14. Costal Origins of the Serratus Major.
15. External Intercostal Muscle.
16.16. Two Internal Intercostal Muscles.

FIG. 184.

A VIEW OF THE ABDOMINAL MUSCLES AND THE
ABDOMINAL OR INGUINAL CANAL.

1. External Oblique Muscle of the Abdomen.
2. Its Aponeurosis.
3. Its Tendon slit up and turned back to show
   the Canal.
4. Anterior Superior Spinous Processes.

5. Upper portion of Poupar's Ligament.
6. External Column of the External Ring.
7. Internal Column of the External Ring.
8. Intercrossing of the Tendons of each Side.
9. Body of the Pubes.
10. Upper Boundary of the External Abdominal
    Ring—the Line points to the Ring.
11. Fascia Transversalis.
12.
13. Fibres of the Internal Oblique turned up.
14. Fibres of the Transversalis Muscle.
15. Points to the Internal Ring, the Opening is
    enlarged for the demonstration.
16. Sartorius.
17. Fascia Lata Femoris.
18. Rectus Femoris.
19. Adductor Longus.
20. Penis.
21. Fascia Lata of the opposite Thigh.
22. Point where the Saphena Vein enters the
    Femoral.
23. Fascia Lata as applied to the Vessels.
24. Insertion of the Transversalis Muscle on the
    Pubis.
25.26. Correspond to 11.12. of the opposite side
    and indicate the Fascia Transversalis.
27. Poupart's Ligament turned off from the In-
    ternal Muscles.
28. Transversalis Abdominis.
29. Internal Oblique.
30. Rectus Abdominis.

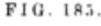

FIG. 185.

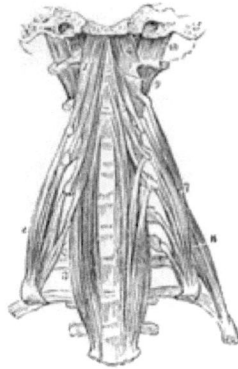

FIG. 186.

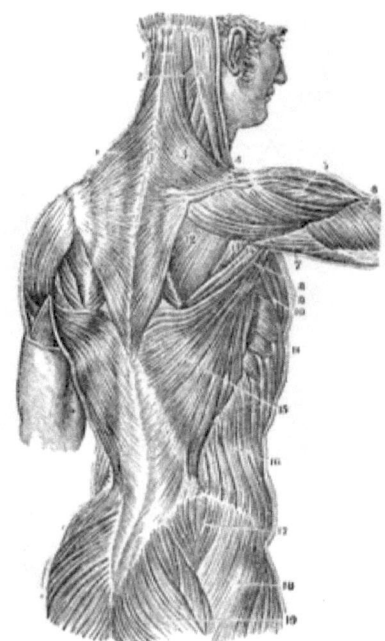

MUSCLES OF THE BACK.

FIG. 185.

A VIEW OF THE MUSCLES ON THE FRONT AND SIDES OF THE CERVICAL VERTEBRÆ.

1. Rectus Capitis Anticus Major.
2. Scalenus Anticus.
3. Lower portion of the Longus Colli on the Right Side.
4. Rectus Capitis Anticus Minor.
5. Upper portion of the Longus Colli on the Left Side.
6. Seventh Cervical Vertebra.
7. Scalenus Medius.
8. Scalenus Posticus.
9. One of the Inter-Transversales Muscles.
10. Rectus Capitis Lateralis.

FIG. 186.

A VIEW OF THE MUSCLES OF THE BACK AS SHOWN AFTER THE REMOVAL OF THE INTEGUMENTS.

1. Occipital Origin of the Trapezius.
2. Sterno-Cleido-Mastoideus.

3. Middle of the Trapezius.
4. Insertion of the Trapezius into the Spine of the Scapula.
5. Deltoid.
6. Second Head of the Triceps Extensor Cub' i
7. Its Superior Portion.
8. Scapular portion of the Latissimus Dorsi
9. Axillary Border of the Pectoralis Major
10. Axillary Border of the Pectoralis Minor
11. Serratus Major Anticus.
12. Infra-Spinatus.
13. Teres Minor.
14. Teres Major.
15. Middle of the Latissimus Dorsi.
16. External Oblique of the Abdomen.
17. Gluteus Medius.
18. Gluteus Minimus.
19. Gluteus Magnus.
20. Fascia Lumborum.

FIG. 187.

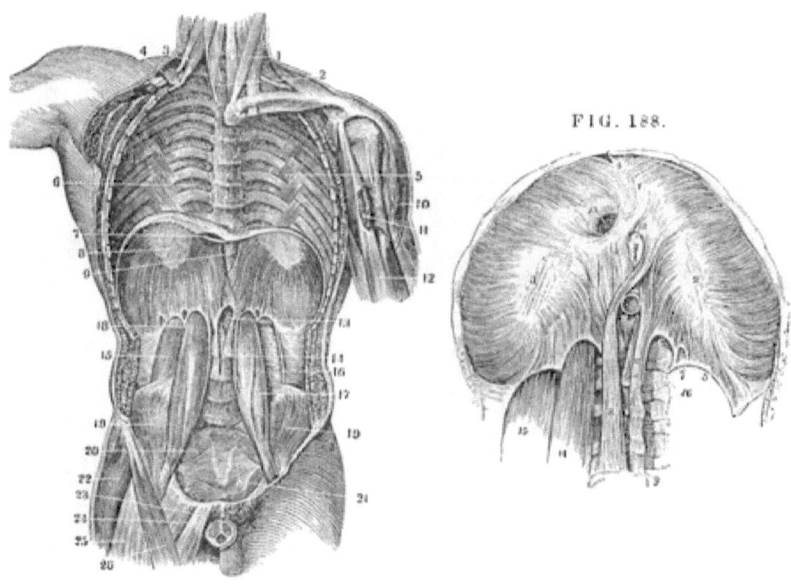

FIG. 188.

MUSCLES OF THE TRUNK

FIG. 187.

A VERTICAL SECTION OF THE FRONT OF THE
TRUNK, SHOWING ITS POSTERIOR PARIETIES
AND THE CAVITIES OF THE CHEST AND ABDO-
MEN.

1. Sterno-Cleido-Mastoid.
2. Longus Colli.
3. Scalenus Anticus.
4. Upper portion of the Serratus Major Anticus.
5. Infra Costales Muscles or Appendices to the
   Internal Intercostal Muscles.
6. Internal Intercostal Muscles.
7. Foramen Quadratum for the Inferior Vena-
   Cava.
8. Back part of the Cordiform Tendon of the
   Diaphragm.
9. Middle of the Diaphragm showing the Foramen Œsophageum.
10. Deltoid.
11. Insertion of the Pectoralis Major.
12. Biceps Flexor Cubiti.
13. Foramen Aorticum of the Diaphragm.
14. Origin of the Lesser Muscle of the Dia-
    phragm.
15. Quadratus Lumborum.
16. Its Sheath.
17. Psoas Magnus.
18. Origin of the Psoas Parvus.
19. Iliacus Internus.

20. Pyriformis.
21. Levator Ani and Coccygeus.
22. Tensor Vaginæ Femoris.
23. Adductor Longus.
24. Pectineus.
25. Rectus Femoris.
26. Sartorius.

———

FIG. 188.

A VIEW OF THE UNDER SIDE OF THE DIAPHRAGM.

1.
2. } The Greater Muscle of the Diaphragm in-
3. } serted into the Cordiform Tendon.
4. The small triangular space behind the Sternum, covered only by Serous Membrane and
   through which Hernia sometimes pass.
5. Ligamentum Arcuatum of the Left Side.
6. Point of Origin of the Psoas Magnus.
7. A small Opening for the Lesser Splanchnic
   Nerve.
8. One of the Crura of the Diaphragm.
9. Fourth Lumbar Vertebra.
10. Another Crus or portion of the Lesser Muscle
    of the Diaphragm.
11. Hiatus Aorticus.
12. Foramen Œsophageum.
13. Foramen Quadratum.
14. Psoas Magnus Muscle.
15. Quadratus Lumborum.

FIG. 189.
FIG. 190.

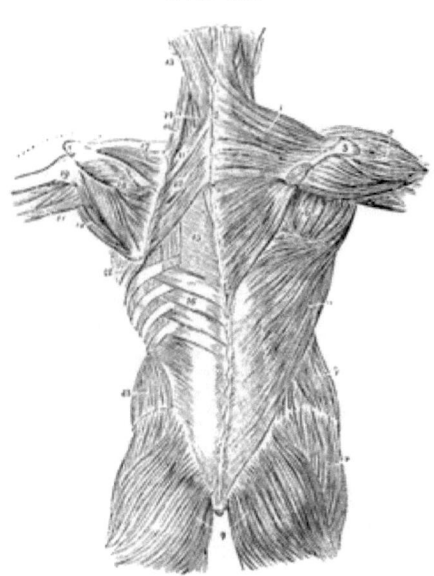
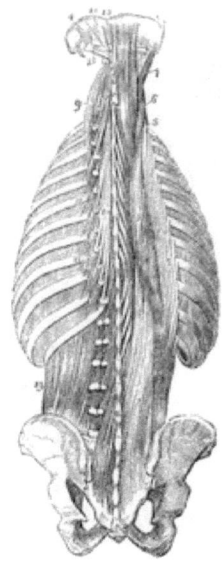

MUSCLES OF THE BACK.

FIG. 189.

A VIEW OF THE SECOND LAYER OF MUSCLES OF THE BACK.

1. Trapezius.
2. A portion of the Tendinous ellipse formed by the Trapezius on both sides.
3. Spine of the Scapula.
4. Latissimus Dorsi.
5. Deltoid.
6. Infra-Spinatus and Teres Minor.
7. External Oblique of the Abdomen.
8. Gluteus Medius.
9. Gluteus Magnus of each side.
10. Levator Scapulæ.
11. Rhomboideus Minor.
12. Rhomboideus Major.
13. Splenius Capitis.
14. Splenius Colli.
15. A portion of the Origin of the Latissimus Dorsi.
16. Serratus Inferior Posticus.
17. Supra-Spinatus.
18. Infra-Spinatus.
19. Teres Minor.
20. Teres Major.
21. Long Head of the Triceps Extensor Cubiti.
22. Serratus Major Anticus.
23. Internal Oblique of the Abdomen.

FIG. 190.

A VIEW OF THE MUSCLES OF THE BACK WHICH FILL UP THE FOSSA ON EITHER SIDE OF THE SPINOUS PROCESSES OF THE VERTEBRÆ.

1. Tendinous Origin of the Longissimus Dorsi.
2. Upper portion of the Sacro-Lumbalis.
3. Upper portion of the Longissimus Dorsi.
4. Spinalis Dorsi.
5. Cervicalis Descendens.
6. Transversalis Cervicis.
7. Trachelo-Mastoideus.
8. Complexus.
9. Insertion of the Transversalis Cervicis.
10. Semi-Spinalis Dorsi.
11. Semi-Spinalis Cervicis.
12. Rectus Capitis Posticus Minor.
13. Rectus Capitis Posticus Major.
14. Obliquus Capitis Superior.
15. Obliquus Capitis Inferior.
16. Multifidus Spinæ at its Lower Part. The rest is concealed by other Muscles.
17.17. Levatores Costarum.
18. Inter-Transversarii.
19. Quadratus Lumborum.

FIG. 191.

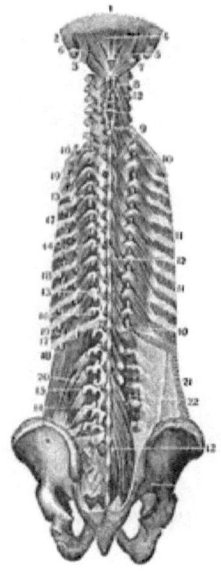

FIG. 192.

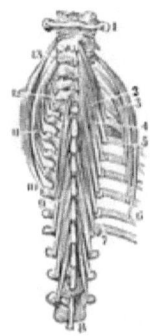

MUSCLES OF THE BACK.

FIG. 191.

A VIEW OF THE DEEP-SEATED OR FOURTH LAYER OF MUSCLES ON THE BACK OF THE HEAD AND TRUNK.

1. Occiput.
2. Mastoid Process of the Temporal Bone.
3. First Cervical Vertebra.
4. Rectus Capitis Posticus Minor.
5. Rectus Capitis Posticus Major.
6. Obliquus Capitis Superior.
7. Obliquus Capitis Inferior.
8.8. Inter-Spinales of the Neck.
9. Inter-Spinales of the Dorsal Vertebræ.
10.10. Levatores Costarum.
11.11. Intercostales.
12.12.12. Multifidus Spinæ from its Origin to its Insertion.
  13.13. Cut Origins of the Multifidus Spinæ.
    14. Cut Insertions of the Multifidus Spinæ.
    15. Quadratus Lumborum.
  16.16. Insertions of the Longissimus Dorsi.
17.17.18. Insertions of the Sacro-Lumbalis.

19. External Intercostals.
20. Outer portion of the Quadratus Lumborum.
21. Section of the Fascia Lumborum.
22. Inter-Transversarii.

FIG. 192.

AN ENLARGED VIEW OF THE MUSCLES ATTACHED TO THE CERVICAL VERTEBRÆ BEHIND.

1. Atlas.
2. Semi-Spinalis Cervicis at its Upper part.
3. Insertions of the Cervicalis Descendens.
4. Middle of the Semi-Spinalis Cervicis.
5.6. Origins of the Cervicalis Descendens.
7. Lower portion of the Semi-Spinalis Cervicis.
8. Tenth Dorsal Vertebra.
9. Semi-Spinalis Dorsi.
10.11. Origins of the Transversalis Cervicis.
12.13. Its Insertions.

FIG. 193. FIG. 194.

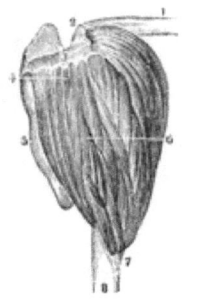

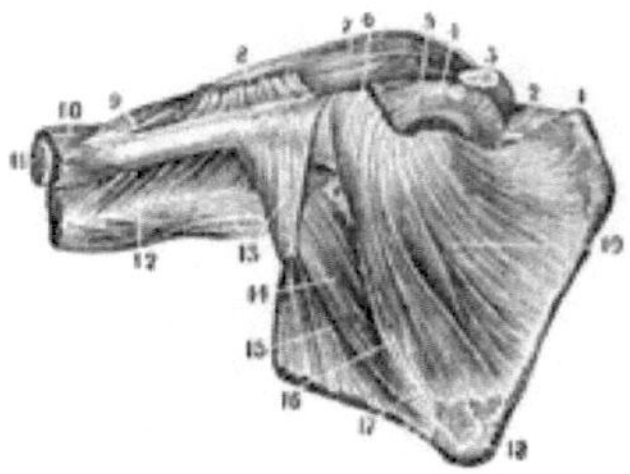

FIG. 195. FIG. 196.

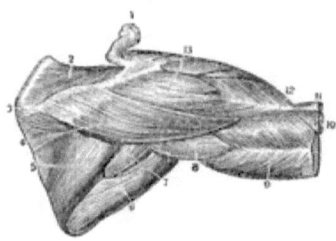
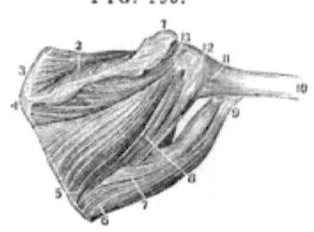

MUSCLES OF THE SHOULDER.

FIG. 193.

A VIEW OF THE DELTOID MUSCLE.

1. Clavicle.
2. Origin of the Deltoid from the Clavicle, Acromion
3. and Spine of the Scapula.
4.
5. Body of the Scapula.
6. Middle of the Deltoid, showing the Fasciculated character of its Fibres.
7. Its Insertion.
8. Shaft of the Os Humeri.

FIG. 194.

AN ANTERIOR VIEW OF THE MUSCLES OF THE SHOULDER.

1. Upper part of the Body of the Scapula.
2. Supra Spinatus Muscle.
3. Section of Acromion Process.
4. Coracoid Process.
5. Origin of the Second or short Head of the Biceps.
6. Sub-Scapularis near its Insertion.
7. Deltoid.
8. Tendon of the Pectoralis Major.
9. Insertion of the Deltoid Muscle.
10. Brachialis Internus.
11. Cut Extremity of the Os Humeri.
12. Triceps Extensor Cubiti.
13. Tendon of the Latissimus Dorsi.
14. Teres Major.
15. Axillary portion of the Latissimus Dorsi.
16. Axillary portion of the Sub-Scapularis.
17. Origin of the Teres Major.
18. Lower portion of the Scapula.

FIG. 195.

A POSTERIOR VIEW OF THE MUSCLES OF THE SHOULDER WITH THE DELTOID.

1. Acromion Scapulæ.
2. Supra-spinatus Muscle.
3. Spine of the Scapula.
4. Posterior portion of the Origin of the Deltoid.
5. Infra-Spinatus Muscle.
6. Teres Major.
7. Teres Minor.
8. Long Head of the Triceps Extensor.
9. Its Second Head.
10. The Shaft of the Os Humeri.
11. Brachialis Internus.
12. Insertion of the Deltoid.
13. Its middle portion forming the round part of the Shoulder.

FIG. 196.

A POSTERIOR VIEW OF THE MUSCLES OF THE SHOULDER WHICH STRENGTHEN THE ARTICULATION.

1. Acromion Scapulæ.
2. Supra-Spinatus Muscle.
3. Upper Angle of the Scapula.
4. Spine of the Scapula.
5. Origin of the Infra-Spinatus Muscle.
6.7. Origin of the Teres Major.
8. Origin of the Teres Minor.
9. Insertion of the Teres Major.
10. Shaft of the Os Humeri.
11. Lower part of the Capsular Ligament.
12. Insertion of the Teres Minor.
13. Insertion of the Infra-Spinatus.

FIG. 197.

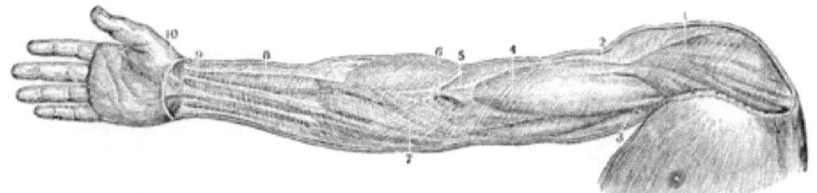

FIG. 198.

FIG. 199.

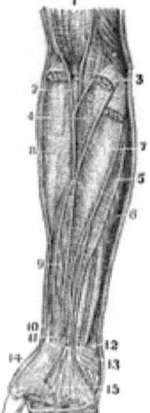

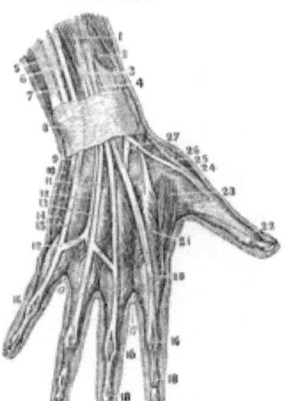

FASCIA AND MUSCLES OF THE UPPER EXTREMITY.

FIG. 197.

A VIEW OF THE FASCIA BRACHI-
ALIS IN ITS WHOLE EXTENT.

1. Portion covering the Deltoid Muscle.
2. Portion covering the upper part of the Biceps.
3. Portion covering the Coraco-Brachialis.
4. Portion covering the lower part of the Biceps.
5. Tendon of the Biceps.
6. Opening for the Vein.
7. Aponeurosis as strengthened by the Expansion from the Tendon of the Biceps.
8. Fascia over the Flexor Sublimis.
9. Fascia over the Flexor Carpi Radialis.
10. Commencement of the Palmar Fascia.

FIG. 198.

A VIEW OF THE INTER-MUSCU-
LAR FASCIÆ OR SHEATHS OF
THE MUSCLES OF THE FORE-
ARM. THE THICKNESS OF THE
SHEATHS HAS BEEN EXAGGE-
RATED IN ORDER TO SHOW
THEM BETTER.

1. Inferior Extremity of the Sheath of the Biceps Flexor Cubiti.
2. Tendon of the Biceps cut off just above its Insertion.

3. Aponeurotic Attachment at the Internal Condyle of the Flexors of the Fore-Arm.
4. Sheath of the Pronator Radii Teres.
5. Sheath of the Palmaris Longus.
6. Sheath of the Flexor Carpi Ulnaris.
7. Sheath of the Flexor Carpi Radialis.
8. Sheath of the Supinator Radii Longus.
9. Fibro Cellular Tissue covering the Flexor Sublimis.
10. Tendon of the Supinator Radii Longus cut off near its Insertion.
11. Tendon of the Flexor Carpi Radialis cut off near its Insertion.
12. Tendon of the Flexor Carpi Ulnaris cut off near its Insertion.
13. Palmaris Brevis.
14. Openings in the Palmar Fascia for the Superficial Nerves.
15. Fascia Palmaris.

FIG. 199.

A VIEW OF THE MUSCLES AND
TENDONS ON THE BACK OF
THE HAND.

1. Lower portion of the Extensor Communis Digitorum.
2. Extensor Minor Pollicis Manus.
3. Tendons of the Extensor Communis.

4. Extensor Major Pollicis.
5. The Ulna.
6. Tendon of the Auricularis.
7. Extensor Carpi Ulnaris Tendon.
8. Posterior Carpal Ligament.
9. Insertion of the Extensor Carpi Ulnaris into the Metacarpal Bone of the Little Finger.
10. Abductor Minimi Digiti.
11. Middle Tendon of the Extensor Communis.
12. Tendon to the Ring Finger.
13. Prior Annularis.
14. Flexor Parvus Minimi Digiti Manus.
15. Interosseous Digiti Auricularis.
16.16.16. Arrangement of the Extensor Communis Tendons at the Phalangial Articulations.
17. Points to the Interossei Muscles on the Palm of the Hand.
18. Insertions of the Extensor Communis.
19. Cross Slips connecting the different Tendons of the Extensor Communis.
20. Tendon of the Indicator.
21. Prior Indicis.
22. Insertion of the Extensor Major Pollicis.
23. Abductor Indicis Manus.
24. Insertion of the Extensor Carpi Radialis Longior.
25. Extensor Minor Pollicis Tendon.
26. Extensor Major Pollicis Tendon.
27. Insertion of the Tendon of the Extensor Carpi Radialis Brevior.

FIG. 200.

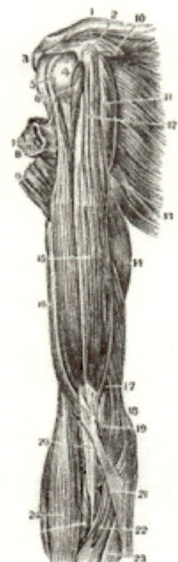

FIG. 202.

FIG. 201.

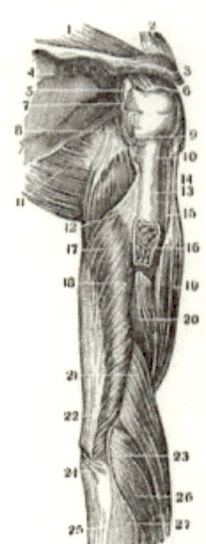

MUSCLES OF THE ARM AND FORE-ARM

FIG. 200.

A VIEW OF THE MUSCLES ON THE FRONT OF THE ARM.

1. Clavicle.
2. Coracoid Process and Origin of the Short Head of the Biceps.
3. Acromion Scapulæ.
4. Head of the Os Humeri.
5. Tendon of the Biceps Muscle in the Bicipital Groove.
6. Ligamentum Adscititium dissected off.
7. Cut portion of the Pectoralis Major.
8. Long Head of the Biceps.
9. Insertion of the Deltoid.
10. Cut portion of the Tendinous Insertion of the Pectoralis Minor.
11. Coraco-Brachialis.
12. Short Head of the Biceps.
13. Latissimus Dorsi.
14. Inner portion of the Triceps.
15. Body of the Biceps.
16. Outer portion of the Triceps.
17. Brachialis Internus.
18. Origin of the Flexor Muscles.
19. Brachialis Internus near its Insertion.

20. Tendon of the Biceps.
21. Fasciculus from the Biceps Tendon to the Fascia Brachialis.
22. Flexor Carpi Radialis.
23. Palmaris Longus.
24. Supinator Radii Longus.

FIG. 201.

A VIEW OF THE MUSCLES ON THE BACK OF THE ARM.

1. Supra-Spinatus Muscle.
2. Section of the Clavicle.
3. Acromion Process.
4. Fossa Infra-Spinata.
5. Head of the Os Humeri.
6. Capsular Ligament.
7. Tendon of the Infra-Spinatus Muscle.
8. Origin of the Long Head of the Triceps.
9. } Teres Minor Tendon.
10. }
11. Serratus Major Anticus.
12. Origin of the Second Head of the Triceps.
13. Shaft of the Humerus.
14. Long Head of the Biceps Flexor.
15. Insertion of the Pectoralis Major.
16. Insertion of the Deltoid.
17. Body of the Triceps.

18. Origin of its Third Head, sometimes called Brachialis Externus.
19. Middle of the Biceps Flexor.
20. Middle of the Brachialis Externus.
21. Origin of the Supinator Radii Longus.
22. Lower portion of the Triceps.
23. Origin of the Extensor Carpi Radialis Longior.
24. Insertion of the Triceps.
25. Shaft of the Ulna.
26. Middle of the Extensor Carpi Radialis Longior.
27. Extensor Communis Digitorum.

FIG. 202.

A VIEW OF THE PRONATORS OF THE FORE-ARM.

1. Os Humeri.
2. Radius.
3. Ulna.
4. Capsular Ligament of the Elbow.
5. Interosseous Ligament.
6. Origin of the Pronator Radii Longus.
7. Its Insertion.
8. Supinator Radii Brevis.
9. Pronator Quadratus.
10. Tendon of the Biceps.
11. Carpal Articulation.

Page 64

FIG. 203.   FIG. 204.

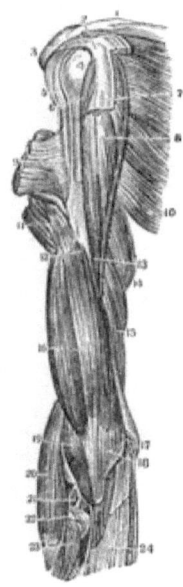 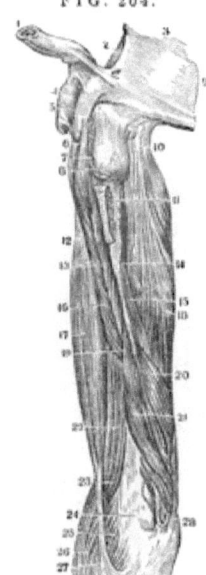

MUSCLES OF THE ARM.

FIG. 203.

AN ANTERIOR VIEW OF THE DEEP-SEATED MUS-
CLES OF THE ARM.

1. Clavicle.
2. Coracoid Process of the Scapula.
3. Acromion Scapulæ.
4. Head of the Os Humeri.
5. Tendon of the Long Head of the Biceps.
6. Upper portion of the Coraco-Brachialis.
7. Origin of the Short Head of the Biceps.
8. Body of the Coraco-Brachialis.
9. Insertion of the Pectoralis Major.
10. Latissimus Dorsi.
11. Insertion of the Deltoid.
12. Origin of the Brachialis Internus.
13. Insertion of the Coraco-Brachialis.
14 Middle portion of the Triceps.
15. Its Lower Anterior Portion.
16. Body of the Brachialis Internus.
17. Internal Condyle.
18. 19. } Insertion of the Brachialis Internus.
20. Supinator Radii Longus.
21. Opening in the Capsular Ligament.
22. Cut Tendon of the Biceps at its Insertion.
23. Supinator Radii Brevis.
24. Fascia.

FIG. 204.

A LATERAL VIEW OF THE DEEP-SEATED MUS-
CLES ON THE BACK OF THE ARM.

1. Section of the Clavicle.
2. Fossa Supra-Spinata of the Scapula.
3. Base of the Scapula.
4. Coraco-Acromial Ligament.
5. Coracoid Process.
6. Origin of the Coraco-Brachialis.
7. Section of the Sub-Scapularis Muscle.
8. Head of the Os Humeri.
9. Section of the Body of the Scapula.
10. Origin of the Long Head of the Triceps.
11. Insertion of the Latissimus Dorsi.
12. Edge of the Biceps Flexor Cubiti.
13. Coraco-Brachialis.
14. 15. } Origin of the Second Head of the Triceps.
16. Lower portion of the Coraco-Brachialis.
17. Body of the Biceps.
18. Body of the Triceps.
19. Origin of the Third Head of the Triceps.
20. Its middle portion, known as the Brachialis
21. } Externus.
22. Brachialis Internus.
23. Its Insertion.
24. Capsular Ligament of the Elbow.
25. 26. } Origin of the Flexors of the Fore-Arm.
27. Prolongation of the Tendon of the Biceps to the Fascia Brachialis.
28. Olecranon.

FIG. 205. FIG. 207.

FIG. 206.

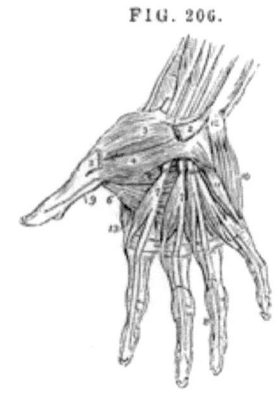
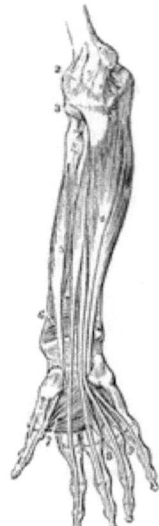

MUSCLES OF THE FORE-ARM AND HAND.

FIG. 205.

A VIEW OF THE OUTER LAYER OF THE MUSCLES ON THE FRONT OF THE FORE-ARM (FLEXORS).

1. Lower portion of the Biceps Flexor Cubiti.
2. Brachialis Internus.
3. Lower Internal portion of the Triceps.
4. Pronator Radii Teres.
5. Flexor Carpi Radialis.
6. Palmaris Longus.
7. Part of the Flexor Sublimis Digitorum.
8. Flexor Carpi Ulnaris.
9. Palmar Fascia.
10. Palmaris Brevis Muscle.
11. Abductor Pollicis Manus.
12. Portion of the Flexor Brevis Pollicis Manus. The Line crosses the Adductor Pollicis.
13. Supinator Longus.
14. Extensor Ossis Metacarpi Pollicis.

FIG. 206.

A VIEW OF THE MUSCLES ON THE PALM OF THE HAND.

1. Annular Ligament.
2.2. Origin and Insertion of the Abductor Pollicis.
3. Opponens Pollicis.

4.5. Two Bellies of the Flexor Brevis Pollicis.
6. Adductor Pollicis.
7.7. Lumbricales arising from Tendons of the Flexor Profundus Digitorum.
8. Shows how the Tendon of the Flexor Profundus passes through the Flexor Sublimis.
9. Tendon of the Flexor Longus Pollicis.
10. Abductor Minimi Digiti.
11. Flexor Parvus Minimi Digiti.
12. Pisiform Bone.
13. First Dorsal Interosseous Muscle.

FIG. 207.

A VIEW OF THE UNDER LAYER OF MUSCLES ON THE FRONT OF THE FORE-ARM (FLEXORS).

1. Internal Lateral Ligament of the Elbow-Joint.
2. Capsular Ligament of the Elbow-Joint.
3. Coronary Ligament of the Head of the Radius.
4. Flexor Profundus Digitorum Perforans.
5. Flexor Longus Pollicis.
6. Pronator Quadratus.
7. Adductor Pollicis Manus.
8. Lumbricales.
9. Interossei.

FIG. 208.   FIG. 209.

FIG. 210.

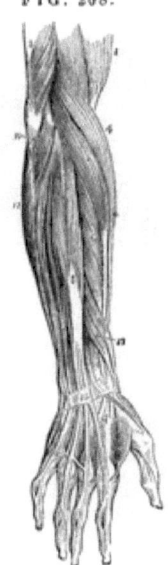
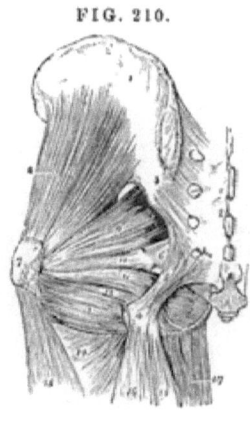
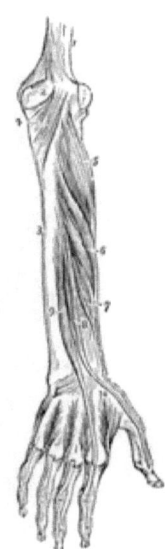

MUSCLES OF THE FORE-ARM AND HIP.

FIG. 208.

A VIEW OF THE OUTER LAYER OF MUSCLES ON
THE BACK OF THE FORE-ARM (EXTENSORS).

1. Lower portion of the Biceps Flexor.
2. Part of the Brachialis Internus.
3. Lower part of the Triceps Extensor.
4. Supinator Radii Longus.
5. Extensor Carpi Radialis Longior.
6. Extensor Carpi Radialis Brevier.
7. Tendinous Insertions of these two Muscles.
8. Extensor Communis Digitorum.
9. Portion of the Extensor Communis Digitorum called Auricularis.
10. Extensor Carpi Ulnaris.
11. Anconeus.
12. Portion of the Flexor Carpi Ulnaris.
13. Extensor Minor Pollicis. The Muscle nearest the Figure is the Extensor Ossis Metacarpi Pollicis.
14. Extensor Major Pollicis.
15. Posterior Annular Ligament. The distribution of the Tendons of the Extensor Communis, is seen on the backs of the Fingers.

FIG. 209.

A VIEW OF THE DEEP-SEATED MUSCLES ON THE
BACK OF THE FORE-ARM (EXTENSORS).

1. Lower part of the Humerus.
2. Olecranon.
3. Shaft of the Ulna.

4. Anconeus Muscle.
5. Supinator Radii Brevis.
6. Extensor Ossis Metacarpi Pollicis.
7. Extensor Minor Pollicis.
8. Extensor Major Pollicis.
9. Indicator.
10. First Dorsal Interosseous Muscle. The others are also shown.

FIG. 210.

A VIEW OF THE DEEP-SEATED MUSCLES AT THE
HIP-JOINT.

1. Os Ilium.
2. Os Sacrum.
3. Posterior Sacro-Iliac Ligaments.
4. Tuber Ischii.
5. Greater Sacro-Sciatic Ligament.
6. Lesser Sacro-Sciatic Ligament.
7. Trochanter Major.
8. Gluteus Minimus.
9. Pyriformis.
10. Geminus Superior.
11. Obturator Internus.
12. Geminus Inferior.
13. Quadratus Femoris.
14. Adductor Magnus.
15. Vastus Externus.
16. Biceps.
17. Gracilis.
18. Semi-Tendinosus.

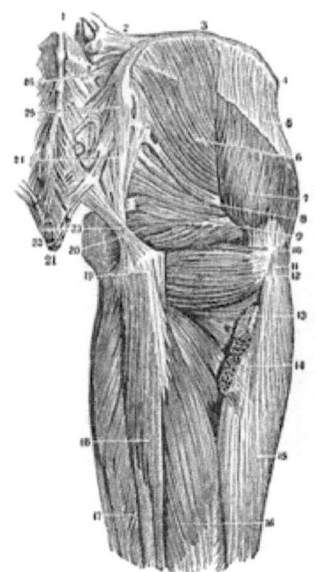 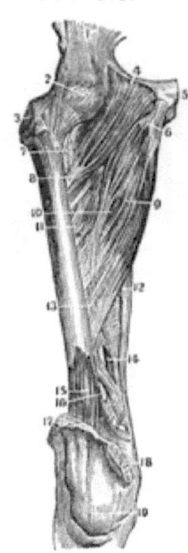

MUSCLES OF THE THIGH

FIG. 211.

A VIEW OF THE DEEP-SEATED MUSCLES ON THE
POSTERIOR PART OF THE HIP-JOINT.

1. Fifth Lumbar Vertebra.
2. Ilio-Lumbar Ligament.
3. Crest of the Ilium.
4. Anterior Superior Spinous Process.
5. Origin of the Fascia Femoris.
6. Gluteus Medius.
7. Its Lower and Anterior portion.
8. Pyriformis.
9. Gemini.
10. Trochanter Major.
11. Insertion of the Gluteus Medius.
12. Quadratus Femoris.
13. Part of the Adductor Magnus.
14. Insertion of the Gluteus Magnus.
15. Vastus Externus.
16. Long Head of the Biceps.
17. Semi-Membranosus.
18. Semi-Tendinosus.
19. Tuber Ischii.
20. Obturator Internus.
21. Point of the Coccyx.
22. Posterior Coccygeal Ligament.
23.
24. } Greater Sacro-Sciatic Ligament.
25. Posterior Superior Spinous Process of Ilium.
26. Posterior Sacro-Iliac Ligaments.

FIG. 212.

A VIEW OF THE DEEP-SEATED MUSCLES ON THE
FRONT OF THE THIGH.

1. Os Ilium.
2. Capsular Ligament of the Hip-Joint.
3. Trochanter Major.
4. Origin of the Pectineus Muscle.
5. Symphysis Pubis.
6. Origin of the Adductor Longus.
7. Insertion of the Iliacus Internus and Psoas
 Magnus.
8. Insertion of the Pectineus.
9. Middle of the Adductor Longus.
10. Tendinous Insertion of the Adductor Longus.
11. Part of the Adductor Brevis seen between
 the Pectineus and Adductor Longus.
12. Cut edge of the Vastus Internus.
13. Aperture for the passage of Blood-Vessels.
14. Opening for the Femoral Vessels.
15. Portion of the Cruræus.
16. Another Opening for Vessels.
17. Cut Tendon of the Quadriceps Femoris.
18. Internal portion of the Knee-Joint.
19. Tendon of the Patella.

FIG. 213.   FIG. 215.   FIG. 214.

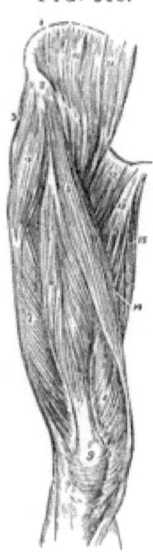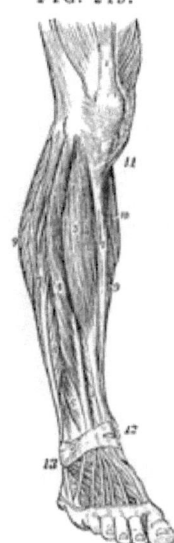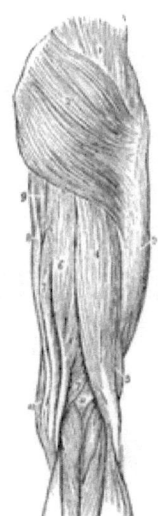

MUSCLES OF THE THIGH AND LEG.

FIG. 213.

A VIEW OF THE MUSCLES ON THE FRONT OF THE THIGH.

1. Crest of the Ilium.
2. Its Anterior Superior Spinous Process.
3. Gluteus Medius.
4. Tensor Vaginæ Femoris.
5. Sartorius.
6. Rectus Femoris.
7. Vastus Externus.
8. Vastus Internus.
9. Patella.
10. Iliacus Internus.
11. Psoas Magnus.
12. Pectineus.
13. Adductor Longus.
14. Adductor Magnus
15. Gracilis.

FIG. 214.

A VIEW OF THE MUSCLES ON THE BACK OF THE THIGH.

1. Gluteus Medius.
2. Gluteus Magnus.
3. Fascia Lata covering the Vastus Externus.
4. Long Head of the Biceps.
5. Short Head of the Biceps.
6. Semi-Tendinosus.
7.7. Semi-Membranosus.
8. Gracilis.
9. Edge of the Adductor Magnus.
10. Edge of the Sartorius.
11. Popliteal Space.
12. Gastrocnemius.

FIG. 215.

A VIEW OF THE MUSCLES ON THE FRONT OF THE LEG.

1. Tendon of the Quadriceps Femoris.
2. Spine of the Tibia.
3. Tibialis Anticus.
4. Extensor Communis Digitorum.
5. Extensor Proprius Pollicis.
6. Peroneus Tertius.
7. Peroneus Longus.
8. Peroneus Brevis.
9.9. Borders of the Soleus.
10. Portion of the Gastrocnemius.
11. Extensor Brevis Digitorum

FIG. 218.   FIG. 219.

MUSCLES OF THE LEG AND FOOT.

FIG. 216.

A VIEW OF THE MUSCLES ON THE BACK OF THE LEG.

1. Tendon of the Biceps.
2. Inner Hamstring Tendons.
3. Popliteal Space.
4. Gastrocnemius.
5. Soleus.
6. Tendo-Achillis.
7. Its Insertion on the Os Calcis.
8. Tendons of the Peroneus Longus and Brevis.
9. Tendons of the Tibialis Posticus and Flexor Longus Digitorum behind the Internal Malleolus.

FIG. 217.

A VIEW OF THE DEEP-SEATED MUSCLES ON THE BACK OF THE LEG.

1. Lower portion of the Femur.
2. Ligament of Winslow.
3. Tendon of the Semi-Membranosus.
4. Internal Lateral Ligament of the Knee-Joint.
5. External Lateral Ligament of the Knee.
6. Popliteus Muscle.
7. Flexor Longus Digitorum.
8. Tibialis Posticus.
9. Flexor Longus Pollicis.
10. Peroneus Longus.
11. Peroneus Brevis.
12. Insertion of the Tendo-Achillis.
13. Tendons of the Tibialis Posticus and Flexor Longus Digitorum.

FIG. 218.

A VIEW OF THE MUSCLES ON THE SOLE OF THE FOOT IMMEDIATELY UNDER THE PLANTAR FASCIA.

1. Os Calcis.
2. Section of the Fascia Plantaris.
3. Abductor Pollicis.
4. Abductor Minimi Digiti.
5. Flexor Brevis Digitorum.
6. Tendon of the Flexor Longus Pollicis.
7.7. Lumbricales.

FIG. 219.

A VIEW OF THE DEEPER-SEATED MUSCLES ON THE SOLE OF THE FOOT.

1. Section of the Plantar Fascia.
2. Flexor Accessorius.
3. Tendon of the Flexor Longus Digitorum.
4. Tendon of the Flexor Longus Pollicis.
5. Flexor Brevis Pollicis.
6. Adductor Pollicis.
7. Flexor Brevis Minimi Digiti.
8. Transversalis Pedis.
9. Interossei.
10. Course of the Peroneus Longus Tendon across the Foot.

PART THIRD.

ORGANS OF DIGESTION
AND
GENERATION:
ONE HUNDRED AND NINETY-ONE FIGURES.

FIG. 220.

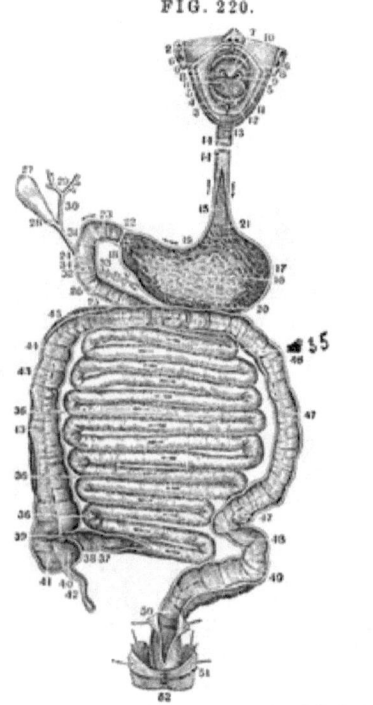

FIG. 221.

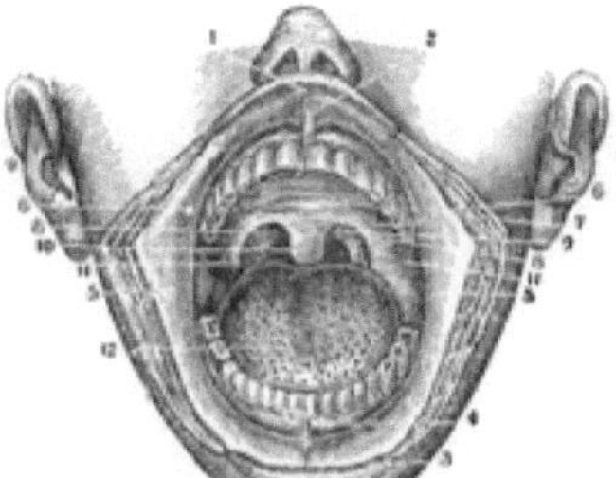

FIG. 222.

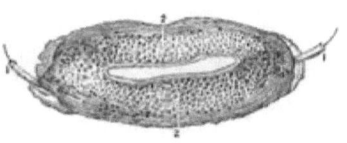

ORGANS OF DIGESTION.

FIG. 220.

A VIEW OF THE ORGANS OF DIGESTION, OPENED IN NEARLY THEIR WHOLE LENGTH. A PORTION OF THE ŒSOPHAGUS HAS BEEN REMOVED ON ACCOUNT OF WANT OF SPACE IN THE FIGURE. THE ARROWS INDICATE THE COURSE OF SUBSTANCES ALONG THE CANAL.

1. The Upper Lip, turned off the Mouth.
2. Its Frænum.
3. The Lower Lip, turned down.
4. Its Frænum.
5.5. Inside of the Cheeks, covered by the lining Membrane of the Mouth.
6. Points to the opening of the Duct of Steno.
7. Roof of the Mouth.
8. Lateral Half Arches.
9. Points to the Tonsils.
10. Velum Pendulum Palati.
11. Surface of the Tongue.
12. Papillæ near its point.
13. A portion of the Trachea.
14. The Œsophagus.
15. Its internal surface.
16. Inside of the Stomach.
17. Its greater extremity or great Cul-de-Sac.
18. Its lesser extremity or smaller Cul-de-Sac.

19. Its lesser Curvature.
20. Its greater Curvature.
21. The Cardiac Orifice.
22. The Pyloric Orifice.
23. Upper portion of Duodenum.
24.25. The remainder of the Duodenum.
26. Its Valvulæ Conniventes.
27. The Gall Bladder.
28. The Cystic Duct.
29. Division of Hepatic Ducts in the Liver.
30. Hepatic Duct.
31. Ductus Communis Choledochus.
32. Its opening into the Duodenum.
33. Ductus Wirsungii, or Pancreatic Duct.
34. Its opening into the Duodenum.
35. Upper part of Jejunum.
36. The Ileum.
37. Some of the Valvulæ Conniventes.
38. Lower extremity of the Ileum.
39. Ileo-Colic Valve.
40.41. Cæcum, or Caput Coli.
42. Appendicula Vermiformis.
43.44. Ascending Colon.
45. Transverse Colon.
46.47. Descending Colon.
48. Sigmoid Flexure of the Colon.
49. Upper portion of the Rectum.
50. Its lower Extremity.

51. Portion of the Levator Ani Muscle.
52. The Anus.

FIG. 221.

A VIEW OF THE CAVITY OF THE MOUTH, AS SHOWN BY DIVIDING THE ANGLES OF THE MOUTH AND TURNING OFF THE LIPS.

1. The Upper Lip, turned up.
2. Its Frænum.
3. The Lower Lip, turned down.
4. Its Frænum.
5. Internal Surface of the Cheeks.
6. Opening of Duct of Steno.
7. Roof of the Mouth.
8. The anterior portion of the Lateral Half Arches.
9. The posterior portion of the Lateral Half Arches.
10. The Velum Pendulum Palati.
11. The Tonsils.
12. The Tongue.

FIG. 222.

A VIEW OF THE INNER SIDE OF THE LIPS. THE MUCOUS MEMBRANE HAS BEEN REMOVED SO AS TO SHOW THE LABIAL AND BUCCAL GLANDS.

1.1. Ducts of Steno: a Bristle has been introduced to show the opening into the Mouth.
2.2. The Labial Glands.

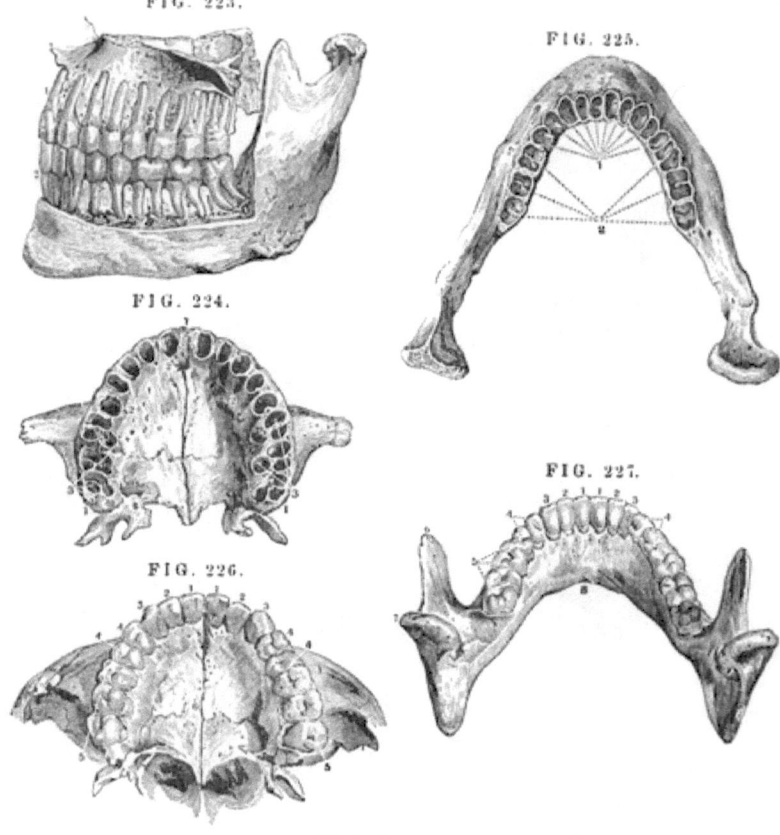

FIG. 223.

FIG. 225.

FIG. 224.

FIG. 227.

FIG. 226.

THE TEETH.

FIG. 223.

A SIDE VIEW OF THE UPPER AND LOWER JAW, SHOWING THE TEETH IN THEIR SOCKETS. THE OUTER PLATE OF THE ALVEOLAR PROCESSES HAS BEEN TAKEN OFF SO AS TO EXPOSE THE FANGS OF THE TEETH AND SHOW THE KIND OF ARTICULATION AND RELATIVE POSITION OF EACH.

1. First Incisores of the Upper Jaw.
2. First Incisores of the Lower Jaw.

FIG. 224.

A VIEW OF THE UNDER SIDE OF THE UPPER JAW WITHOUT THE TEETH.

1.1. The outer Plate of the Alveolar Process.
2.2. The inner Plate.
3.3. The three double Sockets for the Molares, the first two of which have three Sockets and the last two.

The ten single Sockets are seen in advance of these on each side of the Middle Line. They are for the Incisores, the Cuspidati and the Bicuspidati.

FIG. 225.

A VIEW OF THE UPPER PART OF THE LOWER JAW, SHOWING THE SOCKETS OF THE TEETH.

1. The Sockets of the ten single-fanged Teeth.
2. The Sockets of the three double-fanged Teeth.

FIG. 226.

A VIEW OF THE UNDER SIDE OF THE UPPER JAW, SHOWING THE CUTTING EDGES AND GRINDING SURFACES OF THE TEETH OF THIS JAW.

1.1. The two Central Incisores.
2.2. The two Lateral Incisores.
3.3. The two Cuspidati.
4.4. The four Bicuspidati.
5.5. The six Molares or Grinders.

FIG. 227.

A VIEW, FROM ABOVE AND BEHIND, OF THE LOWER JAW WITH A FULL SET OF TEETH, SHOWING THE CUTTING EDGES AND GRINDING SURFACES OF THE TEETH IN THAT JAW, WITH THE CORONOID AND CONDYLOID PROCESSES.

1.1. The two Central Incisores.
2.2. The two Lateral Incisores.
3.3. The two Cuspidati.
4.4. The four Bicuspidati.
5.5. The six Molares or Grinders.
6. Coronoid Process.
7. Condyloid Process.
8. Base of Jaw.

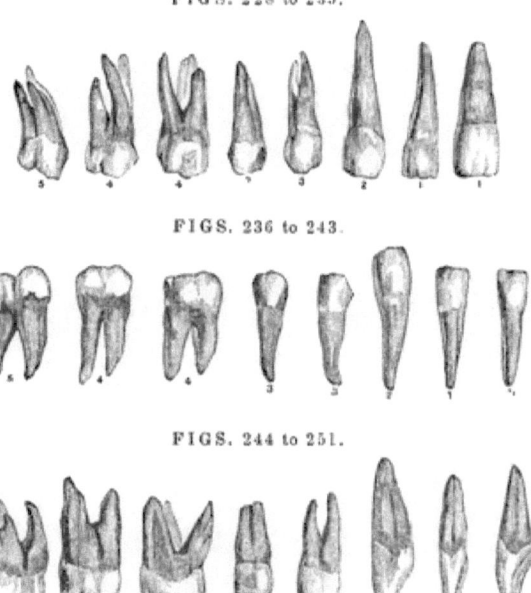

FIGS. 228 to 235.

FIGS. 236 to 243.

FIGS. 244 to 251.

THE TEETH.

FIGS. 228 to 235.

A VIEW OF THE EIGHT TEETH OF ONE SIDE OF
THE UPPER JAW, TAKEN FROM THEIR SOCKETS
SO AS TO SHOW THE WHOLE TOOTH; SEEN
FROM THE OUTSIDE.

1.1. The two Incisores.
2. The Cuspidatus, showing how much it is longer than the others.
3.3. The two Bicuspidati.
4.4. The first two Molares, having three Fangs.
5. The third Molar or Dens Sapientiæ, having also three Fangs.

FIGS. 236 to 243.

THE SAME VIEW OF THE TEETH OF THE LOWER
JAW: THE FIVE SINGLE ONES ARE SIMILAR TO
THOSE IN THE UPPER JAW, BUT THE GRINDERS
IN THIS JAW HAVE ONLY TWO FANGS. THE

FIGURES IN THIS CUT HAVE THE SAME REFER-
ENCES AS IN THE PRECEDING CUT.

FIGS. 244 to 251.

A SIDE VIEW OF THE TEETH OF ONE SIDE OF THE
UPPER JAW, SHOWING HOW THE INCISORES AND
CUSPIDATI IN THIS VIEW DIFFER FROM THE
FORMER VIEW MORE THAN THE BICUSPIDATI
OR MOLARES.

1.1. The two Incisores, showing the hollowed inner Surface of the Body of these Teeth.
2. The Cuspidatus, showing the same.
3.3. The Bicuspidati, showing the two points on the basis of each. The first of them has a forked Fang.
4.5. The Molares.

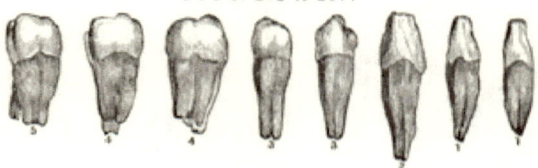

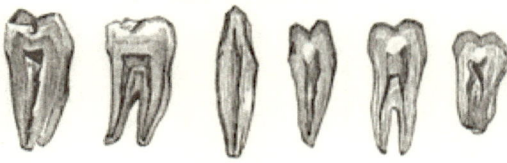

FIGS. 266 and 267.

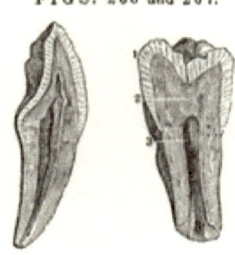

THE TEETH.

FIGS. 252 to 259.

A SIDE VIEW OF THE TEETH OF ONE SIDE OF THE LOWER JAW, SHOWING THAT THE INCISORES AND CUSPIDATI IN THIS VIEW DIFFER FROM THE VIEW IN FIG. 236, MORE THAN THE BICUSPIDATI OR GRINDERS.

1.1. The two Incisores.

2. The Cuspidatus, showing how much longer it is than the others.

3.3. The two Bicuspidati.

4.5. The three Molares.

FIGS. 260 to 265.

A VIEW OF THE CAVITIES OF THE TEETH, AS SEEN IN LONGITUDINAL SECTIONS OF THE INCISORES, CUSPIDATUS, BICUSPIDATI AND MOLARES.

FIGS. 266 and 267.

A VIEW OF AN INCISOR AND OF A MOLAR TOOTH, GIVEN BY A LONGITUDINAL SECTION, AND SHOWING THAT THE ENAMEL IS STRIATED AND THAT THE STRIÆ ARE ALL TURNED TO THE CENTRE. THE INTERNAL STRUCTURE IS ALSO SEEN.

1. The Enamel.
2. The Ivory.
3. The Cavitas Pulpi.

FIG. 268.

FIG. 269.

FIG. 270.

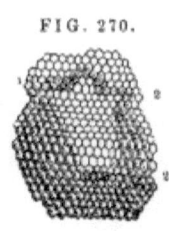

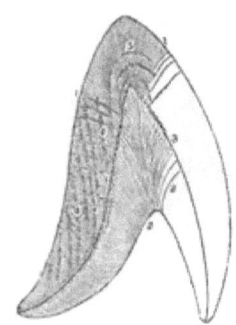

FIG. 271.

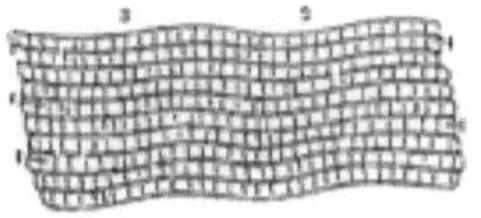

FIG. 272.

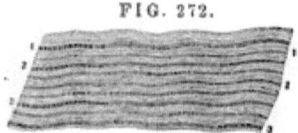

STRUCTURE OF THE TEETH.

FIG. 268.

A VERTICAL SECTION OF AN ADULT BICUSPID, CUT FROM WITHOUT INWARDS; MAGNIFIED FOUR TIMES.

1.1. The Cortical Substance which surrounds the Root up to the commencement of the Enamel.
2.2. The Ivory of the Tooth, in which are seen the greater Parallel Curvatures, as well as the position of the Main Tubes.
3. Apex of the Tooth, where the Tubes are almost perpendicular.
4.4. The Enamel.
5. The Cavity of the Pulp, in which are seen, by means of the Glass, the Openings of the Tubes of the Dental Bone.

FIG. 269.

A VERTICAL SECTION OF AN IMPERFECTLY DEVELOPED INCISOR, TAKEN FROM THE FOLLICLE IN WHICH IT WAS ENCLOSED. THIS SECTION IS MEANT TO SHOW THE POSITION OF THE ENAMEL FIBRES; AND ALSO THAT A PART OF THE APPEARANCES WHICH ARE SEEN IN THIS SUBSTANCE UNDER A LESS MAGNIFYING POWER, ORIGINATE IN PARALLEL CURVATURES OF THE FIBRES.

1.1. The Enamel.
2.2. The Dental Bone, or Ivory.
3.3. The minute Indentations and Points on the Surface of the Ivory, on which the Enamel Fibres rest.

4.4. Brown Parallel Fibres.
5. Parallel Flexions of the Fibres of the Dental Bone in these Stripes.

FIG. 270.

A PORTION OF THE SURFACE OF THE ENAMEL ON WHICH THE HEXAGONAL TERMINATIONS OF THE FIBRES ARE SHOWN; HIGHLY MAGNIFIED.

1.2.3. Are more strongly marked dark crooked Crevices, running between the rows of the Hexagonal Fibres.

FIG. 271.

THE FIBRES OF THE ENAMEL VIEWED SIDEWAYS UNDER A MAGNIFYING POWER OF 350 TIMES.

1.1. The Enamel Fibres.
2.2. The Transverse Stripes upon them.

FIG. 272.

A SMALL PORTION OF FIG. 268 COVERED WITH TURPENTINE VARNISH, VIEWED UNDER A MAGNIFYING POWER OF 350 TIMES.

1.2.3. Are the Tubes containing a powdery lumpy substance. They are regular, and closely undulating; but the Branches do not appear because they are penetrated by the Varnish.

FIG. 273.

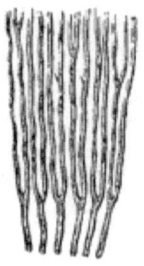

FIG. 274.

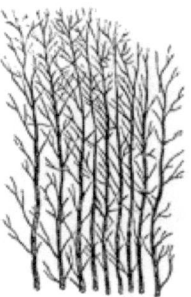

FIG. 277.

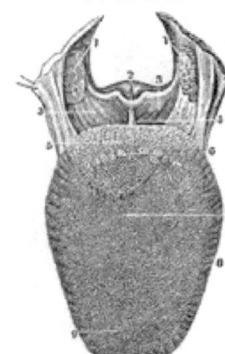

FIG. 275.

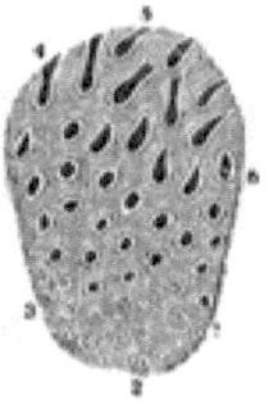

FIG. 276.

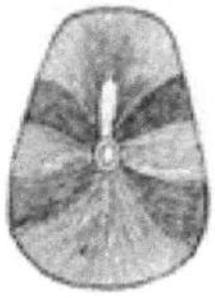

STRUCTURE OF THE TEETH.

FIG. 273.

A View of the most Interior Portion of the Main Tubes of the Dental Bone in an Incisor of a Child two years old, close to their commencement in the Cavitas Pulpi, in order to show their first division.

FIG. 274.

A View of the External Portion of the Tubes of the same Tooth, exhibiting their more minute Ramifications, which, for the most part, turn towards the Crown.

FIG. 275.

A View of a small Portion of a Transverse Section of the Crown of the Tooth, seen in Fig. 268, viewed under a magnifying power of 350 times.

1.2.3. Are the round openings of the Tubes, with Parieties of a peculiar Substance.

4.5.6. Are the Tubes cut more obliquely, in consequence of their more External Position.

FIG. 276.

A View of the Position of the same Main Tubes, in a Transverse Section near the Root of a Bicuspid, magnified five diam's. The dark patches in this Figure mark the places in which the Bone was especially White, and less Transparent than in the clearer Intermediate Tracts.

FIG. 277.

A Front View of the Upper Surface of the Tongue, as well as of the Palatine Arch.

1.1. The Posterior Lateral Half Arches, with the Palato Pharingeal Muscles, as also the Tonsils.

2. The Epiglottis Cartilage, seen from before.

3.3. The Ligament and Mucous Membrane, extending from the Root of the Tongue to the Base of the Epiglottis Cartilage.

4. One of the Pouches on the side of the Posterior Frænum, in which food sometimes lodges.

5. The Foramen Cœcum, or central one of the Papillæ Maximæ.

6. Papillæ Conicæ, or Maximæ.

7. The white point at the end of the line, and all like it, are the Papillæ Fungiformes.

8. The Side of the Tongue, and the Rugæ Transversæ of Albinus.

9. The Papillæ Filiformes.

10. Point of the Tongue.

FIG. 278.

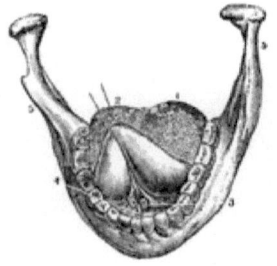

FIG. 279.

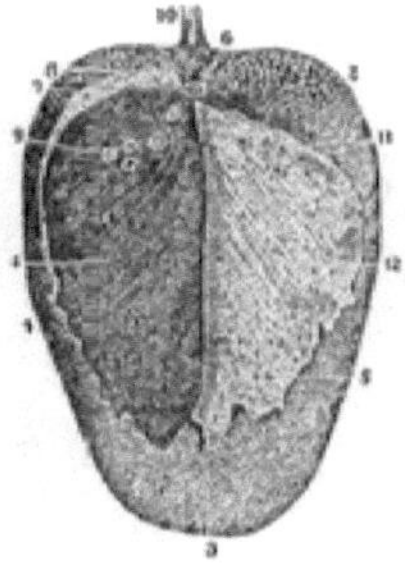

FIG. 280.

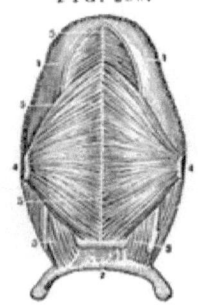

FIG. 281.

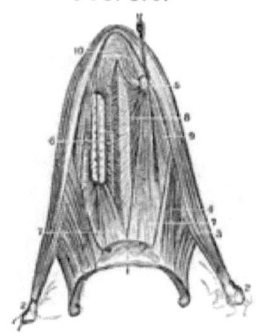

THE MOUTH.

FIG. 278.

A VIEW OF THE LOWER JAW, WITH THE TONGUE DRAWN UPWARDS, SO AS TO SHOW ITS UNDER SURFACE IN SITU.

1. ⎱ The Posterior Superior Surface of the Tongue,
2. ⎰ with the Papillæ Maximæ.
3. The Opening of the Duct of the Sub-Maxillary Gland, or the Duct of Wharton.
4. The Sub-Lingual Gland, seen under the Mucous Membrane of the Mouth.
5. The Lower Jaw.

———

FIG. 279.

A VIEW OF THE DORSUM OF THE TONGUE, FROM WHICH, BY MACERATION, THE PERIGLOTTIS HAS BEEN REMOVED, AND TURNED BACK ON THE RIGHT SIDE.

1. The Sides of the Tongue.
2. Its Base.
3. Its Tip or Point.
4. The denuded portion of the Tongue, showing the Papillæ deprived of the Epidermis or Periglottis.
5. The Under Surface of the detached Epidermis, showing its depressions.
6. Foramen Cœcum.
7. The Truncated Papillæ near it.
8. The other Papillæ, denuded of the Epidermis.
9. Impression of the Periglottis around the denuded Papillæ.
10. Frænum to the Epiglottis Cartilage.
11.12. Depressions on the Periglottis, which fits the Elevations on the Tongue.

FIG. 280.

A VIEW OF THE UNDER SURFACE OF THE TONGUE, WITH THE MUSCLES CONNECTED WITH IT.

1.1. The Inferior Surface of the Tongue.
2. The Os Hyoides.
3.3. Origin of Hyo-Glossus Muscle.
4.4. The Genio-Hyo-Glossus of each side dissected off and turned to one side.
5⁵. The White Central Vertical Septum of the Tongue.

———

FIG. 281.

A VIEW OF THE MUSCLES OF THE TONGUE, AS SEEN ON ITS LOWER SURFACE.

1. Body of the Os Hyoides.
2.2. Styloid Processes of the Temporal Bones.
3. Horizontal Portion of the Stylo-Glossus Muscle.
4. The Hyo-Glossus.
5. The Genio-Hyo-Glossus held up by a hook near its origin.
6. Section of the Glossal Portion of the same Muscle.
7. Its Insertion into the Os Hyoides.
8. The Middle Fissure and Fatty Matter between the Muscles of each side.
9. The Lingualis Muscle.
10. The Transversales Linguæ at the Point of the Tongue.

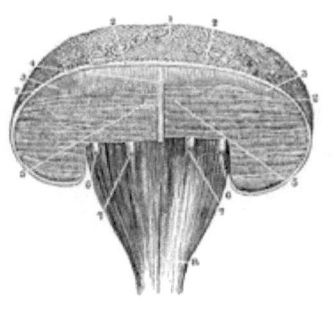

FIG. 282.

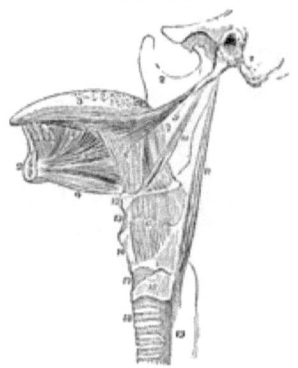

FIG. 283.

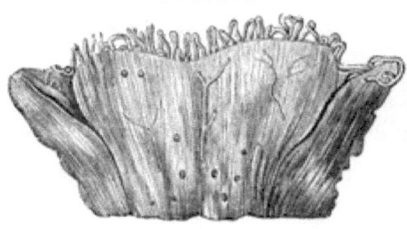

FIG. 284.

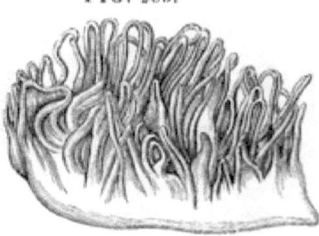

FIG. 285.

THE MOUTH.

FIG. 282.

A VIEW OF A SECTION OF THE ANTERIOR POR-
TION OF THE TONGUE, AS SEEN FROM BEHIND.

1. The Upper Surface.
2.2. The Tongue uncovered by the Epidermis, which is slightly drawn forward.
3.3. The Verticales Linguæ Muscle.
4. The Middle Septum.
5.5. The Transversales Linguæ.
6. The Ranine Arteries.
7. The Glosso-Pharyngeal Nerves.
8. The Genio-Hyo-Glossus Muscle of each side.

FIG. 283.

A LATERAL VIEW OF THE STYLOID MUSCLES, AND ALSO OF THOSE OF THE TONGUE.

1. Mastoid Portion of Temporal Bone.
2.2. Right Half of the Lower Jaw Bone.
3. Upper Surface of the Tongue.
4. Genio-Hyoideus Muscle.
5. Genio-Hyo-Glossus Muscle.
6.7. } Hyo-Glossus Muscle.
8. Anterior Fibres of the Lingualis issuing from between Hyo-Glossus and Genio-Hyo-Glossus.

9. Stylo-Glossus Muscle.
10. Stylo-Hyoid Muscle.
11. Stylo-Pharyngeus Muscle.
12. Os Hyoides.
13. Thyreo-Hyoid Ligament.
14. Thyroid Cartilage.
15. Thyro-Hyoideus Muscle.
16. Cricoid Cartilage.
17. Crico-Thyroid Ligament.
18. Trachea.
19. Œsophagus.

FIG. 284.

A VERTICAL SECTION OF ONE OF THE GUSTA-
TORY PAPILLÆ OF THE LARGEST CLASS, SHOW-
ING ITS CONICAL FORM, ITS SIDES, AND THE
FISSURE BETWEEN THE DIFFERENT PAPILLÆ.
THE LENGTH OF SOME OF THE DIVIDED BLOOD-
VESSELS, A TRANSVERSE SECTION OF OTHERS,
AND THE VESSELS WHICH RISE UP FROM THE
SURFACE LIKE LOOPS OR MESHES, ARE ALSO
SHOWN; HIGHLY MAGNIFIED.

FIG. 285.

A VIEW OF A PAPILLA OF THE SMALLEST CLASS,
MAGNIFIED 25 DIAMETERS. THE LOOPS OF
BLOOD-VESSELS ARE HERE SHOWN, EACH LOOP
CONTAINING USUALLY ONLY ONE VESSEL.

Page 100.

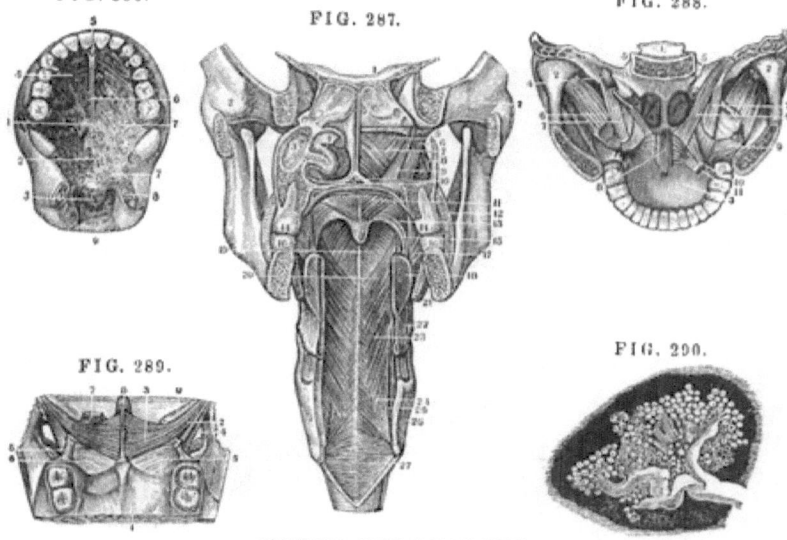

FIG. 286.

FIG. 287.

FIG. 288.

FIG. 289.

FIG. 290.

MOUTH AND PHARYNX.

FIG. 286.

A VIEW OF THE ROOF OF THE MOUTH AND OF THE SOFT PALATE.

1. The Roof of the Mouth, bounded by the Superior Dental Arch.
2. The Soft Palate.
3. The Velum Pendulum Palati.
4. The Ridges seen on the Roof of the Mouth.
5. The Tubercle behind the Incisor Teeth.
6. The Middle Line of the Hard Palate.
7. Orifices of some of the Mucous Follicles.
8. The Tonsil.
9. The Pharynx.

FIG. 287.

A FRONT VIEW OF THE MUSCLES OF THE PALATE AND OF THE POSTERIOR PORTION OF THE PHARYNX, AS GIVEN BY A VERTICAL SECTION OF THE SPHENOIDAL SINUSES—OF THE SPACE BETWEEN THE LAST MOLAR TEETH, AND OF THE TONGUE, OS HYOIDES AND THYROID CARTILAGES.

1. Sphenoidal Sinuses.
2.2. Petrous portions of the Temporal Bones.
3. Back part of Antrum Highmorianum.
4. Middle and Inferior Spongy Bones.
5. Shows the upper portion of the Palatine Walls, after the removal of 3 and 4.
6. The Circumflexus Palati Muscle.
7. Constrictor Pharyngis Superior.
8. Part of its Origin.
9. Levator Palati.
10. Anterior face of the posterior extremity of the middle Suture of the Palate Bones; above is the Septum Narium.
11. Palatine portion of Levator Palati.
12. Section of the Buccinator Muscle.
13. Anterior Half Arch.
14. Last Molar Tooth of Upper Jaw.
15. Constrictor Isthmi Faucium.
16. Last Molar of Lower Jaw.
17. Portion of Constrictor Pharyngis Superior, where the Tonsil rests.
18. Front portion of the section of the Tongue.
19. Constrictor Pharyngis Superior.
20.23.24. Constrictor Pharyngis Medius.

21. Mylo-Hyoideus Muscle.
22. Attachment of Hyo-Glossus.
25. Stylo-Pharyngeus, and Thyreo-Hyoid Ligament.
26. Thyroid Cartilage.
27. Constrictor Pharyngis Inferior Muscle.

FIG. 288.

A POSTERIOR VIEW OF THE MUSCLES OF THE SOFT PALATE, AS SHOWN BY A SECTION OF THE CRANIUM THROUGH THE GLENOID CAVITIES.

1. Basilar portion of the Sphenoid Bone.
2. Condyles of Lower Jaw.
3. Hard Palate.
4. Levator Palati, on one side entire, on the other partially removed.
5. Eustachian Tubes.
6. External Pterygoid Muscle.
7. Circumflexus Palati.
8. Azygos Uvulae.
9. Mylar Attachment of Constrictor Pharyngis Superior.
10. Palato-Pharyngeus.

FIG. 289.

A VIEW OF THE MUSCLES OF THE SOFT PALATE, AS SEEN FROM BELOW AND IN FRONT.

1. The Roof of the Mouth or Hard Palate, sawed across at the second Molar Tooth.
2. Origin of the Levator Palati Muscle.
3. Its expansion near its insertion.
4. Origin of the Circumflexus or Tensor Palati.
5. The Pterygo-Maxillary Ligament, which converts the notch through which this Muscle plays into a Foramen.
6.6. Palatine Aponeurosis.
7. A section of the Constrictor Pharyngis Superior Muscle.
8. Extremity of Azygos Uvulae Muscle.
9. Section of the Eustachian Tube.

FIG. 290.

A LOBULE OF THE PAROTID GLAND OF AN INFANT, INJECTED WITH MERCURY AND MAGNIFIED FIFTY DIAMETERS.

FIG. 291.

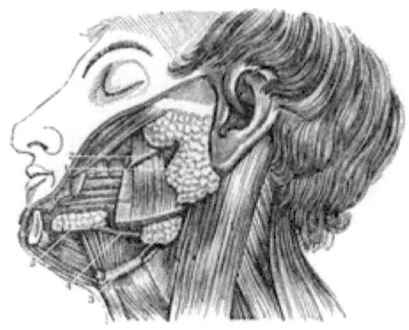

FIG. 292.

FIG. 293.

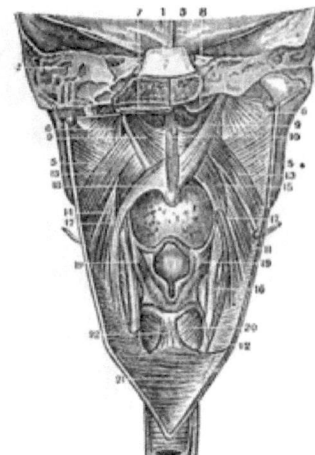

MOUTH AND PHARYNX.

FIG. 291.

A View of the Salivary Glands in situ.

1. The Parotid Gland in situ and extending from the Zygoma above to the Angle of the Jaw below.
2. The Duct of Steno.
3. The Sub-Maxillary Gland.
4. Its Duct.
5. Sub-Lingual Gland.

FIG. 292.

A Posterior View of the Internal Surface of the Pharynx. A vertical cut has been made, and the parts turned off on each side.

1. Basilar portion of Sphenoid Bone.
2. Section of Temporal Bones.
3. Orbitar Plate of Os Frontis.
4. Condyle of Lower Jaw.
5. Constrictor Pharyngis Superior.
6. The Walls of the Pharynx turned to each side by a section through their origin.
7. Cut portion of the Sphenoidal attachment of the Pharynx.
8. Points to the Eustachian Tube.
9. Circumflexus Palati. On the right side it is in situ; on the left it is partially turned downwards.
10. Azygos Uvulæ Muscle.
11. Fibres of the Middle Constrictor of the Pharynx.
12. Fibres of the Inferior Constrictor.
13. Portion of Superior Constrictor.
14. Palato-Pharyngeus.
15. Its upper portion.
16. Its insertion into Thyroid Cartilage.
17. The Palato-Pharyngeus of the opposite side.
18. Origin of Palato-Pharyngeus.
19. Insertion of Stylo-Pharyngeus.
20. Crico-Arytenoideus-Posticus.
21. Internal Muscular Coat of the Œsophagus.

FIG. 293.

A Posterior View of the Muscles of the external portion of the Pharynx, as shown by removing the back of the Head and Thorax.

1. Basilar portion of the Sphenoid Bone.
2. Inferior anterior portion of the Os Frontis, and Crista Galli of the Ethmoid.
3. Petrous portion of Temporal Bones.
4. Levator Palati Muscle.
5. Constrictor Pharyngis Superior.
6. Constrictor Pharyngis Medius.
7. Constrictor Pharyngis Inferior.
8. Upper part of posterior Face of the Lining Membrane of Pharynx, after removing the Muscle.
9. Longitudinal Muscular Fibres of the Œsophagus.
10. Internal Pterygoid Muscle.
11. Stylo-Pharyngeus.
12. Myloid attachment of the Constrictor Pharyngis Superior.
13. Stylo-Hyoideus.
14. Temporal Belly of Digastricus.
15. Platysma Myodes Muscle.
16. Sterno-Cleido-Mastoideus.
17. Omo-Hyoideus.
18. Sterno-Thyroid Muscle.
19. Sterno-Hyoid.
20. Section of Sterno-Thyroideus.
21. Section of the Trapezius Muscle.

FIG. 294.

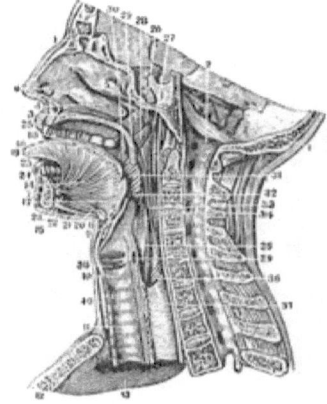

FIG. 295.

FIG. 296.

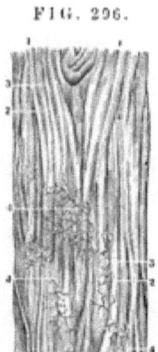

THE MOUTH AND ŒSOPHAGUS.

FIG. 294.

A VIEW OF THE MUSCLES OF THE TONGUE, PA-
LATE, LARYNX, AND PHARYNX—AS WELL AS
THE POSITION OF THE UPPER PORTION OF THE
ŒSOPHAGUS, AS SHOWN BY A VERTICAL SEC-
TION OF THE HEAD.

1.1. The Vertical Section of the Head.
2. Points to the Spinal Canal.
3. Section of the Hard Palate.
4. Inferior Spongy Bone.
5. Middle Spongy Bone.
6. Orifice of the Right Nostril.
7. Section of Inferior Maxilla.
8. Section of Os Hyoides.
9. Section of the Epiglottis.
10. Section of the Cricoid Cartilage.
11. The Trachea covered by its Lining Membrane.
12. Section of Sternum.
13. Inside of the upper portion of the Thorax
14. Genio-Hyo-Glossus Muscle.
15. Its origin.
16.17. The fan-like Expansion of the Fibres of
this Muscle.
18. Superficialis Linguæ Muscle.
19. Verticales Linguæ Muscle.
20. Genio-Hyoideus Muscle.
21. Mylo-Hyoideus Muscle.
22. Anterior Belly of Digastricus.
23. Section of Platysma Myodes.
24. Levator Menti.
25. Orbicularis Oris.
26. Orifice of Eustachian Tube.
27. Levator Palati.
28. Internal Pterygoid.
29. Section of Velum Pendulum Palati, and
Azygos Uvulæ Muscle.

30. Stylo-Pharyngeus.
31. Constrictor Pharyngis Superior.
32. Constrictor Pharyngis Medius.
33. Insertion Stylo-Pharyngeus.
34. Constrictor Pharyngis Inferior.
35.36.37. Muscular Coat of Œsophagus
38. Thyreo-Arytenoid Muscle and Ligaments;
and above is the Ventricle of Galen.
39. Section of Arytenoid Cartilage.
40. Border of Sterno-Hyoideus.

FIG. 295.

A VIEW OF A PORTION OF THE ŒSOPHAGUS OF
AN ADULT, SEEN ON ITS OUTER SIDE.

1.1. External or Longitudinal Muscular Fibres.
2.2. Internal or Circular Fibres, as shown after
the removal of the Longitudinal ones.
3.3. The cut edges of the Longitudinal Fibres,
from which a portion has been removed, so
as to show the Circular ones.

FIG. 296.

A LONGITUDINAL SECTION OF THE ŒSOPHAGUS,
NEAR THE PHARYNX, SEEN ON ITS INSIDE.

1.1. Superior part near the Pharynx.
2.2. Longitudinal folds of its Mucous Membrane.
3.3. Prominences formed by its Muciparous
Glands.
4.4. Capillary Blood-Vessels.
5. Shows the Muscular Coat after the Mucous
Coat has been turned off.

FIG. 297.　　　　　　FIG. 298.

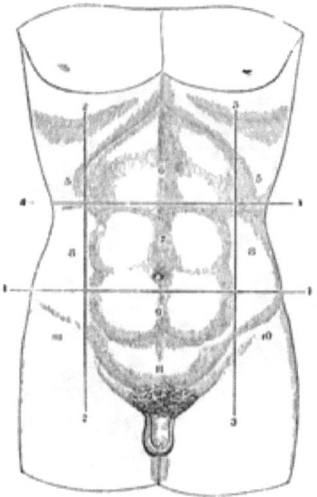 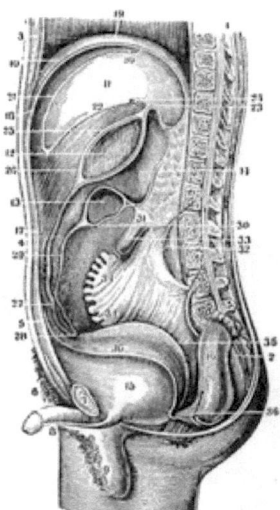

ABDOMINAL VISCERA.

FIG. 297.

A VIEW OF THE EXTERNAL PARIETES OF THE ABDOMEN, WITH THE POSITION OF THE LINES; DRAWN TO MARK OFF ITS REGIONS.

1.1. A line drawn from the highest point of one Ilium to the same point of the opposite one.
2.2. A line drawn from the Anterior Superior Spinous Process to the Cartilages of the Ribs.
3.3. A similar one for the opposite side.
4.4. A line drawn perpendicularly to these, and touching the most prominent part of the Costal Cartilages, thus forming nine regions.
5.5; The Right and Left Hypochondriac Regions.
6. The Epigastric Region.
7. The Umbilical Region.
8.8. The Right and Left Lumbar Regions.
9. The Hypogastric Region.
10.10. The Right and Left Iliac Regions.
11. The lower part of the Hypogastric, sometimes called Pubic.

FIG. 298.

A VIEW OF THE REFLEXIONS OF THE PERITONEUM, AS GIVEN BY A VERTICAL SECTION OF THE BODY OF A MAN.

1. A section of the Spinal Column and Canal.
2. A section of the Sacrum.
3. A section of the Sternum, &c.
4. The Umbilicus.
5. A section of the Linea Alba and Abdominal Muscles.
6. The Mons Veneris.
7. Section of the Pubes.
8. The Penis divided at the Corpora Cavernosa.
9. A section of the Scrotum.
10. The Superior Right Half of the Diaphragm.
11. A section of the Liver.
12. A section of the Stomach, showing its cavity.

13. A section of the Transverse Colon.
14. A section of the Pancreas.
15. A section of the Bladder, deprived of the Peritoneum.
16. The Rectum, cut off, tied and turned back on the promontory of the Sacrum.
17. The Peritoneum covering the anterior Parietes of the Abdomen.
18. The Peritoneum on the inferior under side of the Diaphragm.
19. The Peritoneum on the Convex side of the Diaphragm.
20. Reflection of Peritoneum from Diaphragm to Liver.
21. The Peritoneum on Front of Liver.
22. The same, on its under surface.
23. The Hepato-Gastric Omentum.
24. A large pin passed through the Foramen of Winslow into the Cavity behind the Omentum.
25. The anterior Face of the Hepato-Gastric Omentum, passing in front of the Stomach.
26. The same Membrane leaving the Stomach to make the anterior of the four layers of the Great Omentum.
27.28. The junction of the Peritoneum from the front and back part of the Stomach, as they turn to go up to the Colon.
29. The Gastro-Colic, or Greater Omentum.
30. The separation of its Layers, so as to cover the Colon.
31. The posterior Layer passing over the Jejunum.
32. The Peritoneum in front of the right Kidney.
33. The Jejunum cut off and tied.
34.34. The Mesentery cut off from the small Intestines.
35. The Peritoneum reflected from the posterior Parietes of the Bladder to the anterior of the Rectum.
36. The Cul-de-Sac between the Bladder and Rectum.

FIG. 299.   FIG. 300.

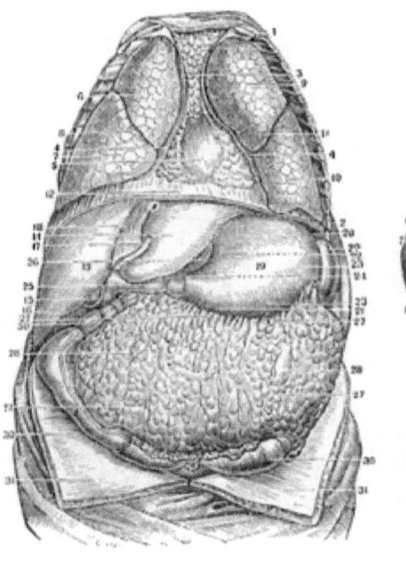
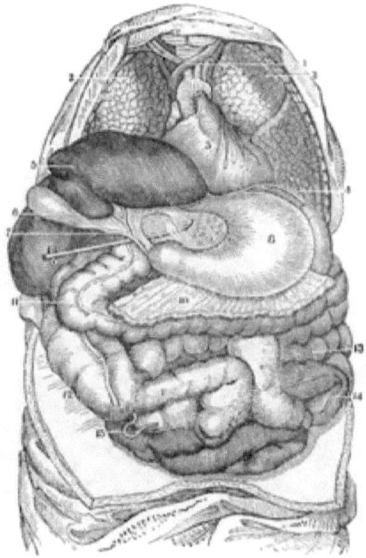

THE VISCERA.

FIG. 299.

A VIEW OF THE VISCERA OF THE CHEST AND
ABDOMEN, IN THEIR NATURAL POSITION, AS
GIVEN BY THE REMOVAL OF THE ANTERIOR
PARIETES OF EACH CAVITY.

1.2. The Ribs forming the side of the Chest.
3. Fatty tissue in the anterior Mediastinum.
4.4. The section of the Pleura of each side.
5. The Pericardium enclosing the Heart.
6. Superior Lobe of the right Lung.
7. Inferior Lobe of the right Lung.
8. The Fissure which separates them.
9. Upper Lobe of the left Lung.
10. Lower Lobe of the left Lung.
11. Fissure between them.
12. A transverse section of the Diaphragm
13. Superior Face of the right Lobe of the Liver.
14. Superior Face of the left Lobe of the Liver.
15. Lower end of the Gall Bladder.
16. Inferior and anterior Edge of the Liver.
17. Round Ligament of the Liver.
18. Suspensory Ligament of the Liver.
19. Anterior Face of the Stomach.
20. Its greater Extremity.
21. Its lesser Extremity.
22. Its lesser Curvature.
23. Its greater Curvature.
24. The Pylorus.
25. The Duodenum.
26. A part of the Gastro-Hepatic Omentum.
27.27. The Gastro-Colic Omentum.
28.28. Convolutions of the Small Intestines, seen
through this Omentum.

29. The Spleen.
30.30. The Large Intestines.
31.31. Parietes of the Abdomen turned down.

FIG. 300.

A VIEW OF THE SAME VISCERA, AFTER THE RE-
MOVAL OF THE FAT IN THE CHEST AND THE
OMENTUM MAJUS OF THE ABDOMEN. THE
LIVER ALSO HAS BEEN TURNED BACK TO SHOW
ITS UNDER SURFACE AND THE LESSER OMEN-
TUM.

1. The great Blood-Vessels of the Heart.
2. The Lungs of each side.
3. The Heart.
4. The Diaphragm.
5. Under surface of the Liver.
6. The Gall Bladder.
7. Union of the Cystic and Hepatic Ducts to
form the Ductus Choledochus.
8. Anterior Face of the Stomach.
9. The Gastro-Hepatic, or lesser Omentum. A
female Catheter has been passed through the
Foramen of Winslow, and is seen through
the Omentum.
10. Gastro-Colic, or greater Omentum, cut off, so
as to show the small Intestines.
11. The Transverse Colon, pushed slightly
downwards.
12. Its ascending portion, also pushed down.
13. Small Intestines.
14. The Sigmoid Flexure.
15. Appendicula Vermiformis.

FIG. 301.   FIG. 302.

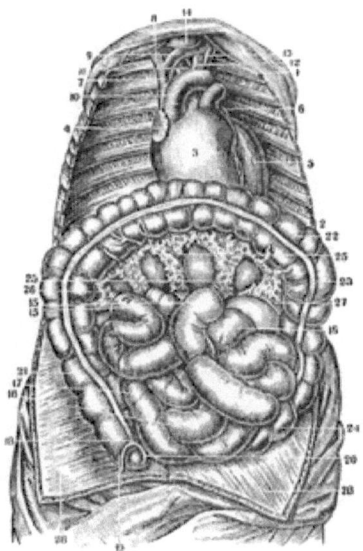

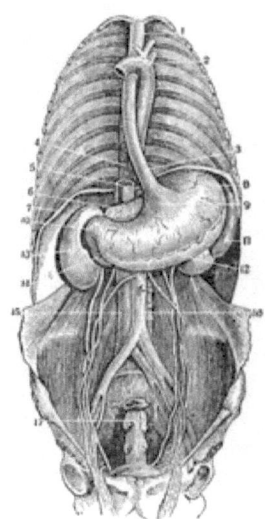

THE VISCERA.

FIG. 301.

A VIEW OF THE HEART AND INTESTINES IN SITU. THE LUNGS, TRACHEA, AND OMENTUM MAJUS, HAVING BEEN REMOVED, AND THE COLON TURNED UPWARDS.

1.2. The Ribs on one side of the Chest.
3. The right Ventricle of the Heart.
4. The right Auricle of the Heart.
5. The left Ventricle.
6. The left Auricle.
7. The Descending Vena Cava.
8.9. Right Subclavian and Vena Innominata.
10. Arch of the Aorta.
11. Arteria Innominata.
12. Left Primitive Carotid Artery.
13. Left Subclavian Artery.
14. Lower portion of the Thyroid Gland.
15.15. The Jejunum.
16.17. The Ileum.
18. One of the Longitudinal Bands of the Colon.
19. The Cœcum.
20. Appendicula Vermiformis.
21. Ascending Colon.
22. Left end of the transverse Colon.
23. Descending Colon.
24. Sigmoid Flexure.
25. Transverse Mesocolon.
26. Right Lumbar portion of Mesocolon.

27. Left Lumbar portion of Mesocolon.
28.28. Parietes of the Abdomen turned down.

FIG. 302.

A VIEW OF THE STOMACH AND ŒSOPHAGUS, IN THEIR NATURAL POSITION. THE THORACIC VISCERA—NEARLY ALL THE DIAPHRAGM AND THE INTESTINES HAVE BEEN REMOVED—THE PERITONEUM HAS BEEN DETACHED FROM THE KIDNEYS, AND THE DUODENUM IS LEFT.

1. Upper portion of the Œsophagus.
2. Arch of the Aorta.
3. Lower portion of the Œsophagus.
4. Vertebral Column.
5. Vena Cava Ascendens.
6. The Pancreas.
7. The cut edge of the Diaphragm.
8. Great Cul-de-Sac of the Stomach.
9. Cardiac orifice of the Stomach.
10. Pyloric orifice of the Stomach.
11. The Spleen.
12. The Peritoneal Coat of the Stomach partially turned off.
13. The right Kidney.
14. Lower curvature of the Duodenum.
15. Ascending Vena Cava.
16. Abdominal Aorta.
17. A section of the Rectum.

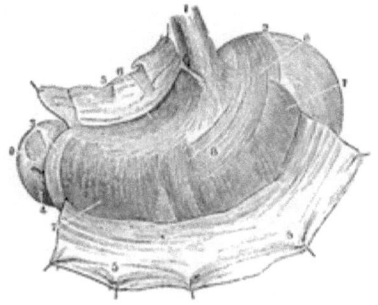

FIG. 303.

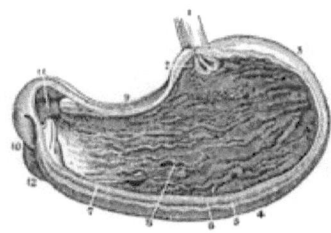

FIG. 304.

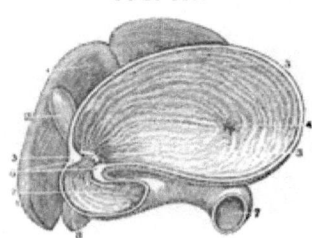

FIG. 305.

THE STOMACH.

FIG. 303.

A FRONT VIEW OF THE STOMACH, DISTENDED BY FLATUS, WITH THE PERITONEAL COAT TURNED OFF.

1. Anterior Face of the Œsophagus.
2. The Cul-de-Sac, or greater Extremity.
3. The lesser or Pyloric Extremity.
4. The Duodenum.
5.5. A portion of the Peritoneal Coat turned back.
6. A portion of the Longitudinal Fibres of the Muscular Coat.
7. The Circular Fibres of the Muscular Coat.
8. The Oblique Muscular Fibres, or Muscle of Gavard.
9. A portion of the Muscular Coat of the Duodenum, where its Peritoneal Coat has been removed.

———

FIG. 304.

A VIEW OF THE INTERIOR OF THE STOMACH, AS GIVEN BY THE REMOVAL OF ITS ANTERIOR PARIETES.

1. Œsophagus.
2. Cardiac Orifice of the Stomach.

3. Its greater Extremity, or Cul-de-Sac.
4. The greater Curvature.
5. Line of attachment of the Omentum Majus.
6. The Muscular Coat.
7. The anterior cut Edge of the Mucous Coat.
8. The Rugæ of the Mucous Coat.
9. The lesser Curvature.
10. The beginning of the Duodenum.
11. Pyloric Orifice, or Valve.
12. The first turn of the Duodenum downwards

———

FIG. 305.

A VIEW OF THE INTERIOR OF THE STOMACH AND DUODENUM IN SITU, THE INFERIOR PORTION OF EACH HAVING BEEN REMOVED.

1.1. The under side of the Liver.
2. The Gall Bladder.
3.3. The lesser Curvature and anterior Faces, as seen from below.
4. The Rugæ, about the Cardiac Orifice.
5. The Pyloric Orifice.
6. The Rugæ, and thickness of this Orifice.
7.7. The Duodenum.
8. Lower End of the Right Kidney.

FIG. 306.

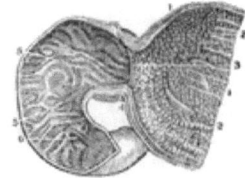

FIG. 307.

FIG. 310.

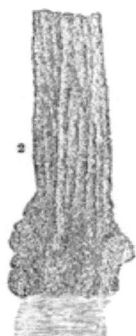

FIG. 309.

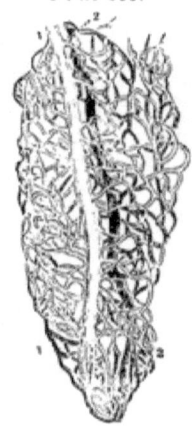

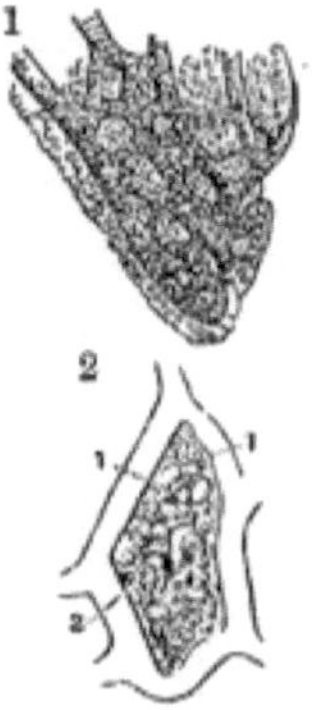

FIG. 308.

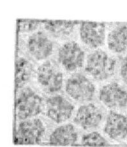

FIG. 311.

FIG. 312.

THE STOMACH.

FIG. 306.

A PORTION OF THE STOMACH AND DUODENUM LAID OPEN TO SHOW THEIR INTERIOR.

1.1. The Right or Pyloric Extremity of the Stomach.
2.2. The Folds and Mucous Follicles of the Mucous Coat of the Stomach.
3. Points into the Pylorus.
4. The thickness of the Pylorus.
5.5. The Rugæ of the Internal Coat of the Duodenum.
6. The Opening of the Ductus Communis Choledochus into the Duodenum.

FIG. 307.

A SECTION OF THE COATS OF THE STOMACH NEAR THE PYLORUS, SHOWING THE GASTRIC GLANDS.

1. Magnified three times.
2. Magnified twenty times.

FIG. 308.

A PORTION OF THE MUCOUS MEMBRANE OF THE STOMACH, SHOWING THE ENTRANCES TO THE SECRETING TUBES, IN THE CELLS UPON ITS SURFACE.

FIG. 309.

(1.) The apex of an Intestinal Villus from the Duodenum of the Human Female.
(2.) A Mesh of the Vascular Network.
1. The Net-work.
2. Delicate Vesicular Tissue, magnified nearly 45 Diam's.

FIG. 310.

THE VESSELS OF AN INTESTINAL VILLUS OF A HARE, FROM A DRY PREPARATION BY DOL-

LINGER, MAGNIFIED ABOUT 45 DIAMETERS.

1. Veins filled with white injection.
2. Arteries injected with red.

FIG. 311.

THE GLANDS IN THE COATS OF THE STOMACH, MAGNIFIED 45 DIAMETERS.

1. A Gastric Gland, from the middle of the Stomach.
2. Another, of more complex structure, and appearing to contain Mucus — from the neighbourhood of the Pylorus.

FIG. 312.

ONE OF THE INTESTINAL VILLI, WITH THE COMMENCEMENT OF A LACTEAL. MAGNIFIED.

FIG. 313.

FIG. 314.

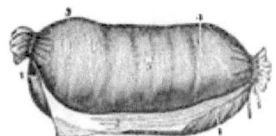

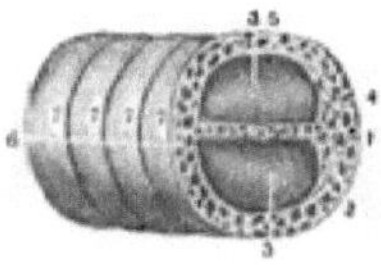

FIG. 315.

FIG. 317.

FIG. 316.

FIG. 318.

FIG. 319.

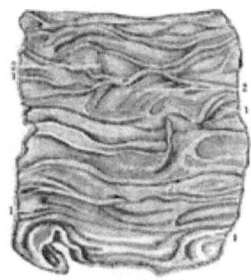

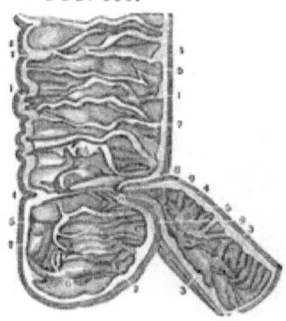

THE INTESTINAL CANAL.

FIG. 313.

A VIEW OF THE MUSCULAR COAT OF THE ILEUM.

1,1. The Peritoneal Coat.
2. A portion of this Coat turned off and showing a portion of the Longitudinal Fibres of the Muscular Coat adherent to it.
3,4,5. The Circular Muscular Fibres in different parts of the Intestine.

FIG. 314.

A PORTION OF THE JEJUNUM, INVERTED, DISTENDED AND DRIED.

1. The Sub-Mucous Cellular Tissue distended by the inflation.
2. The Cellular Tissue of the Mesentery close to the Intestine.
3,3. The Peritoneal Coat.
4. The Muscular Coat.
5. The Union of the Peritoneal and Muscular Coats.
6. The Mucous or Villous Coat.
7,7,7. Valvulæ Conniventes, seen thus in consequence of the inflation of the Sub-Mucous Cellular Tissue.

FIG. 315.

A PORTION OF THE MUCOUS COAT OF THE SMALL INTESTINES AS ALTERED IN FEVER. THE FOLLICLES OF LIEBERKÜHN BEING FILLED WITH A WHITE TENACIOUS MUCUS.

FIG. 316.

ONE OF THE CONGLOMERATE GLANDS OF BRUNNER, FROM THE COMMENCEMENT OF THE DUODENUM. MAGNIFIED AN HUNDRED TIMES.

FIG. 317.

A VIEW OF ONE OF THE GLANDULÆ MAJORES SIMPLICES OF THE LARGE INTESTINE, AS SEEN FROM ABOVE, AND ALSO IN A SECTION. MAGNIFIED.

FIG. 318.

A LONGITUDINAL SECTION OF THE UPPER PART OF THE JEJUNUM EXTENDED UNDER WATER.

1,1. Valvulæ Conniventes.
2,2. The Summits of two of the Valvulæ placed side by side.

The Villi cover the whole Membrane, but are best seen on its edges in this cut.

FIG. 319.

A LONGITUDINAL SECTION OF THE END OF THE SMALL INTESTINES, OR ILEUM, AND OF THE BEGINNING OF THE LARGE INTESTINES, OR COLON.

1,1. A portion of the Ascending Colon.
2,2. The Cœcum, or Caput Coli.
3,3. Lower portion of the Ileum.
4,4. The Muscular Coat, covered by the Peritoneum.
5,5. The Cellular and Mucous Coats.
6,6. Folds of the Mucous Coat at this end of the Colon.
7,7. Prolongations of the Cellular Coat into these Folds.
8,8. Ileo-Colic Valve.
9,9. The Union of the Coats of the Ileum and Colon.

FIG. 320.

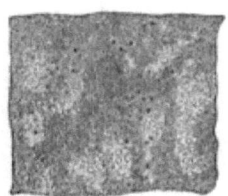

FIG. 321.

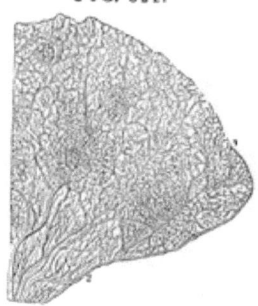

FIG. 322.

FIG. 323.

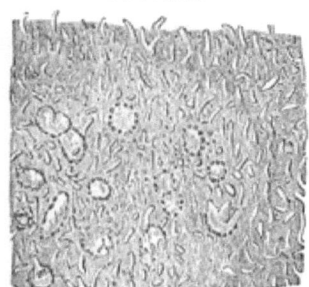

FIG. 324.

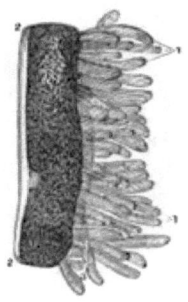

THE INTESTINAL CANAL.

FIG. 320.

A View of a Longitudinal Section of the Ileum, extended under Water. The Villi and Mucous Follicles, known as the Glands of Brunner, are well seen. The Follicles are rendered more apparent by their being indurated, and their Orifices seen at the Surface of the Intestine. There are no Valvulæ Conniventes in this piece.

FIG. 321.

A View of a portion of the Ileum with the Veins injected.

1. The Intestine.
2 The Mesentery.

FIG. 322.

A View of a portion of two of the Valvulæ Conniventes with their Villi, taken from a Woman who was drowned shortly after eating. The Villi are filled with Chyle and appear as small cylindrical prolongations, curved towards their free Extremity.

FIG. 323.

A portion of one of the Patches of Peyer's Glands from the end of the Ileum, highly magnified. The Villi are also seen.

FIG. 324.

A View of a Longitudinal Section of the Jejunum, showing the Villi as seen under the Microscope.

1.1. The Terminal Orifices of the Villi.
2.2. The Internal Coats of the Intestine.
3. The Peritoneal Coat.

FIG. 325. FIG. 326.

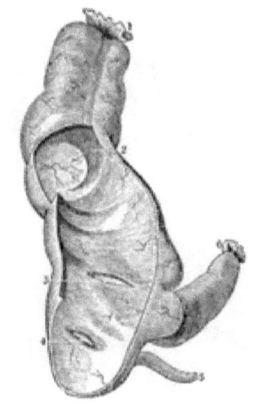

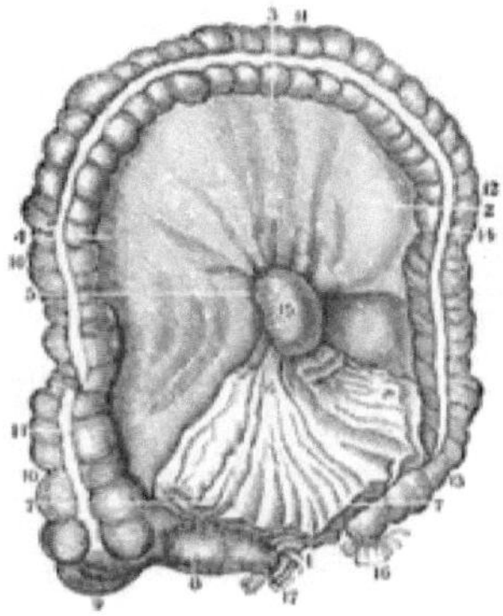

FIG. 328.

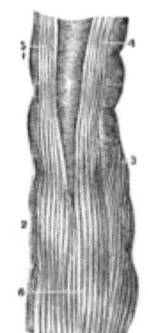

FIG. 327.

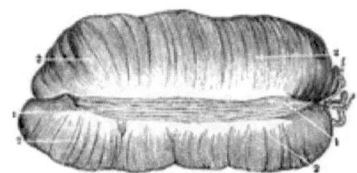

THE INTESTINAL CANAL.

FIG. 325.

A VIEW OF THE CŒCUM—AFTER
IT HAS BEEN DISTENDED—DRIED
AND LAID OPEN IN FRONT.

1. The Ascending Colon.
2. One of the Cells of the Colon.
3. The Ileo-Colic Valve.
4. The Opening into the Appendicula Vermiformis.
5. Appendicula Vermiformis.
6. A Section of the Lower End of the Ileum.

FIG. 326.

A VIEW OF THE MESOCOLON IN
ITS CONNEXION WITH THE MESENTERY, AS WELL AS THE CONNEXIONS OF THE COLON WITH
THE MESOCOLON—THE OPENING OF THE ILEUM INTO THE
CŒCUM, AND THE PASSAGE OF
THE DUODENUM FROM THE SUPERIOR TO THE INFERIOR PART
OF THE ABDOMEN.

1. The Peritoneum of the Lumbar Region, and the Origin of
the Left Lumbar Mesocolon.

2. The Left Lumbar Portion of the Mesocolon.
3. The Transverse Mesocolon.
4. The Right Lumbar Mesocolon.
5. The Union of the Mesocolon with the Mesentery.
6. The Mesentery.
7.7. The Folds of the Mesentery cut off from the small Intestines.
8. Lower End of the Ileum.
9. The Cœcum.
10.10. The Ascending Colon.
11. The Transverse Colon.
12. The Descending Colon.
13. The Sigmoid Flexure.
14. The Anterior Muscular Band of the Colon.
15. The Duodenum, passing from the Superior to the Inferior Portion of the Abdomen.
16. The Colon ending in the Rectum.
17. Section of the Ileum.

FIG. 327.

A VIEW OF THE MUSCULAR COAT
OF THE COLON, AS SEEN AFTER
THE REMOVAL OF THE PERITONEUM.

1.1. One of its three Bands of
Longitudinal Muscular Fibres.
2.2. The Circular Fibres of the Muscular Coat.

FIG. 328.

A VIEW OF THE LONGITUDINAL
MUSCULAR FIBRES OF A SECTION OF THE RECTUM.

1. Termination of the Sigmoid
Flexure in the Rectum.
2. Upper Portion of the Rectum.
3.) The three Bands of Longitu-
4.) dinal Fibres of the Colon
5.) continued upon the Rectum.
6. The Longitudinal Muscular
Fibres of the Rectum formed
by the expansion of those of
the Colon.

FIG. 329.

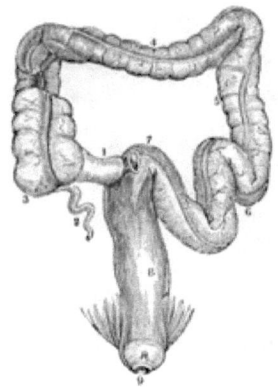

FIG. 330.

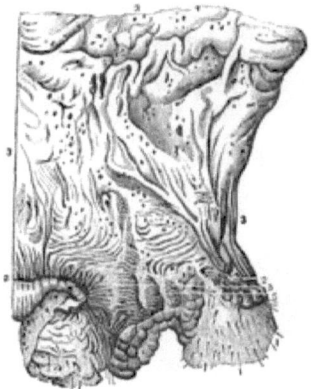

FIG. 331.

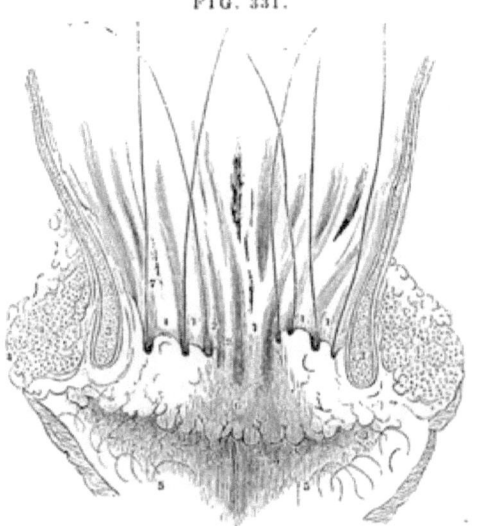

THE INTESTINAL CANAL.

FIG. 329.	FIG. 330.	FIG. 331.
A VIEW OF THE POSITION AND CURVATURES OF THE LARGE INTESTINES.	A VIEW OF A PORTION OF THE RECTUM, CUT OFF LONGITUDINALLY AND EXTENDED UNDER WATER.	A VERTICAL SECTION OF THE PARIETES OF THE ANUS, WITH THE RECTUM, SO AS TO SHOW THE RELATION OF THE RECTAL POUCHES TO THE SURROUNDING PARTS, THEIR ORIFICES BEING MARKED BY BRISTLES.

FIG. 329.

A VIEW OF THE POSITION AND CURVATURES OF THE LARGE INTESTINES.

1. The End of the Ileum.
2. Appendicula Vermiformis.
3. The Cæcum, or Caput Coli.
4. The Transverse Colon.
5. The Descending Colon.
6. The Sigmoid Flexure.
7. Commencement of Rectum.
8.8. The Rectum.
9. The Anus. — The Levator-Ani Muscle is seen on each side.

FIG. 330.

A VIEW OF A PORTION OF THE RECTUM, CUT OFF LONGITUDINALLY AND EXTENDED UNDER WATER.

1.1. A Portion of the Perineum.
2.2. The Anus laid open.
3.3. The Folds and Doublings of the Mucous Coat.
4.4. Orifices of the Mucous Follicles.
5.5. The Mucous Lacunæ, or Pouches near the Anus.

FIG. 331.

A VERTICAL SECTION OF THE PARIETES OF THE ANUS, WITH THE RECTUM, SO AS TO SHOW THE RELATION OF THE RECTAL POUCHES TO THE SURROUNDING PARTS, THEIR ORIFICES BEING MARKED BY BRISTLES.

1.1. Columns of the Rectum.
2.2. Rudiments of Columns.
3. Section of Internal Sphincter.
4. Section of External Sphincter.
5.5. Radiated Folds of the Skin on the Surface of the Nates.
6. Imperfect Pouches.
7. Bristles in the Rectal Pouches.

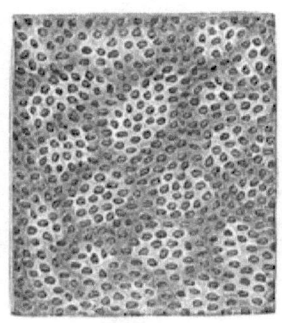

FIG. 332.

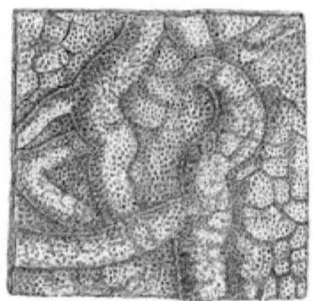

FIG. 333.

FIG. 334.

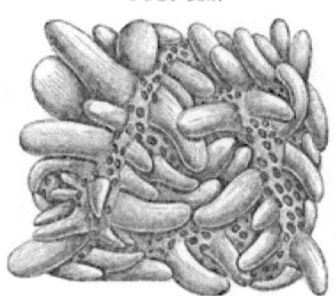

FIG. 335.

MINUTE ANATOMY OF MUCOUS COAT.

FIG. 332.

A VIEW OF THE FOLLICLES OF THE COLON, MAGNIFIED ABOUT 115 TIMES. (*Wistar Museum*.)

In the Mucous Coat of the Alimentary Canal is to be found a Cribriform Texture of Veins, almost without an Artery. The fine Venous Trunks of a deeper Layer have their originating extremities directed vertically towards the cavity of the Gut, and the meshes of the Venous Intertexture are exceedingly minute, producing in the Colon an appearance resembling a plate of metal pierced with round holes closely bordering on each other. These holes are the Follicles of Lieberkuhn, are gaping Orifices, the Edges of which are rounded off, and their depth is that of the thickness of the Venous Anatomosis. The aggregate number of these Follicles in the Colon, is estimated at Nine Million Six Hundred and Twenty Thousand. (*Horner's Anat. Vol. 2, p. 48*.)

FIG. 333.

A VIEW OF THE FOLDS AND FOLLICLES OF THE STOMACH, HIGHLY MAGNIFIED. (*W. Museum*.)

In the Stomach the Follicles vary much in size, and many of the smaller ones open into the larger.

On an average, about Two Hundred and Twenty-Five are found upon every square of an eighth of an inch, which, by calculation from this preparation, would give One Million Two Hundred and Ninety-Six Thousand Follicles to the entire Stomach. (*Horner's Anat. Vol. 2d, page 48, &c.*)

FIG. 334.

A VIEW OF THE FOLLICLES AND VILLI OF THE JEJUNUM, HIGHLY MAGNIFIED. (*W. Museum*.)

The Villi, being erected by injection, here run into each other and press one upon another like the convolutions of the Cerebrum. Some of them are merely semi-oval plates, the Transverse Diameter of which exceeds the length or elevation. The Follicles are seen between them and at their Bases.

FIG. 335.

A VIEW OF THE VILLI AND FOLLICLES OF THE ILEUM, HIGHLY MAGNIFIED. (*W. Museum*.)

These Villi are curved with their Edges bent in, or concave; but there is, in the whole Canal, every variety of shape, from oblong, curved and serpentine Ridges, to the laterally flattened Cone standing on its Base.

FIG. 336.

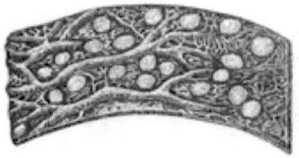

FIG. 337.

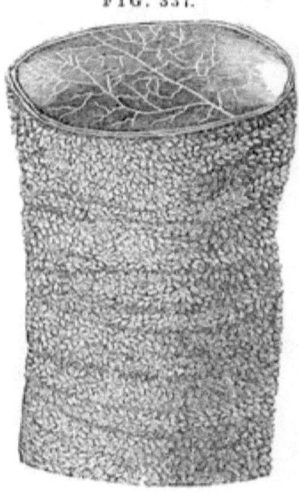

FIG. 338.

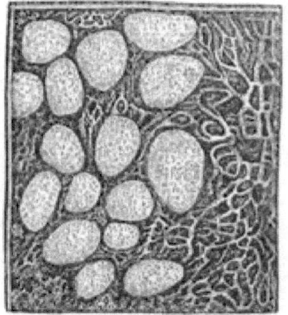

MINUTE ANATOMY OF THE MUCOUS COAT.

FIG. 336.

A MAGNIFIED VIEW OF THE FAVOUS DEPRESSIONS OF THE MUCOUS COAT OF THE STOMACH, AND THE MUCIPAROUS GLANDS. (*W. Museum.*)

———

FIG. 337.

A SECTION OF THE ILEUM, INVERTED SO AS TO SHOW THE APPEARANCE AND ARRANGEMENT OF THE VILLI ON AN EXTENDED SURFACE, AS WELL AS THE FOLLICLES OF LIEBERKÜHN; THE WHOLE SEEN UNDER THE MICROSCOPE. (*W. Museum.*)

A close examination of this Cut, will show a great number of black points in the spaces be-tween the projections or Villi: these are the Follicles of Lieberkuhn.

———

FIG. 338.

A SECTION OF THE SMALL INTESTINE CONTAINING SOME OF THE GLANDS OF PEYER, AS SHOWN UNDER THE MICROSCOPE. (*Wistar Museum.*)

These Glands appear to be small Lenticular Excavations, containing, according to Boehm, a white, milky and rather thick Fluid, with numerous round Corpuscules of various sizes, but mostly smaller than Blood Globules. The Meshes seen in the Cut are the ordinary tripe-like Folds of the Mucous Coat, and not the Venous Texture spoken of under the Follicles.

FIG. 339.

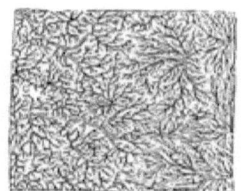

FIG. 340.

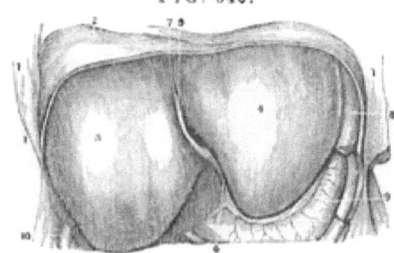

FIG. 341.

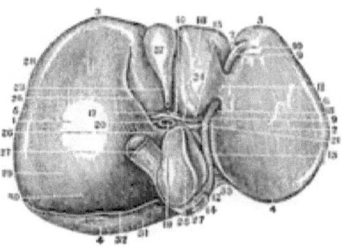

FIG. 342.

FIG. 343.

THE LIVER

FIG. 339.

A View of a portion of the Peritoneum covering the Liver, with its Capillary Vessels Injected.

FIG. 340.

A View of the Liver in Situ, together with the parts adjoining, in a new-born Infant.

1.1. The Integuments of the Abdomen turned back.
2.2. The Thoracic Surface of a Section of the Diaphragm.
3. Anterior Face of the Right Lobe of the Liver.
4. The Left Lobe.
5. The Suspensory Ligament.
6. The Round Ligament.
7. Point of Origin of the Coronary Ligament.
8. The Spleen.
9. Section of the Stomach.
10. Upper portion of the Colon.

FIG. 341.

The Inferior or Concave Surface of the Liver, showing its Subdivisions into Lobes.

1. Centre of the Right Lobe.
2. Centre of the Left Lobe.

3. Its Anterior, Inferior or Thin Margin.
4. Its Posterior, Thick or Diaphragmatic Portion.
5. The Right Extremity.
6. The Left Extremity.
7. The Notch on the Anterior Margin.
8. The Umbilical or Longitudinal Fissure.
9. The Round Ligament or remains of the Umbilical Vein.
10. The Portion of the Suspensory Ligament in connexion with the Round Ligament.
11. Pons Hepatis, or Band of Liver across the Umbilical Fissure.
12. Posterior End of Longitudinal Fissure.
13. } Attachment of the Obliterated Ductus Venosus to
14. } the Ascending Vena Cava.
15. Transverse Fissure.
16. Section of the Hepatic Duct.
17. Hepatic Artery.
18. Its Branches.
19. Vena Portarum.
20. Its Sinus, or Division into Right and Left Branches.
21. Fibrous remains of the Ductus Venosus.
22. Gall Bladder.
23. Its Neck.
24. Lobulus Quartus.

25. Lobulus Spigelii.
26. Lobulus Caudatus.
27. Inferior Vena Cava.
28. Curvature of Liver to fit the Ascending Colon.
29. Depression to fit the Right Kidney.
30. Upper portion of its Right Concave Surface over the Renal Capsule.
31. Portion of Liver uncovered by the Peritoneum.
32. Inferior Edge of the Coronary Ligament in the Liver.
33. Depression made by the Vertebral Column.

FIG. 342.

A View of the Connexion of the Lobules of the Liver with the Hepatic Vein.

1. Trunk of the Vein.
2.2. Lobules depending from its Branches like leaves on a tree, the centre of each being occupied by a venous twig—the Intra-Lobular Vein.

FIG. 343.

1. Nucleated Cells composing the Parenchyma of the Gland.
2. Lobules of Human Liver with Ramifications of the Hepatic Vein.

Page 113

FIG. 344.
FIG. 347.

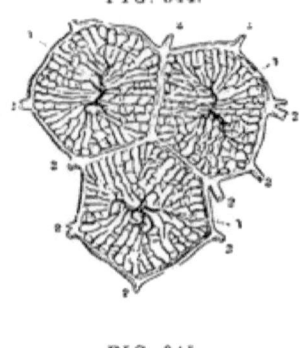

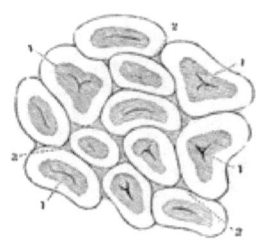

FIG. 348.

FIG. 345.

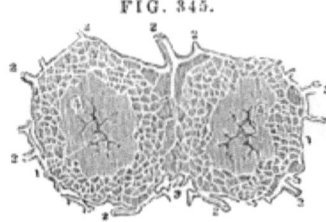

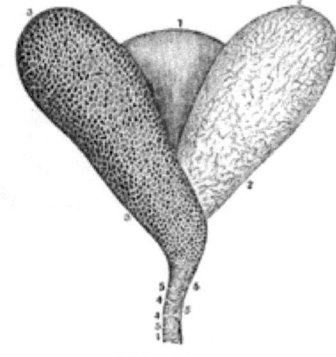

FIG. 346.

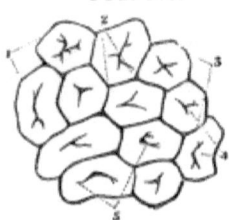

FIG. 349.

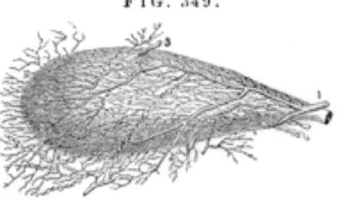

THE LIVER AND GALL BLADDER.

FIG. 344.

A HORIZONTAL SECTION OF THREE SUPERFICIAL LOBULES OF THE LIVER, SHOWING THE TWO PRINCIPAL SYSTEMS OF BLOOD-VESSELS.

1.1. Intra-Lobular Veins proceeding from the Hepatic Veins.
2.2. Intra-Lobular Plexus formed by branches of the Portal Veins.

FIG. 345.

A HORIZONTAL SECTION OF TWO SUPERFICIAL LOBULES, SHOWING THE INTRA-LOBULAR PLEXUS OF BILIARY DUCTS.

1.1. Intra-Lobular Veins.
2.2. Trunks of Biliary Ducts, proceeding from the Plexus which traverses the Lobules.
3. Inter-Lobular Tissue.
4. Parenchyma of the Lobules.

FIG. 346.

ANGULAR LOBULES IN A STATE OF ANÆMIA AS THEY APPEAR ON THE EXTERNAL SURFACE OF THE LIVER.

1. The Surface.
2. Inter-Lobular Spaces.
3. Inter-Lobular Fissures.
4. Intra-Lobular Veins occupying the Centres of the Lobules.
5. Smaller Veins terminating in the central Veins.

FIG. 347.

A VIEW OF THE ROUNDED LOBULES IN THE FIRST STAGE OF HEPATIC VENOUS CONGESTION AS THEY APPEAR ON THE SURFACE OF THE LIVER.

1.1. The Lobules.
2.2. Inter-Lobular Spaces and Fissures.

FIG. 348.

SHOWS THE THREE COATS OF THE GALL-BLADDER SEPARATED FROM EACH OTHER.

1. The External or Peritoneal Coat.
2. The Cellular Coat with its vessels injected.
3. The Mucous Coat covered with Wrinkles.
4.4. Valves formed by this Coat in the Neck of the Gall-Bladder.
5.5. Orifices of the Mucous Follicles at this point.

FIG. 349.

A VIEW OF THE GALL-BLADDER DISTENDED WITH AIR, AND WITH ITS VESSELS INJECTED.

1. Cystic Artery.
2. The Branches of it which supply the Peritoneal Coat of the Liver.
3. The Branch of the Hepatic Artery which goes to the Gall-Bladder.
4. The Lymphatics of the Gall Bladder.

FIG. 351.

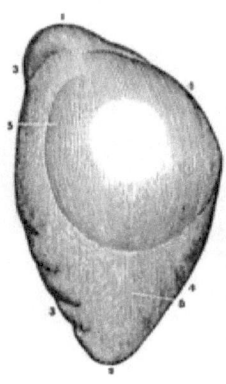

FIG. 350.

FIG. 352.

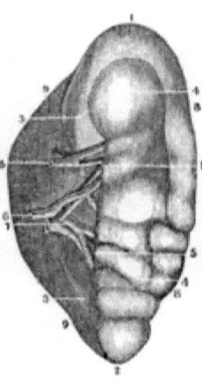

FIG. 353.

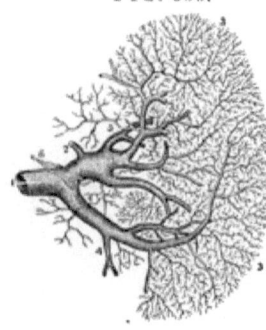

FIG. 354.

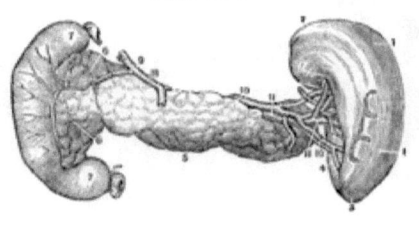

THE SPLEEN AND PANCREAS.

FIG. 350.

A VIEW OF THE ROOTS, TRUNK AND DIVISIONS OF THE VENA PORTARUM.

1.1. The Veins coming from the Intestines.
2. Trunk of the Vena Portarum.
3.3. Branches as distributed in the Liver.

FIG. 351

REPRESENTS THE CONVEX OR EXTERNAL FACE OF THE SPLEEN OR THE SIDE WHICH CORRESPONDS TO THE DIAPHRAGM.

1. Its Superior Extremity.
2. Its Inferior Extremity.
3.3. Anterior Edge.
4.4. Posterior Edge.
5.5. Its Convex Surface.

FIG. 352

SHOWS THE INTERNAL FACE OF THE SPLEEN WHERE IT TOUCHES THE STOMACH.

1. Superior Extremity.
2. Inferior Extremity.
3. Posterior Part of the Concave Face.
4. Anterior Part of the same.
5. Fissure of the Spleen.
6. Splenic Artery.
7. Splenic Vein.
8.8. Anterior Edge of the Spleen.
9.9. Its Posterior Edge.

FIG. 353

REPRESENTS THE SPLENIC VEIN WITH ITS BRANCHES AND RAMIFICATIONS.

1. Trunk of the Vein.
2. Gastric Branch of this Vein coming from the Stomach.

3. Branches coming from the Substance of the Spleen.
4. A small Mesenteric Vein cut off.
5. Branches coming from the External Coat of the Spleen.
6. Branches of the Lymphatic Vessels of the Spleen.

FIG. 354.

AN ANTERIOR VIEW OF THE PANCREAS, SPLEEN AND DUODENUM WITH THEIR BLOOD-VESSELS INJECTED.

1. The Spleen.
2. Its Diaphragmatic Extremity.
3. Its Inferior Portion.
4. The Fissure for its Vessels.
5. The Pancreas.
6. Its Head, or the Lesser Pancreas.
7. Duodenum.
8. Coronary Arteries of the Stomach.
9. The Hepatic Artery.
10. The Splenic Artery.
11. The Splenic Vein.

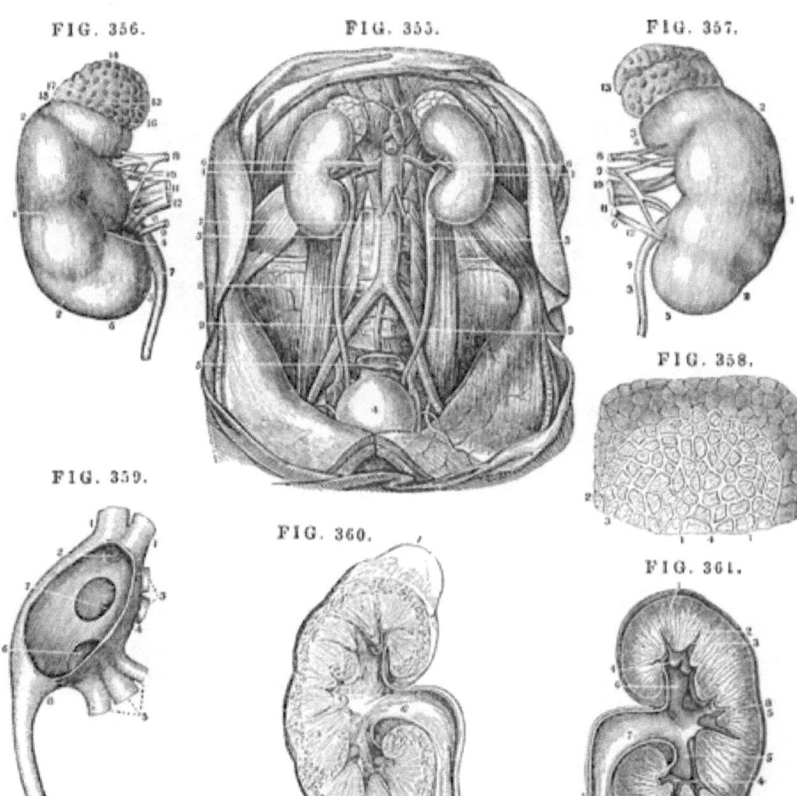

FIG. 356. FIG. 355. FIG. 357.

FIG. 358.

FIG. 359. FIG. 360. FIG. 361.

THE KIDNEYS AND RENAL CAPSULES.

FIG. 355.

A VIEW OF THE URINARY OR-
GANS IN SITU.

1.1. The Kidneys.
2.2. The Capsulæ Renales.
3.3. The Ureters in their course to
the Bladder, and their relations
to the Blood-Vessels.
4. Bladder distended with Urine.
5. The Rectum.
6. The Emulgent Arteries.
7. The Abdominal Aorta.
8. Its Division into the Iliacs.
9. The Primitive Iliacs at the point
where the Ureters cross them.

FIG. 356.

A VIEW OF THE RIGHT KIDNEY
WITH ITS RENAL CAPSULE.

1. Anterior Face of the Kidney.
2. External or Convex Edge.
3. Its Internal Edge.
4. Hilum Renale.
5. Inferior Extremity of the Kidney.
6. Pelvis of the Ureter.
7. Ureter.
8. } Superior and Inferior Branches
9. } of the Emulgent Artery.
10. }
11. } The three Branches of the
12. } Emulgent Vein.
13. Anterior Face of the Renal Capsule.
14. Its Superior Edge.
15. Its External Edge.

16. Its Internal Extremity.
17. The Fissure on the Anterior
Face of the Capsule.

FIG. 357.

A FRONT VIEW OF THE LEFT
KIDNEY. — THE NUMBERS
POINT TO THE SAME PARTS OF
THE GLAND AS IN THE PRE-
CEDING CUT.

FIG. 358.

A PORTION OF THE SURFACE OF
THE KIDNEY SEEN THROUGH
THE MICROSCOPE.

1. Superficial Veins forming a net-
work on the Surface.
2. The Capillary Vessels that these
Veins receive from the Cortical
Substance of the Kidney.
3. Areolæ formed on the Surface by
the Superficial Veins.
4. Smaller Veins forming Stars over
this Surface.

FIG. 359.

A VIEW OF THE PELVIS OF THE
URETER WITH THE CALICES.

1.1. Two small Calices at the Upper Portion.
2. A larger Calix formed by the
union of the two preceding.
3.4. Two other Calices.

5. Three smaller Inferior Calices.
6. A larger Calix formed by the
union of these and opening into
the Pelvis.
7. Opening of 3 and 4.
8. Origin of the Ureter.
9. The Ureter.

FIG. 360.

A SECTION OF THE RIGHT KID-
NEY SURMOUNTED BY THE RE-
NAL CAPSULE.

1. Supra-Renal Capsule.
2. Cortical Portion.
3. Medullary or Tubular.
4. Two of the Calices receiving the
Apex, of their corresponding
Cones.
5. The Infundibula.
6. The Pelvis.
7. The Ureter.

FIG. 361.

A VERTICAL SECTION OF THE
LEFT KIDNEY.

1. Cortical or Vascular Structure.
2. Pyramids of Malpighi or Tubular
Structure.
3. Papillæ or Apices of Pyramids.
4. Terminations of other Papillæ in
Infundibula.
5. Calices.
6. The three Infundibula.
7. Pelvis of the Ureter.
8. The Ureter.

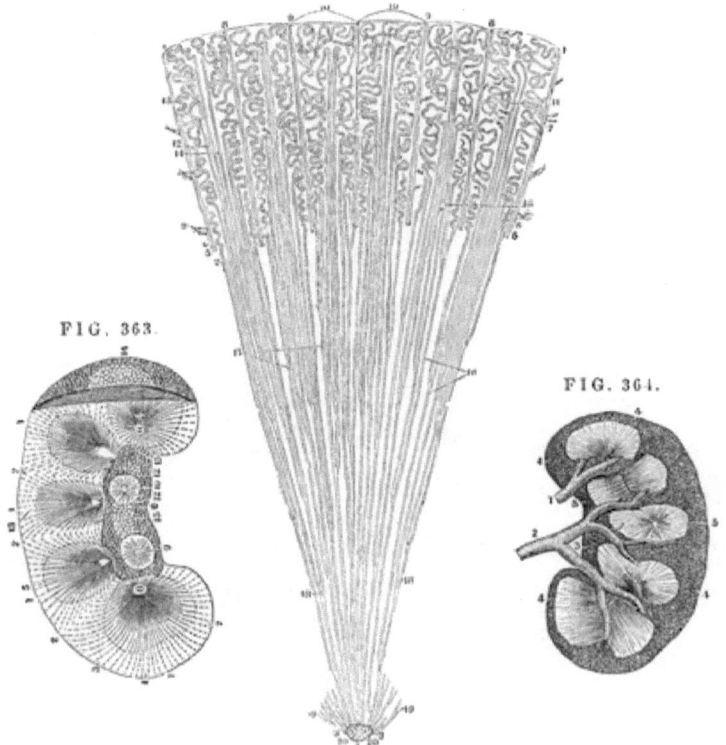

FIG. 362.

FIG. 363.

FIG. 364.

MINUTE STRUCTURE OF THE KIDNEY.

FIG. 362.

A SECTION OF ONE OF THE PYRA-
MIDS OF MALPIGHI, AND OF
ITS CORRESPONDING CORTICAL
SUBSTANCE, AS SEEN UNDER
THE MICROSCOPE.

1. Portion of the Surface of the Kidney.
2. From this Figure up to 1, is the Cortical Substance of the Kidney.
3. From 2 to this number is the Tubular portion.
4. The Foveola.
5.6. Arteries and Veins ramifying through the Kidney.
7. Arteries to the Acini of the Kidney.
8. Capillary Extremities of Veins anastomosing with corresponding Arterioles.
9. Tortuous Extremities of the Arteries directed into the Interior of the Gland.
10. Bases of the Cones of the Cortical and Pyramidal Substance of the Kidney. From 10 to 4 is a collection of these Cones.
11. The Envelope of the Cortical Layer.

12. Prolongations of the Tubular portion.
13. Tortuous Tubes, or those of Ferrein.
14. Straight Tubes, or those of Bellini.
15. Vessels which wind between them.
16. Course of the Uriniferous Tubes in the Tubular portion.
17. The matter between these Tubes.
18. Bifurcation of the Straight Tubes.
19. Sections of these Tubes.
20. Their Orifices.

FIG. 363.

A VIEW OF HALF A KIDNEY DI-
VIDED VERTICALLY FROM ITS
CONVEX TO ITS CONCAVE
EDGE. ONE OF ITS EXTRE-
MITIES IS PERFECT.

1.1. The Lobes which form the Kidney.
2.2. The Lines of Separation of these Lobes.
3. The Cortical Substance.
4.5. The Pyramids of Malpighi.
6. The Hilum Renale split up and cleared of its Vessels.

7.7. Points to the Tubes of Bellini.
8. One of the Papillæ.
9.10. Two other Papillæ, uncut but deprived of the Calices that surrounded them.
11. One of the Foveolæ in the Papilla.
12.12. The Vascular Circle surrounding the Papillæ.
13. Circumference of the Tubular portion.
14. External Surface of the Kidney.
15. The portion of its External Surface on a Line with its Fissure.

FIG. 364

REPRESENTS THE HALF OF A
KIDNEY DIVIDED VERTICALLY,
AND WITH ITS ARTERIES IN-
JECTED. THE MATTER HAS
ALSO PASSED INTO THE EX-
CRETORY DUCTS.

1.2. Branches of the Emulgent Artery.
3.3. Hilum Renale.
4.4. Cortical Substance, as essentially formed by the Capillary Terminations of the Vessels of the Kidney.
5. Medullary or Tubular portion.

FIG. 365.

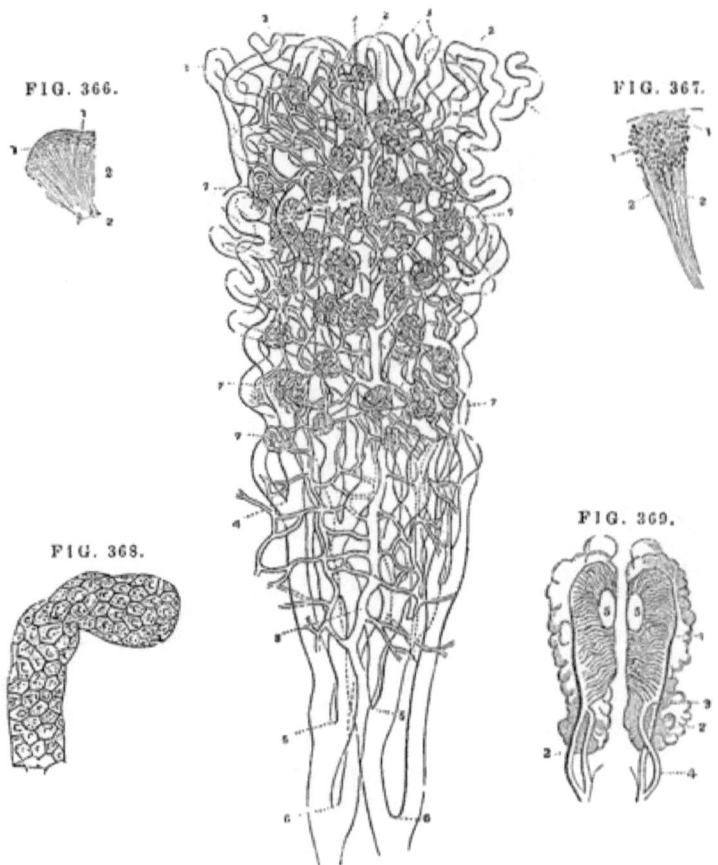

FIG. 366.

FIG. 367.

FIG. 368.

FIG. 369.

MINUTE STRUCTURE OF THE KIDNEY.

FIG. 365.

A SMALL PORTION OF THE KID-
NEY MAGNIFIED ABOUT SIXTY
TIMES.

1. Cœcal Extremity of a Tu-
bulus Uriniferus.
2.2. Recurrent Loops of Tubuli.
3.3. Bifurcations of Tubuli.
4.
5. } Tubuli converging towards
6. } the Papilla.
7.7. { Corpora Malpighiana seen
7.7. { to consist of Plexuses of
Blood-Vessels, connected
with a Capillary net-work.
8. Arterial Trunk.

FIG. 366.

PORTION OF THE KIDNEY OF A
NEW-BORN INFANT. NATURAL
SIZE.

1.1. Corpora Malpighiana as dis-
persed Points in the Cortical Substance.
2.2. Papilla.

FIG. 367.

A SMALLER PART, MAGNIFIED.

1.1. Corpora Malpighiana.
2. Tubuli Uriniferi.

FIG. 368.

EXTREMITY OF ONE OF THE TU-
BULI URINIFERI FROM THE KID-
NEY OF AN ADULT, SHOWING
ITS TESSELATED EPITHELIUM.
MAGNIFIED 250 DIAMETERS.

FIG. 369.

CORPORA WOLFFIANA AS SHOWN
IN THE EMBRYO OF BIRDS,
WITH THE KIDNEY AND TESTES.

1. Kidney.
2.2. Ureters.
3. Corpus Wolffianum.
4. Its Excretory Duct.
5.5. Testicles.—On the top of the
Figure are seen the Supra-
Renal Capsules.

FIG. 370.

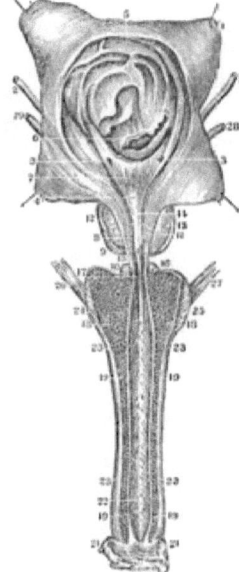

FIG. 371.

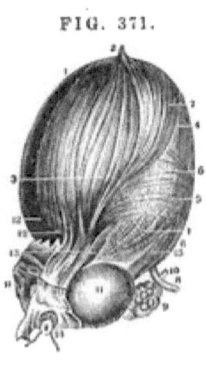

FIG. 372.

THE BLADDER AND URETHRA.

FIG. 370.

THE BLADDER AND URETHRA OF
A MAN, LAID OPEN IN ITS WHOLE
LENGTH.

1.1. The Bladder, cut open by a
crucial Incision and the four
Flaps separated.
2. The Ureters.
3. Their Vesical Orifices.
4. Uvula Vesicæ. The Triangle formed by the Points at
3.4 is the Vesicle Triangle.
5. Superior Fundus of the Bladder.
6. Bas Fond of the Bladder.
7. The smooth Centre of the
Vesical Triangle.
8. Verumontanum or Caput Gal-
linaginis.
9. Orifice of the Ductus Ejaculatorius.
10. Depression near the Verumontanum.
11. Ducts from the Prostate
Gland.
12.13. Lateral Lobes of the Prostate Gland.
14. Prostatic Portion of the Urethra; just above is the Neck
of the Bladder.
15. Its Membranous Portion.
16. One of Cowper's Glands.
17. The Orifices of their Excretory Ducts.
18. Section of the Bulb of the
Urethra with its Erectile Tissue.
19. Cut Edges of the Corpora
Cavernosa.
20. Cut Edges of the Glans Penis.
21. Prepuce dissected off.
22. Internal Surface of the Urethra laid open.
23. Outer Surface of Corpora
Cavernosa.
24.25. Accelerator Urinæ Muscle.
26.27. Erector Penis Muscle.

FIG. 371.

A THREE-QUARTER VIEW OF
THE URINARY BLADDER, DIS-
TENDED WITH AIR AND SHOW-
ING ITS MUSCULAR FIBRES.

1.1. The Bladder.
2. Urachus.
3. Two Planes of Longitudinal
Muscular Fibres on the Anterior and External Portion
of the Bladder.
4. A Band of Fibres separating from these and running
upwards and outwards.
5. Muscular Fibres which form
Loops on the Posterior Surface of the Bladder.
6.7. Other Muscular Fibres forming a Layer between the External and the Internal.
8. Left Ureter.
9. Left Portion of the Vesiculæ
Seminalis.
10. Vas Deferens of the same
Side.
11.11. The Lateral Lobes of the
Prostate Gland.
12. Muscular Fibres which run
on the Sides of the Prostate.
13. Other Fibres on its Anterior.
14. The Urethra tied with a Cord.

FIG. 372.

ANOTHER URINARY BLADDER
DISTENDED WITH AIR, AND
SHOWING A DIFFERENT AR-
RANGEMENT OF THE MUSCULAR
FIBRES.

1. Neck of the Bladder.
2. Two Bands of Fibres on the
Anterior and External Faces
of the Bladder, running up to
its top, and answering to those
marked 3, in Fig. 371.
3. Urachus raised up on the summit of the Bladder.
4. Inferior Fundus.
5. Right Ureter surrounded by
Muscular Fibres.
6. Very strong Muscular Fibres
running upwards to lose themselves under No. 2.
7. Other strong Fibres intercrossing with these.
8. Fibres passing from the Neck
and Inferior Fundus to the Superior Fundus.
9. Internal Layer of Fibres.

FIG. 373.

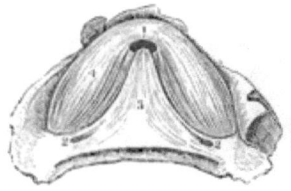 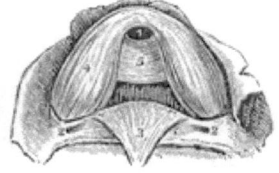 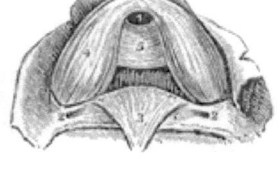

FIG. 374.   FIG. 375.

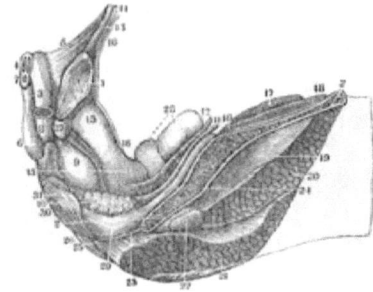 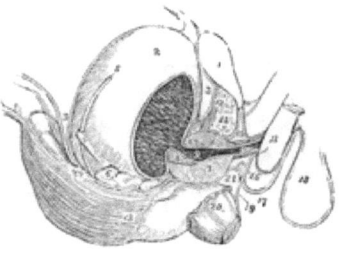

THE GENITO-URINARY ORGANS.

FIG. 373.

A VIEW OF THE SPHINCTER AP-
PARATUS OF THE NECK OF THE
BLADDER, AS DESCRIBED IN
VOL. II., P. 94, HORNER'S SPE-
CIAL ANATOMY. 1843.

1.1. Orifice of the Neck of the
Bladder.
2.2. Orifices of the Ureters.
3.3. The Triangular Muscle under the Vesical Triangle.
4.4. The Crescentic Muscular
Fibres at the Neck of the
Bladder.
  5. The Transverse Fasciculus
of Muscular Fibres.

FIG. 374.

A SIDE VIEW OF THE POSITION
OF THE URINARY BLADDER,
PROSTATE AND VESICULÆ SE-
MINALES, IN THE CAVITY OF
THE PELVIS.

1. Symphysis Pubis.
2. Section of the Ilium.
3. A Section of the Left Corpus
Cavernosum.
4. A Vertical Section of both of
the Corpora Cavernosa.
5. Ligamentum Suspensorium of
the Penis.

6. Bulb of the Urethra.
7. A Vertical Section of the
Urethra.
8. Membranous Portion of the
Urethra.
9. Prostate Gland.
10. Left Seminal Vesicle.
11. Left Vas Deferens.
12. Left Ureter.
13. Urinary Bladder, emptied
and flattened.
14. Tendon of the Rectus Abdominis.
15. Right Pyramidalis Muscle.
16. Peritoneum.
17. Section of the Psoas Magnus.
18. Section of the Iliacus Internus.
19. Gluteus Minimus.
20. Gluteus Medius.
21. Gluteus Maximus.
22. Section of the Pyriformis.
23. Musculus Ischio-Coccygeus.
24. Obturator Internus.
25. Last Bone of the Coccyx.
26. Gluteus Maximus.
27. Right Ramus of the Pubis.
28. Sigmoid Flexure of the Colon.
29. Rectum.
30. Anus.
31. External Sphincter Muscle.

FIG. 375.

A SIDE VIEW OF THE VISCERA
OF THE PELVIS, SHOWING THE
BLADDER AND ITS SURROUND-
ING PARTS.

1. Symphysis Pubis.
2. The Bladder.
3. The Recto-Vesical Fold of
the Peritoneum.
4. The Ureter.
5. The Vas Deferens.
6. Vesicula Seminalis of the
Right Side.
7. Section of the Prostate Gland.
8. Section of the Neck of the
Bladder.
9. Prostatic Portion of Urethra.
10. Membranous Portion.
11. Corpus Spongiosum.
12. Anterior Ligament of the
Bladder.
13. Rectal End of the Pelvic
Fascia.
14. Space between the Deep and
Pelvic Fascia.
15. Triangular Ligament.
16. One of Cowper's Glands.
17. Continuation of Superficial
Perineal Fascia.
18. Scrotum.
19. Deep Fascia prolonged to the
Rectum.
20. Portion of the Levator Ani.
21.22. Course of Deep Fascia.

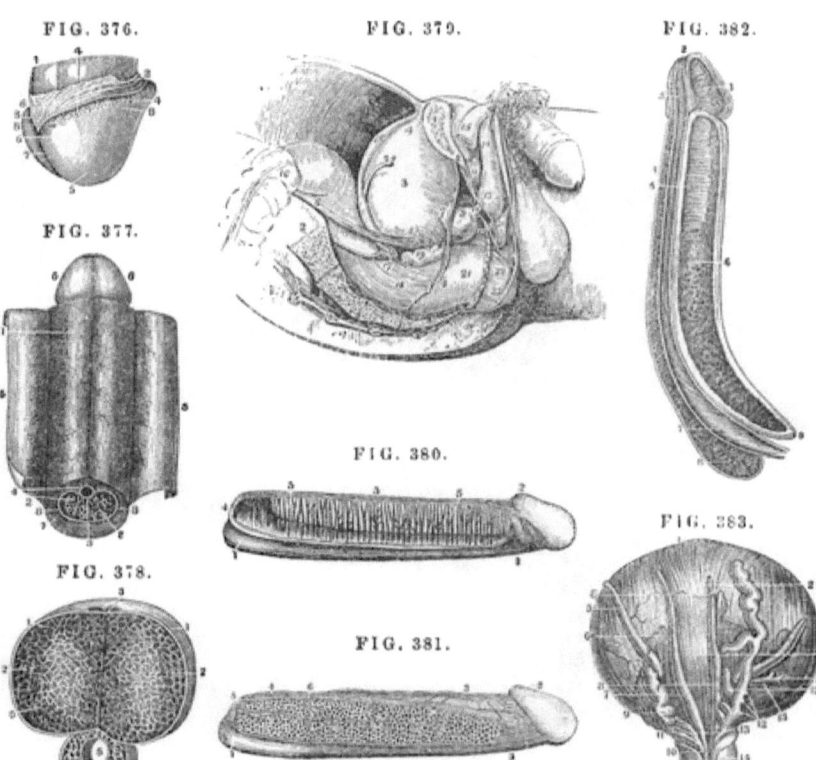

FIG. 376.   FIG. 379.   FIG. 382.

FIG. 377.

FIG. 380.

FIG. 383.

FIG. 378.

FIG. 381.

THE PENIS.

FIG. 376.

A View of the Glans Penis Injected.

1.1. Portions of the Corpora Cavernosa.
2. The Prepuce turned back.
3. Its Frænum.
4.4. Glandulæ Odoriferæ Tysoni.
5. Point of the Glans Penis.
6. Prominences of the Glans on each side of the Frænum.
7. The Furrow which separates the Sides of the Glans.
8. Corona Glandis.

FIG. 377.

The Penis deprived of its Skin, distended, dried and seen on its Inferior Surface.

1. Surface of the Cellular Membrane of the Penis separated from the Skin.
2. The Corpora Cavernosa.
3. Septum Pectiniforme as seen from behind.
4. Urethra, surrounded by the Corpora Cavernosa.
5. Internal Surface of the Skin.
6. Glans Penis.
7. Thickness of the Cellular Membrane as shown in a Section of the Penis.
8. Fibrous Membrane of the Corpora Cavernosa.

FIG. 378.

A Section of the Penis inflated, dried, and deprived of its External Cellular Membrane.

1. Fibrous Coat of the Corpora Cavernosa.
2. Corpora Cavernosa.
3. Their Septum.
4. Corpus Spongiosum Urethræ.
5. Canal of the Urethra.
6. Internal Filaments of the Corpora Cavernosa which pass from the Median Septum to the External Fibrous Membrane.

FIG. 379.

A Side View of the Viscera of the Male Pelvis in Situ, as given by a Vertical Section through the Bones of the Pelvis.

1. Section of the Pubis.
2. Section of the Sacrum.
3. Body of the Bladder.
4. Its Fundus.
5. The Base of the Bladder.
6. The Ureter.
7. The Neck of the Bladder.
8. Pelvic Fascia.
9. Prostate Gland.
10. Membranous Portion of the Urethra.
11. Triangular Ligament.
12. One of Cowper's Glands.
13. The Bulb of the Corpus Spongiosum.
14. Body of Corpus Spongiosum.
15. End of Corpus Cavernosum.
16. Sigmoid Flexure of the Colon.
17. Recto-Vesical Fold of the Peritoneum.
18. Muscular Fibres of the Rectum.

19. Right Vesicula Seminalis.
20. Vas Deferens.
21. Rectum covered by the Pelvic Fascia.
22. Portion of the Levator Ani Muscle.
23. Sphincter Ani.
24. Space between the Deep and Superficial Perineal Fascia.

FIG. 380.

A View of the Septum Pectiniforme of the Corpora Spongiosa.

1. Course of the Urethra.
2. Glans Penis.
3. Vena Dorsalis Penis.
4. Posterior Portion of the Septum.
5. Comb-like Processes of Septum Pectiniforme.

FIG. 381.

A View of the Arteries of the Penis Injected. The Penis is distended and dried.

1.2.3. Represent the same parts as in the previous Figure.
4. Arteria Dorsalis Penis.
5.6. Deep Arteries of the Corpora Cavernosa giving off Branches to these Bodies.

FIG. 382.

A Vertical Section of the Penis and Urethra.

1. Glans Penis.
2. Orifices of the Urethra.
3. Fossa Navicularis.
4. Corpus Spongiosum Urethræ.
5. Anterior Portion of the Septum Pectiniforme.
6. Its Posterior Portion.
7. Bulbous portion of the Urethra.
8. Bulb of the Corpus Spongiosum.
9. Posterior End of the Corpus Cavernosum.

FIG. 383.

The Vesiculæ Seminales, Bladder and Prostate, the Right Seminal Vesicle only is opened, the Left is injected and distended.

1. The Urinary Bladder.
2. The Posterior Longitudinal Layer of Muscular Fibres.
3. The Prostate Gland.
4. Membranous Portion of the Urethra.
5. The Ureters.
6. Blood-Vessels.
7. Right Vas Deferens.
8. Left Vas Deferens.
9. Right Seminal Vesicle in its Natural Position.
10. Ductus Ejaculatorius of the Right Side traversing the Prostate Gland.
11. Left Seminal Vesicle injected with wax and diverted out.
12. Blind Pouches of Vesicula.
13. Other Appendices.
14. Left Ductus Ejaculatorius traversing the Prostate

FIG. 384.

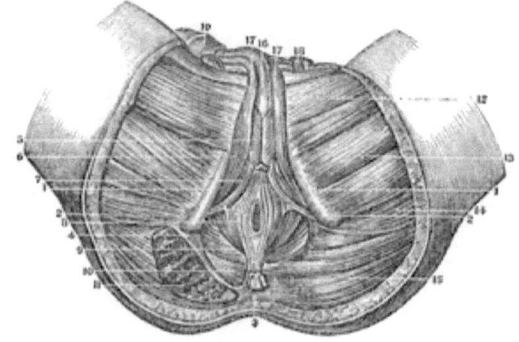

FIG. 385.

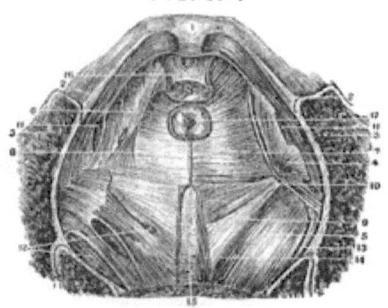

THE MALE PERINEUM

FIG. 384.

A VIEW OF THE MUSCLES OF THE PERINEUM OF
THE MALE. ONLY ONE SIDE IS REFERRED TO.

1. Ascending Ramus of the Ischium.
2. Tuber Ischii.
3. Posterior Face of the Coccyx.
4. Portion of the Great Sacro-Sciatic Ligament.
5. Musculus Accelerator Urinæ.
6. Erector Penis Muscle.
7. Transversus Perinei.
8. Sphincter Ani.
9. Levator Ani.
10. Musculus Coccygeus.
11. Section of the Gluteus Magnus.
12. Adductor Longus.
13. Adductor Brevis.
14. Adductor Magnus.
15. Extremity of the Gluteus Magnus.
16. The Urethra.
17. Corpora Cavernosa turned up.
18. Spermatic Cord turned up.
19. Free Extremity of the Penis with its Integuments.

FIG. 385.

A VIEW OF THE INTERIOR OF THE PELVIS, AS
SEEN FROM ABOVE.

1. Symphysis Pubis.
2. Ileo-Pectineal Protuberance.
3. A Section of the Body of the Ilium.
4. Obturator Internus freed from the Pelvic Fascia.
5. Pyriformis Muscle.
6. Ischio-Pubic Bands of the Pelvic Fascia.
7. Part of the Levator Ani Muscle.
8. The Portion of the Fascia of the opposite side which covers it.
9. Lesser Sacro-Sciatic Ligament.
10. Spine of the Ischium.
11. Opening for the Obturator Vessels.
12. Openings for the Sacral Plexi of Nerves and the Blood-Vessels.
13. Top of the Greater Ischiatic Foramen.
14. A little Muscle, occasionally seen and known as the Curvator Coccygis of Sömmerring.
15. Section of the End of the Sacrum and Coccyx.

FIG. 386.

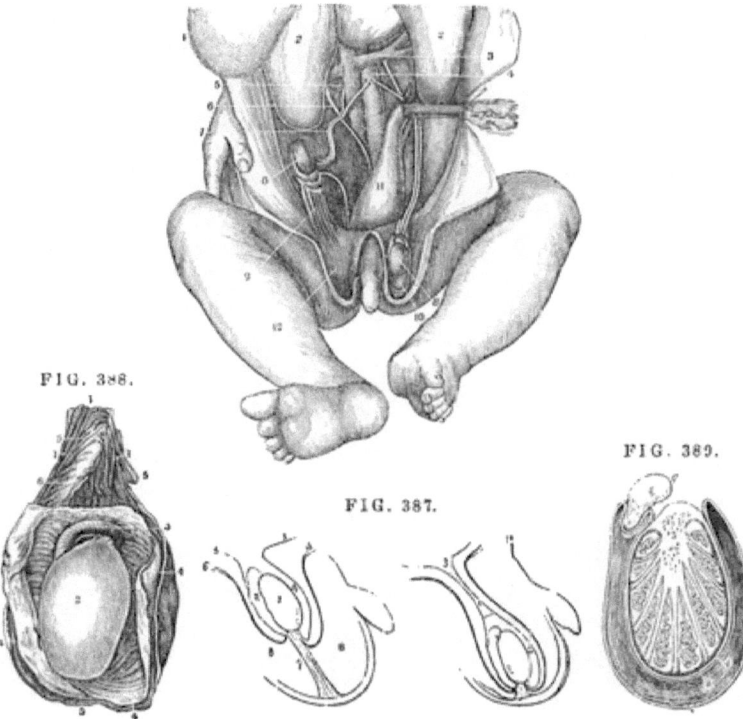

FIG. 388.

FIG. 387.

FIG. 389.

THE TESTICLE.

FIG. 386.

A VIEW OF THE POSITION OF THE TESTICLE IN A FŒTUS OF ABOUT SIX MONTHS, SHOWING THE GUBERNACULUM TESTIS.

1. Lower Portion of the Liver.
2. The Kidneys.
3. The Emulgent Vessels.
4. The Aorta.
5. The Ascending Cava.
6. The Ureter.
7. Spermatic Vessels.
8.8. Testicle in the Iliac Fossa and also in the Scrotum.
9. Gubernaculum Testis of one Side.
10. Tunica Vaginalis in advance of the Testis.
11. Rectum filled with Meconium.
12. Tunics of Scrotum.

FIG. 387.

A DIAGRAM OF THE DESCENT OF THE TESTIS AS SHOWN BY A LATERAL SECTION.

1. The Testis.
2. The Epididymis.

3. The Peritoneum.
4. The Portion of it thrust downward by the Testis in its descent.
5. Point of Insertion of the Cremaster Muscle.
6. The Portion of its Fibres coming from the Fibres of the Internal Oblique and Transversalis.
7. Gubernaculum Testis.
8. Cavity of the Scrotum.

In the other Figure the Testis has completed its descent, the Gubernaculum is shortened to its utmost, and the Cremaster everted. The Pouch of the Peritoneum above the Testis is compressed so as to form a Tubular Canal. The Dotted Line at 1 marks where the Tunica Vaginalis will terminate.

FIG. 388.

THE TUNICA VAGINALIS TESTIS AND COVERINGS OF THE SPERMATIC CORD.

1.1. The Spermatic Cord.

2. The Testicle covered by the Tunica Albuginea.
3. The Epididymis covered by the same Membrane.
4.4. Tunica Vaginalis Testis.
5.5. Common Covering of the Testicle and Spermatic Cord.
6. Proper Sheath of the Spermatic Cord.

FIG. 389.

A TRANSVERSE SECTION OF THE TESTICLE.

1. The Cavity of the Tunica Vaginalis.
2. The Tunica Albuginea.
3. Corpus Highmorianum or Mediastinum Testis. The cut ends of the vessels below the figure belong to the Rete Testis; those above, to the Blood-Vessels of the Testicle.
4. Tunica Vasculosa of the Testis.
5. One of the Lobules of the Tubuli Seminiferi terminating in the Vas Rectum.
6. A Section of the Epididymis.

FIG. 390.   FIG. 391. 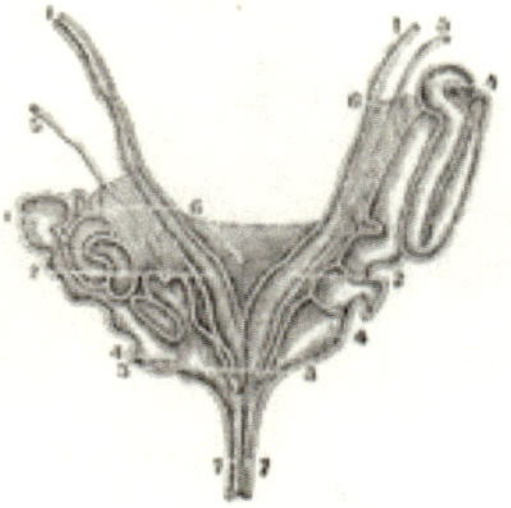   FIG. 392.

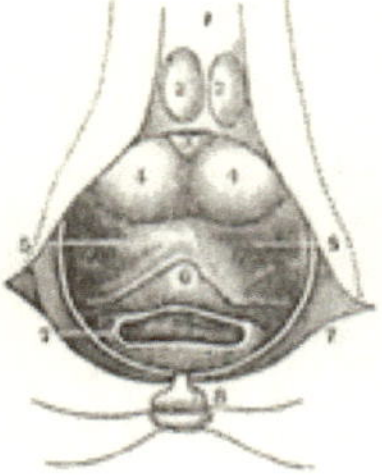

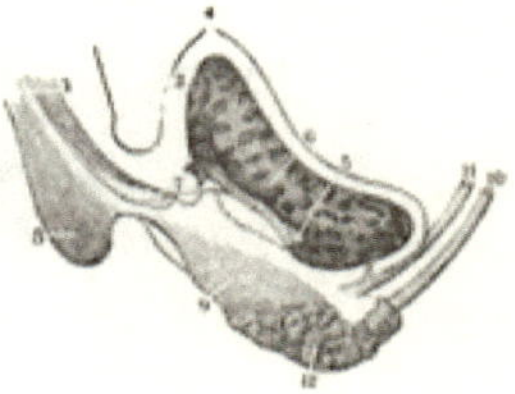

FIG. 393. 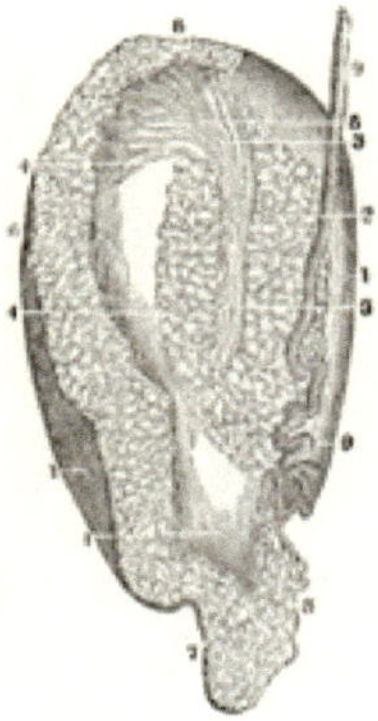   FIG. 394. 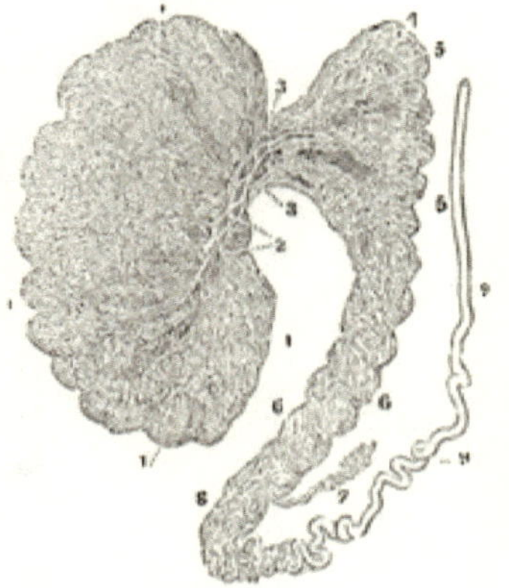   FIG. 395.

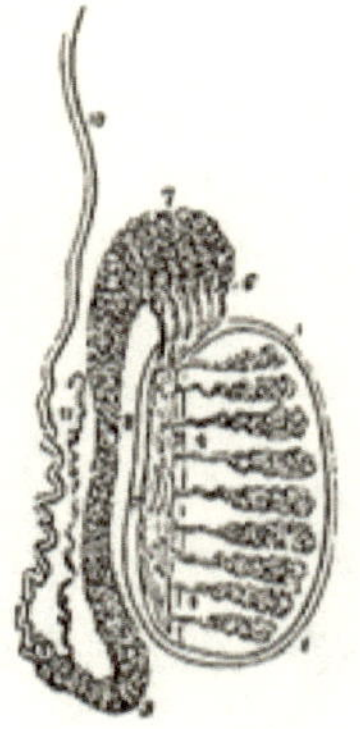

THE TESTICLE AND MUCOUS GLANDS.

FIG. 390.

THE RELATIVE POSITION OF THE PROSTATE, VESICULÆ SEMINALES AND BLADDER, AS SEEN FROM BEFORE, AFTER THE REMOVAL OF THE PERINEAL MUSCLES.

1. Section of the Urethra.
2. Prominences formed by the Bulb of the Urethra.
3. Membranous Portion of the Urethra.
4. Prostate Gland.
5. Vesiculæ Seminales.
6. Fundus of the Bladder lying upon the Rectum.
7. Section of the Rectum.
8. Portion of the Coccyx.

FIG. 391.

A VERTICAL SECTION OF THE UNION OF THE VAS DEFERENS AND VESICULÆ SEMINALES SO AS TO SHOW THEIR CAVITIES.

1.1. Vas Deferens with thick Parietes and narrow Cavity.
2.2. Portion of the same where the Cavity is enlarged.
3.3. The Extremities of the Vas Deferens from each side where they join the Vesiculæ Seminales and Ductus Ejaculatorius.
4.4. Vesiculæ Seminales distended with air and dried.

5.5. Arteries to the Vesiculæ.
6. Portion of the Peritoneum covering the Posterior Part of the Vesiculæ.
7. Ejaculatory Ducts.

FIG. 392.

A VERTICAL SECTION OF THE BLADDER AND URETHRA.

1. The Urethra laid open.
2. Fundus of the Bladder.
3. Anterior Parietes of the Bladder.
4. Urachus.
5. Orifice of the Left Ureter.
6. Orifice of the Right Ureter.
7. Verumontanum.
8. Bulb of the Urethra.
9. Prostate Gland.
10. Vas Deferens.
11. Ureter.
12. Vesicula Seminalis.

FIG. 393.

THE TESTICLE INJECTED WITH MERCURY.

1. Tunica Albuginea.
2. Seminiferous Tubes.
3. The Rete Vasculosum Testis.
4. A Globule of Mercury which has ruptured the Tubes.
5. The Vasa Efferentia which form the Coni Vasculosi.
6. Coni Vasculosi forming the Head of the Epididymis.
7. Epididymis.

8. Globus Minor of the Epididymis.
9. Vas Deferens.

FIG. 394.

THE TESTIS MORE MINUTELY INJECTED WITH MERCURY.

1.1. Lobules of the Tubuli Seminiferi.
2. Rete Testis.
3. Vasa Efferentia.
4.5. Coni Vasculosi forming the Globus Major.
6. The Epididymis.
7. Vasculum Aberrans.
8. Globus Minor.
9. Vas Deferens.

FIG. 395.

A VIEW OF THE MINUTE STRUCTURE OF THE TESTIS.

1.1. Tunica Albuginea.
2.2. Corpus Highmorianum.
3.3. Tubuli Seminiferi Convoluted into Lobules.
4. Vasa Recta.
5. Rete Testis.
6. Vasa Efferentia.
7. Coni Vasculosi constituting the Globus Major of the Epididymis.
8. Body of the Epididymis.
9. Its Globus Minor.
10. Vas Deferens.
11. Vasculum Aberrans or Blind Duct.

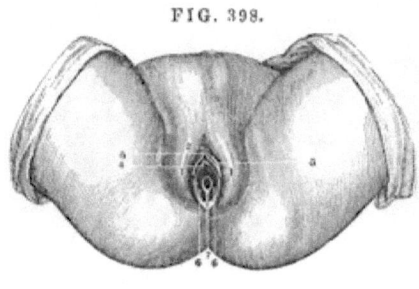

FIG. 398.

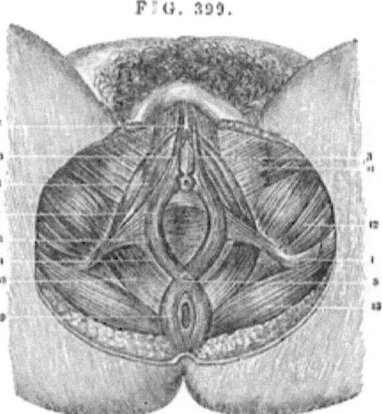

FIG. 399.

FEMALE ORGANS OF GENERATION.

FIG. 396.

THE EXTERNAL ORGANS OF GE-
NERATION IN THE UNMARRIED
FEMALE, THE LABIA MAJORA
BEING CLOSED TOGETHER.

1.1. Labia Majora.
2. Rima or Fissura Vulvæ.
3. Fourchette or Posterior Commissure—the Line of Reference is a
little too high.
4. The Anterior Commissure.
5. Perineum.

FIG. 397.

A VIEW OF THE EXTERNAL OR-
GANS OF GENERATION IN THE
UNMARRIED FEMALE — THE
VULVA BEING PARTIALLY
OPEN.

1.1. Labia Majora.
2. Fourchette.
3. Mons Veneris.

4. Prepuce of the Clitoris around
the Glans Clitoris.
5. Vestibulum.
6. The Nymphæ.
7.8. The Hymen, open in its central portion and surrounding the
Inferior extremity of the Vagina.
9. The Perineum.
10. The Anus.

FIG. 398.

THE EXTERNAL ORGANS OF GE-
NERATION IN A FEMALE FŒ-
TUS AT TERM.

1.1. Labia Majora.
2. Clitoris covered by its Prepuce.
3. The Nymphæ.
4. Meatus Urinarius.
5. Vestibulum.
6. The Hymen pierced with its ordinary Opening.
7. A thicker Portion of the Hymen forming a sort of Frænum.

FIG. 399.

A VIEW OF THE MUSCLES OF THE
PERINEUM IN THE FEMALE.

1. Tuber Ischii.
2. Sphincter Vaginæ Muscle.
3. Its Origin from the Base of the
Clitoris.
4. Vaginal Ring of the same Muscle, which receives a part of the
Fibres of the Levator Ani.
5. Intercrossing of the Sphincter
Ani and Sphincter Vaginæ Muscles at the Perineal Centre.
6. Erector Clitoridis Muscle.
7. The Clitoris covered by its Prepuce.
8. Transversus Perinei Muscle of
the Female.
9. Sphincter Ani.
10. Levator Ani.
11. The Gracilis.
12. Adductor Magnus.
13. Posterior Par. of the Gluteus
Magnus.

Page 127.

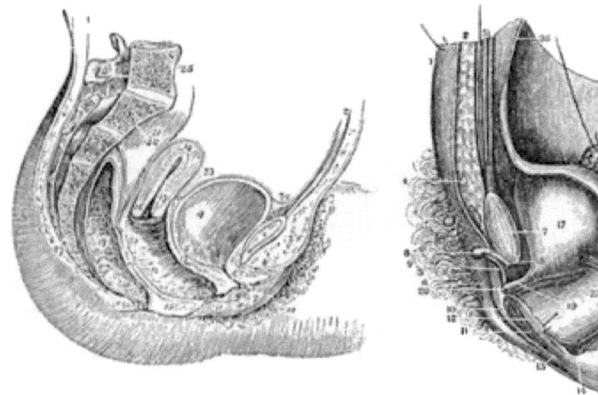
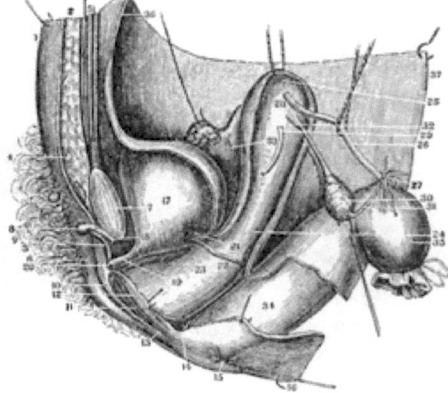

FIG. 402.

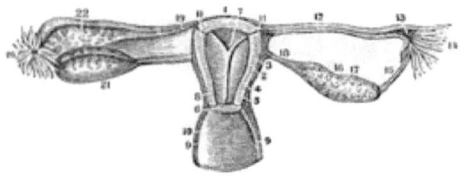

FEMALE ORGANS OF GENERATION.

FIG. 400.

A SIDE VIEW OF THE VISCERA OF THE FEMALE PELVIS.

1. Symphysis Pubis.
2. Abdominal Parietes.
3. The Fat forming the Mons Veneris.
4. The Bladder.
5. Entrance of the Left Ureter.
6. Canal of the Urethra.
7. Meatus Urinarius.
8. The Clitoris and its Prepuce.
9. Left Nympha.
10. Left Labium Majus.
11. Orifice of the Vagina.
12. Its Canal and Transverse Rugæ.
13. The Vesico-Vaginal Septum.
14. The Vagino-Rectal Septum.
15. Section of the Perineum.
16. Os Uteri.
17. Cervix Uteri.
18. Fundus Uteri.
19. The Rectum.
20. The Anus.
21. Upper Portion of the Rectum.
22. Recto-Uterine Fold of the Peritoneum.
23. Utero-Vesical Reflection of the Peritoneum.
24. The Peritoneum reflected on the Bladder from the Abdominal Parietes.
25. Last Lumbar Vertebra.
26. The Sacrum.
27. The Coccyx.

FIG. 401.

A VERTICAL SECTION THROUGH THE LINEA ALBA AND SYMPHYSIS PUBIS SO AS TO SHOW THE BLADDER, VAGINA, UTERUS AND RECTUM IN SITU.— THE PERITONEUM HAS BEEN CUT AT THE POINTS WHERE IT IS REFLECTED.

1. Anterior Parietes of the Abdomen.
2. Sub-Cutaneous Cellular Tissue.
3. Hairs on the Mons Veneris.
4. Cellular Tissue on the Mons Veneris.
5. Rectus Abdominis of the Right Side.
6. Right Labia Majora.
7. Symphysis Pubis.
8. The Clitoris.
9. Its opposite Crus.
10. Right Labia Minora.
11. Orifice of the Vagina.
12. Portion of the Left Labia Minora.
13. The Fourchette, or Posterior Commissure of the Vulva.
14. The Perineum.
15. The Anus.
16. A Portion of the Integuments of the Buttock.
17. Left side of the Bladder.
18. Neck of the Bladder.
19. The Urethra.
20. Meatus Urinarius.

21. Entrance of the Left Ureter into the Bladder.
22. Left Ureter cut off.
23. Left Side of the Vagina.
24. Left Side of the Neck of the Uterus outside of the Vagina.
25. Fundus of the Uterus.
26. Left Fallopian Tube separated from the Peritoneum.
27. Its Fimbriated Extremity.
28. Its Entrance into the Uterus.
29. Left Round Ligament.
30. Left Ovary.
31. Fimbriated Portion which unites the Tube to the Ovary.
32. Insertion of the Ligament of the Ovary to the Uterus.
33. Right Broad Ligament of the Uterus.
34. Lower Portion of the Rectum.
35. Rectum turned off and tied.
36. The Peritoneum lining the Anterior Parietes of the Abdomen.
37. The Peritoneum which covers the Posterior Parietes of the Abdomen.

FIG. 402.

THE UTERUS, FALLOPIAN TUBES, OVARIES AND A PART OF THE VAGINA OF A FEMALE OF SIXTEEN YEARS. ON ONE SIDE THE TUBE AND OVARY IS DIVIDED VERTICALLY; THE OTHER SIDE IS UNTOUCHED. THE ANTERIOR PORTION OF THE UTERUS AND VAGINA HAVE ALSO BEEN REMOVED.

1. Fundus of the Uterus.
2. Thickness of its Parieties anteriorly.
3. External Surface of the Uterus.
4. Section of the Neck of the Uterus.
5. Section of the Anterior Lip.
6. Its Posterior Lip untouched.
7. Cavity of the Uterus.
8. Cavity of its Neck.
9. Thickness of the Walls of the Vagina.
10. Its Cavity and Posterior Parietes.
11. Openings of Fallopian Tubes into the Uterus.
12. Cavity of the Left Tube.
13. Its Pavilion.
14. Corpus Fimbriatum.
15. Its Union with the Ovary.
16. Left Ovary vertically divided.
17. The Vesicles in its Tissue.
18. Ligament of the Ovary.
19. Right Fallopian Tube, untouched.
20. Its Corpus Fimbriatum.
21. Right Ovary.
22. The Broad Ligament.

FIG. 403.

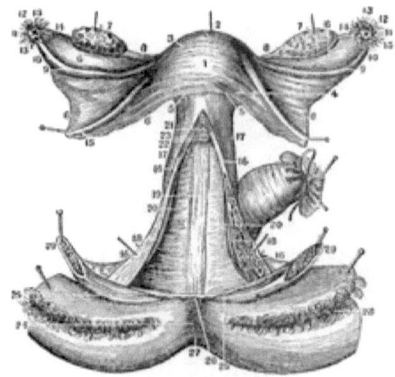

FIG. 404.

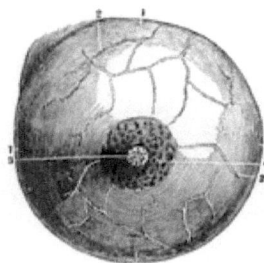

FIG. 405.

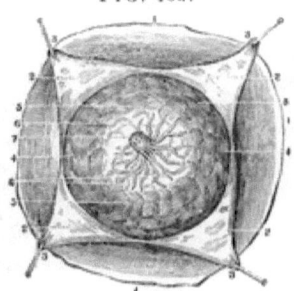

FEMALE ORGANS OF GENERATION

FIG. 403.

A View of the Uterus, Ovaries, Fallopian Tubes, Round Ligaments, Vagina and a Portion of the External Parts of the Female.

1. Anterior Face of the Uterus covered by the Peritoneum.
2. Its Fundus.
3. One of its Superior Lateral Angles near the Origin of the Fallopian Tubes.
4. Sides of the Uterus.
5. Its Neck embraced by the Upper End of the Vagina.
6. Portion of the Broad Ligaments.
7. The Ovaries drawn up by Hooks above their natural position.
8. The Ligaments which unite the Ovaries to the Uterus.
9. Fallopian Tubes.
10. The Enlargement near their Extremities.
11. Their Trumpet-shaped Mouths.
12. The Pavilion.
13. Corpus Fimbriatum.
14. A Portion of the Fimbriated Processes running to the Ovary.
15. Section of the Round Ligaments.
16. A Longitudinal Section of the Vagina.
17. Portion of the External Surface of the Vagina.
18. A Portion of its Internal Anterior Parietes.
19. Longitudinal Lines forming a sort of Raphe on its Posterior Part.
20. Transverse Wrinkles or Folds.
21. Anterior Lip of the Os Uteri.
22. Its Posterior Lip.
23. Os Externum.
24. Perineum.
25. Caruncula Myrtiformes drawn out.
26. Posterior Commissure of the Vulva forcibly drawn out.
27. The Anus.
28. Labia Majora everted.
29. The two Halves of the Clitoris and the Labia Minora forcibly separated.

The Rectum, cut off and tied, is seen behind, and the Bladder and other parts have been removed in front.

FIG. 404.

A Front View of the Mammary Gland of a Female recently Delivered.

1.1. Circumference of the Gland.
2.2. The Sub-Cutaneous Veins as seen through the Skin.
3.3. The Nipple pierced by the Lactiferous Tubes.
4. The Areola.

FIG. 405.

The Mammary Gland after the removal of the Skin, as taken from the Subject three days after Delivery.

1. The Surface of the Chest.
2. Sub-Cutaneous Fat.
3. The Skin covering the Gland.
4. Circumference of the Gland.
5. Its Lobules separated by Fat.
6. The Lactiferous Ducts converging to unite in the Nipple.
7. The Nipple slightly raised and showing the openings of the Tubes at its Extremity.

FIG. 406.

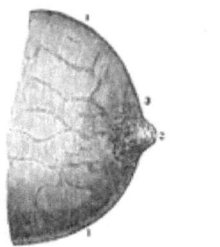

FIG. 407.

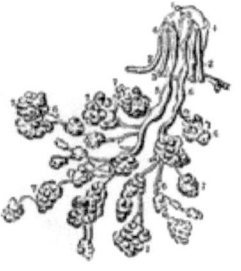

FIG. 408.

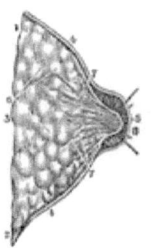

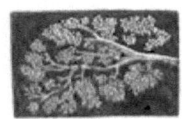

FIG. 409.

FIG. 410.

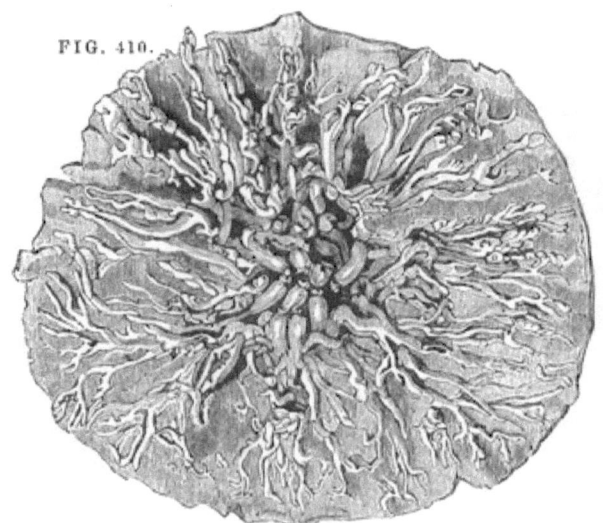

THE LACTIFEROUS GLANDS.

FIG. 406.

A SIDE VIEW OF THE GLAND AS BEFORE SHOWN IN FIG. 404.

FIG. 407.

A VERTICAL SECTION OF THE MAMMARY GLAND, SHOWING ITS THICKNESS AND THE ORIGINS OF THE LACTIFEROUS DUCTS.

1.2.3. Its Pectoral Surface.
    4. Section of the Skin on the Surface of the Gland.
    5. The thin Skin covering the Nipple.
    6. The Lobules and Lobes composing the Gland.

    7. The Lactiferous Tubes coming from the Lobules.
    8. The same Tubes collected in the Nipple.

FIG. 408.

A PREPARATION OF THE LACTIFEROUS TUBES, DURING LACTATION.

1.2. Top and Base of the Nipple.
    3. Lactiferous Tubes in the Natural State.
    4. Two in the Nipple which are injected.
    5. These Tubes dilated and forming a kind of Sinus at the Base of the Nipple.

    6. The Roots of the Lactiferous Ducts.
    7. Lobules of the Gland.
    8. The Orifices of the prepared Tubes.

FIG. 409.

TERMINATION OF A PORTION OF A LACTIFEROUS DUCT IN THE CELLS OF THE LOBULES, FROM A MERCURIAL INJECTION BY SIR A. COOPER; ENLARGED FOUR TIMES.

FIG. 410.

THE DISTRIBUTION OF THE LACTIFEROUS DUCTS DURING LACTATION; INJECTED WITH WAX, (AFTER SIR A. COOPER).

PART FOURTH.

ORGANS OF RESPIRATION

AND

CIRCULATION:

NINETY-EIGHT FIGURES.

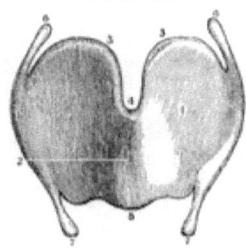

FIG. 411.

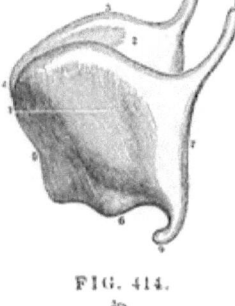

FIG. 412.

FIG. 415.

FIG. 413.

FIG. 414.

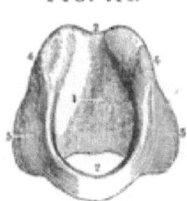

FIG. 416.

THE LARYNX.

FIG. 411.

A FRONT VIEW OF THE THYROID CARTILAGE.

1. Left Half of the Cartilage.
2. Anterior projecting Angle.
3. Superior Margin.
4. Its Notch.
5. Inferior Margin.
6.6. Cornu Majus of each Half.
7.7. Cornu Minus of each Half.

FIG. 412.

A LATERAL VIEW OF THE THYROID CARTILAGE.

1. Its Left Half.
2. Its Right Half.
3. The Superior Margin.
4. The Notch.
5. Anterior Angle.
6. Inferior Margin.
7. Posterior Margin.
8.8. Cornu Majus of each Side.
9. Cornu Minus.

FIG. 413.

A POSTERIOR VIEW OF THE LEFT ARYTENOID CARTILAGES.

1. Its Posterior Face.
2. The Summit.
3. The Base and Cavity for Articulating with the Cricoid Cartilage.

4. Its External Angle.
5. Its Internal Angle.

FIG. 414.

AN ANTERIOR VIEW OF THE LEFT ARYTENOID CARTILAGES.

1. Its Anterior Face.
   The other References as in Fig. 413.

FIG. 415.

A LATERAL VIEW OF THE EPIGLOTTIS CARTILAGE.

1. Anterior or Convex Surface.
2. Posterior or Concave Surface.
3. Superior Margin.
4. Inferior Margin or Pedicle.
5. Its Sides. The Openings of the Muciparous Ducts are also shown.

FIG. 416.

A FRONT VIEW OF THE CRICOID CARTILAGE.

1. Its Internal Face.
2. The Cavity of the Larynx as formed by this Cartilage.
3. Its Inferior Surface.
4. The little Head or Convexity for Articulating with the Arytenoids.
5. The Surface of the Superior Edge for the Attachment of the Lateral Crico-Arytenoid Muscles.

FIG. 417.

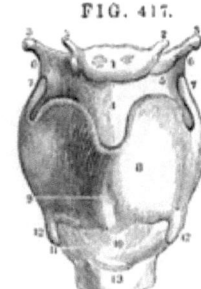

FIG. 418.

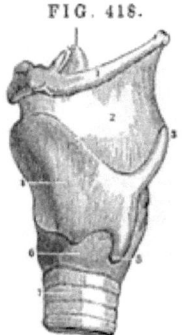

FIG. 419.

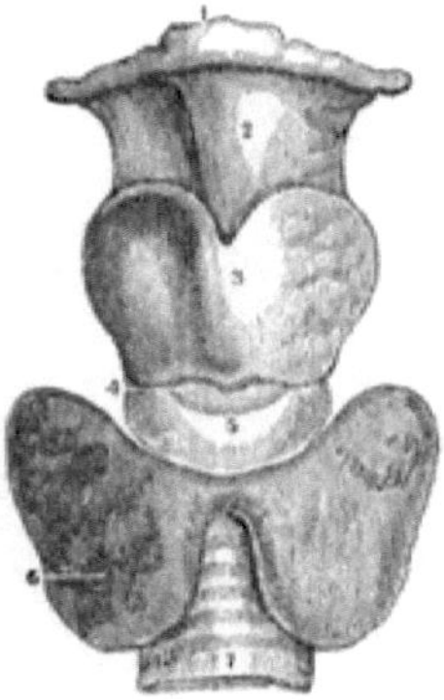

FIG. 420.

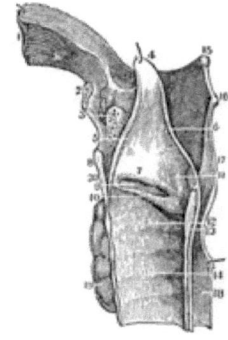

THE LARYNX.

FIG. 417.

A FRONT VIEW OF THE LIGAMENTS OF THE LA-
RYNX.

 1. Body of the Os Hyoides.
 2. Its Appendices.
 3. Its Cornua.
4.5. Thyreo-Hyoid Ligament.
 6. Lateral Thyreo-Hyoid Ligament.
 7. Cornu Majus of each Half of the Thyroid
    Cartilage.
 8. Sides of the Thyroid Cartilage.
 9. Its Projecting Angle.
10.11. Crico-Thyroid Ligament.
 12. Cornu Minus of each Side of the Thyroid
    Cartilage.
 13. First Ring of the Trachea.

FIG. 418.

A LATERAL VIEW OF THE SAME.

1. Os Hyoides.
2. Thyreo-Hyoid Ligament.
3. Cornu Majus of the Thyroid Cartilage.
4. Its Angle and Side.
5. Cornu Minus.
6. Lateral Portion of the Cricoid Cartilage.
7. Rings of the Trachea.

FIG. 419.

A FRONT VIEW OF THE THYROID GLAND IN SITU.

1. Os Hyoides.

2. Thyreo-Hyoid Ligament.
3. Thyroid Cartilage.
4. Crico-Thyroid Ligament.
5. Cricoid Cartilage.
6. Thyroid Gland.
7. Trachea.

———

FIG. 420.

A VERTICAL SECTION OF THE LARYNX TO SHOW
ITS INTERNAL SURFACE.

 1. Section of the Root of the Tongue.
 2. Os Hyoides.
 3. The Muciparous Gland of the Epiglottis.
 4. Top of the Epiglottis Cartilage.
 5. A Section of its Anterior Face.
 6. A Fold of Mucous Membrane from the Ary-
    tenoids to the Epiglottis.
 7. Superior Vocal Ligament.
 8. Section of Thyroid Cartilage.
 9. Ventricle of Galen or Morgagni.
10. Lower Vocal Ligament.
11. Arytenoid Cartilages.
12. Inside of the Cricoid Cartilage.
13. Its Posterior Portion.
14. Lining Membranes of the Trachea.
15. End of the Cornu Majus of the Os Hyoides.
16. Cornu Majus of the Thyroid Cartilage.
17. Mucous Membrane of the Pharynx.
18. Œsophagus.
19. Thyroid Gland.

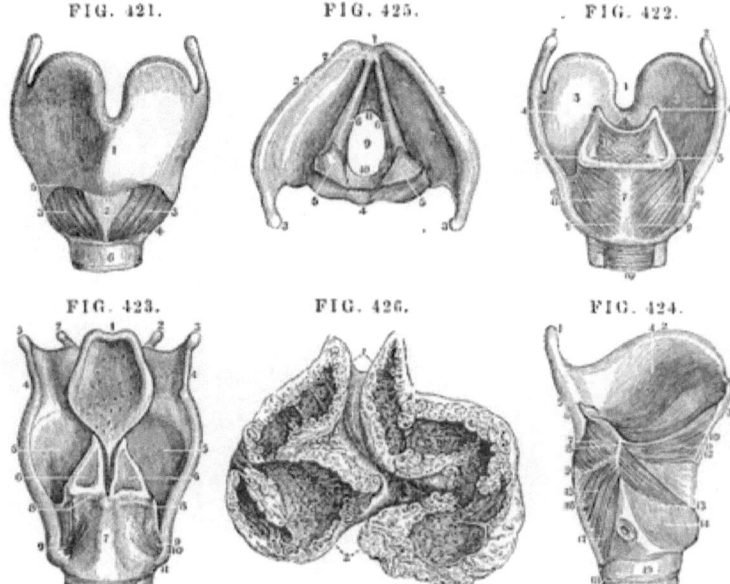

FIG. 421.   FIG. 425.   FIG. 422.

FIG. 423.   FIG. 426.   FIG. 424.

THE LARYNX AND THYMUS GLAND.

FIG. 421.

A FRONT VIEW OF THE CRICO-THYROID MUSCLES.

1. Thyroid Cartilage.
2. Crico-Thyroid Ligament.
3. Right Crico-Thyroid Muscle.
4. Its Origin.
5. Its Insertion.
6. First Ring of the Trachea.

FIG. 422.

A POSTERIOR VIEW OF THE ARYTENOID AND CRICO-ARYTENOIDEUS MUSCLES.

1.2.3. Thyroid Cartilage.
    4. Summit of the Arytenoid Cartilages.
    5. Insertion of Arytenoid Muscles.
    6. Cricoid Cartilage.
    7. Its Middle Portion.
    8.9. Crico-Arytenoideus Muscles.
    10. Posterior Portion of the Trachea.
    11. Arytenoid Muscles.

FIG. 423.

A POSTERIOR VIEW OF THE ARTICULATIONS OF THE CARTILAGES OF THE LARYNX.

1. Posterior Face of the Epiglottis.
2. Appendices of the Os Hyoides.
3. Its Cornua.
4. Lateral Thyreo-Hyoid Ligaments.

5. Posterior Face of the Thyroid Cartilage.
6. Arytenoid Cartilages.
7. Cricoid Cartilage.
8. Crico-Arytenoid Articulation.
9. Posterior Crico-Thyroid Ligament.
10. Cornu Minus of the Thyroid Cartilage.
11. Anterior Crico-Thyroid Ligament.
12. Ligamentous Portion of the first Ring of the Trachea.

FIG. 424.

A VERTICAL SECTION OF THE LARYNX TO SHOW SOME OF ITS MUSCLES.

1. Cornu Majus of the Thyroid Cartilage.
2. Its Superior Border.
3. Section of its Body.
4. Its Internal Surface.
5. Arytenoid Cartilage.
6. Posterior Surface of the Thyroid Cartilage.
7.8.9. Arytenoid Muscles.
10.11.12. Thyreo-Arytenoid Muscle.
13. Crico-Arytenoideus Lateralis Muscle.
14. Cricoid Cartilage.
15.16.17. Crico - Arytenoideus Posticus.
18.19. First Rings of the Trachea as united by Ligaments.

FIG. 425.

A VIEW OF THE LARYNX FROM ABOVE, SHOWING THE THYREO-ARYTENOID OR VOCAL LIGAMENTS.

1. Superior Edge of the Larynx.
2. Its Anterior Face.
3. Cornua Majores of the Thyroid Cartilage.
4. Posterior Face of the Cricoid Cartilage.
5.5. Arytenoid Cartilages.
6.6. Thyreo-Arytenoid Ligam'ts.
7. Their Origin within the Angle of the Thyroid Cartilage.
8. Their Terminations at the Base of the Arytenoid Cartilages.
9. The Glottis.
10. Anterior Part of the Inferior Surface of the Cricoid Cartilage.

FIG. 426.

A SECTION OF THE THYMUS GLAND AT THE 8TH MONTH.

1. Cervical Portion of the Gland.
2. Secretory Cells seen upon its Surface.
3. The Pores or Openings of the Cells and Pouches. The continuity of the Reservoir of the Lower and Cervical Portion of the Gland is also seen.

FIG. 427.

FIG. 428.

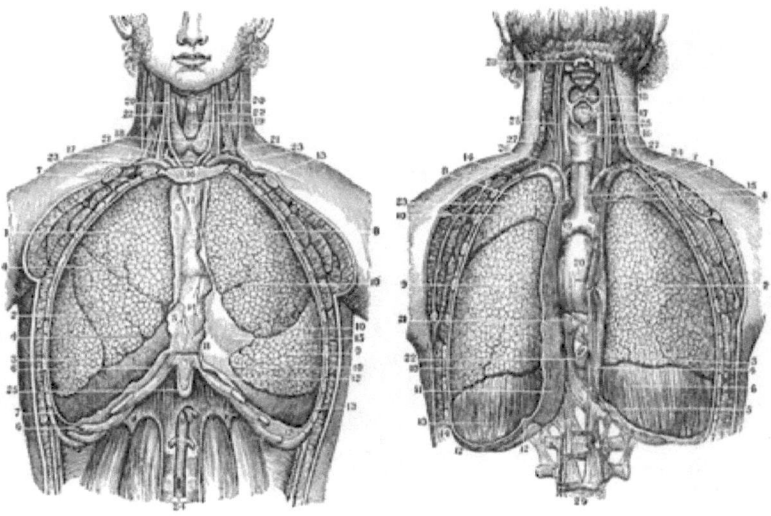

ORGANS OF RESPIRATION.

FIG. 427.

AN ANTERIOR VIEW OF THE THORACIC VISCERA
IN SITU, AS SHOWN BY THE REMOVAL OF THEIR
ANTERIOR PARIETES.

1. Superior Lobe of the Right Lung.
2. Its Middle Lobe.
3. Its Inferior Lobe.
4.4. Lobular Fissures.
5.5. Internal Layer of the Costal Pleura forming
the Right Side of the Anterior Mediastinum.
6.6. The Right Diaphragmatic Portion of the Pleura
Costalis.
7.7. The Right Pleura Costalis on the Ribs.
8. Superior Lobe of the Left Lung.
9. Its Inferior Lobe.
10.10. Interlobular Fissures.
11. The Portion of the Pleura Costalis which forms
the Left Side of the Anterior Mediastinum.
12. The Left Diaphragmatic Portion of the Pleura
Costalis.
13. Left Pleura Costalis.
14.14. The Middle Space between the Pleuræ, known
as the Anterior Mediastinum.
15. The Pericardium.
16. Fibrous Partition over which the Pleuræ are reflected.
17. The Trachea.
18. Thyroid Gland.
19. Anterior Portion of the Thyroid Cartilage.
20. Primitive Carotid Artery.
21. Subclavian Vein.
22. Internal Jugular Vein.
23. Brachio-Cephalic Vein.
24. Abdominal Aorta.
25. Xiphoid Cartilage.

FIG. 428.

A POSTERIOR VIEW OF THE THORACIC VISCERA,
SHOWING THEIR RELATIVE POSITIONS BY THE
REMOVAL OF THE POSTERIOR PORTION OF THEIR
PARIETES.

1.2. Upper and Lower Lobes of the Right Lung.
3. Interlobular Fissures.
4. Internal Portion of the Pleura Costalis, forming
one of the Sides of the Posterior Mediastinum.
5. Twelfth Rib and Lesser Diaphragm.
6. Reflection of the Pleura over the Greater Muscle of the Diaphragm on the Right Side.
7.7. Right Pleura Costalis adhering to the Ribs.
8.9. The two Lobes of the Left Lung.
10.10. Interlobular Fissures.
11.11. The Left Pleura, forming the Parietes of the
Posterior Mediastinum.
12.13. Its Reflections over the Diaphragm on this side.
14.14. The Left Pleura Costalis on the Parietes of the
Chest.
15. The Trachea.
16. The Larynx.
17. Opening of the Larynx and the Epiglottis Cartilage in Situ.
18. Root and Top of the Tongue.
19.19. Right and Left Bronchia.
20. The Heart enclosed in the Pericardium.
21. Upper Portion of the Diaphragm on which it
rests.
22. Section of the Œsophagus.
23. Section of the Aorta.
24. Arteria Innominata.
25. Primitive Carotid Arteries.
26. The Subclavian Arteries.
27. Internal Jugular Veins.
28. Second Cervical Vertebra.
29. Fourth Lumbar.

FIG. 429.　　　　　　　FIG. 430.

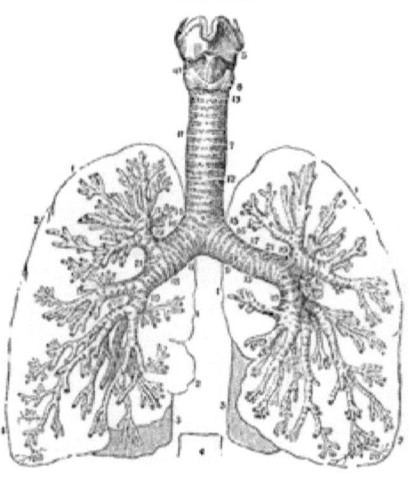

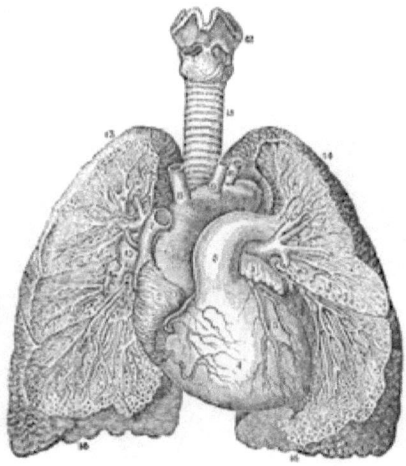

ORGANS OF RESPIRATION.

FIG. 429.

The Larynx, Trachea and Bronchia, deprived of their Fibrous Covering, and with
the outline of the Lungs.

1.1. Outline of the Upper Lobes of the Lungs.
2. Outline of the Middle Lobe of the Right
Lung.
3.3. Outline of the Inferior Lobes of both Lungs.
4. Outline of the 9th Dorsal Vertebra, showing its relation to the Lungs and the Vertebral Column.
5. Thyroid Cartilage.
6. Cricoid Cartilage.
7. Trachea.
8. Right Bronchus.
9. Left Bronchus.
10. Crico-Thyroid Ligament.
11.12. Rings of the Trachea.
13. First Ring of the Trachea.
14. Last Ring of the Trachea, which is Corset-
shaped.
15.16. A complete Bronchial Cartilaginous Ring.
17. One which is Bifurcated.
18. Double Bifurcated Bronchial Rings.
19.19. Smaller Bronchial Rings.
20. Depressions for the Course of the large
Blood-Vessels.

FIG. 430.

A View of the Bronchia and Blood-Vessels
of the Lungs as shown by Dissection, as
well as the relative Position of the
Lungs to the Heart.

1. End of the Left Auricle of the Heart.
2. The Right Auricle.
3. The Left Ventricle with its Vessels.
4. The Right Ventricle with its Vessels.
5. The Pulmonary Artery.
6. Arch of the Aorta.
7. Superior Vena Cava.
8. Arteria Innominata.
9. Left Primitive Carotid Artery.
10. Left Sub-Clavian Artery.
11. The Trachea.
12. The Larynx.
13. Upper Lobe of the Right Lung.
14. Upper Lobe of the Left Lung.
15. Trunk of the Right Pulmonary Artery.
16. Lower Lobes of the Lungs.

The Distribution of the Bronchia and of the
Arteries and Veins, as well as some of the Air-
Cells of the Lungs, are also shown in this dis-
section.

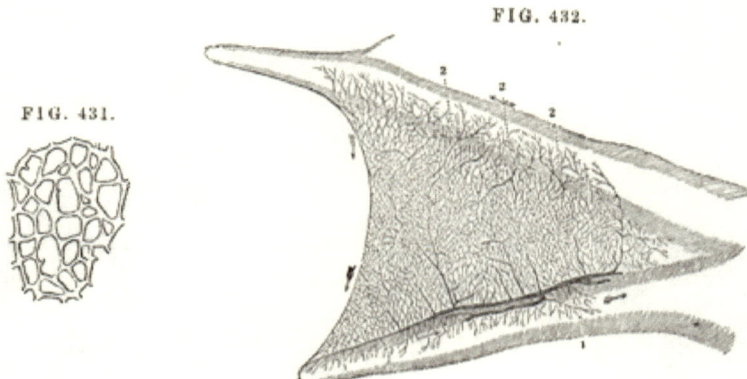

FIG. 432.

FIG. 431.

FIG. 433.

FIG. 434.

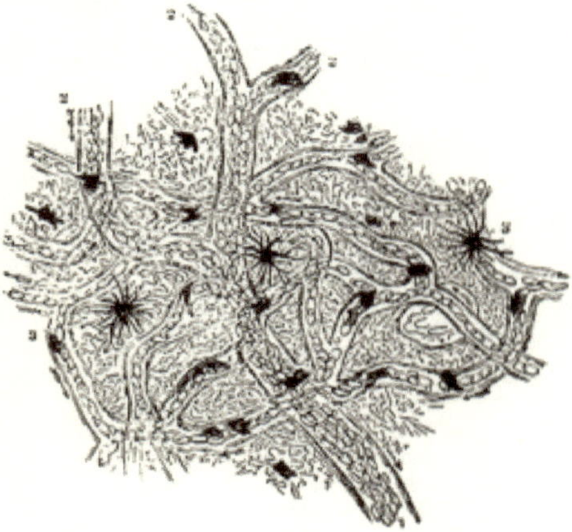

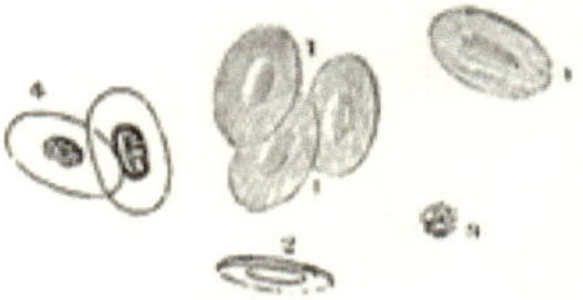

FIG. 435.

THE CIRCULATORY SYSTEM.

FIG. 431.

FIRST APPEARANCE OF BLOOD-VESSELS IN THE VASCULAR LAYER OF THE GERMINAL MEMBRANE OF A FOWL AT THE THIRTY-SIXTH HOUR AFTER INCUBATION.

FIG. 432.

A VIEW OF THE TERMINATION OF THE ARTERIES IN THE VEINS AS SHOWN IN THE WEB OF A FROG'S FOOT—MAGNIFIED 3 DIAMETERS.

1.1. The Veins.
2.2. The Arteries.

FIG. 433.

A MAGNIFIED VIEW OF THE CAPILLARY CIRCULATION IN THE WEB OF A FROG'S FOOT—MAGNIFIED 110 DIAMETERS.

1. Trunk of a Vein.
2.2. Its Branches.
3.3. Pigment Cells.

FIG. 434.

PARTICLES OF FROG'S BLOOD, MAGNIFIED ABOUT 500 DIAMETERS.

1.1. Their Flattened Face.
2. A Particle turned Edgeways.
3. A Lymph Globule.
4. Blood Corpuscles altered by dilute Acetic Acid.

FIG. 435.

CORPUSCLES OF HUMAN BLOOD, MAGNIFIED ABOUT 500 DIAMETERS.

(1). Single Particles.
    1.1. Their Flattened Face.
    2. A Particle seen Edgeways.
(2). Aggregation of Particles in a Columnar Form.

FIG. 436.

FIG. 437.

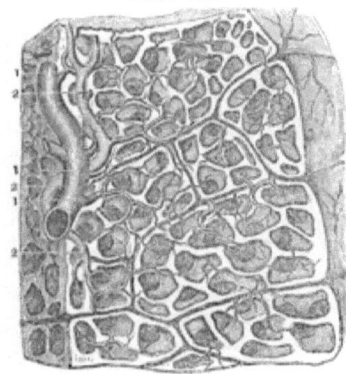

FIG. 439.

FIG. 438.

FIG 440.

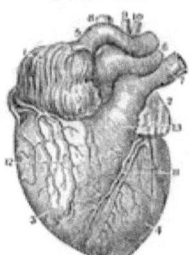

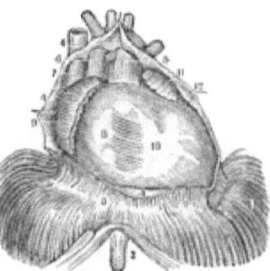

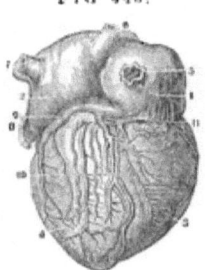

THE LUNGS AND HEART.

FIG. 436.

An Outline of a Transverse Section of the Chest, showing the relative Position of the Pleura to the Thorax and its Contents.

1. The Skin on the Front of the Chest drawn up by a Hook.
2. The Skin on the Sides of the Chest.
3. That on the Back.
4. The Sub-Cutaneous Fat and Muscles on the outside of the Thorax.
5. Section of the Muscles in the Vertebral Gutter.
6. Section of the 5th Dorsal Vertebra.
7. The Spinal Canal.
8. Spinous Process.
9.9. } Sections of the Ribs and In-
10.10. } tercostal Muscles.
11. Their Cartilages.
12. The Sternum.
13. The Division of the Pulmonary Artery.
14. The Exterior Surface of the Lungs.
15. Posterior Face of the Lungs.
16. Anterior Face of the Lungs.
17. Inner Face of the Lungs.
18. Anterior Face of the Heart covered by the Pericardium.
19. Pulmonary Artery.
20. } Its Division into Right and Left
21. } Branches.
22. Portion of the Right Auricle.
23. Descending Cava cut off at the Right Auricle.
24. Section of the Left Bronchus.
25. Section of the Right Bronchus.

26. Section of the Œsophagus.
27. Section of the Thoracic Aorta.

The space between Figures 12 and 18 and the two 16's is the Anterior Mediastinum, and the space which contains 26 and 27 is the Posterior Mediastinum. These spaces are formed by the Reflections of the Pleuræ.

FIG. 437.

A Magnified View of a Section of the Lung, showing the Arrangement of some of the Lobules, the Communication of the Air-Cells in one Lobule and their Separation from those of the adjoining Lobule. The Ramifications of the Blood-Vessels in the Texture of the Lung and their Course through the Air-Cells are also seen.

1.1. Branches of the Pulmonary Veins.
2.2. Branches of the Pulmonary Artery.

FIG. 438.

An Anterior View of the Heart in Situ, the Pericardium being divided and drawn back.

1. The Greater Muscle of the Diaphragm.
2. The Xiphoid Cartilage.
3. Tendinous Centre of the Diaphragm.
4.4. Section of the Pericardium drawn off from the Heart.
5. The Aorta.
6. Descending Vena Cava.
7. The Pulmonary Artery.

8. Right Ventricle.
9. Right Auricle.
10. Left Ventricle.

FIG. 439.

An Anterior View of the Heart in a Vertical Position with its Vessels injected.

1. Right Auricle.
2. Left Auricle.
3. Right Ventricle.
4. Left Ventricle.
5. Descending Vena Cava.
6. Aorta.
7. Left Pulmonary Artery.
8. The Arteria Innominata.
9. Left Primitive Carotid.
10. Left Sub-Clavian Artery.
11. Anterior Cardiac Vessels in the Vertical Fissure.
12. Posterior Vessels from the Transverse Fissure.
13. Main Trunk of the Pulmonary Artery.

FIG. 440.

A Posterior View of the Heart in a Vertical Position and with its Vessels injected.

1. Right Auricle.
2. Left Auricle.
3. Right Ventricle.
4. Left Ventricle.
5. Ascending Vena Cava.
6. Right Posterior Pulmonary Vein.
7. Left Posterior Pulmonary Vein.
8. End of the Left Auricle.
9. Great Coronary Vein.
10. Posterior Cardiac Vessels in the Vertical Fissure.
11. The same in the Transverse Fissure.

FIG. 441.

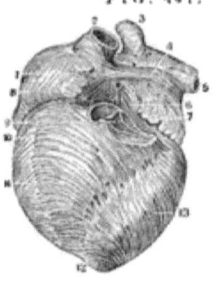

FIG. 442.

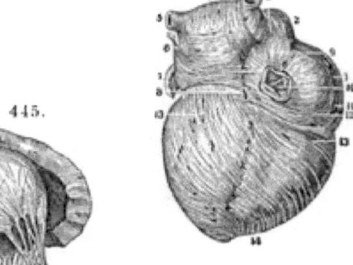

FIG. 445.

FIG. 443.

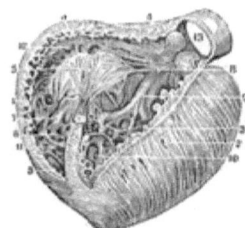

FIG. 444.

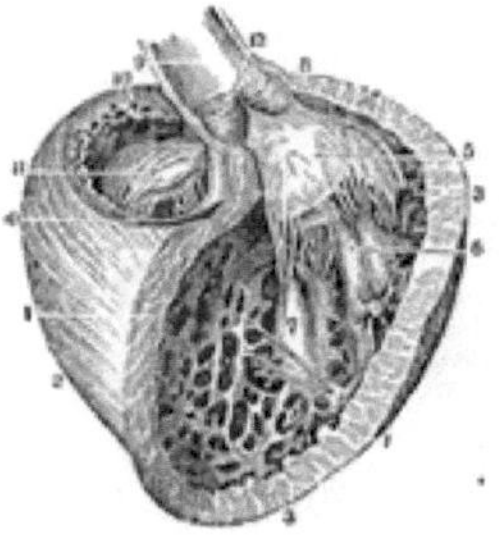

THE HEART.

FIG. 441.

AN ANTERIOR VIEW OF THE EXTERNAL MUSCU-
LAR LAYER OF THE HEART AFTER THE REMO-
VAL OF ITS SEROUS COAT, &c.

1. Right Auricle.
2. Descending Vena Cava.
3. Right Anterior Pulmonary Vein.
4. A Horizontal Band of Fibres passing across
   the Base of the Auricles.
5. Left Anterior Pulmonary Vein.
6. Muscular Fibres between the Auricles.
7. The Fringed or Ring-shaped Bands of Fibres
   at the Extremity of the Left Auricle.
8. The Muscular Fibres at the Base of the Right
   Auricle.
9. Section of the Pulmonary Artery, showing
   the Semi-Lunar Valves.
10.11. The Anterior Bis-Ventricular Muscular Fibres.
12.13. Their Continuation on to the Left Ventricle.

FIG. 442.

A POSTERIOR VIEW OF THE SAME.

1. Right Auricle.
2. Descending Vena Cava.
3. Right Posterior Pulmonary Vein.
4. Muscular Fibres of the Left Auricle.
5. Left Posterior Pulmonary Vein.
6.7. The Arrangement of the Muscular Fibres at
   the end of the Left Auricle.
8. Orifice of the Great Coronary Vein.
9. Band of Fibres between the two Venæ Cavæ.
10. The Orifice of the Ascending Vena Cava; the
   Eustachian Valve is at the end of the Line.
11.12. Muscular Fibres at the Base of the Auricle.
13.14. Muscular Fibres in the Ventricles.

FIG. 443.

A VIEW OF THE INTERIOR OF THE RIGHT VEN-
TRICLE. THE REST OF IT HAS BEEN REMOVED,
BUT THE LEFT VENTRICLE IS ENTIRE.

. Section of the Parietes of the Right Ventricle.
2. Left Ventricle.
3. Thickness of the Parietes of the Right Ventricle.

4. Thickness at the commencement of the Pulmonary Artery.
5. Anterior Fold of the Tricuspid Valve.
6. A Portion of the Right Ventricle untouched.
7.8. Columnæ Carneæ of the Right Ventricle with
   their Chordæ Tendineæ.
9. The Right Side of the Ventricular Septum.
10.11. Cavities between the Bases of the Columnæ
   Carneæ.
12. The Depression leading to the Pulmonary Artery.
13. Interior of the Pulmonary Artery. Two of the
   Sigmoid Valves are seen, the third has been
   removed.

FIG. 444.

A THREE-QUARTER VIEW OF THE LEFT VENTRI-
CLE AFTER THE REMOVAL OF ITS ANTERIOR PA-
RIETES.

1. Outer Side of the Left Ventricle.
2. Outer Side of the Right Ventricle.
3. Thickness of its Outer Parietes.
4. Thickness of a Section near the Side of the
   Right Ventricle.
5. The Mitral Valve.
6.7. Two of the Columnæ Carneæ with their Chordæ
   Tendineæ as attached to the Valve.
8. Thickness of the Ventricular Parietes at the
   Origin of the Aorta.
9. Cavity of the Aorta.
10.10. Section of the Superior Surface of the Right
   Ventricle, showing the Ostium Venosum and
   Tricuspid Valve from above.
11. Tricuspid Valve.
12. Semilunar Valves of the Aorta.

FIG. 445.

A VIEW OF THE MITRAL VALVE AS SEEN FROM
BELOW.

The Drawing shows its two Folds, its Chordæ Tendineæ arising from the Columnæ Carneæ and those
coming from the other Columnæ of the Ventricle.
The lower part of the Figure is the portion of the Left
Ventricle from which the main Columnæ arise; the
upper portion is the Left Auriculo-Ventricular Septum
around the Left Ostium Venosum.

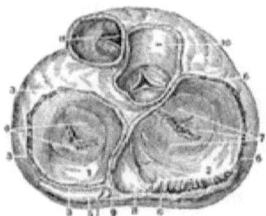

FIG. 446.

FIG. 447.

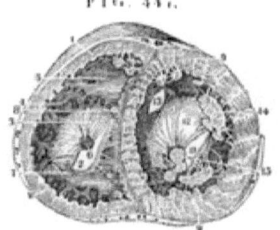

FIG. 448.

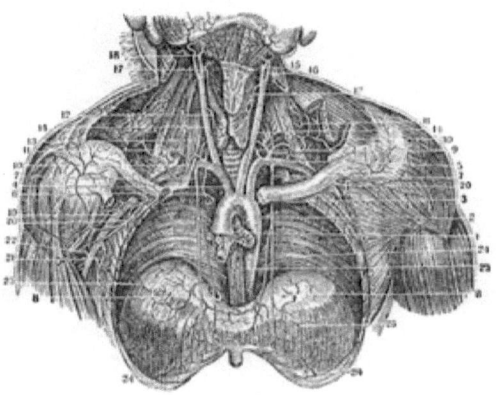

THE HEART AND ARTERIES.

FIG. 446.

A VERTICAL VIEW OF THE AURICULO-VENTRICULAR AND ARTERIAL VALVES, AS GIVEN BY A SECTION OF THE HEART AT THE OSTIUM VENOSUM AND OF THE ARTERIES AT THEIR VALVES.

1. Depression in the Left Auricle at the Left Ostium Venosum.
2. Depression in the Right Auricle at the Right Ostium Venosum.
3.3. Section of the Parietes of the Left Auricle.
4. Superior or Auricular Face of the two Folds of the Mitral Valve.
5. Section of the Greater Coronary Vein.
6.6. Section of the Parietes at the Base of the Right Auricle.
7. Auricular Face of the three Folds of the Tricuspid Valve.
8. The Orifice of the Greater Coronary Vein.
9. Septum of the Auricles.
10. A Section of the Aorta to show its Sigmoid Valves.
11. The Pulmonary Artery with its Valves.

FIG. 447.

A TRANSVERSE SECTION OF THE TOP OF THE VENTRICLES JUST BELOW THE BASE OF THE AURICLES.

1.1. Section of the Right Ventricle.
2. Right Auriculo-Ventricular Opening or Ostium Venosum.
3. The largest Fold of the Tricuspid Valve.
4. Depression to direct the Blood to the Pulmonary Artery.
5. Funnel-shaped enlargement near the Pulmonary Artery.
6. Section of one of the Columnæ Carneæ attached by the Chordæ Tendineæ to the Tricuspid Valve.
7.8. Other Columnæ Carneæ.
9. Section of the External Parietes of the Left Ventricle.
10. Section showing the thickness of the Ventricular Septum.
11. Left Ostium Venosum

12. The Mitral Valve.
13. Ventricular Opening of the Aorta.
14.15. Columnæ Carneæ of the Mitral Valve.

FIG. 448.

A VIEW OF THE ARTERIES OF THE CHEST AND NECK.

1. The Aorta at its Exit from the Heart.
2. Ascending Portion of its Arch. One of the Coronary Arteries is just below the Line.
3. Arch of the Aorta.
4. Arteria Innominata.
5. Left Subclavian Artery.
6. Bronchial and Thymic Arteries, which are here not from the Aorta but from the Sub-Clavian Artery.
7. External Mammary Arteries.
8. The Superior Phrenic Arteries, branches of the last.
9. The Vertebral Artery.
10. The Superior Scapular Artery; on the Right it goes to the Fossa Supra-Spinata, and on the Left it is lost in the Trapezius Muscle.
11. Transverse Cervical.
12. Inferior Thyroid Artery seen on the Body of the Gland.
13. The Cervicalis Ascendens.
14. Primitive Carotid on the Neck.
15. Internal Carotid.
16. External Carotid.
17. Superior Thyroid Artery.
18. Arteria Facialis.
19. Arteria Axillaris.
20. Superior Thoracic, which furnishes the Acromial.
21. Trunk of the Anterior Circumflex and Inferior Thoracic.
22. Posterior Circumflex.
23. Thoracic Aorta.
24.24. Intercostal Arteries.
25. Distribution of the Phrenic Arteries upon the Diaphragm.

FIG. 449.

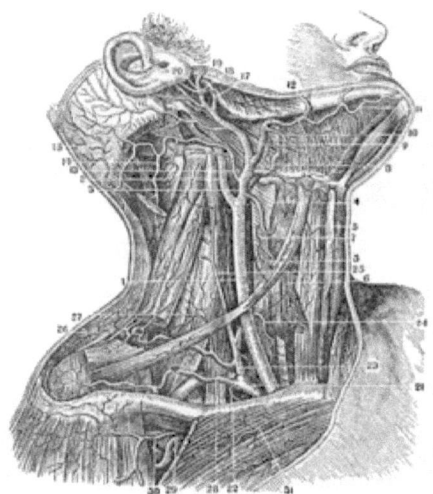

THE CAROTID ARTERY AND ITS BRANCHES

FIG. 449.

A VIEW OF THE ARTERIES OF THE NECK AND SHOULDER.

1. Primitive Carotid Artery.
2. Internal Carotid Artery.
3. External Carotid Artery.
4. The Superior Thyroid Artery.
5. Branches to the Muscles.
6. Main Branch to the Gland.
7. Inferior Pharyngeal Artery.
8. Lingual Artery.
9. Facial Artery.
10. Its Branches to the Sub-Maxillary Gland.
11. Sub-Mental Branch.
12. Principal Branch of the Facial as it goes over the Jaw.
13. Occipital Artery.
14. Branches to the Muscles on the back of the Neck.
15. Main Trunk to the Occiput.
16. Posterior Auricular Artery.
17. A Branch cut off, which goes to the Parotid Gland.
18. Origin of the Internal Maxillary Artery.
19. Origin of the Temporal Artery.
20. Origin of the Anterior Auricular.
21. The Sub-Clavian.
22. Origin of the Internal Mammary.
23. Trunk of the Inferior Thyroid, from which arise in this subject the Anterior and Posterior Cervical Arteries.
24. Branch of the Inferior Thyroid going to the Thyroid Gland.
25. Anterior Cervical going up the Neck.
26. Posterior or Transverse Cervical.
27. Branches to the Scaleni and Levator Scapulæ Muscles.
28. The Superior Scapular Artery.
29. The Thoracica Superior of the Axillary Artery.
30. A Branch to the Deltoid.
31. Recurrent Branches of the Intercostals

FIG. 450.   FIG. 451.

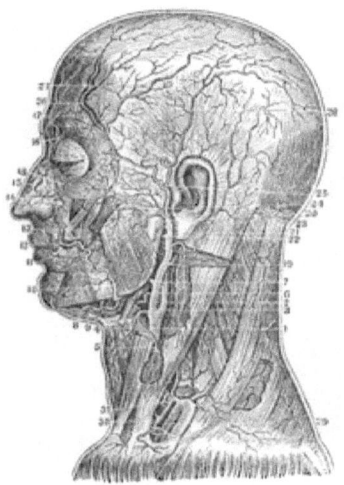 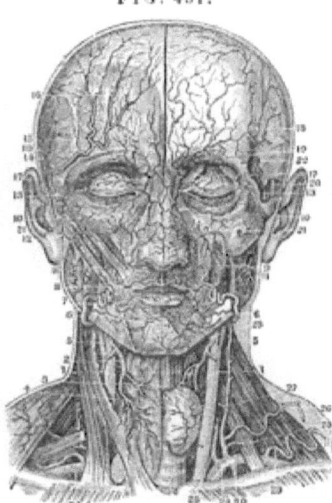

THE CAROTID ARTERY AND ITS BRANCHES

FIG. 450.

A VIEW OF THE EXTERNAL CAROTID ARTERY
AND ITS BRANCHES.

1. Left Primitive Carotid Artery, seen through a Section of the Sterno-Cleido-Mastoid Muscle.
2. Internal Carotid Artery.
3. External Carotid Artery.
4. Superior Thyroid Artery.
5. A Branch to the Sterno-Cleido Muscle.
6. Lingual Artery.
7. Origin of the Facial Artery.
8. Sub-Mental Branch.
9. Branch to the Sub-Maxillary Gland.
10. Facial Artery passing over the Jaw.
11. Inferior Coronary Artery.
12. Superior Coronary.
13. Branch to anastomose with the Infra-Orbitar.
14. Branch to the Alæ Nasi.
15. Anastomosis of Facial with Ophthalmic.
16. Nasal Branch of Ophthalmic.
17. Its Frontal Branch.
18. Branch to the Orbicularis Palpebrarum Muscle.
19. Origin of the Occipital Artery.
20. Point where it passes under the Splenius Muscle.
21. Posterior Auricular Artery.
22. Origin of the Internal Maxillary.
23. Temporal Artery.
24. Transverse Facial.
25. Point of Division of the Temporal Artery.
26. Anterior Temporal Artery.
27. Middle Temporal Artery.
28. Posterior Temporal Artery.
29. Internal Mammary Artery.
30. Inferior Thyroid Artery.
31. Transversalis Cervicis Artery.

FIG. 451.

A FRONT VIEW OF THE ARTERIES OF THE HEAD
AND NECK.

1. Primitive Carotid Artery.
2. Superior Thyroid Artery.
3. Its Muscular Branches.
4. Its Main Branch to the Gland.
5. External Carotid Artery.
6. Facial Artery passing over the Jaw.
7. Inferior Coronary Artery.
8. Superior Coronary Artery.
9. Buccalis Ascendens.
10. Anastomosis of the Facial with the Ophthalmic Artery.
11. Branches of the External Carotid to the Masseter Muscle.
12. Temporal Artery where it divides.
13. Anterior Temporal Artery.
14. }
15. } Its principal Branches.
16. }
17. Nasal Branch of the Ophthalmic Artery.
18. A Branch to the Forehead.
19. Supra-Orbitar Artery.
20. Temporal Artery.
21. Infra-Orbitar Artery.
22. Deep Temporal Artery.
23. Anterior Cervical Artery.
24. Sub-Clavian Artery.
25. Vertebral Artery.
26. Transverse Cervical.
27. Inferior Thyroid Artery.
28. Anterior Cervical.
29. Superior Scapular.
30. Internal Mammary.

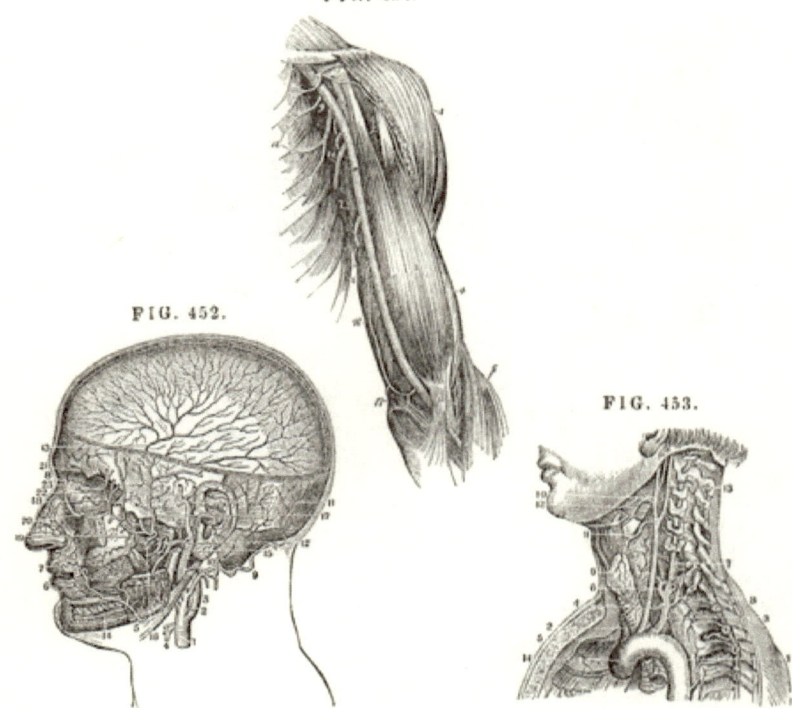

FIG. 454.

FIG. 452.

FIG. 453.

THE CAROTID AND SUBCLAVIAN ARTERIES.

FIG. 452.

A VIEW OF THE INTERNAL MAXILLARY ARTERY, AS GIVEN BY SECTIONS OF THE BONES OF THE HEAD AND FACE.

1. Primitive Carotid Artery.
2. External Carotid.
3. Internal Carotid.
4. Section of the Superior Thyroid Artery.
5. Point where the Facial Artery crosses the Lower Jaw.
6. Inferior Coronary Artery.
7. Superior Coronary Artery.
8. Point of anastomosis of Facial with the Nasal Branch of Ophthalmic.
9. The Occipital Artery.
10. Posterior Auricular.
11. Temporal Artery.
12. Origin of the Internal Maxillary Artery.
13. Meningea Magna of the Dura Mater ramifying over its Surface.
14. Inferior Dental Artery in the Alveolar Processes of the Lower Jaw.
15. The Pterygoid Arteries.
16. The Masseter Arteries.
17. Deep-seated Posterior Temporal Artery.
18. Deep-seated Anterior Temporal Artery.
19. Buccal Arteries.
20. Infra-Orbital.
21. Posterior Palatine.
22. Origin of the Pterygoid Artery.
23. Origin of the Spheno-Palatine.

FIG. 453.

A VIEW OF THE VERTEBRAL ARTERY, CAROTID AND ARCH OF THE AORTA, AS GIVEN BY A VERTICAL SECTION OF THE NECK.

1. Commencement of the Thoracic Aorta.
2. The Innominata at its Origin.
3. The Left Sub-Clavian.
4. The Internal Mammary Artery.
5. The Artery of the Right Side.
6. The Inferior Thyroid.
7. The Vertebral in the Transverse Processes of the Cervical Vertebræ.
8. Superior Inter-Costal Artery.
9. Left Primitive Carotid.
10. External Carotid Artery.
11. Superior Thyroid.
12. The Lingual, which has here a common Trunk with the Facial.
13. Internal Carotid.
14. Origin of the Aorta.

FIG. 454.

THE AXILLARY AND BRACHIAL ARTERIES WITH THEIR BRANCHES.

1. The Deltoid Muscle.
2. The Biceps.
3. The Tendinous Process from the Tendon of the Biceps.
4. Brachialis Internus Muscle.
5. The Supinator Longus.
6. The Coraco-Brachialis.
7. The Middle Portion of the Triceps Muscle.
8. Its Inner Head.
9. The Axillary Artery.
10. The Brachial Artery.
11. The Thoracica Acromialis Artery.
12. The Superior and Inferior Thoracic Arteries.
13. The Serratus Magnus Muscle.
14. The Subscapular Artery.
15. The Profunda Major Artery.
16. The Profunda Minor.
17. The Anastomotica.
18. The Profunda Major inosculating with the Radial Recurrent Artery.

FIG. 455.

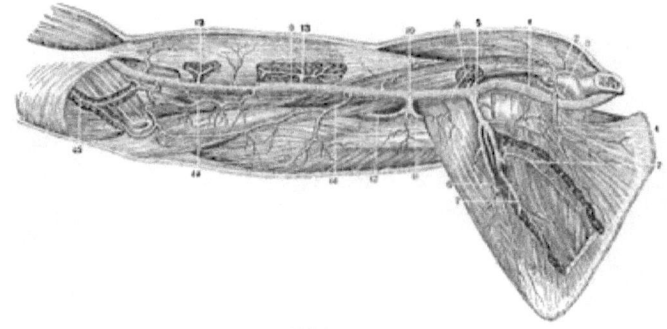

FIG. 456.

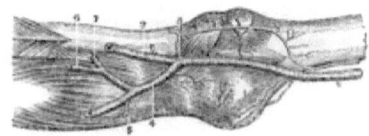

FIG. 457.

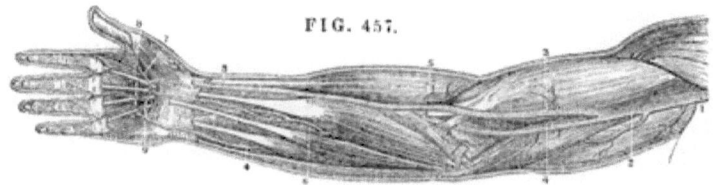

THE AXILLARY AND BRACHIAL ARTERIES.

FIG. 455.

A View of the Arteries on the Anterior Portion of the Arm and Shoulder.

1. Axillary Artery.
2. Thoracica Acromialis Artery.
3. Thoracica Superior.
4. Sub-Scapularis Branch.
5. Inferior Scapulæ.
6.7. Branches to the Teres and Sub-Scapularis Muscles.
8. Anterior Circumflex.
9. Brachial Artery.
10. Profunda Major Humeri.
11. Posterior Circumflex.
12. Main Trunk of the Profunda Major.
13. Muscular Branches of the Brachial to the Biceps Muscle.
14. Branches to the Brachialis Internus.
15. Recurrens Ulnaris anastomosing with the Anastomotica of the Brachial.

FIG. 456.

The Anterior Surface of the Elbow-Joint with its Vessels.

1. The Brachial Artery.

2. The Radial Artery.
3. Recurrens Radialis.
4. The Ulnar Artery.
5. Recurrens Ulnaris.
6. Interosseous Anterior Artery.
7. Interosseous Posterior Artery.

FIG. 457.

A View of one of the Anomalies in the Arrangement of the Brachial Artery. It here divides above the Elbow.

1. Termination of the Axillary Artery
2. The Brachial Artery.
3.3. Radial Artery.
4.4. Ulnar Artery.
5. A Recurrent Branch.
6. Anterior Interosseous Artery.
7. Superficial Palmar Arch formed by the Ulnar Artery.
8. Deep-Seated Palmar Arch.
9. The Anastomosis of the two Arteries, much enlarged.

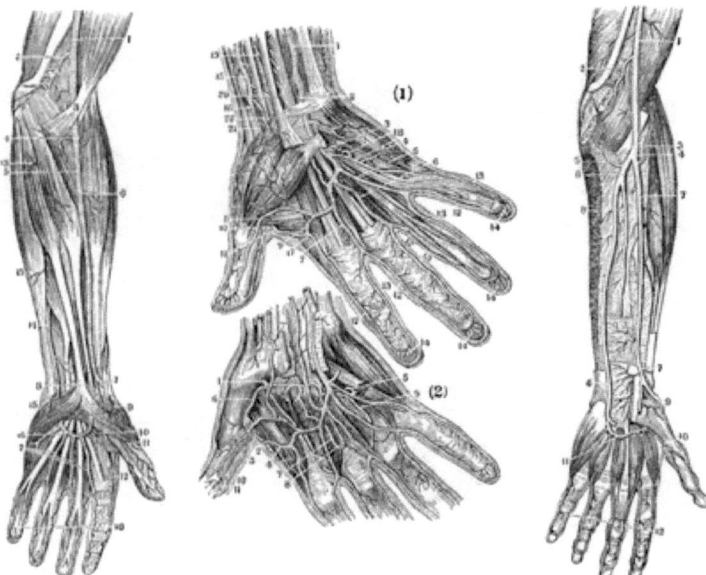

FIG. 458.   FIG. 460.   FIG. 459.

(1)

(2)

THE RADIAL AND ULNAR ARTERIES.

FIG. 458.

A VIEW OF THE ARTERIES OF THE
LOWER PORTION OF THE SU-
PERIOR EXTREMITY, AS SEEN
AFTER THE REMOVAL OF THE
INTEGUMENTS.

1. Lower part of the Brachial Artery.
2. Arteria Anastomotica.
3. Aponeurotic Expansion of the
Tendon of the Biceps.
4. Recurrens Radialis Artery.
5. Radial Artery.
6. Muscular Branches.
7. Superficialis Volæ giving off a
Branch to the Arcus Sublimis.
8. The Tendons passing under the
Annular Ligament of the Wrist
Joint.
9. Branch of the Superficialis Volæ
on the Ball of the Thumb.
10. Points to the Palmaris Profunda.
11. Magna Pollicis Artery.
12. Radialis Indicis.
13. Cubito-Muscular Arteries.
14. Lower part of the Ulnar Artery.
15. Branches to the Palm and Muscles of the Little Finger.
16. The Arcus Sublimis.
17. Branches running to supply the
Fingers.
18. The Digital Arteries.

FIG. 459.

THE ARTERIES OF THE FORE-
ARM AFTER THE REMOVAL OF
A PORTION OF THE MUSCLES.
. Lower part of the Brachial Ar-
tery.

2. Inter-Muscular Aponeurosis.
3. Recurrens Radialis.
4. Division of the Brachial into the
Radial and Ulnar, as usually
seen.
5. Recurrens Ulnaris.
6. Ulnar Artery.
7. Radial Artery.
8. Interosseous Anterior Artery.
9. Dorsalis Carpi Artery.
10. Magna Pollicis Artery.
11. Arcus Profundus formed by the
Palmaris Profundus and anastomosing with a Branch from
the Arcus Sublimis.
12. The Digital Arteries.

FIG. 460.

(1.) A VIEW OF THE MINUTE DI-
VISIONS OF THE ARCUS SUB-
LIMIS AND ITS BRANCHES.

1. The Ulnar Artery at the
lower portion of the Fore-
Arm.
2. Point where it passes between
the Anterior Annular Ligament and the Aponeurosis
Palmaris.
3. Point where it reaches the
Palm of the Hand.
4,5. } The Digital Branches which
6,7. } it gives off in the Palm of the
8,9. } Hand.
10. Point of Anastomosis of its
branch No. 8 with the branch
from the Arcus Profundus.
11. The termination of the Radial
Artery in sending a branch
to the Thumb and Fore-Finger.

12,12. Digito - Radial Branches of
the Arcus Sublimis.
13,13. Digito-Ulnar Branches of the
same.
14,14. Anastomosis and Capillary
Terminations of these Arteries in the Pulps of the Fingers.
15. The Radial Artery.
16. Point where it passes to the
back and outside of the Hand
under the Extensor Tendons
of the Thumb.
17. Last Branch of the Radial
Artery, called Radialis Indicis.
18. End of the Arcus Profundus
on the Ulnar side of the Hand.
19,20. Superficial Muscular Branches
of the Radial at the Wrist.
21,22. Superficialis Volæ and Branches to the Ball of the Thumb.

(2.) THE MINUTE DIVISIONS OF
THE ARCUS PROFUNDUS AND
ITS BRANCHES.

1. Point where the Radial comes
into the Palm of the Hand.
2. Anastomosing Branch to give
off.
3. A Branch on the side of the
Thumb.
4. A Branch to the Fore-Finger.
5. Anastomosis of the Arcus Profundus and a Digital Branch
of the Ulnar.
6. The Magna Pollicis Artery.
7. } A succession of Interosseous
8. } Branches which anastomose
9. } with the Digital Branches of
10. } the Ulnar before their bifur-
11. } cations to each finger. The
12. } Anastomoses are in Arches

FIG. 461.　　　　　　FIG. 462.

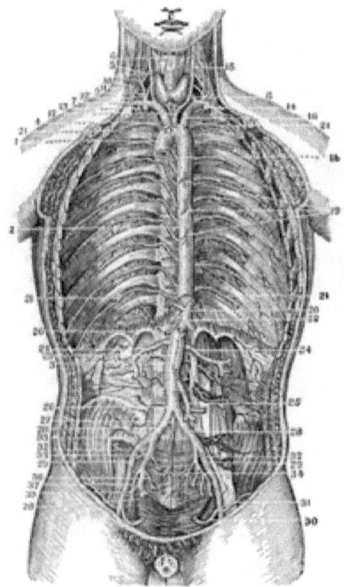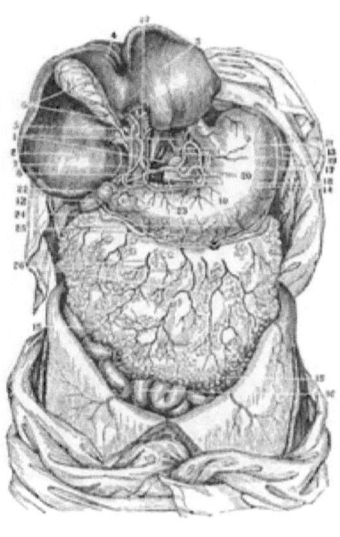

THE ABDOMINAL AORTA.

FIG. 461.

A VIEW OF THE AORTA IN ITS
WHOLE LENGTH, AND OF ITS
BRANCHES, AS GIVEN BY A SEC-
TION OF THE ANTERIOR PARIE-
TES OF THE TRUNK.

1. Commencement and Arch of the
   Aorta.
2. Thoracic Aorta.
3. Abdominal Aorta.
4. Arteria Innominata.
5. Right Primitive Carotid.
6. Superior Thyroid.
7. Right Sub-Clavian.
8. Vertebral.
9. Inferior Thyroid.
10. Anterior Cervical.
11. Transverse Cervical.
12. Superior Scapular.
13. Superior Intercostal.
14. Section of Internal Mammary.
15. Left Primitive Carotid.
16. Left Sub-Clavian.
17. A small Artery to the Superior
    Mediastinum.
18. Some of the Upper Intercostal
    Arteries.

19. Œsophageal Arteries.
20. Phrenic Arteries, here coming
    off from the Cœliac.
21. Remains of the Diaphragm and
    commencement of the Cœliac
    Artery.
22. Tripod of Haller, or Division of
    the Cœliac, into Hepatic, Gastric
    and Splenic Arteries.
23. Superior Mesenteric, cut off.
24. Emulgent Arteries.
25. Inferior Mesenteric.
26. Division of the Aorta into Iliacs.
27. Middle Sacral—last Branch of
    the Aorta.
28. Primitive Iliacs.
29. External Iliacs.
30. Epigastric Artery.
31. Circumflexa Ilii.
32. Internal Iliac Artery.
33. Ileo-Lumbar.
34. Lateral Sacral.
35. Gluteal.
36. Vesical Arteries.
37. Obturator.
38. Ischiatic.
39. Internal Pudic.

FIG. 462.

A VIEW OF THE ARTERIES OF
THE STOMACH AND LIVER.

1.1. Crura of the Diaphragm.
2. The Liver turned upwards.
3. Its Left Lobe.
4. Its Right Lobe.
5. Lobulus Spigelii.
6. Porus of the Liver.
7. Ductus Choledochus.
8. Vena Portarum.
9.10.11. The Stomach.
12. The Duodenum.
13. The Spleen.
14. The Pancreas.
15. The Great Omentum.
16. The Small Intestines.
17. Tripod of Haller.
18. Abdominal Aorta.
19. Phrenic Arteries.
20. Coronary Artery of the Stomach.
21. Splenic Artery.
22. Gastric Artery.
23. Hepatic Artery.
24. Right Gastro-Epiploic Artery.
25. Branches to the Greater Curva-
    ture of the Stomach.
26. Branches to the Omentum Ma-
    jus.
27. Main Trunk of the Hepatic
    dividing into Right and Left
    Branches, and giving off the
    Cystic Artery.

Page 147.

FIG. 463. FIG. 464.

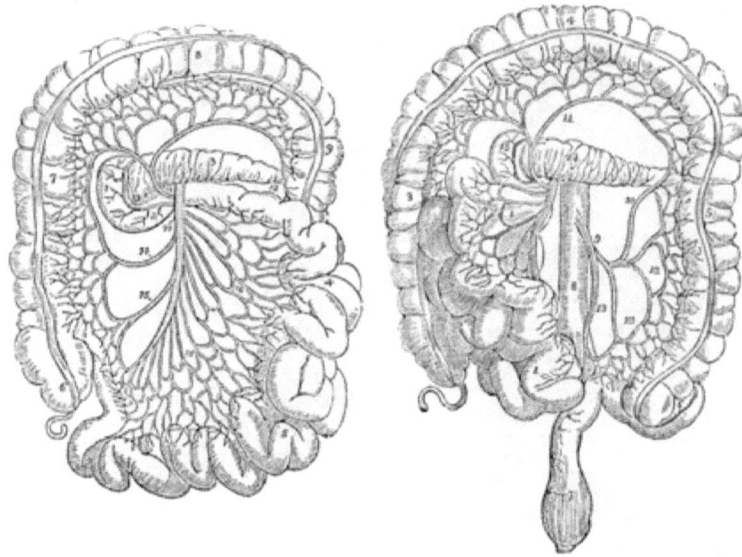

THE MESENTERIC ARTERIES.

FIG. 463.	FIG. 464.
A VIEW OF THE DISTRIBUTION OF THE SUPERIOR MESENTERIC ARTERY.	THE DISTRIBUTION OF THE INFERIOR MESENTERIC ARTERY.

1. Descending portion of the Duodenum.	1. Superior Mesenteric, with its Branches to the small Intestines turned back.
2. The Transverse portion.	2. The Cæcum.
3. The Pancreas.	3. Ascending Colon.
4. The Jejunum.	4. Transverse Colon.
5. The Ileum.	5. Descending Colon.
6. The Cæcum.	6. Sigmoid Flexure.
7. The Ascending Colon.	7. The Rectum.
8. The Transverse Colon.	8. The Aorta.
9. The commencement of the Descending Colon.	9. The Inferior Mesenteric Artery.
10. The Superior Mesenteric Artery.	10. Colica Sinistra.
11. The Colica Media.	11. Colica Media anastomosing with the latter.
12. Anastomosis with the Colica Sinistra.	12. Branches of the Inferior Mesenteric to the Sigmoid Flexure.
13. Anastomosis with the Pancreatico-Duodenalis.	13. Superior Hemorrhoidal.
14. Colica Dextra Artery.	14. The Pancreas.
15. Ileo-Colic Artery.	15. Descending portion of the Duodenum.
16. Branches of the Superior Mesenteric to the small Intestines.	

FIG. 465.   FIG. 466.

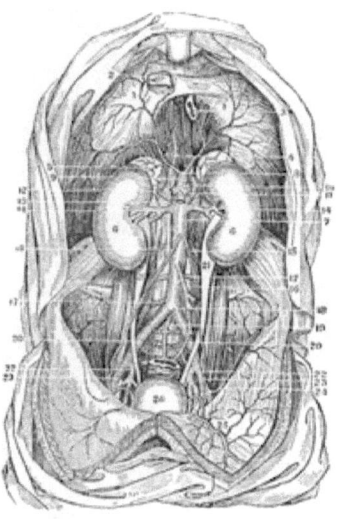

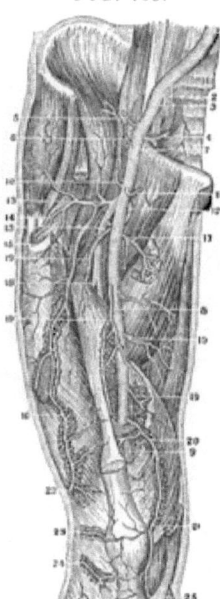

THE AORTA AND FEMORAL ARTERIES.

FIG. 465.

A VIEW OF THE ABDOMINAL AORTA AND ITS BRANCHES.

1,1. The Diaphragm.
2. Foramen Quadratum and Section of the Ascending Vena Cava.
3. Foramen Œsophageum and Section of the Œsophagus.
4. Foramen Aorticum in the Crura of the Diaphragm. The Phrenic Arteries are seen going to the Diaphragm.
5. Capsulæ Renales.
6. The Kidneys.
7. Abdominal Aorta.
8. Phrenic Arteries.
9. Cœliac—giving off.
10. The Splenic.
11. The Gastric.
12. The Hepatic.
13. Section of Superior Mesenteric.
14. Emulgent Arteries.
15. Spermatic Arteries.
16. Inferior Mesenteric.
17,17. Lumbar Arteries.
18. Division of the Abdominal Aorta.
19. Its last Branch—the Middle Sacral.
20. Primitive Iliacs.
21. Ureters—in their Position to the Arteries.
22. Internal Iliacs.
23. External Iliacs.
24. Circumflexa Ilii.
25. Distribution of the Epigastric.
26. Bladder distended with Urine. The Vesical Arteries are seen near it.

FIG. 466.

A FRONT VIEW OF THE FEMORAL ARTERY, AS WELL AS OF THE EXTERNAL AND PRIMITIVE ILIACS OF THE RIGHT SIDE.

1. Primitive Iliac Artery.
2. Internal Iliac Artery.
3. External Iliac Artery.
4. Epigastric Artery.
5. Circumflexa Ilii Artery.
6. Arteria Ad Cutem Abdominis.
7. Commencement of the Femoral just under the Crural Arch.
8. Point where it passes the Vastus Internus Muscle.
9. Point where it leaves the Front of the Thigh to become Popliteal.
10. Muscular Branch to the Psoas and Iliacus.
11. External Pudic Artery cut off.
12. Origin of the Internal Circumflex.
13. Profunda Femoris.
14. Muscular Branch.
15,16. Artery to the Vastus Externus Muscle.
17. Artery to the Pectineus and Adductors
18. First Perforating Artery.
19,19. Muscular Arteries.
20,21. Anastomotica.
22. Superior External Articular.
23. Middle Articular.
24. Inferior External Articular.
25. Inferior Internal Articular

FIG. 467. FIG. 468.

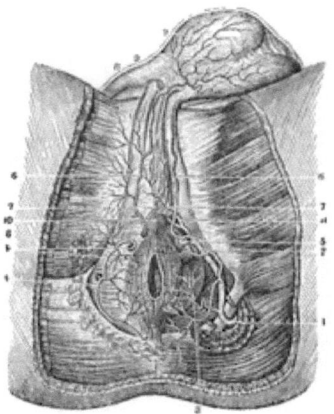 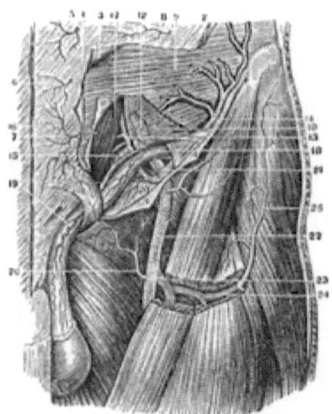

ARTERIES OF THE PERINEUM AND GROIN.

FIG. 467.

THE ARTERIES IN THE PERINEUM OF THE MALE. ON THE RIGHT SIDE THEY ARE SEEN DIRECTLY UNDER THE FASCIA, BUT ON THE LEFT SIDE ARE UNDER THE MUSCLES.

1. Internal Pudic Artery between the two Sacro-Sciatic Ligaments.
2. The same Artery between the Transversus Perinei and Erector Penis Muscles.
3. Inferior Hemorrhoidal Artery.
4. Superficial Arteries to the Fat around the Anus.
5. The Perineal Artery.
6.6. Urethro-Bulbar Artery.
7.7. Branches of the same to the Corpus Spongiosum.
8.9. Branches to the Scrotum and Dartos.
10. Cavernous Artery.
11. Ramus Superficialis Dorsi Penis.

FIG. 468.

A VIEW OF THE ARTERIES IN THE GROIN OF THE LEFT SIDE IN THEIR RELATIVE POSITIONS, THE INGUINAL CANAL BEING OPENED.

1. Aponeurosis of the Obliquus Externus Muscle.
2. Section of this Muscle.
3. Its Tendon turned off and upwards.
4. Its Tendon turned downwards and exposing the Inguinal Canal.
5.6.7. Sub-Cutaneous Arteries.
8. A Branch of the Ad Cutem Abdominis.
9. Surface of the Obliquus Internus Muscle.
10. Surface of the Transversalis Muscle.
11. Section of the Fascia Transversalis.
12. Branch of the Epigastric.
13. Epigastric Artery.
14. Muscular Arteries, Branches from the Epigastric and Circumflexa Ilii.
15. Lower Edge of the Transversalis Muscle, giving off Fibres to form the Cremaster.
16. Section of the Linea Alba.
17. Rectus Abdominis Muscle.
18. Spermatic Cord, entire.
19. An Arteriole from the Epigastric.
20. Another to the Fascia.
21. End of the External Iliac Artery.
22. The Femoral Artery.
23. The Profunda Femoris.
24. External Circumflex.
25. A Branch to the Fascia Lata.
26. External Pudic Artery.

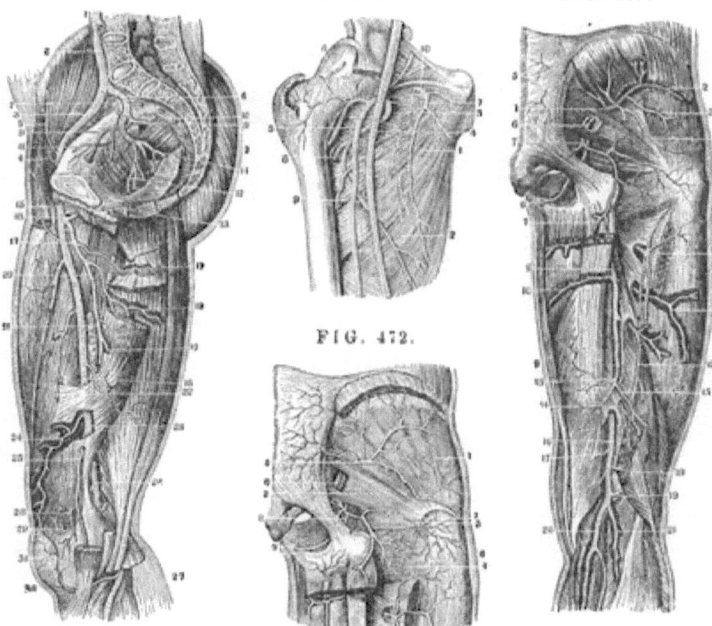

FIG. 469.   FIG. 470.   FIG. 471.

FIG. 472.

THE FEMORAL ARTERY.

FIG. 469.

THE ARTERIES OF THE PELVIS AND THIGH, AS SEEN FROM THE INNER SIDE, BY A VERTICAL SECTION.

1. Inferior Extremity of the Abdominal Aorta, just where it divides into the Iliac Arteries.
2. Right Primitive Iliac.
3. Right External Iliac.
4. Origin of Epigastric Artery.
5. Circumflexa Ilii.
6. Hypogastric or Internal Iliac Artery.
7. Ileo Lumbar.
8. Gluteal.
9. Obturator.
10. Lateral Sacral.
11. Vesical Arteries cut off.
12. Middle Hæmorrhoidal.
13. Internal Pudic.
14. Ischiatic.
15. Origin of the Femoral Artery at the Crural Arch.
16. Point where it passes through the Adductor Muscles.
17. Profunda Major.
18. Internal Circumflex.
19. First Perforatory Artery.
20. Second Perforatory Artery.
21. Third Perforatory Artery.
22. Another Perforatory Artery.
23. Femoral, seen in the Adductors.
24. The Anastomotica of the Femoral.
25. A Branch to the Sartorius Muscle.
26. Popliteal Artery.
27. The same Artery behind the Knee-joint under the Soleus Muscle.
28. A Supernumerary Articular Artery.

29. Superior Internal Articular Artery.
30. Inferior Internal Articular Artery.
31. Anastomosis of these with Anastomotica.

FIG. 470.

A VIEW OF THE FEMORAL ARTERY, AS IT EMERGES FROM POUPART'S LIGAMENT.

1. Adductor Brevis Muscle.
2. Adductor Magnus.
3. Obturator Externus Muscle.
4. Femoral Artery.
5. Profunda Femoris.
6. External Circumflex Artery.
7. Origin of Internal Circumflex Artery.
8. First Perforating Artery.
9. Another Branch to the Adductor Muscles.
10. The Obturator Artery.

FIG. 471.

A VIEW OF THE ARTERIES ON THE BACK OF THE THIGH AND BUTTOCK, AS WELL AS ON THE BACK OF THE HAM.

1. Gluteal Artery as it escapes from the Pelvis.
2,3,4. Branches which it furnishes to the Gluteus Medius and Gluteus Minimus Muscles.
5. Small Cutaneous Arteries given off by the posterior Branches of the Sacral Arteries.
6,6. Internal Pudic from its exit from the Pelvis to the root of the Penis.
7,7. Ischiatic Artery as it escapes from the Pelvis to its dis-

tribution to the head of the Biceps and Semi-Tendinous Muscles, as well as its Branches to the Gemini, Pyriformis, and Quadratus Femoris Muscles.
8. Termination and distribution of Internal Circumflex.
9. Profunda Femoris seen in the thickness of the Adductors.
10. A Branch to Adductor Longus and Brevis.
11. First Perforating Artery, going to Vastus Externus.
12. Second Perforating Artery.
13. Third Perforating Artery.
14. Termination of Profunda Femoris in the Biceps Muscle.
15. A Branch to the short Head of the Biceps.
16. Popliteal Artery.
17,18,19. Its Muscular Branches.
20,21. Gastrocnemial Arteries.

FIG. 472.

A VIEW OF THE DISTRIBUTION OF THE DEEP-SEATED EXTERNAL BRANCHES OF THE ISCHIATIC ARTERY.

1. Gluteus Minimus Muscle.
2. Pyriformis.
3. Lower one of the Gemini Muscles.
4. Quadratus Femoris.
5,6. Ischiatic Artery in its course outside the Pelvis to the Rotator Muscles.
7. A Branch to the Capsular Ligament.
8. Internal Pudic just after it leaves the Pelvis.
9. Its position on the Ramus of the Ischium.
10. Internal Circumflex Artery.

FIG. 474.　　　　　　　　　　　　　　FIG. 475.

FIG. 473.

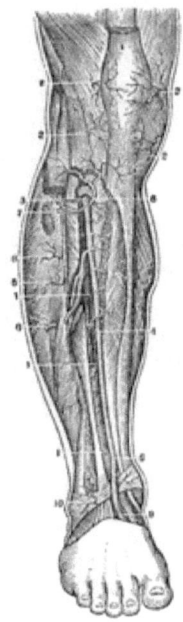

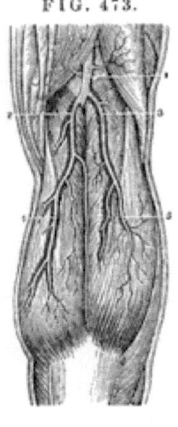

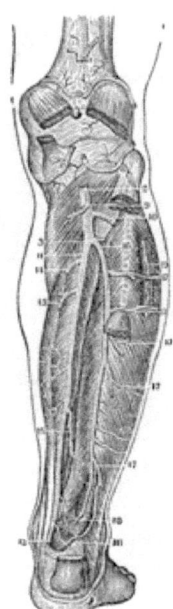

ARTERIES OF THE LEG.

FIG. 473.

A VIEW OF THE ARTERIES IN THE POPLITEAL SPACE.

1. Popliteal Artery.
2. Internal Gastrocnemial Artery.
3. External Gastrocnemial Artery.
4.5. Division of these Arteries in the Substance of the Muscle.

FIG. 474.

A VIEW OF THE ANTERIOR TIBIAL ARTERY AND ITS BRANCHES.

1.1. The remains of the Extensor Proprius Pollicis Pedis Muscle and Tendon.
2.2. Superficial Branches from the Popliteal Artery, known as Articular Arteries.
3. Anterior Tibial Artery, as it comes through the Interosseous Ligament.
4. The same Artery, on the middle of the Leg.
5. Point where it passes under the Extensor Proprius Tendon and the Annular Ligament.
6. Recurrent Branch.
7. Branch to the Extensor Communis, Soleus and Peroneus Longus Muscles.
8.8. Other Muscular Branches.
9. Pedal Artery, or continuation of the Anterior Tibial on the Foot.
10. External Malleolar Artery.

FIG. 475.

A VIEW OF THE ARTERIES ON THE BACK OF THE LEG. THE MUSCLES HAVE BEEN REMOVED SO AS TO DISPLAY THE VESSELS IN THEIR WHOLE LENGTH.

1. The Popliteal Artery, cut off so as to show the Articular Arteries.
2. Lower End of the same Artery on the Popliteus Muscle.
3. Point of Bifurcation into the Posterior Tibial and Peroneal.
4. Superior Internal Articular Artery.
5. Superior External Articular Artery.
6. Middle Articular Artery.
7. Inferior Internal Articular Artery.
8. Inferior External Articular Artery.
9. Branch to the Head of the Soleus Muscle.
10. Origin of the Anterior Tibial Artery.
11. Origin of the Posterior Tibial Artery.
12. Point where it passes behind the Annular Ligament to become the Plantar.
13.14.15. Muscular Branches.
16. Origin of the Peroneal Artery.
17.17. Muscular Branches.
18.18. Anastomosis of the Posterior Tibial and Peroneal Arteries near the Heel.
19. Muscular Branch from the Anterior Tibial.

FIG. 476.

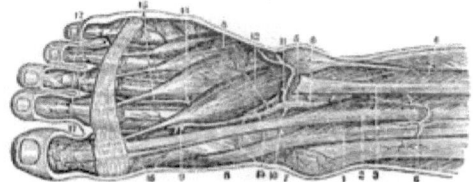

FIG. 477.

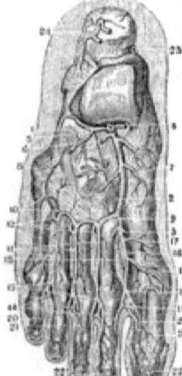

FIG. 478.

FIG. 479.

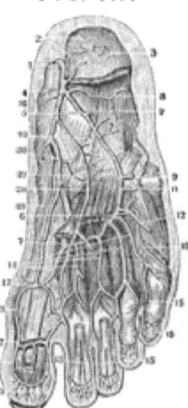

BRANCHES OF THE ANTERIOR AND POSTERIOR TIBIAL ARTERIES.

FIG. 476.

THE SUPERFICIAL ARTERIES ON THE TOP OF THE FOOT.

1. Tibialis Anticus Muscle.
2. Extensor Proprius Pollicis Pedis.
3. Extensor Communis Tendon, cut off.
4. Extensor Brevis Digitorum Pedis.
5. Anterior Tibial Artery, between the Extensor Tendons.
6. Some of its Muscular Branches.
7. Internal Malleolar Artery.
8. Lower portion of the Anterior Tibial Artery.
9. Point where it sinks to anastomose with the Plantar.
10.11. Two Malleolar Arteries.
12.13. Muscular Branches of the Anterior Tibial on the Foot.
14. Metatarsal Artery.
15.16.17. Its Interosseal Branches and their distribution.

FIG. 477.

THE DEEP-SEATED ARTERIES ON THE TOP OF THE FOOT.

1. Point where the Anterior Tibial comes on to the Foot.
2. The same Artery on the Tarsal Bones.
3. Point where it dips to the Plantar Arteries.
4. Internal Malleolar Artery.
5. External Malleolar Artery.
6. A Branch to the Extensor Brevis Muscle.
7. Branches of the Tarsal Artery.
8. Branches to the Ligaments.
9. Metatarsal Artery.

10. Superior Branches of the Metatarsal Artery.
11. Interosseal Arteries.
12. Posterior Perforating Branches of the Metatarsus.
13. Plantar Interosseous Arteries, seen through the Metatarsus.
14. Anterior Perforating Branches of the Metatarsal.
15. Bifurcation of the Interosseal to give the Digital of the Toes.
16. Dorsalis Hallucis.
17. A Branch to the inside of the Great Toe.
18. Bifurcation of the Dorsalis Hallucis.
19. Its Perforating Branch.
20.21.22. Distribution of the Digitals of the Toes.
23. Section of the Posterior Tibial.
24. Branch of the Posterior Peroneal Artery.

FIG. 478.

A VIEW OF THE ARTERIES ON THE BACK OF THE LEG AND THEIR CONTINUATION ON TO THE SOLE OF THE FOOT.

1.1. Tendons of the Flexor Communis and Flexor Longus Pollicis Pedis.
2. Tendon of the Peroneus Longus.
3. Posterior Tibial Artery at the Ankle.
4.4. External and Internal Plantar Arteries.
5. Point where it dips to form the Arcus Plantaris.
6. Peroneal Artery.
7. A Branch to anastomose with the Posterior Tibial.

8. Posterior Inferior Branch of the Peroneal.

FIG. 479.

THE DEEP-SEATED BRANCHES OF THE ARTERIES ON THE SOLE OF THE FOOT.

1. Posterior Tibial Artery by the side of the Astragalus.
2. Branches to the Calcis.
3. Branch of the Posterior Peroneal Artery.
4. Bifurcation of the Posterior Tibial into the Internal and External Plantar.
5. Origin of the External Plantar Artery.
6. Point where it forms the Plantar Arch.
7. Anastomosis of the Anterior Tibial with the Plantar Arch.
8.9.10. Muscular Branches of the External Plantar Artery.
11. Anastomosis of this Artery with the Metatarsal.
12.13. External Digital of the Little Toe.
14. Digital Arteries of the other Toes.
15.15. Their distribution on the Toes.
16. Origin of the Internal Plantar Artery.
17. Its anastomosis with the Arcus Plantaris.
18.19.20. Muscular Branches of the Internal Plantar Artery.
21. Digital of the Big Toe, as formed by the anastomosis of the Internal Plantar and Arcus Plantaris.
22. Sub-Articular Branch of the Great Toe.
23. Anastomosis in the Pulp of the Toe.

FIG. 480.

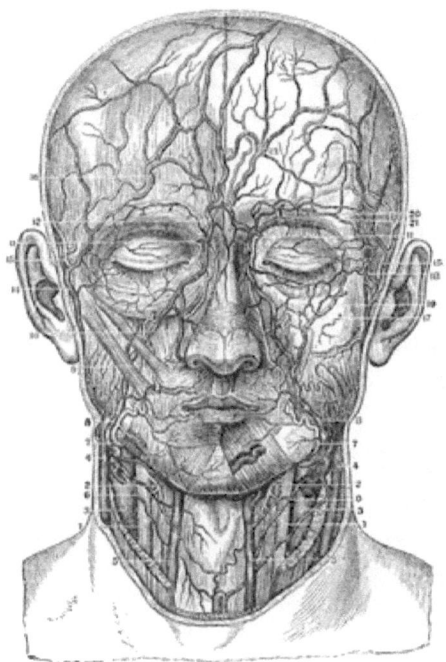

ARTERIES AND VEINS OF THE HEAD AND NECK.

FIG. 480.

A Front View of the relative Positions of
the Veins and Arteries of the Face and
Neck. On the Right Side the Superficial
Vessels are seen, and the Deep-seated
ones on the Left.

1. Primitive Carotid Arteries.
2. Superior Thyroid Arteries.
3. Internal Jugular Veins.
4. External Jugular Veins.
5. A Branch known as the Anterior Jugular
   Vein.
6. Superior Thyroid Veins.
7. Facial Arteries.
8. Facial Veins.

9. Zygomatic Branch of the Facial Artery.
10. Nasal Branch of the Facial Vein.
11. Anastomosis of the Facial Artery and
    Vein with the Ophthalmic Artery.
12. Venous Arch above the Nose.
13. Frontal Vein.
14. Temporal Vein.
15. Temporal Artery.
16. Frontal Branches of the Temporal Artery
    and Vein.
17. Infra-Orbitar Vessels.
18. Sub-Aponeurotic Branch of the Temporal
    Vein.
19.20. Venous Anastomosis around the Eye-Lids.
21. Frontal Branches of the Ophthalmic Ves-
    sels of Willis.

FIG. 481.   FIG. 482.

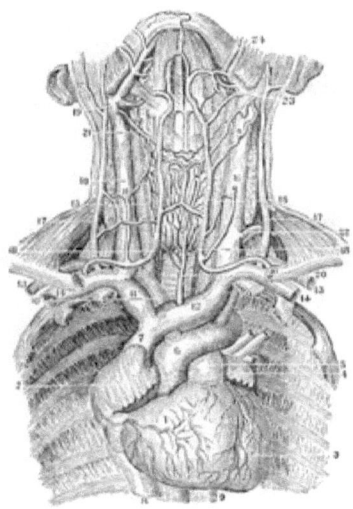 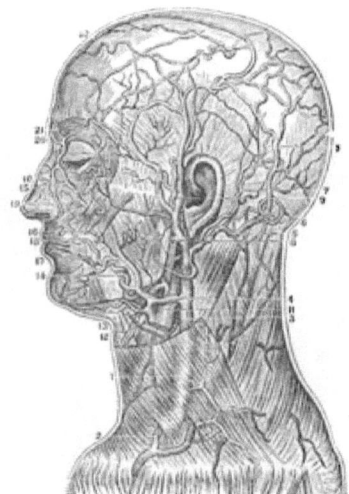

THE VESSELS OF THE HEAD AND NECK.

FIG. 481.	FIG. 482.

A VIEW OF THE HEART, WITH THE GREAT VES-
SELS OF THE NECK IN SITU.

1. Right Ventricle of the Heart.
2. Right Auricle.
3. Left Ventricle.
4. Left Auricle.
5. Pulmonary Artery.
6. Arch of the Aorta.
7. Descending Vena Cava at its entrance
into the Right Auricle.
8. Ascending Vena Cava.
9. Thoracic Aorta.
10. Arteria Innominata.
11. Right Brachio-Cephalic Vein.
12. Left Brachio-Cephalic Vein.
13. Section of the Sub-Clavian Artery.
14. Section of the Sub-Clavian Vein.
15,15. Primitive Carotid Arteries.
16,16. Internal Jugular Veins.
17,17. External Jugular Veins. Between these
Veins is seen the Section of the Sterno-
Cleido-Mastoid Muscle.
18. The Trunk formed by the Superficial Cervical Veins, known sometimes as the Anterior Jugular Vein.
19. A Branch from it to the Facial.
20. Main Trunk from the Inferior Thyroid
Veins.
21. Superior Thyroid Vein.
22. Transverse Cervical Artery and Vein.
23. Lingual Artery and Vein.
24. Facial Artery and Vein.

A SIDE VIEW OF THE SUPERFICIAL ARTERIES
AND VEINS OF THE FACE AND NECK.

1. External Jugular Vein, seen under the
Platysma Myodes Muscle.
2. Anastomosing Branch from the Cephalic
Vein of the Arm to the External Jugular.
3. External Jugular after the removal of the
Platysma Muscle.
4. Communication of the External and Internal Jugulars by means of the Facial Vein.
5. Occipital Vein and Branches.
6. Occipital Artery.
7. Posterior Auricular Artery and Vein.
8. Point where the External Jugular is formed
by the union of the Temporal and Internal
Maxillary Veins.
9. Temporal Artery and Parietal Vein.
10. Frontal Branches of the same: on the
top of the Head are seen the Anastomoses
of these Vessels with the Occipital.
11. Internal Jugular Vein.
12. Superior Thyroid Artery and Vein.
13. Lingual Artery and Vein.
14. Facial Artery.
15. Point of its Anastomosis with the Nasal
Branch of the Ophthalmic.
16. Facial Vein separated from the Artery, except at its Origin and Termination.
17. Inferior Coronary Artery and Vein.
18. Superior Coronary Artery and Vein.
19. Ascending Nasal Vein.
20. Nasal Branches of the Ophthalmic Artery
and Vein.
21,22. Frontal Vein.

FIG. 484.   FIG 483.   FIG. 485.

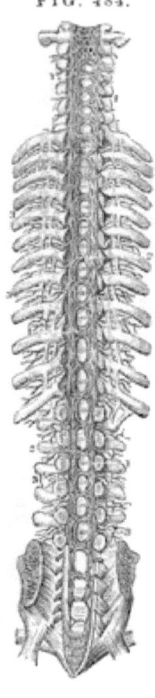 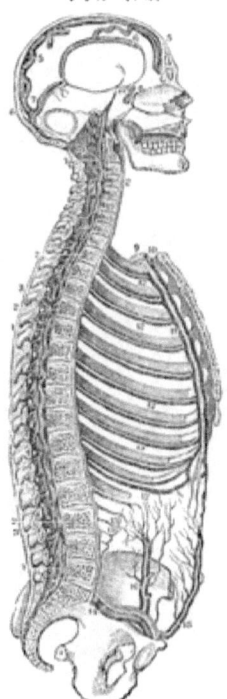 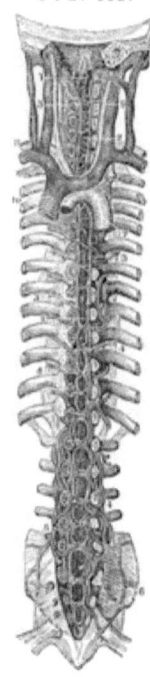

THE VERTEBRAL SINUSES.

FIG. 483.

A LONGITUDINAL SECTION OF THE SKULL AND SPINAL COLUMN TO SHOW THEIR SINUSES.

1.1.1. The Vertebral Sinus in its whole length.
2.2. Venous Trunks from the Bodies of the Vertebræ, opening into the Vertebral Sinus.
3.3. Foramen for the Vessels which connect the Internal and External Veins of the Spine.
4. Anastomosis of the Petrous and Transverse Sinuses with the Vertebral.
5. Superior Longitudinal Sinus of the Cerebrum.
6. Inferior Longitudinal Sinus.
7. Sinus Quartus, or Rectus.
8. Torcular Herophili.
9. Sub-Clavian Artery.
10. Sub-Clavian Vein.
11. Internal Mammary Artery between its two Veins.
12. Inter-Costal Veins.
13. Lumbar Veins.
14. External Iliac Artery and Vein.
15. Epigastric Artery and Vein.
16. Circumflex Iliac Artery and Vein.

FIG. 484.

THE VERTEBRAL SINUSES SEEN IN THE WHOLE LENGTH OF THE SPINAL CANAL, BY CUTTING OFF THE SPINOUS PROCESSES OF THE VERTEBRÆ.

1.1. A succession of Sinuses, commencing inferiorly in the Sacral Canal.
2.2. Circles formed throughout the Canal by the Veins which come out of the Vertebræ.
3.3. Venous Branches which form the communication of the Internal and External Veins of the Spinal Column by the Posterior Foramina of the Sacrum, or by openings between adjacent Vertebræ.

FIG. 485.

AN ANTERIOR VIEW OF THE VERTEBRAL SINUSES, AS SHOWN BY A SECTION OF THE SPINAL COLUMN, AND THE REMOVAL OF THE BODIES OF THE VERTEBRÆ, AND ALSO OF THE SPINAL MARROW.

1.1. The Veins on the Posterior portions of the Vertebræ.
2. The Transverse Veins of each individual Vertebra running to empty into
3.3. The Main Trunks or Sinuses.
4.4.5. The Openings of the Veins from the Foramina on the Posterior Faces of the Vertebræ and the Plexuses of each Vertebra.
6. The Sacral Veins.
7. The Aorta.
8. The Sub-Clavian Artery and Vein.
9. The Carotid Artery.
10. The Descending Vena Cava.

FIG. 486.

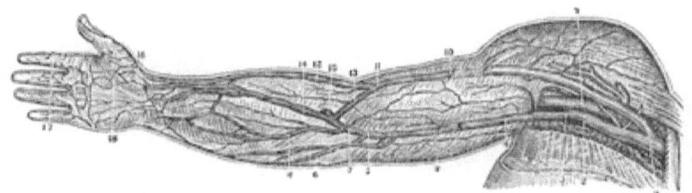

FIG. 487.

FIG. 488.

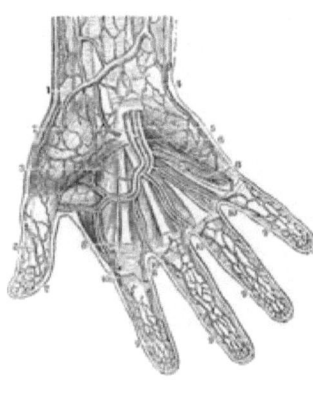

THE VEINS OF THE UPPER EXTREMITY.

FIG. 486.

THE SUPERFICIAL VEINS ON THE FRONT OF THE UPPER EXTREMITY.

1. Axillary Artery.
2. Axillary Vein.
3. Basilic Vein where it enters the Axillary.
4.4. Portion of the Basilic Vein which passes under the Brachial Fascia—a portion of the Vein is freed from the Fascia.
5. Point where the Median Basilic joins the Basilic Vein.
6. Points to the Posterior Basilic Vein.
8. Anterior Basilic Vein.
9. Point where the Cephalic enters the Axillary Vein.
10. A portion of the same Vein as seen under the Fascia; the rest is freed from it.
11. Point where the Median Cephalic enters the Cephalic Vein.
12. Lower Portion of the Cephalic Vein.
13. Median Cephalic Vein.
14. Median Vein.
15. Anastomosing Branch of the Deep and Superficial Veins of the Arm.
16. Cephalica-Pollicis Vein.
17. Sub-Cutaneous Veins of the Fingers.
18. Sub-Cutaneous Palmar Veins.

FIG. 487.

THE VEINS OF THE FORE-ARM AND BEND OF THE ELBOW.

1. Lower part of Cephalic Vein.
2. Upper part of Cephalic Vein.
3. Anterior Basilic Vein.
4. Posterior Basilic Vein.
5. The Trunk formed by their union.
6. The Basilic Vein piercing the deep Fascia at 7.
8. The Median Vein.
9. A communicating Branch between the deep Veins of the Fore-Arm and the upper part of the Median Vein.
10. The Median Cephalic Vein.
11. The Median Basilic.
12. A slight convexity of the deep Fascia, formed by the Brachial Artery.
13. The process of Fascia derived from the Tendon of the Biceps, and separating the Median Basilic Vein from the Brachial Artery.
14. The External Cutaneous Nerve piercing the deep Fascia.
15. The Internal Cutaneous Nerve dividing into Branches which pass in front of the Median-Basilic Vein.
16. The Musculo-Cutaneous Nerve.
17. The Spiral Cutaneous Nerve, a Branch of the Musculo-Spiral.

FIG. 488.

THE SUPERFICIAL ARCH AND VEINS OF THE HAND.

1. Cephalic Vein of the Thumb.
2. The Anastomosis of Veins, whence it comes.
3. A Branch of the Anastomosis of the Roots of the Cephalic Vein with those of the Hand.
4. Superficial Veins from the Palmar Aponeurosis.
5. Ulnar Artery, with its Venæ Satellites.
6.7. Its Venæ Satellites in the Superficial Arch.
8. Digital Branches both of Arteries and Veins to the Fingers.
9. Superficial Veins forming a net-work on the Fingers.
10.11. Main Digital Vessels formed by their junction.

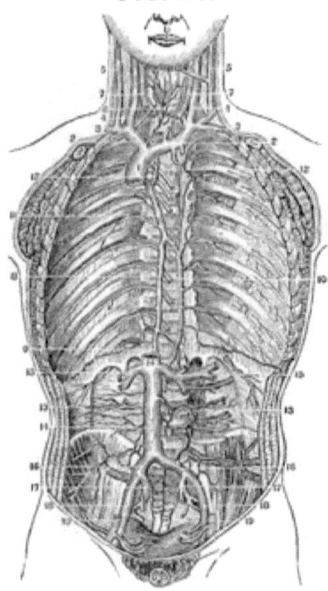 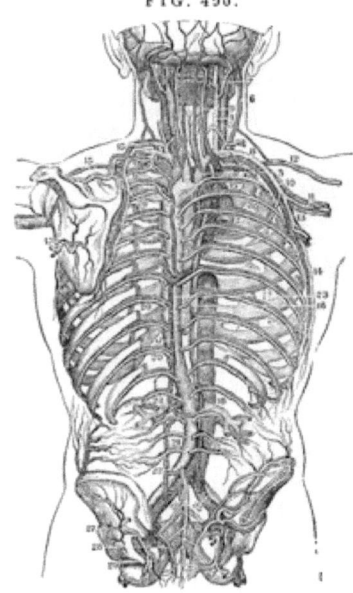

THE VEINS OF THE TRUNK.

FIG. 489.

AN ANTERIOR VIEW OF THE GREAT VEINS OF THE TRUNK.

1. Descending or Superior Vena Cava.
2. Right and Left Brachio-Cephalic Veins.
3. Sub-Clavian Veins.
4. Internal Jugular Veins.
5. External Jugular Veins.
6. Inferior Thyroid Vein.
7. Primitive Carotid Arteries, cut off below.
8. Vena Azygos receiving the ten Intercostal Veins.
9. Anastomosis of the Vena Azygos with the Ascending Vena Cava.
10. Vena Hemi-Azygos.
11. Trunk of the Vena Azygos after the junction of the Vena Hemi-Azygos; above this it empties into the Descending Vena Cava.
12. Superior Inter-Costal Veins emptying into the Vena Azygos and the Brachio-Cephalic Vein.
13. Lumbar Arteries and Veins.
14. Ascending Vena Cava.
15. Emulgent Veins.
16. Primitive Iliac Veins.
17. Internal Iliac Veins.
18. External Iliac Veins.
19. External Iliac Arteries cut off.

FIG. 490.

A POSTERIOR VIEW OF THE ARTERIES AND VEINS OF THE TRUNK, SHOWING THEIR RELATIVE POSITIONS.

1. The Aorta, cut off at its origin in the Heart.
2. The Descending Vena Cava, cut off at the Heart.
3. Arteria Innominata. The Right Brachio-Cephalic Vein is seen near it.
4. Right Primitive Carotid.
5. Right Internal Jugular Vein.
6. Right External Jugular Vein.
7. Occipital Artery and Vein.
8. Sub-Clavian Artery and Vein.
9. Vertebral Artery and Vein.
10. Axillary Artery and Vein.
11. Humeral Artery and Vein.
12. Cephalic Vein of the Arm.
13. Sub-Scapular Artery and Vein.
14. External Mammary Artery and Vein.
15. Scapular Artery and Vein.
16. Great Vena Azygos.
17. Smaller Vena Azygos, or Hemi-Azygos.
18. Opening or Origin of the Vena Azygos in the Ascending Vena Cava.
19. Point where the Vena Azygos enters the Descending Vena Cava.
20.20. Inter-Costal Arteries and Veins.
21. Lumbar Arteries and Veins.
22. Anastomosing Branch of the Lumbar Vena Azygos and the Primitive Iliac Veins.
23. Lower portion of the Thoracic Aorta.
24. Emulgent Artery and Vein.
25. Primitive Iliac Artery and Vein.
26. Middle Sacral Artery and Vein.
27. Gluteal Artery and Vein.
28. Lateral Sacral Artery and Vein.
29. Internal Pudic Artery and Vein.

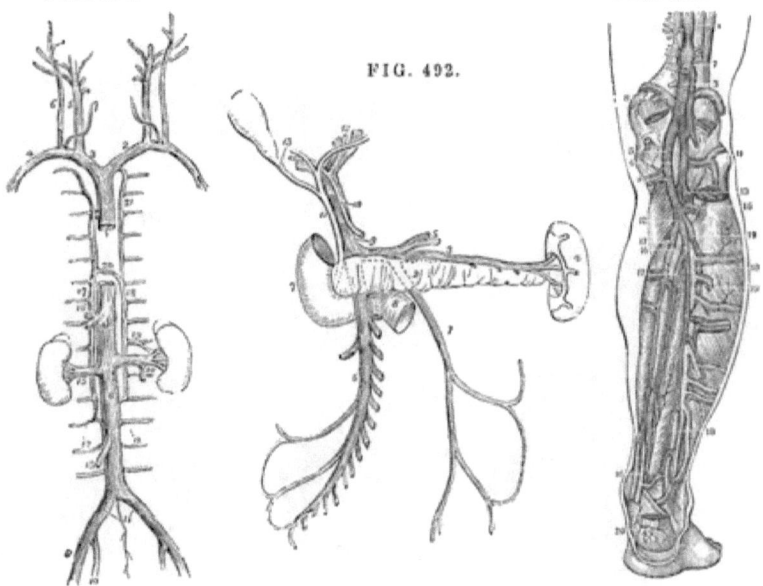

FIG. 491.   FIG. 492.   FIG. 493.

VENÆ CAVÆ AND VEINS OF THE LEG.

FIG. 491.

A VIEW OF THE VEINS OF THE TRUNK AND NECK.

1. The Descending Vena Cava.
2. The Left Vena Innominata.
3. The Right Vena Innominata.
4. The Right Sub-Clavian Vein.
5. The Internal Jugular Vein.
6. The External Jugular.
7. The Anterior Jugular.
8. The Inferior Vena Cava.
9. The External Iliac Vein.
10. The Internal Iliac Vein.
11. The Primitive Iliac Veins.
12.12. Lumbar Veins.
13. The Right Spermatic Vein.
14. The Left Spermatic Vein.
15. The Right Emulgent Vein.
16. The Trunk of the Hepatic Veins.
17. The Vena Azygos.
18. The Hemi-Azygos.
19. A branch communicating with the Left Renal Vein.
20. The Termination of the Hemi-Azygos in the Vena Azygos.
21. The Superior Inter-Costal Vein.

FIG. 492.

AN ENLARGED VIEW OF THE VENA PORTARUM.

1. The Inferior Mesenteric Vein.
2. The Pancreas.
3. The Splenic Vein.
4. The Spleen.
5. The Gastric Veins, opening into the Splenic Vein.
6. The Superior Mesenteric Vein.

7. The Descending Portion of the Duodenum.
8. Its Transverse Portion.
9. The Vena Portarum.
10. The Hepatic Artery.
11. The Ductus Communis Choledochus.
12. The Divisions of the Duct and Vessels at the Transverse Fissure of the Liver.
13. The Cystic Duct.

FIG. 493.

THE ARTERIES AND DEEP-SEATED VEINS ON THE BACK OF THE LEG.

1. Popliteal Vein.
2. Popliteal Artery.
3.4. Vein and Artery in their relative Position on the Back of the Knee-Joint.
5. Popliteal Vein on the inner side of the joint.
6. Popliteal Artery without and beneath it.
7. Extremity of Saphena Minor Vein.
8.9. Internal Articular Vessels, both Arteries and Veins.
10.11. External Articular Vessels, both Arteries and Veins.
12. Junction of the Peroneal and Posterior Tibial Veins.
13. A Venous Branch from the Anterior Tibial Vein.
14. A Vein from the Gastrocnemius.
15. Anterior Tibial Artery coming through the Interosseous Ligament.
16. Posterior Tibial Artery.
17. Its two Venæ Comites.
18. Peroneal Artery.
19. Its two Venæ Comites.
20. Vessels on the Heel.

FIG. 494.

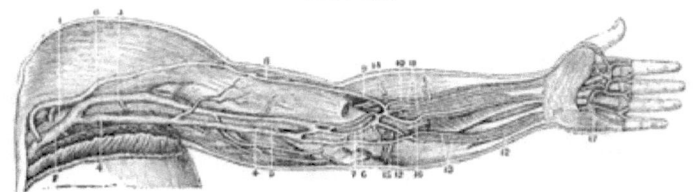

FIG. 496. FIG. 495. FIG. 497.

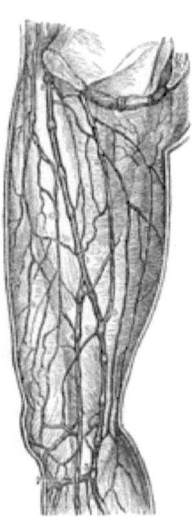

VEINS OF THE EXTREMITIES.

FIG. 494.

THE DEEP-SEATED VEINS ON THE FRONT OF THE UPPER EXTREMITY IN THEIR RELATIONS TO THE ARTERIES.

1. Axillary Artery.
2. Axillary Vein.
3. Humeral Vein.
4. Basilic Vein.
5. Brachial Artery.
6. The same Artery at the bend of the Arm.
7. Median Basilic Vein.
8.8. Cephalic Vein.
9. Median Cephalic Vein.
10. Radial Artery.
11. Its two Venæ Satellites.
12.12. Ulnar Artery.
13. Its two Venæ Satellites.
14. Recurrens Radialis Artery and Vein.
15. Recurrens Ulnaris Artery and Vein.
16. Interosseal Arteries and Veins.
17. Palmar Arch and Digital Vessels, of which there is an enlarged View in Fig. 488.

FIG. 495.

A VIEW OF THE SUPERFICIAL VEINS OF THE THIGH, AS SEEN ON ITS INNER SIDE.

1. Great Saphena Vein.
2. Point where it traverses the Fascia to enter the Femoral Vein.
3. Lower Femoral portion of the Saphena; in its whole course it is on the inner edge of the Sartorius Muscle.
4. A Collateral Branch of the Saphena.
5.6. Anastomosing Branches.
7. An Anastomosis which receives the Veins of the Leg just below the Knee.

FIG. 496.

THE SUPERFICIAL VEINS ON THE INNER SIDE OF THE LEGS.

1. The Saphena Major at the inside of the Knee.
2. A Collateral Branch of the Saphena Major on the Leg.
3. The Anastomosis of the Veins just below the Knee.

4. Internal Saphena at the Middle of the Calf of the Leg.
5. Origin of the Saphena Vein at the Ankle-Joint.
6. Anastomosing Branch of the Saphena Major and Minor.
7. Branches on the back of the Leg.
8. The Great Internal Vein of the Foot.
9. The Arch of Veins on the Meta-Tarsal Bones.
10. A Branch from the Heel.
11. Branches on the Sole of the Foot.

FIG. 497.

THE SUPERFICIAL VEINS OF THE FRONT OF THE LEG.

1. Saphena Major above the Leg.
2. The same Vein on the inner Side of the Leg.
3. A Transverse Branch below the Knee which receives all the Venous Branches from the Front of the Leg.
4. A Branch which Anastomoses with the Deep-seated Veins.
5. The Great Vein on the inner Side of the Foot.
6. The Arch formed by the Veins from the Meta-Tarsus.

FIG. 498.

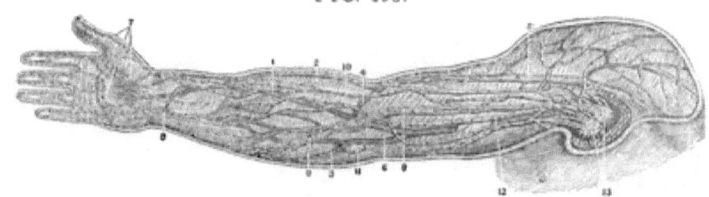

FIG. 499.

FIG. 500.

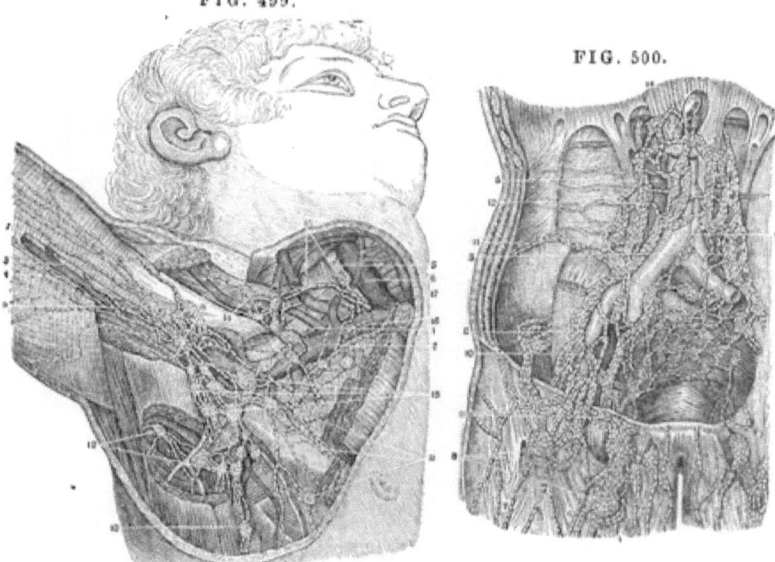

THE LYMPHATICS.

FIG. 498.

THE SUPERFICIAL LYMPHATIC VESSELS OF THE UPPER EXTREMITY.

1. Median Vein.
2. Cephalic Vein.
3. Posterior Basilic Vein.
4. Median Cephalic.
5. Cephalic Vein high up the Arm.
6. Median Basilic Vein.
7. Superficial Lymphatics of the Hand.
8. Lymphatic Trunks from the inside of the Hand.
9.9. Principal Fasciculus of Lymphatics from the Front and Back of the Fore-Arm.
10. A Branch from the Superficial to the Deep Lymphatics of the Fore-Arm.
11. An accidental Lymphatic Gland.
12. Superficial Lymphatics which dip down with the Basilic Vein.
13. The Lymphatic Glands of the Axilla, which receive the Lymphatic Vessels of the Arm.

FIG. 499.

A VIEW OF THE VESSELS AND LYMPHATIC GLANDS OF THE AXILLA.

1. The Axillary Artery.

2. The Axillary Vein.
3. The Brachial Artery.
4. The Brachial Vein.
5. The Primitive Carotid Artery.
6. The Internal Jugular Vein.
7. The Sub-Cutaneous Lymphatics of the Arm at its Upper Part.
8. Two or three of the most Inferior and Superficial Glands into which the Superficial Lymphatics empty.
9. The Deep-seated Lymphatics which accompany the Brachial Artery.
10. The Lymphatics and Glands which accompany the Infra-Scapular Blood-Vessels.
11. The Glands and Lymphatics accompanying the Thoracica Longa Artery.
12. Deeper-seated Lymphatics.
13. The Axillary Chain of Glands.
14. The Acromial Branches of the Lymphatics.
15. The Jugular Lymphatics and Glands.
16.17. The Lymphatics which empty into the Sub-Clavian Vein near its junction with the Right Internal Jugular Vein.

FIG. 500.

A FRONT VIEW OF THE FEMORAL ILIAC AND AORTIC LYMPHATIC VESSELS AND GLANDS.

1. Saphena Magna Vein.
2. External Iliac Artery and Vein.
3. Primitive Iliac Artery and Vein.
4. The Aorta.
5. Ascending Vena Cava.
6.7. Lymphatics which are alongside of the Saphena Vein on the Thigh.
8. Lower Set of Inguinal Lymphatic Glands which receive these Vessels.
9. Superior Set of Inguinal Lymphatic Glands which receive these Vessels.
10. The Chain of Lymphatics in Front of the External Iliac Vessels.
11. Lymphatics which accompany the Circumflex Iliac Vessels.
12. Lumbar and Aortic Lymphatics.
13. Afferent Trunks of the Lumbar Glands, forming the Origin of the Thoracic Duct.
14. Thoracic Duct at its commencement.

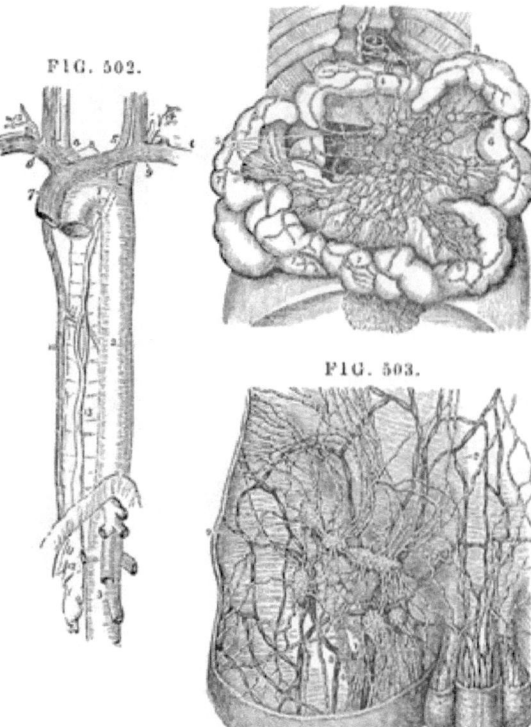

FIG. 501.

FIG. 502.

FIG. 504.

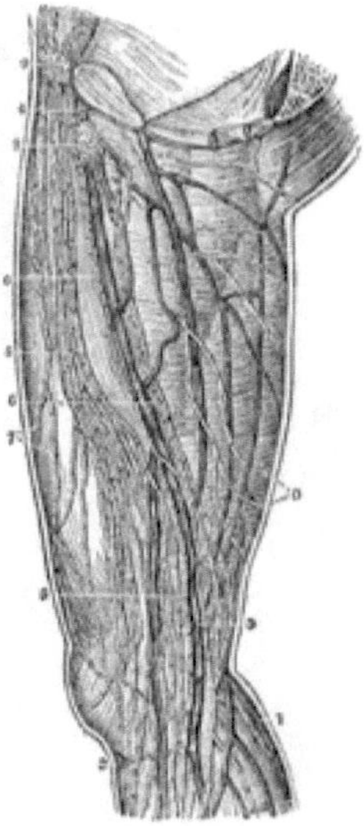

FIG. 503.

THE LYMPHATICS.

FIG. 501.

A VIEW OF THE LYMPHATICS OF THE SMALL INTESTINES OF A MAN DEAD FROM ASCITES.

1. Thoracic Duct.
2. Section of the Aorta.
3. Glands around the Aorta which receive the Lymphatics from the Intestine and give off Vessels to the Thoracic Duct.
4. Superficial Lymphatics on the Intestine.
5.5. More Lymphatic Glands receiving Vessels from the Intestine.
6.7. Lymphatics of the Intestine and Mesentery.

FIG. 502.

A VIEW OF THE COURSE AND TERMINATION OF THE THORACIC DUCT.

1. Arch of the Aorta.
2. Thoracic Aorta.
3. Abdominal Aorta.
4. Arteria Innominata.
5. Left Carotid.
6. Left Sub-Clavian.
7. Superior Cava.
8. The two Venæ Innominatæ.
9. The Internal Jugular and Sub-Clavian Vein at each side.
10. The Vena Azygos.
11. The Termination of the Vena Hemi-Azygos in the Vena Azygos.
12. The Receptaculum Chyli: several Lymphatic Trunks are seen opening into it.
13. The Thoracic Duct dividing, opposite the Middle Dorsal Vertebra, into two branches, which soon re-unite ; the course of the Duct behind the Arch of the Aorta and Left Sub-Clavian Artery is shown by a Dotted Line.
14. The Duct making its turn at the Root of the Neck and receiving several Lymphatic Trunks previous to terminating in the Posterior Angle of the Junction of the Internal Jugular and Sub-Clavian Veins.
15. The Termination of the Trunk of the Lymphatics of the Upper Extremity.

FIG. 503.

THE LYMPHATIC VESSELS AND GLANDS OF THE GROIN OF THE RIGHT SIDE.

1. Saphena Magna Vein.
2. Veins on the Surface of the Abdomen.
3. External Pudic Vein.
4. The Lymphatic Vessels collected in Fasciculi and accompanying the Saphena Vein on its inner side.
5. The External Trunks of the same set of Vessels.
6. The Lymphatic Gland which receives all these Vessels. It is placed on the Termination of the Saphena Vein.
7. The Efferent Trunks from this Gland ; they become Deep-seated and accompany the Femoral Artery.
8. One of the more External Lymphatic Glands of the Groin.
9. A Chain of four or five Inguinal Glands, which receive the Lymphatics from the Genitals, Abdomen, and External Portion of the Thigh.

FIG. 504.

A VIEW OF THE SUPERFICIAL LYMPHATICS OF THE THIGH.

1. The External or Saphena Minor Vein.
2. The Venous Anastomosis below the Patella.
3. Femoral Portion of the Saphena Major.
4. Point where it enters the Femoral Vein.
5. The Great Chain of Superficial Lymphatics on the inner side of the Thigh.
6.6. A Chain of three or four Parallel Trunks, which accompany the Saphena-Major Vein.
7. Branches from the Front of the Thigh.
8. Branches from the Posterior Part.
9.9. The Inguinal Glands into which the Superficial Lymphatics of the Lower Extremity enter.

FIG. 505.

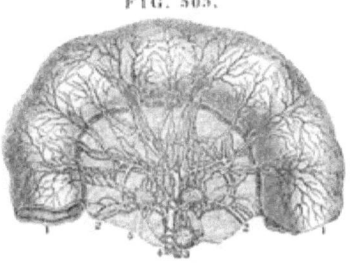

FIG. 506. 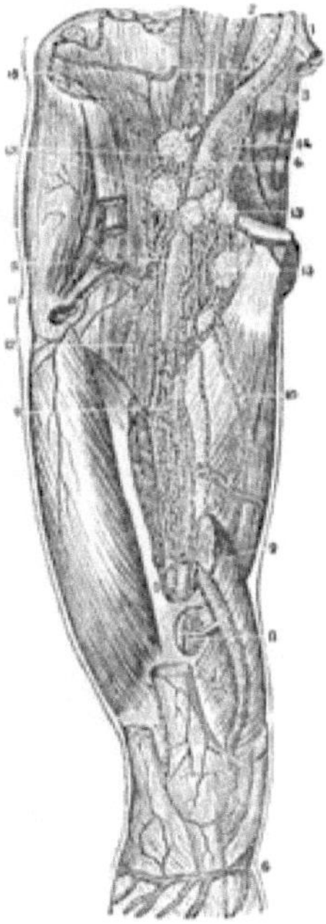   FIG. 508. 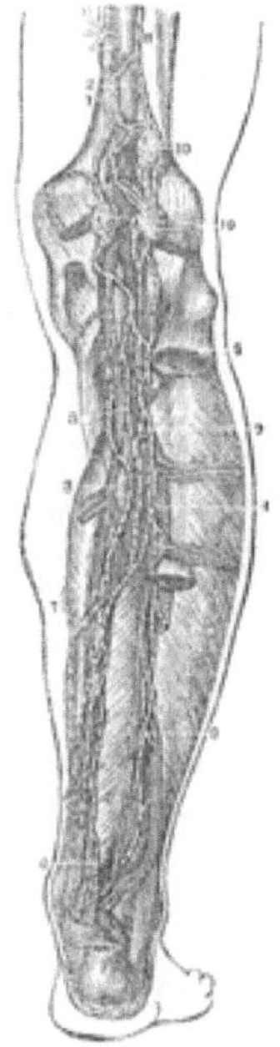   FIG. 507.

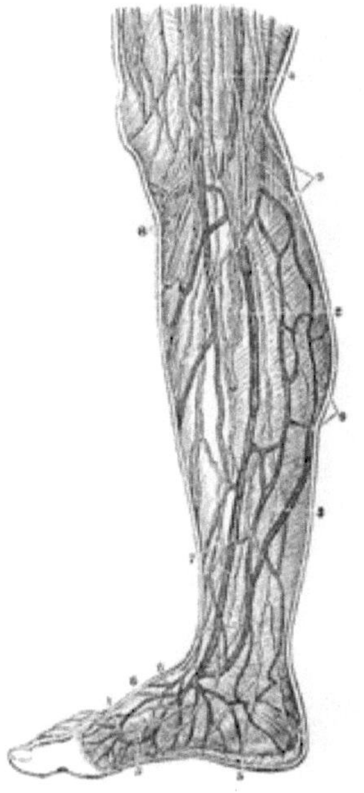

THE LYMPHATICS.

FIG. 505.

A VIEW OF THE LYMPHATICS OF THE JEJUNUM AND MESENTERY, INJECTED: THE ARTERIES ARE ALSO INJECTED.

1. Section of the Jejunum.
2. Section of the Mesentery.
3. Branch of the Superior Mesenteric Artery.
4. Branch of the Superior Mesenteric Vein.
5. Mesenteric Glands receiving the Lymphatics of this Intestine.

FIG. 506.

A FRONT VIEW OF THE DEEP-SEATED LYMPHATICS OF THE THIGH.

1. Lower End of the Aorta.
2. Primitive Iliac Vein.
3,4. External Iliac Artery and Vein.
5. Femoral Artery.
6. Section of the Femoral Vein.
7. Vena Saphena on the Leg.
8. Lymphatics near the Knee.
9. Lymphatics accompanying the Femoral Vessels.
10. Deep Lymphatics going from the inside of the Thigh to the Glands in the Groin.

11. Lymphatics of the External Circumflex Vessels.
12. Lymphatics on the outer side of the Femoral Vessels.
13. A Lymphatic Gland always found outside of the Vessels.
14. A collection of Vessels and Glands from the Internal Iliac Vessels.
15. The Lymphatics of the Primitive Iliac Vessels.

FIG. 507.

THE SUPERFICIAL LYMPHATICS OF THE INNER SIDE OF THE FOOT AND LEG.

1. The Venous Anastomosis on the Phalangial Ends of the Meta-Tarsal Bones.
2. The Saphena Magna Vein.
3. Lymphatics on the back of the Leg.
4. The same Vessels on the lower part of the Thigh.
5,5. Lymphatics coming from the Sole of the Foot.
6,6. Lymphatics from the Dorsal Surface of the Foot.
7. The Lymphatics which accompany the Saphena Vein.

8. Branches of Lymphatics from the Front and Outside of the Leg.
9. Branches from the Posterior and Internal side of the Calf of the Leg.

FIG. 508.

THE DEEP-SEATED LYMPHATIC VESSELS AND GLANDS ON THE BACK OF THE LEG.

1. Popliteal Artery.
2. Popliteal Vein.
3. Posterior Tibial Vessels: the Artery is between its two Veins.
4. Peroneal Artery and Veins.
5. Lymphatic Vessels from the Front of the Leg, coming through the Opening in the Interosseous Ligament.
5. Deep-seated Lymphatic Vessels which arise in the Sole of the Foot and accompany the Blood-Vessels.
7. Anastomosis of the Superficial and Deep-seated Lymphatics.
8,9. Uniting Branches of Posterior Tibial Lymphatics.
10,10. Popliteal Ganglions which receive the Deep Lymphatics of the Leg and Foot.
11,11. Efferent Popliteal Trunks which accompany the Blood-Vessels to the Femoral Ganglions.

PART FIFTH.

THE NERVOUS SYSTEM

AND

THE SENSES:

ONE HUNDRED AND TWENTY-SIX FIGURES.

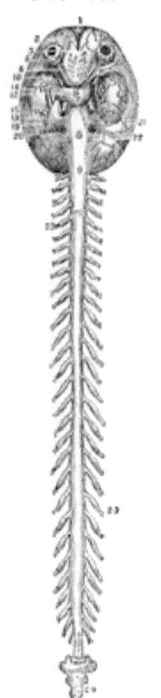 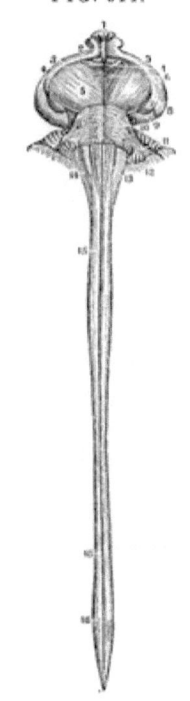 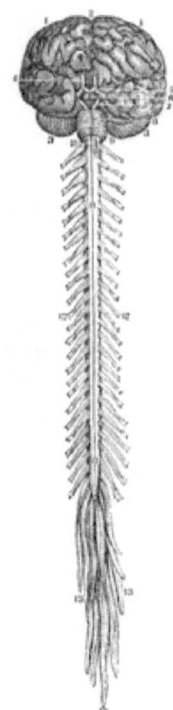

THE MEDULLA SPINALIS.

FIG. 509.

AN ANTERIOR VIEW OF THE EXTERNAL SURFACE OF THE DURA MATER OF THE SPINAL MARROW AND BRAIN.

1. The portion of the Dura Mater Cerebri which is attached to the Crista Galli.
2. The part covering the Anterior Fossæ of the Cranium.
3. A series of little Canals that it furnishes to the Olfactory Nerves.
4. The Fibrous Sheath of the Optic Nerves.
5. The Eye-Ball.
6. The Dura-Mater at the Superior Face of the Sphenoid Bone.
7. The same at the Sella Turcica.
8. The portion which covers the Basilar Gutter.
9. The part which passes through the Foramen Magnum to be continued on to that of the Medulla Spinalis.
10. The Dura Mater at the Foramen Lacerum of the Sphenoid Bone.
11. The 3d, 4th and 6th Pairs of Nerves, piercing the Dura Mater to pass out of the Foramen Sphenoidale.
12. The Dura Mater below the Cavernous Sinus.
13. The Carotid Artery.
14. The Dura Mater at the Temporal Fossa.
15. That on the sides of the Cranium.
16.17.18. Three Branches of the 5th Pair of Nerves piercing the Dura Mater.
19. The Facial and Auditory Nerves passing through their Canal.
20. Enlargement for the Internal Jugular Vein.
21. Glosso-Pharyngeal Nerve.
22. Pneumo-Gastric Nerve piercing the Dura Mater in front of the Enlargement for the Jugular Vein.
23.23. The Fibrous Sheaths furnished to the Spinal Nerves by the Dura Mater of the Medulla Spinalis.
24. The Bones of the Coccyx with the Processes of the Dura Mater inserted into them.
25. The Anterior Face of the Dura Mater of the Medulla Spinalis.

FIG. 510.

AN ANTERIOR VIEW OF THE BRAIN AND SPINAL MARROW, AS EXTRACTED FROM THEIR OSSEOUS CAVITIES.

1.1. The Hemispheres of the Cerebrum.
2. The Great Middle Fissure.
3. The Cerebellum.
4. The Olfactory Nerves.
5. The Optic Nerves.
6. The Corpora Albicantia.
7. The Motor Oculi Nerves.
8. The Pons Varolii.
9. The Fourth Pair of Nerves.
10. The lower portion of the Medulla Oblongata.
11.11. The Medulla Spinalis in its whole length.
12.12. The Spinal Nerves.
13. The Cauda Equina.

FIG. 511.

AN ANTERIOR VIEW OF THE SPINAL MARROW, MEDULLA OBLONGATA, &c., OF A NEW-BORN INFANT.

1. The Pituitary Gland.
2. The Infundibulum.
3. The Optic Nerves.
4. The Corpora Albicantia.
5. Crura Cerebri.
6. The triangular space between the Crura.
7. Corpus Geniculatum Internum.
8. Corpus Geniculatum Externum.
9. Posterior portion of the Thalami Nervi Optici.
10. Pons Varolii.
11. Its Prolongation into the Crus Cerebelli.
12. Eminentia Olivaria.
13. Corpora Pyramidalia.
14. Corpus Restiforme.
15. Anterior Middle Fissure of the Spinal Marrow.
16. Enlargement for the Origin of the Lumbar Nerves.

FIG. 512.

FIG. 514.

FIG. 513.

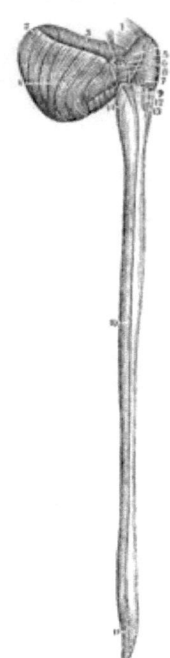

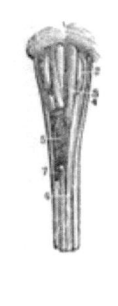

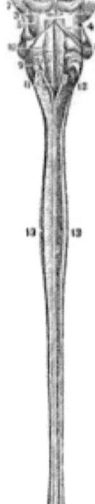

FIG. 515.

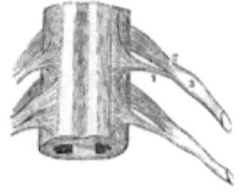

THE MEDULLA SPINALIS.

FIG. 512.

A LATERAL VIEW OF THE SPINAL MARROW, &c., OF A NEW-BORN INFANT, TO SHOW THE LATERAL FASCICULUS, WHICH IS THEN MORE APPARENT.

1. Crura Cerebri.
2.3.4. One of the Hemispheres of the Cerebellum.
5. External Fasciculus of the Crus Cerebelli.
6. Lobulus Amygdaloides and Nervi Pneumogastrici.
7. Point where the Lateral Column of the Spinal Marrow enters the Cerebellum.
8. Pons Varolii.
9.10.11. Continuation of 7, or of the Lateral Fasciculus all the way down the Spinal Marrow. In the new-born Infant it is very nearly white, whilst the matter around is of a light grey.
12. Eminentia Olivaria.
13. Corpora Pyramidalia.
14. Corpus Restiforme.

FIG. 513.

A POSTERIOR VIEW OF THE MEDULLA SPINALIS, WITH THE FASCICULI OF THE CORPORA RESTIFORMIA CUT OFF FROM EACH SIDE OF THE CALAMUS SCRIPTORIUS.

From the top of this section as far as the Lumbar portion of the Medulla Spinalis these posterior Fasciculi have been dissected out down to the Axis of the Medulla.

1. The Pineal Gland.
2. The Tubercula Quadrigemina.
3. Origin of the 4th Pair of Nerves.
4. The Valve of the Vieussens turned up a little.
5. Posterior portion of the Crus Cerebri.
6. Section of the Crus Cerebelli.
7. Anterior portion of the Crus Cerebri.
8. Section of the Corpus Restiforme on one side.
9. The Corpus Restiforme untouched on the other side.
10. A prominent Lateral Fasciculus on the Floor of the Calamus Scriptorius.
11. Point of the Calamus. From its Point to the End of the Medulla Spinalis are seen the junctions of the Fasciculi of each side, which make the Axis of the Medulla Spinalis.
12. The Lateral Fasciculus.
13. The enlargement for the Axillary Nerves.
14. The enlargement for the Lumbar Nerves.

FIG. 514.

AN ANTERIOR VIEW OF THE MEDULLA OBLONGATA AND OF THE TERMINATION OF THE DECUSSATION OF MITISCHELLI.

1. The Pons Varolii.
2. The Eminentia Olivaria.
3. The Corpus Pyramidale.
4. The Corpus Restiforme.
5. The Decussation of Mitischelli.
6. The Anterior Columns of the Spinal Marrow.
7. The Lateral Columns.

FIG. 515.

A VIEW OF A SMALL PORTION OF THE SPINAL MARROW, SHOWING THE ORIGINS OF SOME OF THE SPINAL NERVES.

1. The Anterior or Motor Root of a Spinal Nerve.
2. The Posterior or Sensory Root of a Spinal Nerve.
3. The Ganglion connected with the latter.

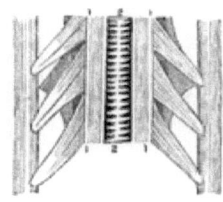

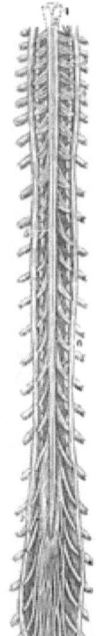

FIG. 519.

FIG. 520.

THE MEDULLA SPINALIS.

FIG. 516.

An Anterior View of the Spinal Marrow, seen in its whole length, after removal from the Spinal Canal.

1. Lines indicating the Corpora Pyramidalia.
2. Eminentia Olivaria.
3. Anterior Face of the Spinal Marrow.
4. Anterior Roots of the Cervical Spinal Nerves.
5. Anterior Roots of the Dorsal Nerves.
6. Anterior Roots of the Lumbar Nerves.
7. Anterior Roots of the Sacral Nerves.
8.9.10.11. The Anterior and Posterior Roots of the Spinal Nerves, united to pass out of the Dura Mater.
12. Dura Mater of the Medulla Spinalis.
13. Ganglia on the Cervical Nerves.
14. Ganglia on the Dorsal Nerves.
15. Ganglia on the Lumbar Nerves.
16. Ganglia on the Sacral Nerves.
17. Cauda Equina.
18. Sub-Occipital Nerve.
19. Ligamentum Denticulatum.

FIG. 517.

A Posterior View of the same Spinal Marrow.

1. Inferior Extremity of the Medulla Oblongata.
2. The Calamus Scriptorius.
3. The Posterior Face of the Spinal Marrow, with the Middle Fissure.
4.5.6.7. The Posterior Roots of the Cervical, Dorsal, Lumbar and Sacral Nerves. The other parts of this cut are the same as in Fig. 516.

FIG. 518.

A View of the Cervical Nerves of a Child of four Years of age, showing the Anterior Fissure laid open and the Suture-like appearance of the Anterior Commissure.

1. The Sides of the Anterior Middle Fissure.
2. The union of the two Halves, or the Anterior Commissure of the Spinal Marrow.

FIG. 519.

A View of the Posterior Commissure of the same Subject.

1. The Sides or Borders of the Posterior Fissure.
2. The union of the two Sides at the bottom of the Fissure, or the Posterior Commissure. This is seen to be formed by Longitudinal Fibres, whilst the Anterior is by Transverse.

FIG. 520.

A Transverse Section of the Spinal Marrow.

1.1. The two Halves of the Spinal Marrow.
2. The Anterior Middle Fissure.
3. The Posterior Middle Fissure.
4. The position of the Cineritous Matter to each Half of the Spinal Marrow.
5. The Origin of one of the Anterior Roots of a Spinal Nerve.
6. The Origin of one of the Posterior Roots.

FIG. 522.

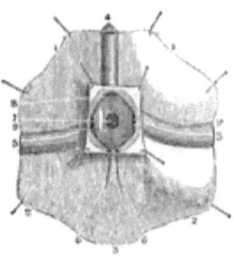

FIG. 521.

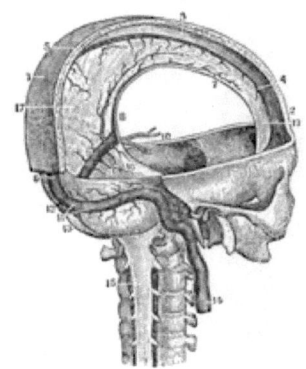

FIG. 523.

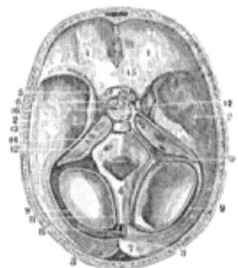

FIG. 524.

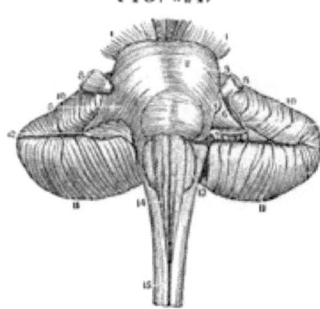

THE CEREBRAL SINUSES AND MEDULLA OBLONGATA.

FIG. 521.

A VIEW OF THE DURA MATER OF THE CRANIUM AND PART OF THE SPI- NAL CANAL, WITH THEIR SINUSES.

1.2.3. A Section of the Bones com- posing the Vault of the Cranium, showing the arched attachment of the Falx Major.
4. Anterior portion of the Superior Longitudinal Sinus.
5. Its Middle Portion.
6. Its Inferior Portion; the outer table of the Cranium is removed.
7. Commencement of the Inferior Longitudinal Sinus.
8. Its Termination in the Straight Sinus.
9. The Sinus Quartus or Rectus.
10. The Venæ Galeni.
11. One of the Lateral Sinuses.
12. The Torcular Herophili.
13. The Sinus of the Falx Cerebelli.
14. The Internal Jugular Vein.
15. The Dura Mater of the Spinal Marrow.
16. The Tentorium Cerebelli.
17.17. The Falx Cerebri.

FIG. 522.

THE JUNCTION OF THE SINUSES OF THE DURA MATER, SEEN FROM BE- HIND AND LAID OPEN.

1.1. A portion of the Dura Mater of the Superior Occipital Fossa.
2.2. Portion of the Dura Mater of the Inferior Occipital Fossa.
3. The Dura Mater from the Fo- ramen Magnum.

4. Posterior Extremity of the Su- perior Longitudinal Sinus.
5. Portions of the Lateral Sinuses.
6. Outline of the Lower Occipital Sinus.
7. The Torcular Herophili.
8.9. The Openings into the Torcu- lar Herophili.

FIG. 523.

A HORIZONTAL SECTION OF THE CRANIUM TO SHOW THE SINUSES AT ITS BASE: THOSE ON THE RIGHT SIDE ARE INJECTED, THOSE ON THE LEFT ARE EMPTY.

1. The Fossæ for the Anterior Lobes of the Brain.
2. The Fossæ for the Middle Lobes.
3. The Fossæ for the Posterior Lobes.
4. The Basilar Gutter lined by the Dura Mater.
5. The Optic Nerves.
6. The Infundibulum.
7. A Section of the Superior Lon- gitudinal Sinus.
8. The Torcular Herophili.
9. The Middle part of the Lateral Sinuses.
10. The same Sinus at the Poste- rior Foramen Lacerum.
11. One of the Occipital Sinuses.
12. The Superior Petrous Sinus.
13. Its Anterior Extremity opening into the Cavernous Sinus.
14. The Inferior Petrous Sinus.
15. The Sella Turcica of the Sphe- noid Bone.

16. The Cavernous Sinus.
17. The Circular Sinus around the Sella Turcica and opening into the Cavernous Sinus.

FIG. 524.

A POSTERIOR SUPERIOR VIEW OF THE PONS VAROLII, THE CERE- BELLUM, AND THE MEDULLÆ OB- LONGATA AND SPINALIS.

1.1. The Crura Cerebri.
2. The Pons Varolii or Tuber Annularis.
3. Its middle Fossa.
4. An Oblique Band of Medullary Matter seen passing from its side.
5. The External Surface of the Crus Cerebelli in its natural state.
6. The same portion deprived of outer layer.
7. The Nervous Matter which united it to 4.
8. The Trigeminus or Fifth Pair of Nerves.
9. Portion of the Auditory Nerve. The white Neurine is seen passing from the Oblique Band which comes from the Corpus Restiforme to the Trigeminus Nerve in front, and the Auditory Nerve behind.
10.11. The Superior portion of the Hemispheres of the Cerebellum.
12. Lobulus Amygdaloides.
13. Corpus Olivare.
14. Corpus Pyramidale.
15. Medulla Spinalis.

FIG. 525.

FIG. 526.

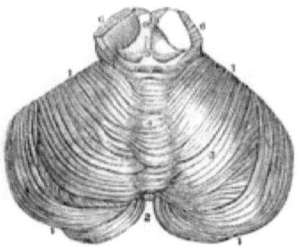

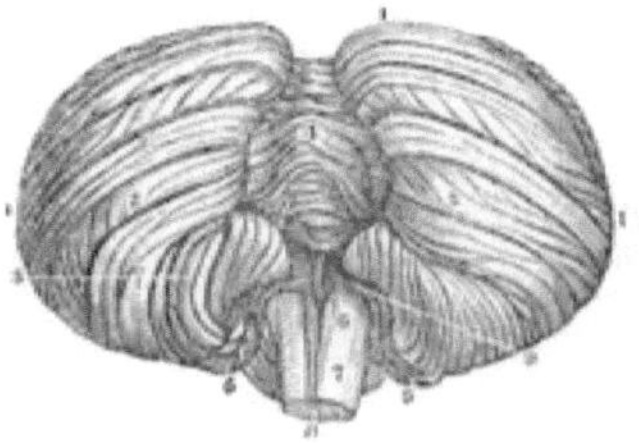

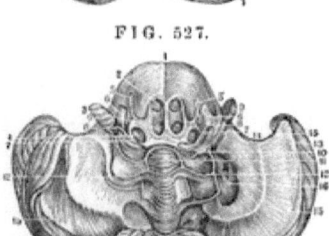

FIG. 527.

FIG. 528.

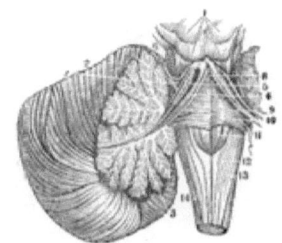

THE CEREBELLUM

FIG. 525.

A VIEW OF THE SUPERIOR FACE OF THE CEREBELLUM.

1.1. The Circumference of the Cerebellum.
2. The Space between its Hemispheres behind.
3. One of the Hemispheres of the Cerebellum, showing the Laminæ which compose it.
4. The Vermis Superior.
5. The Tubercula Quadrigemina.
6. Section of the Crura Cerebri.

FIG. 526.

A VIEW OF THE INFERIOR SURFACE OF THE CEREBELLUM AND A PORTION OF THE MEDULLA OBLONGATA.

1.1. The Circumference of the Cerebellum.
2.2. The two Hemispheres of the Cerebellum.
3. Lobulus Amygdaloides.
4. The Vermis Inferior.
5. Lobulus Nervi Pneumogastrici.
6. The Calamus Scriptorius.
7. Its Point.
8. Section of the Medulla Oblongata.
9. Points to the Origin of the Pneumogastric Nerve.

FIG. 527.

A VIEW OF THE UNDER SIDE OF THE CEREBELLUM. THE PONS VAROLII IS AT THE TOP OF THE CUT, AND THE FASCICULI OF THE SPINAL MARROW WHICH RAN ON TO THE PONS HAVE BEEN CAREFULLY DETACHED.

1. Pons Varolii.

2. Canal for the Corpus Pyramidale.
3. Canal for the Eminentia Olivaria.
4. Canal for the Fasciculi of the Corpus Restiforme.
5. The Seventh Pair of Nerves.
6. The Auditory Nerve.
7. The Roots of these Nerves united to the Floor of the 4th Ventricle.
8. Medullary Layer to unite the Auditory Nerves to the Lobulus Amygdaloides.
9. These Lobules.
10. Medullary Matter by which the Auditory Nerves are connected with the Vermis Inferior.
11. The Vermis Inferior.
12. The Striæ running to the Lobulus Amygdaloides.
13. Posterior Face of the Left Crus Cerebelli.
14. External face of this Crus.
15.15. The Expansion of the Fibres of the Crus Cerebelli.
16. Left Corpus Rhomboideum laid open; on the other side it is untouched.
17. The Fissure between the Hemispheres of the Cerebellum.

FIG. 528.

A VIEW OF THE ARBOR VITÆ AND THE FUNDAMENTAL PORTION OF THE CEREBELLUM, TOGETHER WITH THE FLOOR OF THE FOURTH VENTRICLE.

1. The Tubercula Quadrigemina.
2. The Superior Surface of the Cerebellum.

3. Its Inferior Surface, and also the Arbor Vitæ. In the Trunk of the Arbor Vitæ are seen three Fasciculi running up to the Tubercula Quadrigemina. The most internal of these is
4. A Fibrous Layer in which are collected all the Filaments which pass from the Parietes of the Aqueduct of Sylvius to the Vermis Inferior.
5. Is the Fasciculus outside of the preceding, which runs from the Trunk of the Arbor Vitæ behind the Tubercula Quadrigemina.
6. Is that from which all the Fasciculi of the Vermis Superior pass to the Tubercula Quadrigemina.
7. A very delicate Medullary Layer, which passes from the Anterior Surface of the Crus Cerebelli under the Cineritious Matter of the Cerebrum.
8. The Anterior Extremity of the Fourth Ventricle, drawn back and leading to the Aqueduct of Sylvius.
9. Middle Furrow on the Floor of the Fourth Ventricle.
10. Tracts of Nervous Matter running to the Auditory Nerve.
11. Elevated portion of the same on the Floor of the Fourth Ventricle.
12. Middle Fissure in the Calamus Scriptorius.
13. Corpora Restiformia.
14. Lateral portion of the Spinal Marrow.

FIG. 529.   FIG. 530.

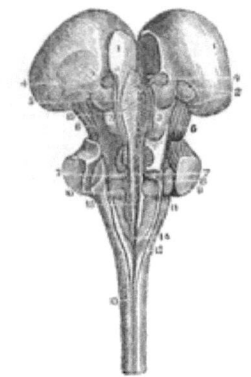
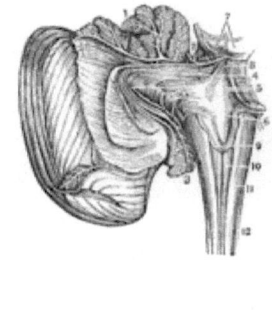

FIG. 531.   FIG. 532.

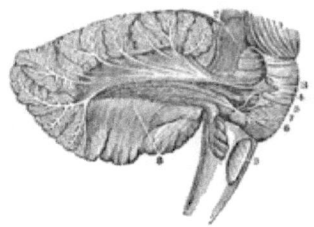
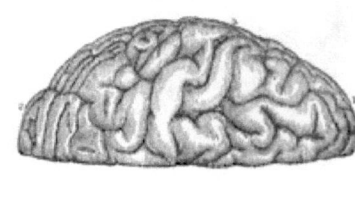

THE MEDULLA OBLONGATA AND CEREBELLUM.

FIG. 529.

A POSTERIOR VIEW OF THE ME-
DULLA OBLONGATA, AS SPLIT
OPEN VERTICALLY ON THE MID-
DLE LINE.

At the bottom of the Fissure is a
succession of Fasciculi which inter-
lock and cross from Right to Left.
The Cerebellum has also been cut
off from its Crura with great care,
so as to show plainly the three principal elements in its composition.

1. The Thalami Nervi Optici slightly separated.
2. The Corpora Geniculata.
3. The Tubercula Quadrigemina.
4. The Pineal Gland divided in the
   middle.
5. The Aqueduct of Sylvius laid
   open.
6. The Fasciculated portion of the
   Crura Cerebelli.
7.8.9. The Internal, Middle and External Fasciculi of the Crura
   Cerebelli.
10. Root of the Auditory Nerve.
11. Corpus Restiforme.
12. Posterior portion of the Corpus
    Pyramidale.
13. Posterior Middle Fissure of the
    Spinal Marrow.
14. Point of the Calamus Scripto-
    rius.
15.15. Between these Figures is seen
    the interlocking of the two
    halves of the Medulla Oblongata.

FIG. 530.

A VIEW OF THE PROLONGATION OF
THE ANTERIOR FASCICULUS OF
THE CRUS CEREBELLI INTO THE
FIBRES OF THE LOBULUS AMYG-
DALOIDES, &c., GIVEN BY A VER-
TICAL SECTION OF THE CEREBEL-
LUM, AND TURNING IT BACK.

1. The Arbor Vitæ of the Vermis
   Superior.
2. The Medullary Matter which
   passes from the Cortical substance of the Cerebellum to the
   Tubercula Quadrigemina.
3. Section of the Lobulus Amygdaloides and Nervi Pneumogastrici.
4. The Internal Fasciculus of the
   Anterior portion of the Crus
   Cerebelli.
5. Prolongations of this Fasciculus
   into the Lobulus Amygdaloides
   and Nervi Pneumogastrici.
6. The Root of the Auditory
   Nerve which forms with the
   preceding parts a system of Fibres which envelope the Inter-
   Cerebellar Prolongations of the
   Corpus Restiforme. All these
   Fibres form the Parietes of the
   4th Ventricle and the Aqueduct
   of Sylvius.
7. The Testes.
8. Anterior extremity of the 4th
   Ventricle; the Medullary streak
   just above the Line is the Valve
   of the Brain.
9. The nervous tracts on the Calamus Scriptorius.
10. Lower portion of the Calamus.
11.12. The Medulla Oblongata and
    Spinalis.

FIG. 531.

IN THIS FIGURE THE EXTERNAL
PORTION OF THE CRUS CERE-
BELLI HAS BEEN REMOVED SO
AS TO SHOW THE DEEPER-SEAT-
ED PARTS, AS THE PROLONGA-
TION OF THE AUDITORY AND
TRIGEMINUS NERVES INTO THE
FUNDAMENTAL PORTION OF
THE CEREBELLUM.

1. Expanding Fibres of the Crus Cerebri.
2. Posterior Surface of the Crus
   Cerebri.
3. Trigeminus Nerve.
4. Its Prolongation to the centre of
   the Cerebellum.
5. Its Prolongation to the Corpus
   Restiforme.
6. Auditory Nerve.
7. Medullary Matter going from this
   Nerve to the Trigeminus.
8. Doubling of the Fibres of the
   Laminæ of the Cerebellum and
   their continuation to Fig. 7.
9. Eminentia Olivaria.

FIG. 532.

A VIEW OF THE APPEARANCE OF
THE CONVOLUTIONS OF ONE
SIDE OF THE CEREBRUM, AS
SEEN FROM ABOVE.

1. The Anterior Lobe of the Cere
   brum.
2. Its Posterior Lobe.
3. The Middle Lobe.

FIG. 533.

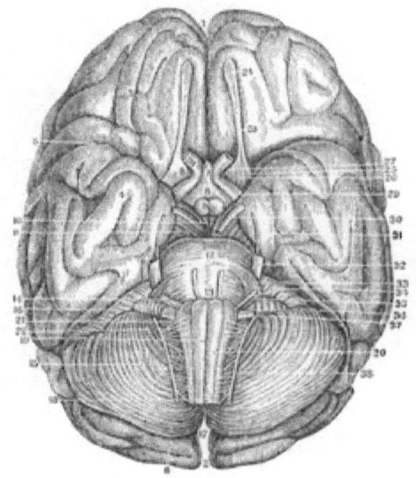

THE CEREBRUM.

FIG. 533.

A View of the Base of the Cerebrum and Cerebellum, together with their Nerves.

1. Anterior Extremity of the Fissure of the Hemispheres of the Brain.
2. Posterior Extremity of the same Fissure.
3. The Anterior Lobes of the Cerebrum.
4. Its Middle Lobe.
5. The Fissure of Sylvius.
6. The Posterior Lobe of the Cerebrum.
7. The Point of the Infundibulum.
8. Its Body.
9. The Corpora Albicantia.
10. Cineritious Matter.
11. The Crura Cerebri.
12. The Pons Varolii.
13. The top of the Medulla Oblongata.
14. Posterior Prolongation of the Pons Varolii.
15. Middle of the Cerebellum.
16. Anterior part of the Cerebellum.
17. Its Posterior part and the Fissure of its Hemispheres.
18. Superior part of the Medulla Spinalis.
19. Middle Fissure of the Medulla Oblongata.
20. The Corpus Pyramidale.
21. The Corpus Restiforme.
22. The Corpus Olivare.
23. The Olfactory Nerve.
24. Its Bulb.
25. Its External Root.
26. Its Middle Root.
27. Its Internal Root.
28. The Optic Nerve beyond the Chiasm.
29. The Optic Nerve before the Chiasm.
30. The Motor Oculi, or Third Pair of Nerves.
31. The Fourth Pair, or Pathetic Nerves.
32. The Fifth Pair, or Trigeminus Nerves.
33. The Sixth Pair, or Motor Externus.
34. The Facial Nerve.
35. The Auditory—the two making the Seventh Pair.
36.37.38. The Eighth Pair of Nerves. (The Ninth Pair are not here seen).

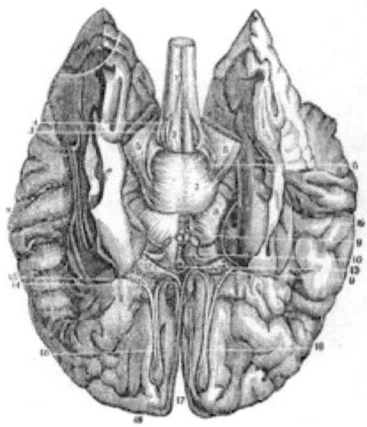 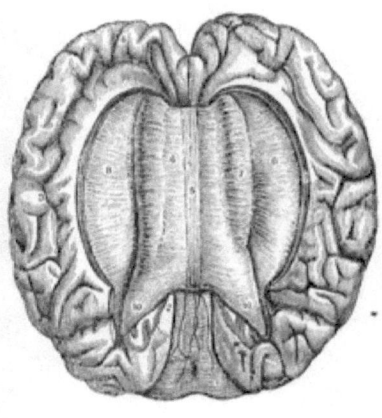

THE CEREBRUM.

FIG. 534.

A VIEW OF THE BASE OF THE CEREBRUM AFTER THE REMOVAL OF ITS MIDDLE AND POSTERIOR LOBES, AS WELL AS OF THE CEREBELLUM.

1. Superficial Intercrossing of the Anterior Cords of the Spinal Marrow.
2. Corpora Pyramidalia.
3. Eminentia Olivaria.
4. Corpora Restiformia.
5. External Surface of the Crura Cerebelli.
6. Oblique Bands extending from the Corpora Restiformia alongside of the Pons Varolii.
7. The Pons Varolii.
8. The Crura Cerebri.
9. The Eminentia Mamillares.
10. The Tract of the Optic Nerves.
11.12. A perforated space near the Roots of the Optic Nerves, and diverging from these Nerves near their Chiasm.
13. The Anterior Commissure shown by the rupture of the Cineritious Matter; this is formed by the union of the Roots of these Nerves.
14. The Internal Root of the Olfactory Nerve.

15. Its External Root coming from the Posterior Margin of the Anterior Lobe of the Cerebrum.
16. The Bulb of the Olfactory Nerve.
17. The Great Middle Fissure of the Cerebrum.
18. The Anterior Lobes of the Cerebrum.
19. The Middle Lobes of the Cerebrum. The rest of the Brain is wanting.

———

FIG. 535.

A VIEW OF THE EXTENT AND SHAPE OF THE CORPUS CALLOSUM AS SEEN FROM ABOVE. ON ITS OUTER SIDE IS SEEN THE CONVERGENCE OF THE FIBRES OF THE HEMISPHERES.

1. The Cerebellum.
2.3.4. The Convolutions on the inner side of the Hemispheres.
5. The Median Tract, or Raphe of the Corpus Callosum.
6. Its Transverse Fibres.
7. The Fibres curved inwards upon its outside.
8. The Converging Fibres of the Hemispheres.
9. The Concave Surface of the Hemispheres which overlaps the sides of the Corpus Callosum.
10.10. Its Posterior Extremities.

FIG. 536.

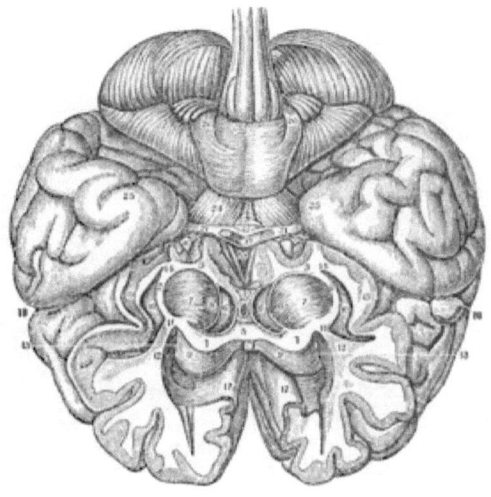

THE CEREBRUM.

FIG. 536.

A VIEW OF THE CONNEXIONS OF THE CEREBRAL CENTRE WITH THE HEMISPHERES, IN THE EXPANSION OF THE DIVERGING FIBRES.

The Cerebrum is lying upon its Convex or Upper Surface, and has been divided Transversely throughout its substance, by a cut which, starting from the Base of the Olfactory Nerves, runs upwards to the superior part of the Cerebrum at the Coronal Suture.

1.1. The Medullary Matter of a Section of the Corpus Callosum.

2.2. Medullary Matter on the outer side of the Corpora Striata.

3.3. Medullary Matter running to the Septum Lucidum.

4. The Point where this Matter unites to form the Septum. To the right and left of this is a black Crescent, marking the Cavity of the Lateral Ventricles.

5. The 5th Ventricle between the Layers of the Septum Lucidum.

6. The Ventricular side of the Corpora Striata.

.8. Medullary and Cineritious Fibres in the Corpora Striata.

9. The Superior Face of the Corpus Callosum.

10. External Face of the Cineritious Layer which envelopes the Corpora Striata.

11. Marks the continuation of the Medullary Matter of 7, in the Corpus Striatum, into that of the Cerebral Hemisphere.

12. The Medullary Matter of the Cerebrum, seen as continued from 11.

13. Shows the Intercrossing of the Fibres of the Fibrous Layer of the Corpus Callosum with that of the Hemispheres.

14.15. Show the continuation of the Medullary and Cineritious Striæ of the Corpora Striata with that of the Hemispheres.

16. Section of the Optic Nerves and their Anterior Gray Root.

17. Portion of the Convolutions of the Cerebrum adjacent and above the Corpus Callosum.

18. The Fissure of Sylvius.

19. Chiasm of the Optic Nerves.

20. The Infundibulum.

21. The Optic Nerves.

22. Tuber Cinerium.

23. Eminentia Mamillares.

24. Crura Cerebri.

25. Temporal portion of the Middle Lobes of the Cerebrum.

26. Pons Varolii with the Oblique Fasciculi coming from the Corpora Restiformia.

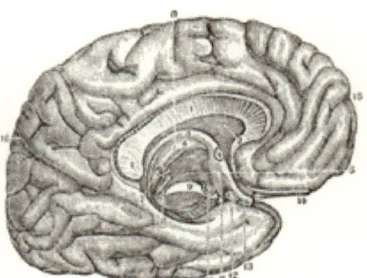

FIG. 537.　　　　FIG. 538.

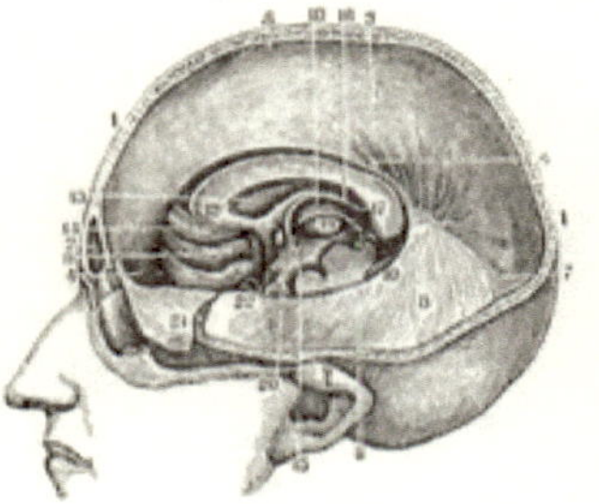

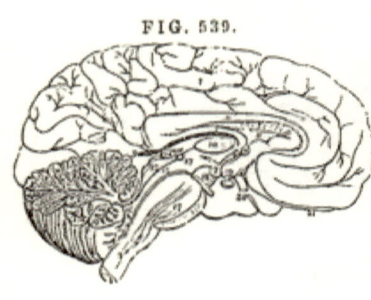

FIG. 539.　　　FIG. 540.

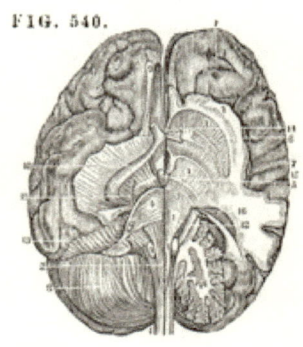

THE CEREBRUM

FIG. 537.

A Section of the Head to show the Falx Major, Tentorium and other parts, found under the Median Line of the Head.

1. Vertical Section of the Head.
2. The Frontal Sinus.
3. The Falx Major Cerebri.
4. Its Origin from the Crista Galli.
5. Its Attachment along the Sagittal Suture.
6. The lower or concave Edge of the Falx.
7. Its continuation to the Tentorium.
8. The Tentorium.
9. Its Attachment to the Petrous portion of the Temporal Bone.
10. The free Edge of the same part.
11. The Convolutions of the Right Anterior Lobe of the Cerebrum.
12. The Anterior Extremity of the Corpus Callosum.
13. The Septum Lucidum.
14. Section of the Anterior Commissure.
15. Anterior Crus of the Fornix.
16. Middle of the Fornix.
17. Its Posterior Extremity joining the Corpus Callosum.
18. Internal side of the Thalami Nervi Optici.
19. Section of the Corpora Striata.
20. Lateral Parietes of the 3d Ventricle.
21. A portion of the Dura Mater turned off.
22. Section of the Internal Carotid Artery.

FIG. 538.

A Vertical Section of the Corpus Callosum through its middle. The Left Internal Side of the Cerebrum is also shown.

1.1. Section of the Corpus Callosum.
2. The Septum Lucidum.

3. Anterior Column of the Fornix.
4. Section of the Anterior Commissure. Another Figure 4 is seen in the convex Surface of the Thalami Nervi Optici.
5. The Thickness or Central Substance of the Thalamus.
6. The Aqueduct of Sylvius.
7. The Pineal Gland.
8. A Medullary Band running from the Pineal Gland to the Anterior Commissure.
9. Section of the Crus Cerebri.
10. One of the Corpora Albicantia.
11. The Tuber Cinereum.
12. Section of the Chiasm of the Optic Nerves.
13. The Optic Nerve beyond the Chiasm.
14. The Olfactory Nerve.
15. Anterior Surface of the Hemisphere.
16. The Fissure between the Posterior and Middle Lobes of the Cerebrum.

FIG. 539.

The Mesial Surface of a Longitudinal Section of the Brain.

1. The Inner Surface of the Left Hemisphere.
2. The Divided Surface of the Cerebellum, showing the Arbor Vitæ.
3. The Medulla Oblongata.
4. The Corpus Callosum.
5. The Fornix.
6. One of the Crura of the Fornix.
7. One of the Corpora Albicantia.
8. The Septum Lucidum.
9. The Velum Interpositum.
10. The Middle Commissure.
11. The Anterior Commissure.
12. The Posterior Commissure; the Commissure is somewhat above and to the left of the Number. The Space between 10 and 11 is the Foramen Commune Ante-

rius. The Space between 10 and 12 is the Foramen Commune Posterius.
13. The Corpora Quadrigemina.
14. The Pineal Gland.
15. The Aqueduct of Sylvius.
16. The Fourth Ventricle.
17. The Pons Varolii, through which are seen passing the Diverging Fibres of the Corpora Pyramidalia.
18. The Crus Cerebri.
19. The Tuber Cinereum, from which projects the Infundibulum, having the Pituitary Gland appended to its extremity.
20. One of the Optic Nerves.
21. The Left Olfactory Nerve.

FIG. 540.

A View of the Course of the Anterior Columns of the Spinal Marrow to their Termination in the Hemispherical Ganglia of the Cerebrum — after the Dissections of Gall.

1.1. } The Motor Tract traced out
1.1. } from the Anterior Columns of
　　 } the Spinal Cord to the Hemispherical Ganglion.
2. Corpus Pyramidale.
3. Eminentia Olivaris.
4. Pons Varolii.
5. Crus Cerebri.
6. Corpus Striatum.
7. Hemispherical Ganglion or Cineritious Neurine of the Cerebrum.
8. The Cerebellum.
9. The Olfactory Nerve.
10. The Optic Nerve.
11. The 4th Pair of Nerves.
12. The Sensory Root of the 5th Pair.
13. The 7th and 8th Pairs of Nerves.
14. The Anterior Commissure.
15. Eminentia Mamillaris.
16. Corpus Geniculatum

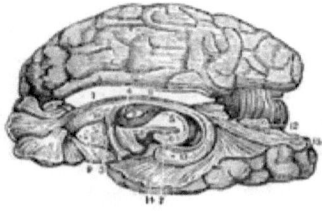
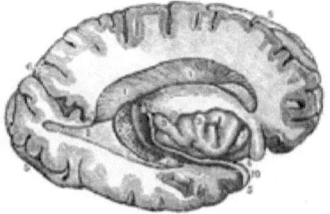

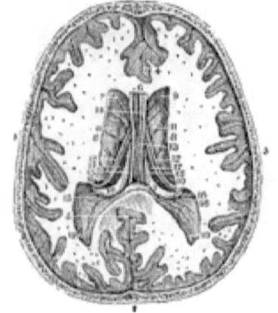
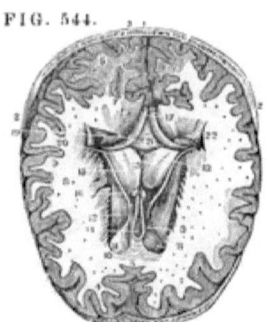

THE VENTRICLES OF THE BRAIN.

FIG. 541.

A VIEW OF THE CONNEXIONS OF THE DIFFERENT PARTS OF THE BRAIN BY MEANS OF THE COMMISSURES—AS GIVEN BY A VERTICAL SECTION.

1. The Great Transverse Commissure or Corpus Callosum divided on its Middle Line.
2. The Commissura Mollis.
3. The Anterior Commissure.
4. The Thalamus.
5. Section of the Crus Cerebri.
6. The Cineritious Matter in the Crus.
7. The commencing Fibres of the Inferior Longitudinal Commissure or Fornix.
8. Corpus Mamillare.
9. The remains of the Corpus Striatum—the rest of it has been scraped away.
10. The Septum Lucidum.
11. Body of the Fornix or Centre of the Commissure.
12. Tænia Hippocampi or Descending Fibres of the Inferior Longitudinal Commissure.
13. Fibres covering the Hippocampus Major.
14. Fibres covering the Pes Hippocampi.
15. Fibres covering the Hippocampus Minor.

It will be thus seen that the different portions of the Convoluted Surface of the Brain are connected together by this Inferior Longitudinal Commissure, called the Fornix.

FIG. 542.

A VIEW OF THE LATERAL VENTRICLES OF THE BRAIN.

The Hemisphere has been divided Vertically so as to lay open the Lateral Ventricle in its greatest extent. Another Section passing from the Fissure of Sylvius has opened the Lateral Ventricle on the External Limit of the Corpus Striatum and all the convexity of the Hemisphere has there been cut away, so as to open the Ventricle outwardly.

1.1. ⎫ Is the whole Cavity of the
2.2. ⎭ Ventricle.
3.3. Convolutions on the under side or Base of the Brain.
4. Points to the opening of the Fissure of Sylvius.
5.5. The External Circumference of the Hemisphere.
6. The Fissure separating the Posterior from the Middle Lobes of the Cerebrum.
7. The bottom of this Fissure towards the Ventricle.
8. The bottom of the Fissure of Sylvius.
9. The Plexus Choroides.
10. The Large Extremity of the Cornu Ammonis.

FIG. 543.

A VIEW OF THE SUPERIOR PART OF THE LATERAL VENTRICLES, CORPORA STRIATA, SEPTUM LUCIDUM, FORNIX, &c., AS GIVEN BY A TRANSVERSE SECTION OF THE CEREBRUM.

1. Section of the Os Frontis.
2. Section of the Os Occipitis.
3. Section of the Ossa Parietalia.
4.5. Anterior and Posterior Extremities of the Middle Fissure of the Cerebrum.
6. Anterior Extremity of the Corpus Callosum.
7. Its Posterior Extremity joining the Fornix.
8.8. Points to where the Corpus Callosum joins the Lateral Medullary Matter of the Cerebrum.
9. Its Place of junction Anteriorly.
10. Posterior point of union.
11. Middle portion of the Corpora Striata (Lateral Ventricle)
12. Tænia Striata.
13. The Septum Lucidum.

14. The Fifth Ventricle.
15. The Fornix.
16. Its Posterior Crura.
17. The Plexus Choroides.
18. The Ergot or Hippocampus Minor.
19. Posterior Crura of the Lateral Ventricle.

FIG. 544.

A TRANSVERSE SECTION OF THE BRAIN ON A LEVEL WITH THE LATERAL VENTRICLES, IN ORDER TO SHOW THE FIFTH VENTRICLE AND THAT PORTION OF THE FORNIX KNOWN AS THE LYRA.

1. Section of the Os Frontis.
2. Section of the Ossa Parietalia.
3. Section of the Os Occipitis.
4. Anterior Lobes of the Cerebrum.
5. Its Posterior Lobes.
6. Anterior Extremity of the Great Middle Fissure.
7. Its Posterior Extremity.
8. The Centrum Ovale, or Medullary Matter of the Cerebrum.
9. The Cortical or Cineritious Matter.
10. Section of the Anterior portion of the Corpus Callosum.
11. Anterior Extremities of the Lateral Ventricles.
12. Corpora Striata.
13. The Sides of the Septum Lucidum.
14. The Cavity between its sides, or the 5th Ventricle.
15. The Thalami Nervi Optici.
16. The Tænia Striata.
17. Section of the Anterior Crura of the Fornix, which is here turned backwards.
18. Cavity of the 3d Ventricle.
19. Lateral Portion of the Fornix.
20. Its Posterior Crura.
21. The Striæ on its under Surface known as the Lyra.
22. Posterior Cornu of the Lateral Ventricle.

FIG. 545.

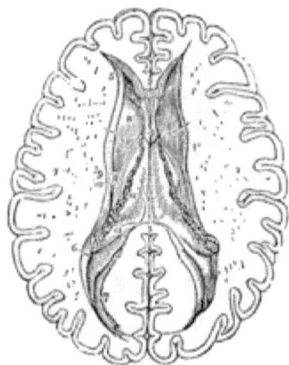

FIG. 546.

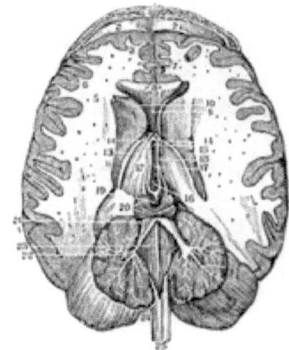

FIG. 547.

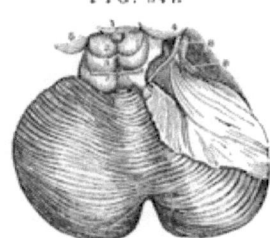

THE CEREBRUM.

FIG. 545.

THE LATERAL VENTRICLES OF THE CEREBRUM.

1.1. The two Hemispheres cut down to a level with the Corpus Callosum, so as to show the Centrum Ovale Majus. The Surface is studded with the small Puncta Vasculosa.
2. A small portion of the Anterior Extremity of the Corpus Callosum.
3. Its Posterior Boundary; the intermediate portion, forming the Roof of the Lateral Ventricles, has been removed so as to completely expose these Cavities.
4. A part of the Septum Lucidum, showing a space between its Layers which is the 5th Ventricle.
5. The Anterior Cornu of one side.
6. The commencement of the Middle Cornu.
7. The Posterior Cornu.
8. The Corpus Striatum of one Ventricle.
9. The Tænia Striata.
10. A small part of the Thalamus Opticus.
11. The Plexus Choroides.
12. The Fornix.
13. The commencement of the Hippocampus Major in the Middle Cornu. The Rounded Oblong Body in the Posterior Cornu of the Lateral Ventricle, directly behind the Figure 13, is the Hippocampus Minor. A Bristle is seen in the Foramen of Munro.

FIG. 546.

A VIEW OF THE VENTRICLES OF THE BRAIN, AS GIVEN BY A TRANSVERSE SECTION OF THE CEREBRUM JUST ABOVE THE TOP OF THE LATERAL VENTRICLES AND A PERPENDICULAR SECTION OF THE CEREBELLUM.

1. Section of the Os Frontis.
2. Its Orbitar Plate.
3. Anterior Lobes of the Cerebrum.
4. Its Posterior Lobes.
5. The Medullary or White Matter of the Cerebrum.
6. The Cineritious or Grey Matter.
7. Anterior portion of the Middle Fissure of the Cerebrum.
8. Section of the Anterior portion of the Corpus Callosum.
9. The curved portion of the Anterior part of the Corpus Callosum placed between the Corpora Striata.
10. Anterior portion of the Corpora Striata.
11. Their Posterior Extremity.
12. The Thalami Nervi Optici.
13. The Tænia Striata.
14. Section of the Anterior Crura of the Fornix.
15. Anterior Extremity of the 3d Ventricle.
16. Its Posterior Extremity.
17. The Commissura Mollis.
18. The Peduncles of the Pineal Gland.
19. The Pineal Gland.

20. The Tubercula Quadrigemina.
21. The Valve of Vieussens divided and turned on each side.
22. Section of the Cerebellum and Arbor Vitæ.
23. The 4th Ventricle.—The dark middle Fissure which leads from the Fourth to the Third Ventricle under the Valve of Vieussens is the Aqueduct of Sylvius.
24. Lower portion of the Calamus Scriptorius.
25. Extremity of the Medulla Spinalis.

FIG. 547.

A VIEW OF A SECTION OF THE BRAIN, SHOWING THE MOTOR ORIGIN OF THE FIFTH PAIR OF NERVES AND THE ORIGIN OF THE FOURTH PAIR, WITH THE POSITION OF THEIR COMMISSURE.

1. The Pineal Gland lying on the Tubercula Quadrigemina, just above the Nates.
2. The Superior of the Tubercula Quadrigemina, or the Nates.
3. The Inferior or Testes.
4. The Motor Root of the 5th Pair of Nerves.
5. The Thalamus Nervi Optici.
6. The Sensory Root of the 5th Pair.
7. The 4th Pair of Nerves.
8. The 5th Pair of Nerves.

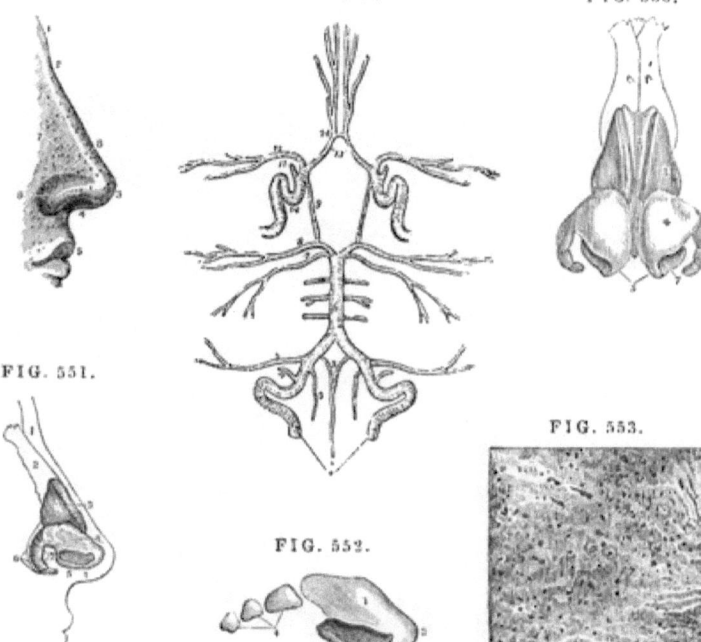

FIG. 549. FIG. 548. FIG. 550.

FIG. 551.

FIG. 553.

FIG. 552.

THE ORGAN OF SMELLING.

FIG. 548.

A VIEW OF THE CIRCLE OF WILLIS.

1. The Vertebral Arteries.
2. The two Anterior Spinal Branches.
3. One of the Posterior Spinal Arteries.
4. The Posterior Meningeal Artery.
5. The Inferior Cerebelli Artery.
6. The Basilar Artery.
7. The Superior Cerebelli Artery.
8. The Posterior Cerebelli.
9. The Posterior Communicans.
10. The Internal Carotid.
11. The Ophthalmic Artery.
12. The Middle Cerebral Artery.
13. The Anterior Cerebri.
14. The Anterior Communicans.

FIG. 549.

A SIDE VIEW OF THE NOSE DEPRIVED OF ITS EPIDERMIS IN ORDER TO SHOW THE SEBACEOUS FOLLICLES OF THE SKIN.

1. Lower part of the Forehead.
2. Root of the Nose.
3. Its Point.

4. Opening of the Right Nostril.
5. The Lips.
6. Ala of the Nose.
7. The Side of the Nose and its Follicles.
8. The same on its Front.

FIG. 550.

A VIEW OF THE CARTILAGES OF THE NOSE.

1. The Nasal Bones.
2. The Cartilaginous Septum.
3. The Lateral Cartilages.
4. The Alar Cartilages.
5. The Central portions of the Alar Cartilages which constitute the Columns.
6. The Appendices of the Alar Cartilage.
7. The Nostrils.

FIG. 551.

A SIDE VIEW OF THE BONES AND CARTILAGES OF THE NOSE, SEEN ON THE RIGHT SIDE.

1.1. An outline of the thickness of the Integuments.
2. The Nasal Bone.

3. The Lateral Cartilage.
4. The External portion of the Cartilage of the Ala Nasi.
5. The Internal portion of the same Cartilage.
6. The Three small Cartilages which support the Ala Nasi.
7. The Fibrous Tissue that holds them together.

FIG. 552.

AN EXTERNAL VIEW OF THE NASAL CARTILAGES AROUND THE NOSTRIL.

1. The Outer Plate of one of the Oval Cartilages.
2. Its Inner Plate.
3. The Columnæ Nasi.
4. The small Cartilages of the Ala Nasi.

FIG. 553.

A PORTION OF THE PITUITARY MEMBRANE OF THE NASAL SEPTUM, MAGNIFIED 9 TIMES, AND SHOWING THE NUMBER, SIZES AND ARRANGEMENT OF THE MUCOUS CRYPTS.

FIG. 554. FIG. 555.

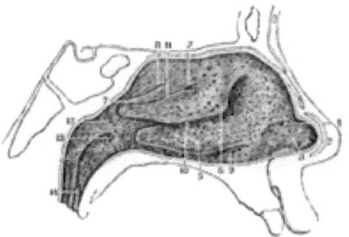
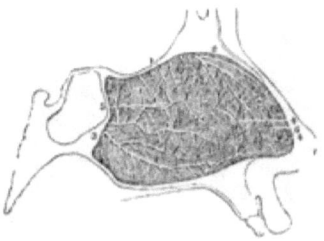

FIG. 556. FIG. 557.

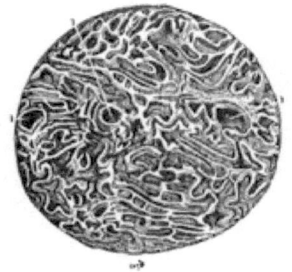

THE ORGAN OF SMELLING.

FIG. 554.

A VIEW OF THE EXTERNAL PARIETES OF THE LEFT NOSTRIL, AS GIVEN BY THE REMOVAL OF THE SEPTUM.

1.2. Sections of the Cartilage of the Nose.
   3. The Hollow on the Inner Side of the Ala Nasi, with the Hairs and Mucous Follicles there found.
   4. The rounded Prominence where the Skin and Mucous Membrane unite.
   5. The Inferior Spongy Bone.
   6. The Middle Spongy Bone.
   7. The Superior Spongy Bone.
   8. An Excavation giving the appearance of a fourth Spongy Bone.
   9. The Inferior Meatus of the Nose.
 10. The Middle Meatus.
 11. The Superior Meatus.
 12. An Elongated Projection which separates the Nose from the Pharynx.
 13. The opening of the Eustachian Tube.
 14. Left half of the Velum Pendulum Palati.

FIG. 555.

THE ARTERIES OF THE LEFT SIDE OF THE NASAL SEPTUM.

1. The Posterior Ethmoidal Artery.
2. The Anterior Ethmoidal Artery.
3. Branches of the Spheno-Palatine Artery.
4.5.6. The minute Anastomoses of the Branches of the Spheno-Palatine with the Ethmoidal Artery, showing the Vascularity of this Surface.

FIG. 556.

A PORTION OF THE PITUITARY MEMBRANE WITH ITS ARTERIES AND VEINS INJECTED—MAGNIFIED 15 DIAMETERS.

The natural size of this piece is seen at the bottom of the Cut.
1.1.1. The Orifices of Three Mucous Crypts surrounded by Veins and Arteries.

FIG. 557.

A VERTICAL SECTION OF THE MIDDLE PART OF THE NASAL FOSSÆ, GIVING A POSTERIOR VIEW OF THE ARRANGEMENT OF THE ETHMOIDAL CELLS, &c.

1. Anterior Fossæ of the Cranium.
2. The same covered by the Dura Mater.
3. The Dura Mater turned up.
4. The Crista Galli of the Ethmoid Bone.
5. Its Cribriform Plate.
6. Its Nasal Lamella.
7. The Middle Spongy Bones.
8. The Ethmoidal Cells.
9. The Os Planum.
10. Inferior Spongy Bone.
11. The Vomer.
12. Superior Maxillary Bone.
13. Its union with the Ethmoid.
14. Anterior Parietes of the Antrum Highmorianum, covered by its Membrane.
15. Its Fibrous Layer.
16. Its Mucous Membrane.
17. Palatine Process of the Superior Maxillary Bone.
18. Roof of the Mouth, covered by the Mucous Membrane.
19. Section of this Membrane. A Bristle is seen in the Orifice of the Antrum Highmorianum.

FIG. 558.

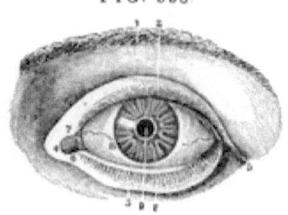

FIG. 559.

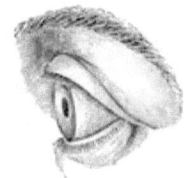

FIG. 560.

FIG. 561.

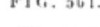

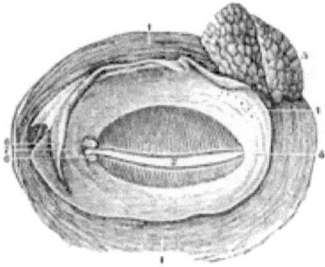
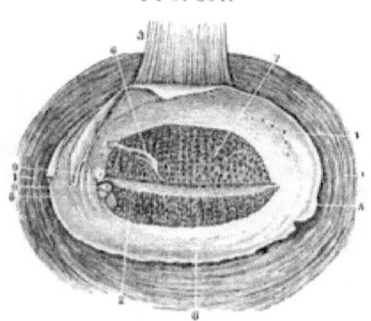

THE EYE.

FIG. 558.

A FRONT VIEW OF THE LEFT EYE—MODERATELY
OPENED.

1. The Supercilia.
2. The Cilia of each Eye-Lid.
3. The Inferior Palpebra.
4. The Internal Canthus.
5. The External Canthus.
6. The Caruncula Lachrymalis.
7. The Plica Semilunaris.
8. The Eye-Ball.
9. The Pupil.

FIG. 559.

A SIDE VIEW OF THE SAME EYE, SHOWING THAT
THE CILIA OF THE UPPER LID ARE CONCAVE
UPWARDS, AND THOSE OF THE LOWER LID CON-
CAVE DOWNWARDS. THE GENERAL CONVEXITY
OF THE EYE-BALL IS ALSO SEEN.

FIG. 560.

A POSTERIOR VIEW OF THE EYE-LIDS AND LACH-
RYMAL GLAND.

1.1. The Orbicularis Palpebrarum Muscle.
2. The Borders of the Lids.

3. The Lachrymal Gland.
4. Its Ducts opening in the Upper Lid.
5. The Conjunctiva covering the Lids.
6. The Puncta Lachrymalia.
7. The Lachrymal Caruncle as seen from behind.

FIG. 561.

A POSTERIOR VIEW OF THE EYE-LIDS—AS SEEN
UNDER THE MICROSCOPE, SO AS TO SHOW CLEARLY
THE GLANDULÆ PALPEBRARUM.

1.1. The Orbicularis Palpebrarum Muscle.
2. The opening of the Lids, through which are
seen the Cilia of the Upper Lid.
3. The Levator Palpebræ Superioris Muscle.
4. The openings of the Ducts of the Lachrymal Gland.
5. The Conjunctiva of the Eye-Lids.
6. The Conjunctiva turned back so as to show
the Glands which are beneath it.
7. The Meibomian Glands of the Upper Eye-
Lid, seen through the Conjunctiva.
8. The same Glands of the Lower Lid.
9. The Puncta Lachrymalia.

FIG. 562.

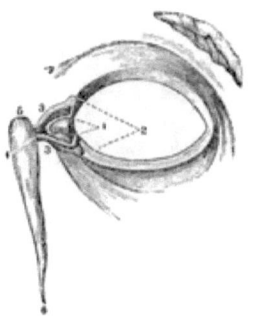

FIG. 563.

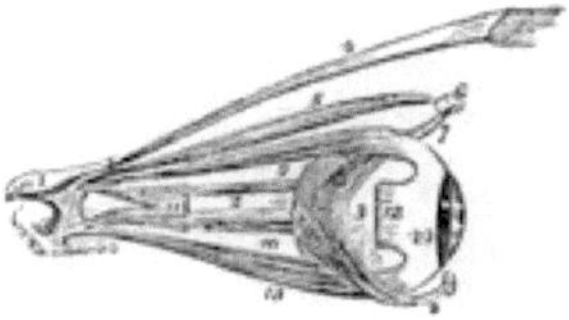

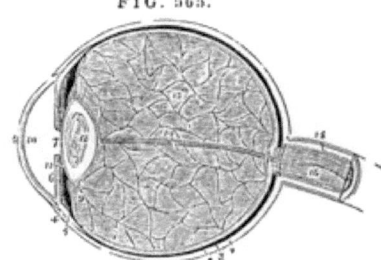

FIG. 565.

FIG. 564.

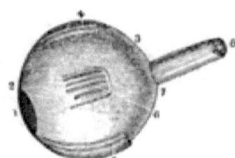

THE EYE.

FIG. 562.

A View of the Shape and Position of the Lachrymal Canals.

1. The Puncta Lachrymalia or openings of the Lachrymal Canals in the Lids.
2. The Cul-de-Sac at the Orbital end of the Canal.
3. The course of each Canal to the Saccus Lachrymalis.
4.5. The Saccus Lachrymalis.
6. The Lower part of the Ductus ad Nasum.

FIG. 563.

A View of the Muscles of the Eye-Ball, taken from the Outer Side of the Right Orbit.

1. A small Fragment of the Sphenoid Bone around the entrance of the Optic Nerve into the Orbit.
2. The Optic Nerve.
3. The Globe of the Eye.
4. The Levator Palpebræ Muscle.
5. The Superior Oblique Muscle.
6. Its Cartilaginous Pulley.
7. Its Reflected Tendon.
8. The Inferior Oblique Muscle; a piece of its Bony Origin is broken off.
9. The Superior Rectus Muscle.
10. The Internal Rectus almost concealed by the Optic Nerve.
11. Part of the External Rectus showing s two Heads.
12. The Extremity of the External Rectus at its Insertion; the intermediate portion of the Muscle having been removed.
13. The Inferior Rectus Muscle.
14. The Sclerotic Coat.

A View of the Tensor Tarsi, or Muscle of Horner, has been already given—see Figures 172.

FIG. 564.

A Side View of the Eye-Ball—entire.

1. The Middle of the Cornea.
2. Its union with the Sclerotic Coat.
3. The Sclerotica.
4.5.6. The Tendons of the Recti Muscles, losing themselves in the Sclerotic Coat.
7. Point where the Optic Nerve penetrates the Coats of the Eye-Ball.
8. The Optic Nerve.

FIG. 565.

A Longitudinal Section of the Globe of the Eye.

1. The Sclerotic Coat.
2. The Cornea.
3. The Choroid Coat.
4. The Ciliary Ligament.
5. The Ciliary Processes.
6. The Iris.
7. The Pupil.
8. The Retina.
9. The Canal of Petit, which encircles the Lens.
10. The Anterior Chamber of the Eye, containing the Aqueous Humour.
11. The Posterior Chamber.
12. The Lens enclosed in its proper Capsule.
13. The Vitreous Humour enclosed in the Hyaloid Membrane.
14. A Tabular Sheath of the Hyaloid Membrane.
15. The Neurilema of the Optic Nerve.
16. The Arteria Centralis Retinæ.

FIG. 566.

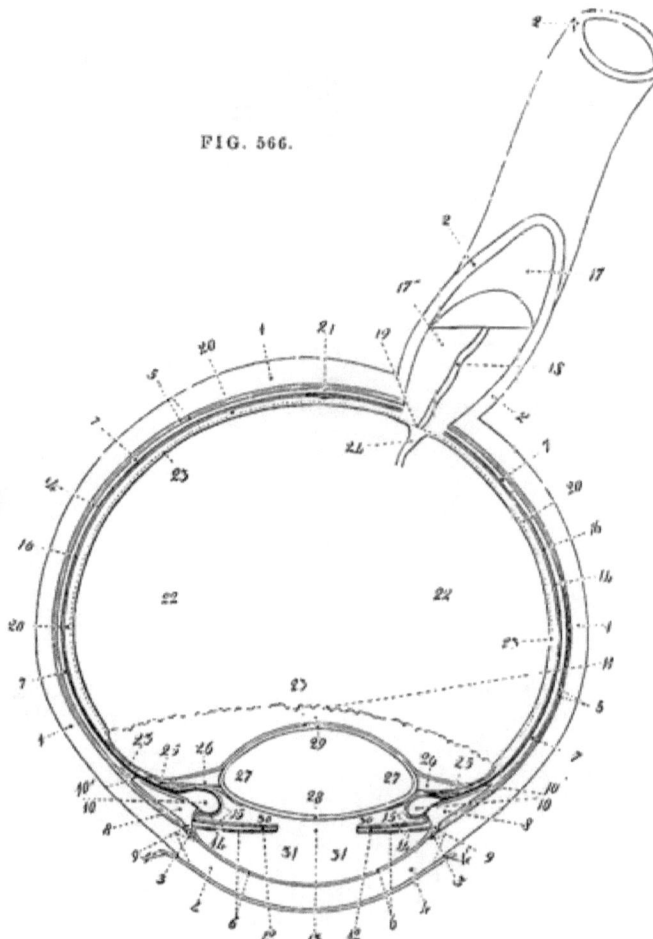

THE EYE BALL.

FIG. 566.

A HORIZONTAL SECTION OF THE EYE-BALL.

1. Sclerotic Coat.
2. Sheath of the Optic Nerve, or Canal of Fontana.
3. Circular Venous Sinus of the Iris.
4. Proper Substance of the Cornea.
5. Arachnoidea Oculi.
6. Membrane of the Anterior Chamber of the Aqueous Humour. Of the Two Dotted Lines one points to the supposed Membrane of Descemet, the other to the supposed continuation of that Membrane over the Anterior Surface of the Iris.
7. Choroid Coat.
8. Annulus Albidus.
9. Ciliary Ligament.

10,10'. Ciliary Body, consisting of (10') a Pars non-Fimbriata, and (10) a Pars Fimbriata formed by the Ciliary Process.
11. Ora Serrata of the Ciliary Body.
12. Iris.
13. Pupil.
14. Membrane of the Pigment.
15. Delicate Membrane lining the Posterior Chamber of the Aqueous Humour.
16. Membrane of Jacob.
17. The Optic Nerve surrounded by its Neurilema.
17'. The Fibres of the Optic Nerve consisting of Fasciculi of Primitive Tubules.
18. Central Artery of the Retina.
19. Papilla Conica of the Optic Nerve.
20. Retina. The situation of its Vas-

cular Layer is indicated by a Dotted Line.
21. Central Transparent Point of the Retina.
22. Vitreous Humour.
23. The Hyaloid Membrane.
24. Canalis Hyaloideus.
25. Zonula Ciliaris. In the Plate, none of its Fimbriated part is seen, being concealed by the Ciliary Processes.
26. Canal of Petit.
27. Crystalline Lens.
28. Anterior Wall of the Capsule of the Lens.
29. Posterior Wall of the Capsule of the Lens.
30. Posterior Chamber of the Aqueous Humour.
31. Anterior Chamber of the Aqueous Humour.

Page 162.

FIG. 567.

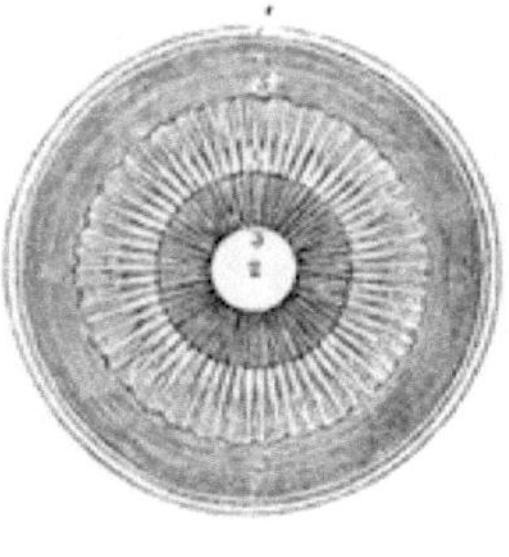

FIG. 569.

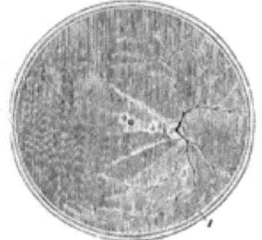

FIG. 570.

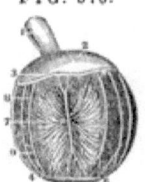

FIG. 568.

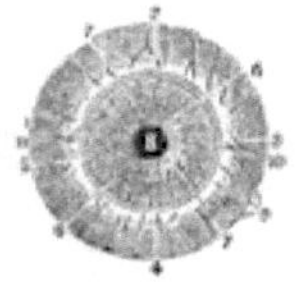

FIG. 571.

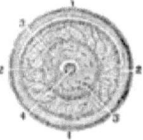

FIG. 572.

THE EYE-BALL.

FIG. 567.

THE ANTERIOR SEGMENT OF A TRANS-
VERSE SECTION OF THE GLOBE OF
THE EYE, SEEN FROM WITHIN.

1. The divided Edge of the Three
   Coats — the Sclerotic, Choroid
   and Retina.
2. The Pupil.
3. The Iris; the surface presented
   to view in this Section being the
   Uvea.
4. The Ciliary Processes.
5. The Anterior Border of the Retina.

FIG. 568.

THE POSTERIOR SEGMENT OF A
TRANSVERSE SECTION OF THE
GLOBE OF THE EYE, SEEN FROM
WITHIN.

1. The divided Edge of the Three
   Coats the Membrane covering
   the whole Internal Surface is the
   Retina.
2. The Entrance of the Optic Nerve
   with the Arteria Centralis Retinæ
   piercing its centre.
3.3. The Ramifications of the Arte-
   rin Centralis.
4. The Foramen of Sömmering; the
   Shade from the sides of the Section obscures the Limbus Luteus
   which surrounds it.

5. A Fold of the Retina, which ge-
   nerally obscures the Foramen of
   Sömmering after the Eye has
   been opened.

FIG. 569.

A VIEW OF THE CHOROID COAT
WITH ITS VESSELS INJECTED.

1. The Optic Nerve.
2. Posterior portion of the Sclerotica, cut off circularly.
3.4. The Ciliary Ligament.
5. The Iris.
6. Ciliary Nerves.
7. Long and Short Arteries of
   the Choroid Coat.
8. Long Internal Ciliary Arteries
   of the Choroid Coat.
9.10. Vasa Vorticosa.

FIG. 570.

A VIEW OF THE VEINS OF THE
CHOROID COAT, AS DISTEND-
ED BY BLOOD.

1. The Optic Nerve.
2.3. Section of the Sclerotic Coat.
4.5. The Circumference of the Iris.
6. The Pupil.
7. The Veins of the Choroid
   Coat.
8.9. The Ciliary Nerves.

FIG. 571.

AN ANTERIOR VIEW OF THE IRIS
AS ATTACHED TO THE CHO-
ROID COAT.

1. The Choroid Coat.
2.3. The Ciliary Ligament.
4. The Great Circumference of
   the Iris.
5. The Anterior Face of the Iris.
6. Its Lesser Circumference.
7. Shows the Striated or Ray-like
   appearance of the Iris.
8. The Pupil.
9. The Ciliary Nerves dividing as
   they penetrate the Ciliary Ligament.
10.11. The Ciliary Blood-Vessels.

FIG. 572.

A FRONT VIEW OF THE RETINA,
WITH THE LENS IN ITS CAP-
SULE.

1.1. The Retina.
2.2. Its Anterior Limits.
3.3. The Lens in its Capsule.
4. The Central Foramen of the
   Retina, seen through the Transparent Lens and Vitreous Humour.

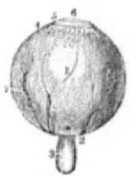

FIG. 573.

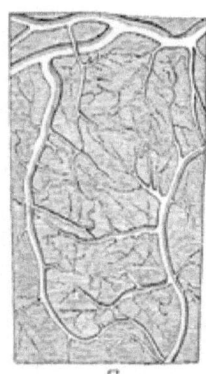

FIG. 575.

FIG. 576.

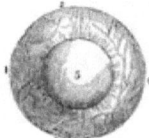

FIG. 574.

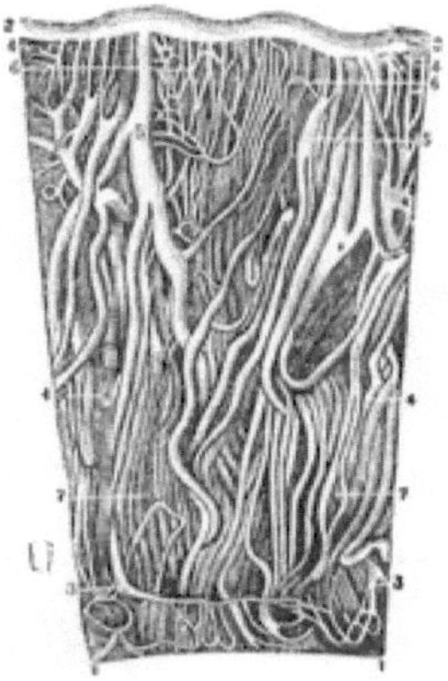

FIG. 577.

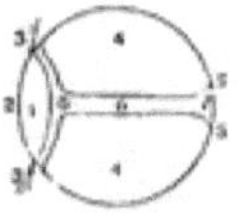

FIG. 578.

FIG. 579.

FIG. 580.

THE EYE-BALL.

FIG. 573.

THE EXTERNAL FACE OF THE RE-
TINA, WITH THE LENS ATTACHED
TO IT.
1. The Retina
2. Its Central Foramen.
3. The Optic Nerve deprived of its
Sheath.
4. The Ciliary Body.
5. The distance of this Body from
the Lens.
6. The Lens in its Capsule.

FIG. 574.

A VIEW OF THE LEFT EYE OF A FŒ-
TUS OF SIX MONTHS, MAGNIFIED 2
DIAMETERS — SHOWING THE VES-
SELS IN THE CONJUNCTIVA.
1.2.3.4. The Internal, Superior, External and Inferior parts of the
Eye-Ball, with the Blood-Vessels
injected.
5. The Transparent Cornea.

FIG. 575.

A PORTION OF THE RETINA OF AN
INFANT, WITH ITS VESSELS INJECT-
ED AND MAGNIFIED 25 DIAMETERS.

An outline of the Natural Size of
this piece is seen just below the
main Cut.

FIG. 576.

A SEGMENT OF THE ANTERIOR FACE
OF THE IRIS WITH ITS VESSELS IN-
JECTED — MAGNIFIED 25 DIAME-
TERS.
1.1. A portion of the Pupillary Circumference of the Iris.
2.2 A part of its Greater Circumference surrounded by a Branch
of the Long Ciliary Artery.
3. Part of the Lesser Circle of the
Iris.
4.4. Part of its Greater Circle.
5.5. Three Arteries which are larger
than the others, and coming
from the Greater Circle are
lost in the Iris.
6. Smaller Arteries arising from
these.
7. Branches of the Larger Arteries, which are lost in the Smaller Circle of the Iris.

An outline of the Natural Size
of this piece is seen on the side of
the Figure between 3 and 7.

FIG. 577.

A SIDE VIEW OF THE VITREOUS HU-
MOUR AND LENS OF A FŒTUS AT
8 MONTHS, SHOWING THE SHAPE
AND DIRECTION OF THE CANAL OF
PETIT.
1. The Lens.
2. Its Anterior Face.

3. Filaments which unite the Circumference of the Lens to the
Ciliary Processes.
4. The Hyaloid Membrane surrounding the Vitreous Humour.
5. The Reflexions of this Membrane at the back of the Eye
Ball.
6. The Hyaloid Canal for the Artery to the Lens.
7. Its Posterior Orifice by which the
Posterior Artery enters.
8. The Canal of Petit around the
Lens.

FIG. 578.

A FRONT VIEW OF THE CRYSTAL-
LINE HUMOUR OR LENS, IN THE
ADULT.

FIG. 579.

A MAGNIFIED VIEW OF THE LENS
OF A FŒTUS OF 8 MONTHS, SEEN
ON ITS ANTERIOR FACE, WITH THE
MARKS OF ITS DIVISION INTO THE
THREE PIECES THAT FORM IT AT
THAT PERIOD.

FIG. 580.

A SIDE VIEW OF THE ADULT LENS.
1. Its Anterior Face.
2. Its Posterior Face.
3.3. Its Circumference.

FIG. 581.

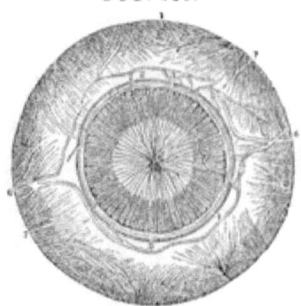

FIG. 582.

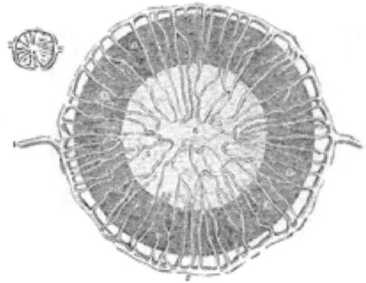

FIG. 583.

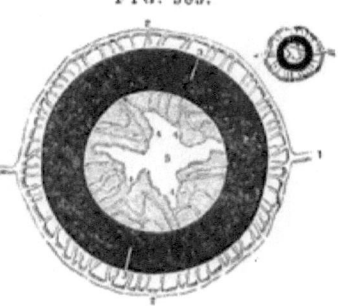

THE EYE-BALL.

FIG. 581.

AN ANTERIOR VIEW OF THE CHOROID, IRIS AND MEMBRANA PUPILLARIS OF A FŒTUS OF 7 MONTHS, HIGHLY INJECTED AND MAGNIFIED 4 DIAMETERS.

1.2. The Choroid Coat.
3. The Ciliary Ligament.
4. The Iris.
5. The Membrana Pupillaris with its Vessels minutely injected.
6.6. The Long Ciliary Arteries.
7.7. The Vasa Vorticosa.

FIG. 582.

AN ANTERIOR VIEW OF THE IRIS AND MEMBRANA PUPILLARIS OF AN INFANT OF 6½ MONTHS, WITH THEIR VESSELS INJECTED—HIGHLY MAGNIFIED.

1.1. The two Long Ciliary Arteries.
2. The Circle around the Iris, formed by their Anastomosing Branches.
3. Branches which arise from this Circle, and run in Front of the Iris.

4. Anterior Face of the Iris.
5. Extremities of the same Arteries, forming Arches between the two Layers of the Membrana Pupillaris.
6. The Centre of the Membrana Pupillaris, usually free from Vessels, where the Membrane ruptures spontaneously.

The Natural Size of this piece is seen on the side of the Cut.

FIG. 583.

A POSTERIOR VIEW OF THE SAME, ALSO MUCH MAGNIFIED, AND WITH THE MEMBRANA PUPILLARIS RUPTURED.

1.1. Long Ciliary Arteries.
2. The Greater Arterial Circle of the Iris.
3. The Posterior Face of the Iris covered with Pigmentum Nigrum.
4. Flaps formed by the remains of the Pupillary Membrane.
5. The Centre of the Pupil.

The Natural Size of the piece is seen on its side.

FIG. 584.   FIG. 585.   FIG. 586.

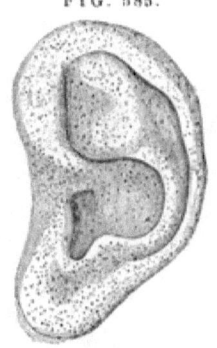
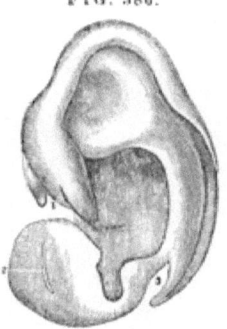

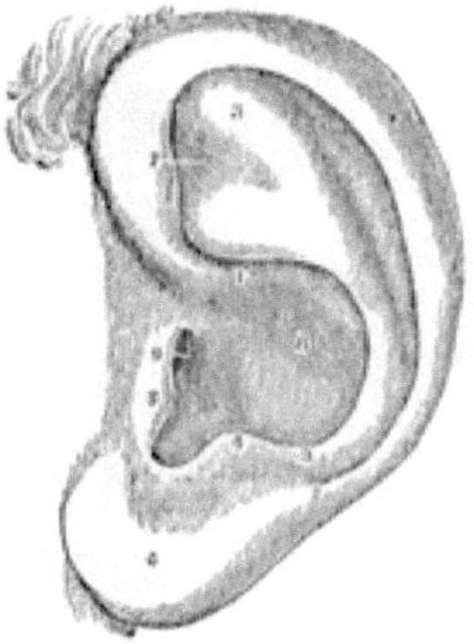

FIG. 587.   FIG. 589.   FIG. 588.

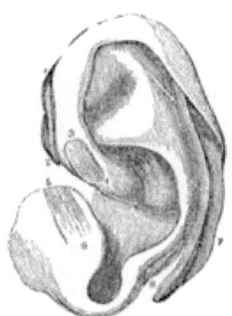
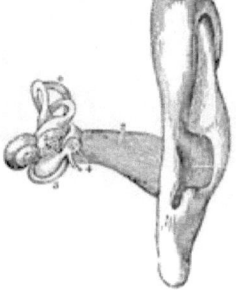
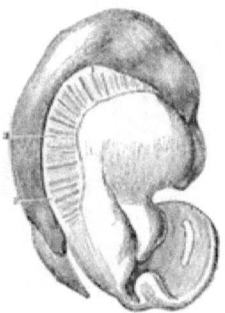

THE EXTERNAL EAR

FIG. 584.

A VIEW OF THE LEFT EAR IN ITS NATURAL STATE.

1.2. The origin and termination of the Helix.
3. The Anti-Helix.
4. The Anti-Tragus.
5. The Tragus.
6. The Lobus of the External Ear.
7. Points to the Scapha, and is on the front and top of the Pinna.
8. The Concha.
9. The Meatus Auditorius Externus.

FIG. 585.

A VIEW OF THE SEBACEOUS FOLLICLES OF THE EXTERNAL EAR. THEY ARE RENDERED MORE APPARENT FROM MACERATION.

FIG. 586.

A VIEW OF THE CARTILAGE OF THE EXTERNAL EAR,—DE-PRIVED OF ITS SKIN AND SHOWING HOW MUCH THE SHAPE OF THE EAR IS DUE TO THE CARTILAGINOUS PLATE.

1. A Fissure found in the lower front portion of the Helix.
2. The Fissure found in the Tragus.
3. The Fissure and Caudate Shape of the lower end of the Helix.

These Fissures favour the Flexion of the different portions of the Cartilaginous Plate of the External Ear.

FIG. 587.

THE CARTILAGE OF THE EXTERNAL EAR, WITH SOME OF ITS MUSCLES.

1.2. The Helicis Major Muscle on the front of the Helix.
3.4. The Helicis Minor Muscle.
5.6. The Tragicus Muscle on the front surface of the Tragus.
7.8. The Anti-Tragicus Muscle.

FIG. 588.

A VIEW OF THE INNER SIDE OF THE CARTILAGE OF THE EXTERNAL EAR, OR THAT NEXT TO THE CRANIUM.

1.2.3. The Transversus Auriculæ Muscle in its usual position.

FIG. 589.

AN ANTERIOR VIEW OF THE EXTERNAL EAR, AS WELL AS OF THE MEATUS AUDITORIUS, LABYRINTH, &c.

1. The Opening into the Ear at the bottom of the Concha.
2. The Meatus Auditorius Externus or Cartilaginous Canal.
3. The Membrana Tympani stretched upon its Ring.
4. The Malleus.
5. The Stapes.
6. The Labyrinth.

FIG. 591.

FIG. 592.

FIG. 593.

FIG. 594.

FIG. 590.

FIG. 595.

FIG. 596.

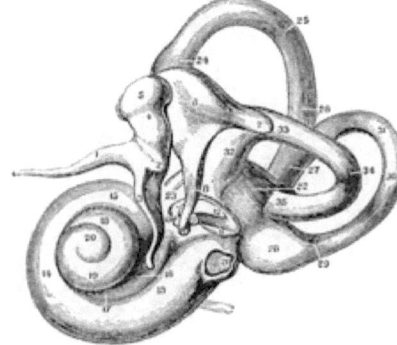

FIG. 597.

THE BONES OF THE EAR.

FIG. 590.

A VIEW OF THE LABYRINTH AND TYMPANUM OF THE EAR, WITH THE BONES IN SITU; HIGHLY MAGNIFIED.

1. Processus Longus of the Malleus.
2. Its Processus Brevis.
3. Its Manubrium.
4. Its Neck.
5. Its Head.
6. Body of the Incus.
7. Its Processus Brevis.
8.8. Its Processus Longus, with the little head for articulating with the Stapes.
9. The Head of the Stapes.
10. Its Anterior Crus.
11. Its Posterior Crus.
12. Its Base.
13.14.15. The first turn of the Cochlea.
16.17.18. Its second turn.
19. Its half turn.
20. The Cupola.
21. The Fenestra Rotunda.
22.23. The Vestibule.
24.25.26. Anterior Semicircular Canal.
27. Its junction with the Posterior Canal.
28.29.30.31. The Posterior Semicircular Canal.
32.33.34.35. The External Semicircular Canal. The Enlargements on these Canals are called Ampullæ.

FIG. 591.

A FULL VIEW OF THE MALLEUS.

1. Processus Longus.
2. Processus Brevis.
3. The Manubrium.
4. The Neck.
5. The Head of the Malleus; near the Figure is seen a small Articulating Face for the Incus.

FIG. 592.

A VIEW OF THE INCUS.

1. Its Body, with the Articular Face for the Convex Head of the Malleus.
2. Its Short or Horizontal Process.
3. Its Long or Perpendicular Process.
4.4. The Head of this Process for articulating with the Head of the Stapes. It is also called the Orbiculare.

FIG. 593.

A VIEW OF THE MALLEUS, SHOWING ITS PROCESSUS BREVIS AND THE ARTICULATING FACE FOR THE INCUS.

1. The Processus Brevis.

FIG. 594.

A FRONT VIEW OF THE STAPES

1.2. The Head of the Stapes with its Articulating Face placed Obliquely
3. Its Neck.
4. Its Anterior Crus.
5. Its Posterior Crus more curved than the other.
6. Its Base, the part which covers the Fenestra Ovalis.

FIG. 595.

A MAGNIFIED VIEW OF THE STAPES FROM ABOVE, SHOWING THE FENESTRUM IN ITS BASE.

1. Cartilaginous Articular Face, with the Orbiculare attached to it.
2. Its Anterior Crus.
3. Its Posterior Crus.
4.4. Its Base slightly open.

FIG. 596.

A MAGNIFIED VIEW OF THE CELLULAR STRUCTURE IN THE CENTRE OF THE INCUS.

FIG. 597.

A MAGNIFIED VIEW OF THE INTERNAL OR CELLULAR STRUCTURE OF THE MALLEUS ON THE SIDE OF ITS PROCESSUS BREVIS.

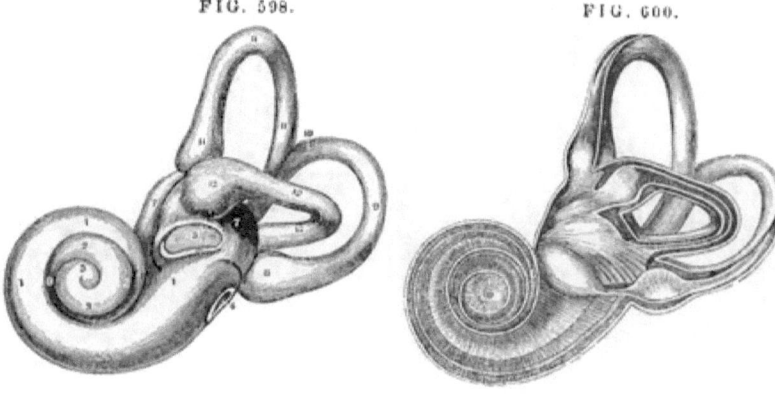

FIG. 598.

FIG. 600.

FIG. 599.

FIG. 601.

THE INTERNAL EAR.

FIG. 598.

A VIEW OF THE LABYRINTH OF THE LEFT EAR OF A FŒTUS OF 8 MONTHS, AS SEEN FROM ABOVE.—MAGNIFIED 4 DIAMETERS.

1.2.3. The Cochlea.
   1.1. Its First Turn.
   2.2. Its Second Turn.
   3.3. Its Third or Half Turn, and Apex or Cupola.
    4. The Foramen Rotundum,
    5. The Foramen Ovale,
    6. The Groove around it.
   7.7. The Vestibule.
8.9.10. The Inferior Semicircular Canal, with its Ampulla at 8.
 11.11. The Superior Semicircular Canal.
   12. The External Semicircular Canal.

FIG. 599.

AN OUTLINE, OF THE NATURAL SIZE, OF FIGURE 598.

FIG. 600.

A VIEW OF THE LABYRINTH OF THE LEFT SIDE LAID OPEN AND SHOWING ITS CONTENTS.

This Figure has the same References as Fig. 598, and is the same as it, except that the Elliptical Sacs and the Membranous Semicircular Canals, &c., are seen within the Bony Cavity as shown in Fig. 602.

FIG. 601.

THE NATURAL SIZE OF FIG. 600.

FIG. 602.   FIG. 603.

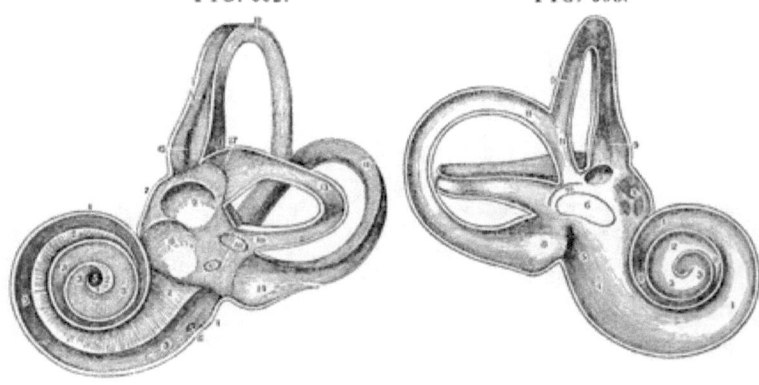

FIG. 604.

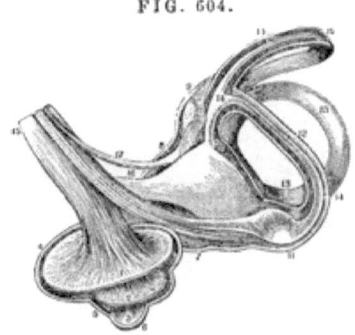

THE INTERNAL EAR.

FIG. 602.

A VIEW OF THE LABYRINTH OF THE LEFT SIDE, LAID OPEN IN ITS WHOLE EXTENT SO AS TO SHOW ITS STRUCTURE. THESE FIGURES ARE ALL MAGNIFIED.

1. The Thickness of the outer Covering of the Cochlea.
2.2. The Scala Vestibuli or upper Layer of the Lamina Spiralis.
3.3. The Scala Tympani or lower Layer of the Lamina Spiralis.
4. The Hamulus Cochleæ.
5. Centre of the Infundibulum.
6. The Foramen Rotundum communicating with the Tympanum.
7. The Thickness of the outer Layer of the Vestibule.
8. The Foramen Rotundum.
9. The Fenestra Ovalis.
10. The Orifice of the Aqueduct of the Vestibule.
11. The Inferior Semicircular Canal.
12. The Superior   do.   do.
13. The External   do.   do.
14. The Ampulla of the Inferior Canal.
15. The Ampulla of the Superior Canal.
16. The common Orifice of the Superior and Inferior Canals.
17. The Ampulla of the External Canal.

FIG. 603.

THE LABYRINTH OF THE LEFT SIDE, LAID OPEN THROUGHOUT ITS WHOLE EXTENT, AND SHOWING ON ITS LOWER HALF, MORE PLAINLY THAN THE PRECEDING FIGURES, THE THICKNESS OF ITS DIFFERENT PARTS.

1.2.3. The lower part of the Cochlea or the Scala Tympani.
1.1. The First Turn or Layer.
2.2. The Second Turn or Layer.
3.3. The Half or Third Turn.
4.5. The Inferior Half of the Vestibule.
6. Is in the Fenestra Ovalis.
7. The External Canal opening into the Vestibule.
8.8. The Inferior Canal.
9.9. The Superior Canal.
10. Part of the Ampulla of the External Canal.
11. The Union of the Superior and Inferior Canals.

FIG. 604.

A VIEW OF THE LABYRINTH IN AN INVERTED POSITION, LAID OPEN SO AS TO SHOW THE DISTRIBUTION OF THE NERVES.

1.2.3. The Cochlea laid open in its fullest extent, so as to show the Lamina Spiralis. The Figures are placed on the Two Turns and a Half.
4.5.6. The remains of the Parietes of the Cochlea.
7.8. The Vestibule.
9.10. Superior Canal.
11.12. Inferior Canal.
13. The External Canal.
14.14. The Semicircular Membranous Canals.
15.16.17. The Auditory Nerve in its course to the Labyrinth.

FIG. 605.   FIG. 606.

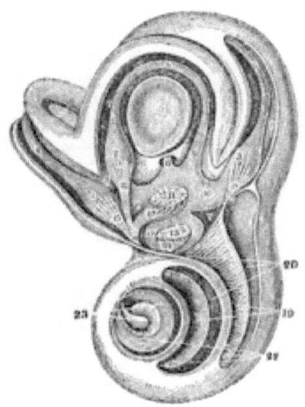

FIG. 607.

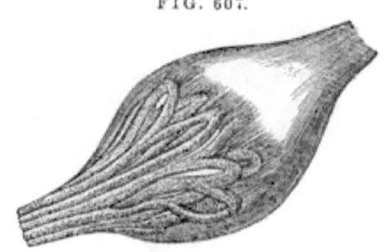

THE INTERNAL EAR.

FIG. 605.

A HIGHLY MAGNIFIED VIEW OF THE EXTERNAL FACE OF THE BONY LABYRINTH OF THE LEFT SIDE, OPENED SO AS TO EXPOSE THE VESTIBULE AND ITS CONTENTS, &c.

The difference of Colour in the shades of this Figure, is intended to assist in distinguishing the external from the internal faces of the Labyrinth, and also the cavities supposed to be occupied by the Liquor of Cotunnius.

1. The Ampulla of the Superior Semicircular Canal.
2. The Ampulla of the External Canal.
3. The Ampulla of the Inferior Canal.
4. The Superior Membranous Semicircular Canal.
5. External Membranous Canal.
6. The Inferior Membranous Canal.
7. The Spaces between the Bony and Membranous Semicircular Canals, thought to be occupied by the Liquor Cotunnii.
8. The common Tube formed by the union of the Superior and Inferior Membranous Canals.

9. The place where the Internal Semicircular Canal opens into the Sacculus Ellipticus of the Vestibule.
10. The Sacculus Ellipticus containing the Otoconie of Breschet, seen at 11.
12. Sacculus Sphericus, containing also some Otoconie, as seen at 13.
14.15.16.17.18. The expansions of the Auditory Nerve to the Membranous Canals and the Sacculus Ellipticus, and also to the Sphericus.
19. The turns of the Lamina Spiralis.
20. The Scala Tympani.
21. The Nervous expansion to the Posterior Ampulla.
22. The Scala Vestibuli.
23. The Modiolus.

FIG. 606.

THE SOFT PARTS OF THE VESTIBULE TAKEN OUT OF THEIR BONY CASE, SO AS TO SHOW THE DISTRIBUTION OF THE NERVES IN THE AMPULLÆ.

1. The Superior Semicircular Membranous Canal or Tube.

2. The External Semicircular Tube.
3. The Inferior Semicircular Tube.
4. The Tube of union of the Superior and Inferior Canals.
5. The Sacculus Ellipticus.
6. The Sacculus Sphericus.
7. The Portio Dura Nerve.
8. The Anterior Fasciculus of the Auditory Nerve.
9. The Nerve to the Sacculus Sphericus.
13.10. The Nervous Fasciculi to the Superior and External Ampullæ.
11. The Nerve to the Sacculus Ellipticus.
12. The Posterior Fasciculus of the Auditory Nerve, furnishing
13. The filaments to the Sacculus Sphericus, and
14. The filaments to the Cochlea, cut off.

FIG. 607.

THE AMPULLA OF THE EXTERNAL SEMICIRCULAR MEMBRANOUS CANAL, SHOWING THE MODE OF TERMINATION OF ITS NERVE.

FIG. 608.

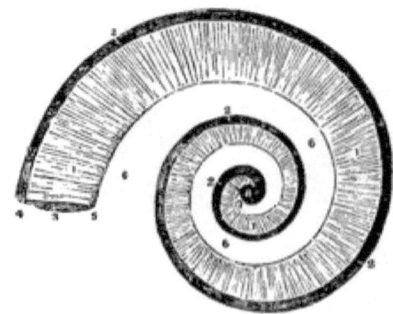

FIG. 609.

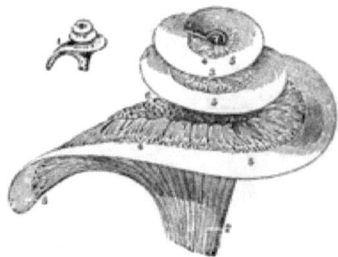

FIG. 610.

THE COCHLEA.

FIG. 608.

AN IMAGINARY FIGURE OR PLAN OF THE COCH-
LEA.

This Figure is designed to show how the two
Scalæ of the Cochlea communicate in its Summit.
The Parietes of the Scala Vestibuli are supposed
to be removed.

1.1. The Osseous portion of the Lamina Spiralis. Its small end is the Hamulus Cochleæ.
2.2. The dark ground here represents the Membranous portion of the Cochlea or the Zona
Membranacea.
3. The commencement of the Scala Tympani.
4. Its External Edge.
5. Its Internal Edge.
6. Corresponds to the Modiolus around which
the Lamina Spiralis is wound.
7. Its Summit.
8. The point of communication of the two
Scalæ.

FIG. 609.

A VIEW OF THE AXIS OF THE COCHLEA AND THE
LAMINA SPIRALIS, SHOWING THE ARRANGE-
MENT OF THE THREE ZONES. THE OSSEOUS
ZONE AND THE MEMBRANE OF THE VESTIBULE
HAVE BEEN REMOVED.

1. The natural size of the parts   The other
Figure is greatly magnified.
2. Trunk of the Auditory Nerve.
3. The distribution of its Filaments in the Zona
Ossea.
4. The Nervous Anastomosis in the Zona Vesicularis.
5. The Zona Membranacea.
6. The Osseous tissue of the Modiolus
7. The opening between the two Scalæ.

FIG. 610.

THE AUDITORY NERVE TAKEN OUT OF THE
COCHLEA.

1.1.1. The Trunk of the Nerve.
2.2. Its Filaments in the Zona Ossea of the
Lamina Spiralis.
3.3. Its Anastomoses in the Zona Vesicularis.

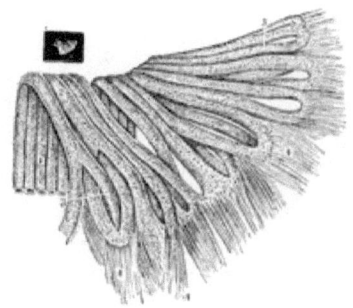

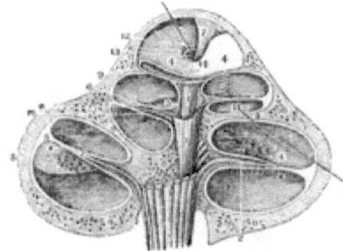

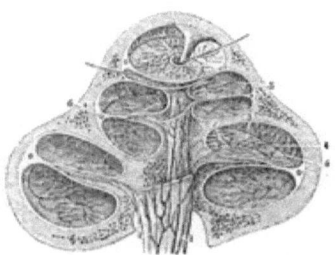

FIG. 612.
FIG. 613.

THE COCHLEA.

FIG. 611.

A HIGHLY MAGNIFIED VIEW OF A SMALL PIECE OF
THE LAMINA SPIRALIS, SHOWING THE GLOBU-
LAR STRUCTURE OF THE NERVES AND THE MAN-
NER IN WHICH THEY LEAVE THEIR NEURILEMA
AS THEY ANASTOMOSE.

The natural size of the piece is seen on the
side of the Figure.

1. Portion of the Auditory Nerve.
2.2. Osseous Canals in the Zona Ossea of the
Lamina Spiralis.
3.3. Anastomoses in the Zona Mollis.
4.4. The Neurilema leaving the Nervous Loops
and interlocking to form the Layer of the
Zona Membranacea.

FIG. 612.

A VERTICAL SECTION OF THE COCHLEA, HIGHLY
MAGNIFIED TO SHOW THE ARRANGEMENT AND
CONNEXION OF ITS PARTS.

1.1. The Trunk of the Auditory Nerve.
2.2. Filaments of it in the Zona Ossea.
3.3. Anastomoses in the Zona Vesicularis.
4.4. Zona Membranacea.

5.5. The doubling up of its external edge.
6.6. The Axis of the Cochlea.
7. The Modiolus.
8.8. Exterior osseous parietes of the Cochlea.
9.9. The bony plates of the Lamina Spiralis.
10. The Scala Tympani.
11. The Scala Vestibuli.
12. The Hamulus Cochleæ.
13. The Infundibulum.
14. A Bristle passed through the course of the
Lamina Spiralis.

FIG. 613.

A MAGNIFIED VIEW OF THE VEINS IN THE INTE-
RIOR OF THE COCHLEA, AS GIVEN BY A VERTI-
CAL SECTION. THE ARTERIES ACCOMPANY
THE VEINS.

1.1. Veins accompanying the Auditory Nerve.
2. The First Anastomosis on a line with the
periphery of the Zona Ossea.
3. The Second Anastomosis on a line with the
periphery of the Zona Coriacea.
4. The last Branches occupying the Zona Membranacea.
5. The Venous Sinus in the periphery of the
Zona Membranacea.

FIG. 614.

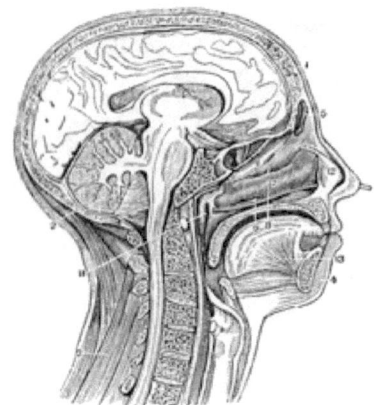

FIG. 615.

FIG. 616.

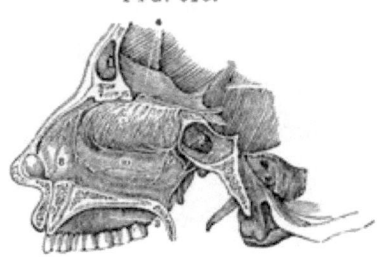

THE NERVES.

FIG. 614.

A VERTICAL SECTION OF THE HEAD AND NECK THROUGH THE MESIAL LINE, IN ORDER TO SHOW THE OPENING OF THE EUSTACHIAN TUBE AND ITS RELATIONS TO THE PHARYNX.

1. Section of the Os Frontis.
2. Section of the Os Occipitis.
3. The Muscles on the back of the Neck.
4. The Integuments on the Chin.
5. The Frontal Sinus.
6. The Middle Spongy Bone.
7. The Inferior Spongy Bone.
8. The Middle Meatus of the Nose.
9. The Inferior Meatus of the Nose.
10. Thickness of the Roof of the Mouth and Floor of the Nostril.
11. Opening of the Eustachian Tube. A Catheter is introduced in the Nostril and about to enter the Tube.
12. Cartilaginous Nasal Septum.
13. Genio-Glossus Muscle.
14. The Soft Palate.

FIG. 615.

A VIEW OF THE ORIGIN AND DISTRIBUTION OF THE PORTIO MOLLIS OF THE SEVENTH PAIR OR AUDITORY NERVE.

1. The Modulla Oblongata.
2. The Pons Varolii.

3.4. The Crura Cerebelli of the Right Side.
5. The Eighth Pair of Nerves.
6. The Ninth Pair.
7. The Auditory Nerve distributed to the Cochlea and Labyrinth.
8. The Sixth Pair of Nerves.
9. The Portio Dura of the Seventh Pair.
10. The Fourth Pair.
11. The Fifth Pair.

FIG. 616.

A VIEW OF THE FIRST PAIR OR OLFACTORY NERVES, WITH THE NASAL BRANCHES OF THE FIFTH PAIR.

1. Frontal Sinus.
2. Sphenoidal Sinus.
3. Hard Palate.
4. Bulb of the Olfactory Nerve.
5. Branches of the Olfactory Nerve on the Superior and Middle Turbinated Bones.
6. Spheno-Palatine Nerves from the Second Branch of the Fifth Pair.
7. Internal Nasal Nerve from the first Branch of the Fifth.
8. Branches of 7 to the Schneiderian Membrane.
9. Ganglion of Cloquet in the Foramen Incisivum.
10. Anastomosis of the Branches of the Fifth Pair on the Inferior Turbinated Bone.

FIG. 617.

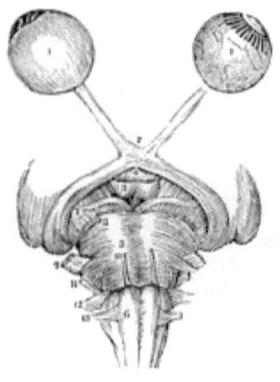

FIG. 619.

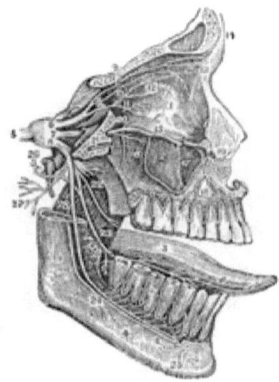

FIG. 618.

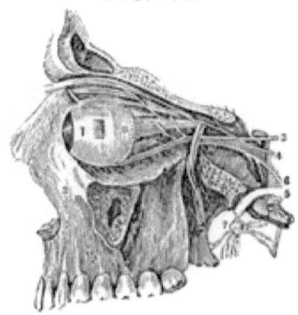

THE SECOND AND FIFTH PAIRS OF NERVES.

FIG. 617.

A VIEW OF THE SECOND PAIR OR OPTIC NERVES, WITH THE ORIGIN OF SEVEN OTHER PAIRS OF NERVES.

1.1. Globe of the Eye; the one on the Left Hand is perfect, but that on the Right has the Sclerotic and Choroid Coats removed in order to show the Retina.
2. The Chiasm of the Optic Nerves.
3. The Corpora Albicantia.
4. The Infundibulum.
5. The Pons Varolii.
6. The Medulla Oblongata.
7. The Third Pair, Motores Oculi.
8. Fourth Pair, Pathetici.
9. Fifth Pair, Trigemini.
10. Sixth Pair, Motor Externus.
11. Seventh Pair, Auditory and Facial.
12. Eighth Pair, Pneumogastric, Spinal Accessory and Glosso-Pharyngeal.
3. Ninth Pair, Hypoglossal.

FIG. 618.

A VIEW OF THE THIRD, FOURTH AND SIXTH PAIRS OF NERVES.

Ball of the Eye and Rectus Externus Muscle.
The Superior Maxilla.
The Third Pair, or Motores Oculi, distributed to all the Muscles of the Eye except the Superior Oblique and External Rectus.
4. The Fourth Pair, or Pathetici, going to the Superior Oblique Muscle.
5. One of the Branches of the Seventh Pair.
6. The Sixth Pair, or Motor Externus, distributed to the External Rectus Muscle.
7. Spheno - Palatine Ganglion and Branches.
8. Ciliary Nerves from the Lenticular Ganglion, the short Root of which is seen to connect it with the Third Pair.

FIG. 619.

A VIEW OF THE DISTRIBUTION OF THE TRIFACIAL OR FIFTH PAIR.

1. Orbit.
2. Antrum Highmorianum.
3. Tongue.
4. Lower Jaw-Bone.
5. Root of the Fifth Pair, forming the Ganglion of Gasser.
6. First Branch of the Fifth Pair, or Ophthalmic.
7. Second Branch of the Fifth Pair, or Superior Maxillary.
8. Third Branch of the Fifth Pair, or Inferior Maxillary.
9. Frontal Branch, dividing into External and Internal Frontal Nerves.
10. Lachrymal Branch of the Fifth Pair.
11. Nasal Branch. Just under the Figure is the long Root of the Lenticular or Ciliary Ganglion and a few of the Ciliary Nerves.
12. Internal Nasal Nerve, disappearing through the Anterior Ethmoidal Foramen.
13. External Nasal Nerve.
14. External and Internal Frontal Nerve.
15. Infra-Orbitary Nerve.
16. Posterior Dental Branches.
17. Middle Dental Branch.
18. Anterior Dental Nerve.
19. Terminating Branches of the Infra-Orbital Nerve, called the Labial and Palpebral Nerves.
20. Subcutaneus Malæ, or Orbitar Branch.
21. Pterygoid, or Recurrent Nerve, from Meckel's Ganglion.
22. Five Anterior Branches of the Third Branch of the Fifth Pair.
23. Lingual Branch of the Fifth, joined by the Chorda Tympani.
24. Inferior Dental Nerve.
25. Its Mental Branches.
26. Superficial Temporal Nerve.
27. Auricular Branches.
28. Mylo-Hyoid Branch.

FIG. 620.   FIG. 621.

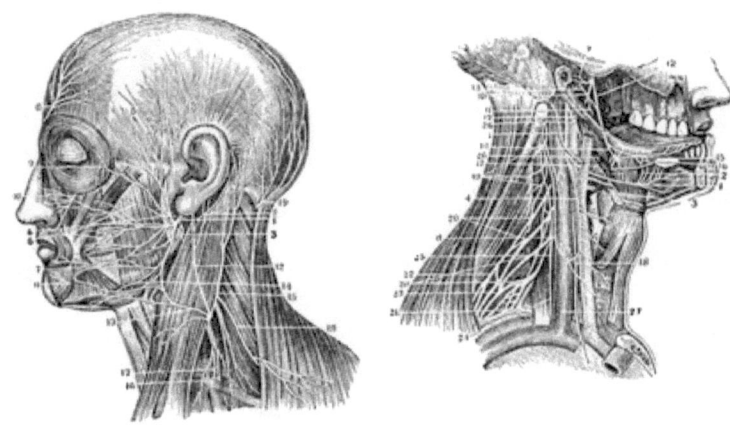

THE FACIAL AND HYPO-GLOSSAL NERVES.

FIG. 620.

A VIEW OF THE FACIAL NERVE, TOGETHER WITH THE BRANCHES OF THE CERVICAL PLEXUS, &c.

1. The Portio Dura or Facial Nerve escaping from the Stylo-Mastoid Foramen. The Parotid Gland has been removed in order to show the Nerve more clearly.
2. Its Posterior Auricular Branch.
3. The Stylo-Hyoid Branch.
4. The Pes Anserinus.
5. Temporal Branches of the Facial Nerve.
6. Malar Branches.
7. Cervico-Facial Branches.
8. Supra-Orbital Nerve.
9. Sub-Cutaneus Malæ, a branch of the Superior Maxillary Nerve.
10. The Infra-Orbital Nerve.
11. Terminal Branches of the Inferior Dental Nerve.
12. Nervus Auricularis of the Cervical Plexus.
13. The Superficialis Colli Nerve.
14. The Plexus formed between the Superficialis Colli and the branches of the Facial.
15. The Occipalis Minor Branch, of the Cervical Plexus.
16. Descending branches of the Cervical Plexus.
17. The Phrenic Nerve.
18. The Nervus Accessorius of the Eighth Pair.
19. The Great or Posterior Occipital Nerve.

FIG. 621.

THE COURSE AND DISTRIBUTION OF THE HYPO-GLOSSAL OR NINTH PAIR OF NERVES. THE DEEP-SEATED NERVES OF THE NECK ARE ALSO SEEN.

1. The Hypo-Glossal Nerve.
2. Branches communicating with the Gustatory Nerve.
3. A Branch to the origin of the Hyoid Muscles.
4. The Descendens Noni Nerve.
5. The Loop formed with the Branch from the Cervical Nerves.
6. Muscular branches to the Depressor Muscles of the Larynx.
7. A Filament from the Second Cervical Nerve, and
8. A Filament from the Third Cervical, uniting to form the communicating branch with the Loop from the Descendens Noni.
9. The Auricular Nerve.
10. The Inferior Dental Nerve.
11. Its Mylo-Hyoidean Branch.
12. The Gustatory Nerve.
13. The Chorda-Tympani passing to the Gustatory Nerve.
14. The Chorda-Tympani leaving the Gustatory Nerve to join the Sub-Maxillary Ganglion.
15. The Sub-Maxillary Ganglion.
16. Filaments of communication with the Lingual Nerve.
17. The Glosso-Pharyngeal Nerve.
18. The Pneumo-Gastric or Par Vagum Nerve.
19. The three upper Cervical Nerves.
20. The four inferior Cervical Nerves.
21. The First Dorsal Nerve.
22,23. The Brachial Plexus.
24,25. The Phrenic Nerve.
26. The Carotid Artery.
27. The Internal Jugular Vein.

FIG. 622.

FIG. 623.

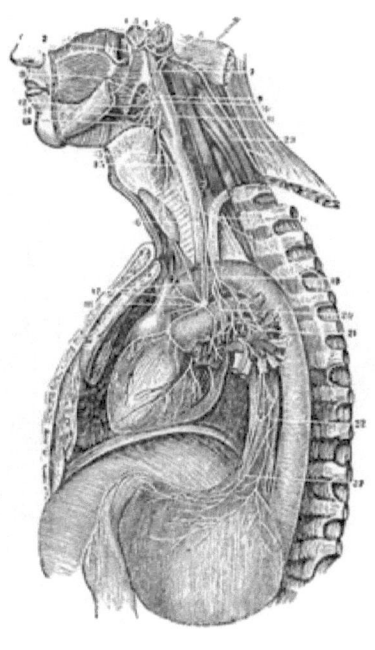

THE EIGHTH PAIR OF NERVES.

FIG. 622.

A PLAN OF THE ORIGIN AND DISTRIBUTION OF THE EIGHTH PAIR OF NERVES.

1. The Corpus Pyramidale of one side.
2. The Pons Varolii.
3. The Corpus Olivare.
4. The Corpus Restiforme.
5. The Facial Nerve.
6. The origin of the Glosso-Pharyngeal Nerve.
7. The Ganglionum Petrosum.
8. The Trunk of the Nerve.
9. The Spinal Accessory Nerve.
10. The Ganglion of the Pneumogastric Nerve.
11. Its Plexiform Ganglion.
12. Its Trunk.
13. Its Pharyngeal Branch, forming (14) the Pharyngeal Plexus, assisted by a branch from the Glosso-Pharyngeal (8), and one from (15) the Superior Laryngeal Nerve.
16. Cardiac Branches.
17. Recurrent Laryngeal Branch.
18. Anterior Pulmonary Branches.
19. Posterior Pulmonary Branches.
20. Œsophageal Plexus.
21. Gastric Branches.
22. Origin of the Spinal Accessory Nerve.
23. Branches to the Sterno-Mastoid Muscle.
24. Branches to the Trapezius Muscle.

FIG. 623.

A VIEW OF THE DISTRIBUTION OF THE GLOSSO-PHARYNGEAL PNEUMO-GASTRIC AND SPINAL ACCESSORY NERVES, OR THE EIGHTH PAIR.

1. The Inferior Maxillary Nerve.
2. The Gustatory Nerve.
3. The Chorda-Tympani.
4. The Auricular Nerve.
5. Its communication with the Portio Dura.
6. The Facial Nerve coming out of the Stylo-Mastoid Foramen.
7. The Glosso-Pharyngeal Nerve.
8. Branches to the Stylo-Pharyngeus Muscle.
9. The Pharyngeal Branch of the Pneumo-Gastric Nerve descending to form the Pharyngeal Plexus.
10. Branches of the Glosso-Pharyngeal to the Pharyngeal Plexus.
11. The Pneumo-Gastric Nerve.
12. The Pharyngeal Plexus.
13. The Superior Laryngeal Branch.
14. Branches to the Pharyngeal Plexus.
15.15. Communication of the Superior and Inferior Laryngeal Nerves.
16. Cardiac Branches.
17. Cardiac Branches from the Right Pneumo-Gastric Nerve.
18. The Left Cardiac Ganglion and Plexus.
19. The Recurrent or Inferior Laryngeal Nerve.
20. Branches sent from the curve of the Recurrent Nerve to the Pulmonary Plexus.
21. The Anterior Pulmonary Plexus.
22.22. The Œsophageal Plexus.

FIG. 624.

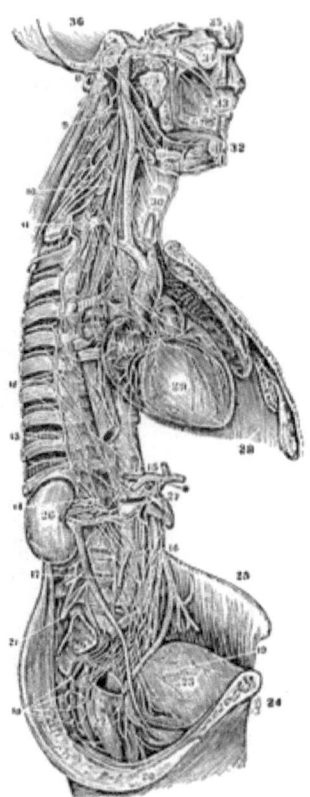

THE GREAT SYMPATHETIC NERVE

FIG. 624.

A VIEW OF THE GREAT SYMPATHETIC NERVE.

1. The Plexus on the Carotid Artery in the Carotid Foramen.
2. Sixth Nerve (Motor Externus).
3. First Branch of the Fifth or Ophthalmic Nerve.
4. A Branch on the Septum Narium going to the Incisive Foramen.
5. The Recurrent Branch or Vidian Nerve dividing into the Carotid and Petrosal Branches.
6. Posterior Palatine Branches.
7. The Lingual Nerve joined by the Corda Tympani.
8. The Portio Dura of the Seventh Pair or the Facial Nerve.
9. The Superior Cervical Ganglion.
10. The Middle Cervical Ganglion.
11. The Inferior Cervical Ganglion.
12. The Roots of the Great Splanchnic Nerve arising from the Dorsal Ganglion.
13. The Lesser Splanchnic Nerve.
14. The Renal Plexus.
15. The Solar Plexus.
16. The Mesenteric Plexus.
17. The Lumbar Ganglia.
18. The Sacral Ganglia.
19. The Vesical Plexus.
20. The Rectal Plexus.
21. The Lumbar Plexus (Cerebro-Spinal).
22. The Rectum.
23. The Bladder.
24. The Pubis.
25. The Crest of the Ilium.
26. The Kidney.
27. The Aorta.
28. The Diaphragm.
29. The Heart.
30. The Larynx.
31. The Sub-Maxillary Gland.
32. The Incisor Teeth.
33. Nasal Septum.
34. Globe of the Eye.
35.36. Cavity of the Cranium.

FIG. 625.

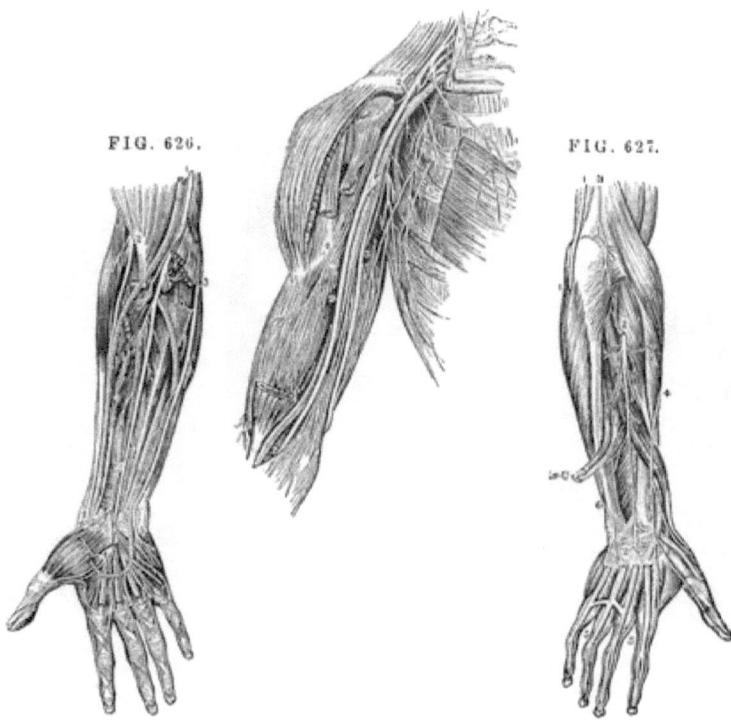

FIG. 626.   FIG. 627.

NERVES OF THE UPPER EXTREMITY.

FIG. 625.

A VIEW OF THE BRACHIAL PLEXUS OF NERVES AND ITS BRANCHES TO THE ARM.

1.1. The Scalenus Anticus Muscle.
2.2. The Median Nerve.
3. The Ulnar Nerve.
4. The Branch to the Biceps Muscle.
5. The Thoracic Nerves.
6. The Phrenic Nerve, from the Third and Fourth Cervical.

___

FIG. 626.

A VIEW OF THE NERVES ON THE FRONT OF THE FORE-ARM.

1. The Median Nerve.
2. Anterior Branch of the Musculo-Spiral or Radial Nerve.
3. The Ulnar Nerve.

4. Division of the Median Nerve in the Palm to the Thumb, First, Second and Radial side of the Third Finger.
5. Division of the Ulnar Nerve to the Ulnar side of the Third and both sides of the Fourth Finger.

___

FIG. 627.

A VIEW OF THE NERVES ON THE BACK OF THE FORE-ARM AND HAND.

1.1. The Ulnar Nerve.
2.2. The Ramus Profundus Dorsalis Nerve.
3. Termination of the Nervus Cutaneus Humeri.
4. The Dorsalis Carpi, a Branch of the Radial Nerve.
5.5. A back view of the Digital Nerves.
6. Dorsal Branch of the Ulnar Nerve.

FIG. 628.

FIG. 629.

FIG. 630.

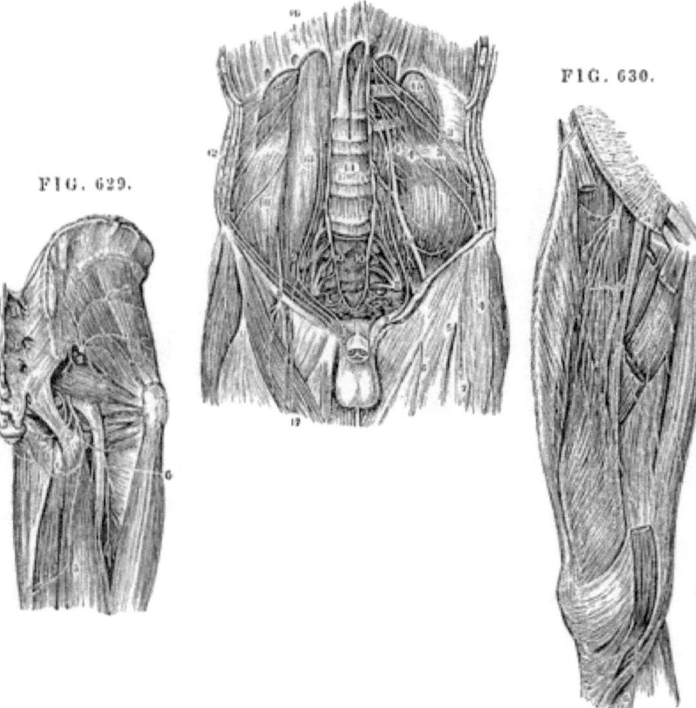

NERVES OF THE LOWER EXTREMITY.

FIG. 628.

A View of the Lumbar and Ischiatic Plexuses and the Branches of the former.

1. The Lumbar Plexus.
2. The Ischiatic Plexus.
3.3. Abdomino-Crural Nerves,
   4. The External Cutaneous Nerve (Inguino-Cutaneous).
5.6.7. Cutaneous Branches from
   8. The Anterior Crural Nerve.
   9. The Genito-Crural Nerve, or Spermaticus Externus.
10.10. The lower termination of the Great Sympathetic.
11. The Iliacus Internus Muscle.
12. The three broad Muscles of the Abdomen.
13. The Psoas-Magnus Muscle.
14. Bodies of the Lumbar Vertebræ.
15. The Quadratus Lumborum Muscle.
16. The Diaphragm.
 7. The Sartorius.

FIG. 629.

A View of the Branches of the Ischiatic Plexus to the Hip and back of the Thigh.

1.1. Posterior Sacral Nerves.
2. Nervi Glutei.
3. The Internal Pudic Nerve.
4. The Lesser Ischiatic Nerve, giving off the Perineal Cutaneus, and
5. The Ramus Femoralis Cutaneus Posterior.
6. Great Ischiatic Nerve.

FIG. 630.

A View of the Anterior Crural Nerve and its Branches.

1. Point where the Nerve comes out under Poupart's Ligament.
2. Division of the Nerve into its Branches.
3. The Femoral Artery.
4. The Femoral Vein.
5. The Branches of the Obturator Nerve.
6. The Nervus Saphenus.

FIG. 631.   FIG. 632.   FIG. 633.

FIG. 634.

 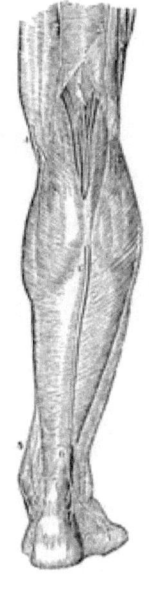  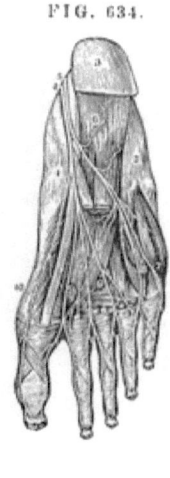

NERVES OF THE LOWER EXTREMITY.

FIG. 631.

A VIEW OF THE ANTERIOR TIBIAL NERVE.

1. The Peroneal Nerve.
2.3. The Anterior Tibial Nerve accompanying the Artery of the same name.

FIG. 632.

A VIEW OF SOME OF THE BRANCHES OF THE POP-LITEAL NERVE.

1. The Popliteal Nerve.
2.3. Terminations of the Ramus Femoralis Cuta-neus Posterior.
4.5. The Saphenous Nerve.
6.6. The External Saphenous or Communicans Tibiæ.

FIG. 633.

A VIEW OF THE POSTERIOR TIBIAL NERVE, IN THE BACK OF THE LEG.

1.2. Indicate its course; the upper part of the Peroneal Nerve being seen to the Right.

FIG. 634.

A VIEW OF THE TERMINATION OF THE POSTERIOR TIBIAL NERVE IN THE SOLE OF THE FOOT.

1. Inside of the Foot.
2. Outer side of the Foot.
3. The Heel.
4. Internal Plantar Nerve.
5. External Plantar Nerve.
6. Branch to the Flexor Brevis Muscle.
7. Branch to the outside of the Little Toe.
8. Branch to the space between the Fourth and Fifth Toes.
9.9.9. Digital Branches to the remaining Spaces.
10. Branch to the internal side of the Great Toe.

www.ingramcontent.com/pod-product-compliance
Lightning Source LLC
Chambersburg PA
CBHW030552040726
47497CB00008B/2683